The Trials of Cairstin Blackwood

A Victorian Gothic Mystery

Sydney F. Grey

The Trials of Cairstin Blackwood

Copyright © 2026 by Sydney F. Grey, Two Mites Publishing

All scripture verses taken from the King James version of the Bible.

All rights reserved. No part of this book may be reproduced, distributed, or transmitted in any form or by any means, including photocopying, recording, or other electronic or mechanical methods, without the prior written permission of the publisher, except in the case of brief quotations embodied in critical reviews and certain other noncommercial uses permitted by copyright law.

ISBN (eBook): 979-8-9931119-3-3, ISBN (Paperback): 979-8-9931119-4-0, ISBN (audiobook): 979-8-9931119-5-7

Cover design by Roseanna White. Author photo by Gayle Yeo.

This is a work of fiction. All incidents are products of the author's imagination or are used fictitiously. Any resemblance to actual events (except railway opening), or persons (except Mr. Arnison), living or dead, is entirely coincidental.

First Edition, 2026. Printed in the USA and UK.

In memory of

Lydia Hiett Coleman
and
Dr. L. Scott Martin

Thank you for believing in me

Chapter One

With a sickening ache in my chest, I climbed the narrow stairs to my parents' bedchamber as silently as I could on the creaking boards. Standing before the door, I gripped the handle and fought down a wave of nausea.

Nothing I had ever said to my cold, silent father lying inside this room had ever seemed to stir his heart. How I wished my brothers had lived so this burden would have fallen on them instead of me. I was certain my father felt the same.

Finally, a familiar numbness covered me like a cool wet blanket, and I welcomed it. It gave me the shield I needed to knock on the door and enter the little sour-smelling bedchamber.

He was asleep, as he usually was these days, his ruddy face pockmarked with lesions that never healed, his breath ragged from a throat constantly parched. I crept to the bedside and took a long look at him, trying to remember what he'd looked like before his illness.

The only times I could remember my Scottish father, the

town tailor, ever being close to happy was after a customer paid their bill in full. Then, though he never smiled, his face would lighten a bit. He would press his lips together in a satisfied way and puff out his broad chest with a deep inhale. Then he would place the money in the little tin box under the floorboard and go back to his normal emotionless self.

I had never been able to truly please him, though I tried hard every day of my life. Both of my older brothers had died young, one as an infant and the other at the age of four from an infection. When I was old enough to thread a needle, I'd worked my tiny fingers until they were raw, my girlish mind trying to understand what he wanted from me. I made a heroic effort each day to see that satisfied look on his face when he examined my work. It never happened.

And now he was desperately ill, no longer able to work at all. It had begun gradually. First his eyes had become red and the skin on his hands irritated. Then he'd complained of strange pains in his stomach and was always asking for tea. Over the last few months, he'd grown worse and worse, until just the week before he could bear it no longer and took to his bed.

The doctor did what little he could but was unable to identify the disease. I was terrified Father would die and my mother, sister, and I would soon be doomed to the workhouse to live destitute, until we also succumbed to illness and joined him in the churchyard.

"Dah," I whispered, half desperate now to rouse him. "Dah, I've come to say good night."

His swollen eyelids flickered, and he wheezed a long exhale.

"Dah, it's Cairy. Do you want a drink of water?"

At this his eyes opened a bit more, and he looked at me coldly. "O' course, lass. Help me up."

I supported him behind his shoulders and held a glass to his cracked lips. It didn't seem to matter how much salve Mother put on them, they were always raw. He drank painfully, then waved off the glass, and I laid him back down. He was much lighter now. The pain in his gut had killed his appetite. My heart threw off its mantle of numbness and gave way to a convulsion of pity.

"Dah, I'm going to start working for Mr. Arnison like you wanted me to. I leave for Penrith in the morning. It'll be very early. Would you like me to come and say goodbye or let you sleep?" I knew what the answer would be even before voicing the question.

"Nay, lass. We'll be sayin' goodbye now." His Scottish burr was ever present, though his voice was hoarse and rattled.

Unexpectedly he took hold of my arm and pushed me toward the chair my mother now slept on every night.

"Set ye down now and listen carefully." His red eyes looked at me long and hard as I waited, holding my breath.

"You're going to that man Arnison now. He ain't the type o' man to put up with any feckless lass. Ya mustn't shame your family. Ya keep your wits about ya and do all he says, eh?"

I nodded, my eyes wide. I had not heard him speak so many words to me in a long time.

He lay back with an exasperated sigh. "Ah, if only your brothers had lived, none o' this t'would be happening now." His eyes found mine again as he took a staggering breath to continue. "You're nothing but a lass, Cairstin, and no lass will 'er be paid as much as a man." His voice cracked, and he hacked out a series of dry coughs.

I reached for the water again, but he held up his hand.

"You'll ne'er be able to earn enough to keep us all living here and fed. It's best you find yourself a husband to take ye, and mind ya, find one 'tis fat with full pockets. 'Tis the only way to keep your mam and sister out o' the workhouse."

He coughed again fiercely, and I brought the glass, my arm under his failing body, to his mouth. He took a long sip and fell back on the pillows, grasping my arm harshly and pulling me down close to his face. I could smell the stench of his breath and see a desperation in his eyes I had never seen there before.

"Cairstin, lass! Ya must marry! Promise me! Promise me now!"

"I . . . I promise, Dah. I promise." I heard myself saying the words in disbelief. Never, ever had my father spoken to me of marriage. It had always been understood that I would work in his tailor shop until the day I died.

He let go of my arm and lay back with a moan. He flung his hand toward the door and covered his eyes with his arm.

"Go, and goodbye to ye."

I closed the door and leaned my back heavily against it. There it was, the plain, hard truth. I wasn't enough, and it wouldn't be enough for me to go to Penrith and work for a successful draper to support my family. It was all just wishful thinking. And now I had promised my father on his deathbed something I had never once given myself a moment to seriously consider. I must marry.

I heard Mother's footsteps on the stairs and tried to pull myself together. Had she known what father would say to me? Did she also feel it was the only way?

"Cairstin, are you all right, love?" Mother put her arm around my shoulders.

I had inherited my father's green eyes and ginger hair, but my slight build and fair complexion were definitely my Mother's. As she rested her hands on my shoulders, I wondered who would break first, her or me. But I mustn't break . . . I could not. It was up to me now, and I might as well get started. I would not worry her with talk of marriage at present.

"It's all right, Mam. It was only difficult to see him so sick and know I may never see him again."

"Oh, child." She took my face in her hands and kissed my cheeks. "May God help us all, especially you. God must give you the strength of a man, my daughter. Have faith, Cairy. He is able."

"I will, Mam. I will be very brave and make you proud. You shall see." I meant what I said, but doubt coursed through me like a poison.

"I believe you, Cairy. We all do."

When she entered her bedchamber and closed the door, I dashed down the stairs. Throwing on my coat and bonnet, I quietly left out the rear door of the residence at the back of my father's tailoring shop. Hoping I wouldn't be seen, I flew down the narrow passage between the back of businesses and the iron fence bordering the churchyard.

I almost slipped on the ice as I ran to the bridge crossing the River Eden and made my way to my favored place, a little break in the dense trees and bramble on the river's bank across from the town. It was a place I had come many times in my seventeen years of life to find solace.

Unable to control my tears any longer, I sobbed a prayer in the frigid mist of sunset and tried to fill my eyes to overflowing with the view before me. "Please, God. Please let me see this place again."

My aching thoughts were broken by the distant bark of a dog and the muted trickling of the river as it flowed between its icy edges just down the bank from where I stood shivering. The frosted dried grasses quivered around me in the faint breeze, while the shadows lengthened and reached out for one another over the surface, like spirits deprived of one another's touch by the light of day.

The river had been the keeper of all my secrets, all my childish dreams, and it never betrayed me or thought me foolish that I could still find a place in my heart for hope and longing.

But now I was being torn from the only place I had ever known, my little town of Appleby in the beauty of the rolling dells, and from this simple refuge by the river.

"Cairy! Cairy!" my little sister Rose's worried voice called for me. If it had been any other voice but hers or Mother's, I might not have stirred ever again.

"Coming, love." My voice sounded like a stranger's, my throat tight and lips salty with tears. "I will never forget you," I whispered to the river and the trees. "Please don't forget me."

I strode up the embankment and met little Rose on the path. I could see the worry in her pale, fragile face, her chin shaking with the cold.

"Are ye all right, Cairy? It's getting late, and Mam's worried ya won't be rested enough for your ride to Penrith in the morning."

I wouldn't lie to her and tell her I was fine. She could read my face better than anyone. "I was just saying goodbye to the Eden. Let's go. Your hands are like ice, Rosie—where are your gloves?"

We walked up the path to the street, then crossed the bridge over the river, which curled its way around Appleby like a mother's arm cradling a child. Passing into the narrow walkway, I paused to look wistfully at the church where I'd prayed so many childish prayers. The silent tombstones stood hard against the frosted lawns as the last of the sun glinted off the church's large mullioned windows. I thought about my two brothers, who lay at the far end of the yard.

"Are ya going to be all right, Cairy? Your face is so pale that it frightens me."

Rosie's whisper sent a stab of loneliness through my heart. "I will be all right, Rose. I have to be."

After a brief embrace, we reached the back door to our home and stepped in out of the cold.

Mother stood in the kitchen and scolded me. "Cairy! What were you thinking? You'll catch a cold before you even start your journey to Penrith!"

My mother's pure and still elegant Southern accent worried over me like salt on a wound. How was I ever going to manage without her?

She pulled my coat from my shoulders, one end dropping from her left hand, the one deformed since birth. I wondered again, as I had a thousand times, what her life would have been like had she been born whole. Such a pretty little thing she was, so delicate and fine. Even under her years of servitude to my father, you could still see the grace in her face, one I was sure had once shone brightly. I was convinced she would never have married my coarse Scottish father if she had not been crippled in this way.

"Your supper is on the table now, and the tea is still hot. You must be off to bed soon or you won't be in any condition to travel in the morning."

"Thank you, Mam." I wasn't sure I could eat anything, with the large lump in my throat, but for her sake I would try.

After saying good night to Mother, I lay next to my sweet Rose, twelve years of innocence shaking with cold and fear. I held her tight to me and couldn't let go of her, nor she me. How I loved her.

"Everything will be all right now, Rosie. If I weren't suitable for a position as a dressmaker in Mr. Arnison's business, Dah would never have written him. They know each other well, since their apprenticing days at the very same shop before Mr. James died and Mr. Arnison bought it. I am sure Dah would never have written if he didn't think I was capable of the work."

"Aye, Cairy, t'isn't that I'm worried about. 'Tis how lonesome Mam and I will be without ye."

I wondered anew how my sister managed to take her accent from my father instead of my mother, as I had. Father spoke little to me and not much more to Rose. I suppose Father's speech was much more like the local Northern dialect than Mother's, and Rose was still influenced by the neighboring children she saw much more of than I.

"Shhh, now. We mustn't talk anymore. I need my sleep if I'm going to be fit for morning."

Eventually Rose's slender body grew limp, and I carefully rolled over so she wouldn't see my tears if she woke. Sleep was evasive, as all that was before me raced through my mind like horses on a track.

What was he like, this Nathan Arnison, who had been so successful in building up his draper and silk mercer's business that he had hired on a whole team of tailoring and dressmaking apprentices?. He'd built his large family of a wife and seven children what was rumored to be a formidable house on a fashionable street in Penrith.

I wish Father had let me see the letter he'd written to Mr. Arnison, and the one he'd received in return saying Mr. Arnison would make a place for me. If only I could stay and make a living here in Appleby, but Father had made it clear why I would never be successful in drawing enough clientele.

First, I'd been sternly told that no man would ever come to

a woman to have his clothes made, so even my father's lifelong clients, including Mayor Milner, would take their business to Mr. Hudspeth's tailoring apprentice now. What a terrible thought. That witless apprentice of his wasn't half the tailor I was. How perfectly unjust to snub my work only because I wasn't a man!

Second, I'd been informed that I couldn't possibly change Father's tailoring business to a dressmaker's shop for fear it would do a great injustice to the only dressmaker in town, Karen Lowthrop, who had done our family many a good turn by recommending the women who came to her that they should take their husbands' business to Father. There simply weren't enough dresses to be made in Appleby to support two dressmakers, as most women couldn't afford one and made their own clothes. Mrs. Lowthrop could not even afford to take me on as an apprentice.

That had left only one other possibility, that Father would call upon his old acquaintance and sometimes supplier, Mr. Arnison of Penrith, some fourteen miles to the northwest. Fourteen long miles that would keep me from being able to easily visit my family and come home even for holidays.

Holidays. My stomach lurched. It was only mid-November, but no one had time to think of Christmastide now, not with Father so ill and my family in a near panic. Another layer of loneliness settled over me as I buried a sob in my pillow and pulled the blankets over my head.

I could see my breath in the cold light of dawn as I made my toilet, moving quietly so as not to wake up Rose. Donning my undergarments and lacing my corset, I drew over my head a creation of my own hands, a subtle gray-and-blue plaid wool dress tailored to perfection with its full skirt, pointed waist, fanned bodice, sloping shoulders, and fitted sleeves. My father always saw to it that his family was well dressed and could furnish me with suitable fabrics to make my own clothes, so every time a customer saw me in the shop, or I was out and about in the town, they would be impressed and know my father was good at his job. Actually, Father never touched my dresses, and I was self-taught on the stitches that differed from those required to make menswear.

A light tap at the door made me jump.

"Breakfast is ready, love," Mother whispered before retreating down the stairs.

I used our small looking glass on the burrow to perfect the low sweeps of my abundant red hair, covering my ears and carefully tucking the rest into a neat bun on the back, suitably demure and plain for my station in life.

I must have been numb since waking, because it wasn't until my eyes met with the girl's in the mirror that a streak of panic shot through my heart. I saw her eyes grow wide with fear and her lips tremble, but I placed my hands on each side of her face and told her, *Hold fast now, Cairy. Hold fast.*

With a nod our eyes unlocked, and I went about packing the rest of my few possessions into my carpetbag, then quietly whisked down the stairs to Mother, who waited at the table with a bowl of warm milk and bread and a cup of steaming-hot tea with sugar.

"I've packed you a bite to eat on the way, Cairy, and some for Mr. Oldcorn too. Here is a jug of water as well, and you mustn't send the basket home. Keep it, as you might have need of it in Penrith. Who knows what Mr. Arnison's staff are given in the way of handy things."

Then she stood in front of me and, to my dismay, unclasped the chain around her neck, on which hung her most prized possession, a small pendant of gold filigree holding a dainty emerald.

"Oh, Mother! No! You must keep it! How could I ever sell it?"

She went behind me and reached around my neck to hang the necklace there. "No, child, hush now. I want you to have it, Cairstin, and wear it for me, and know that my love goes with you wherever you are."

Mother sobbed, and I whirled around to embrace her. "Oh, Mam, don't cry. I can hardly bear to leave you."

She held me close as we swayed by the hearth, the warmth of her love filling me with sorrow and strength.

"You look out for yourself, my dear," she whispered, with urgency. "There is a great, wide world out there you are off to, and not everyone will be someone to trust. You are a beauty, Cairy, and men will take notice. Keep your heart guarded at all times and focus on your work. And you'll have my prayers to watch over you."

I swallowed a sob myself and turned from her embrace, hastily dashing the tears from my cheeks. "I will, Mam. I will be careful and work as hard as ever." Then I turned with determination to face her and said as confidently as I could, "If there is anything I know, Mam, it's that I can sew as well as anyone with a needle, and I will show them how well Father has taught me. I will not fail you and Rosie."

She caught me in another hard embrace and kissed me. "You are more than you know, Cairstin Blackwood. More than you know."

I felt Rosie's lean arms encircle us both as she slipped into the kitchen just then. I scooped her up and swung her around like I did when she was small, and planted a kiss on each of her freckled cheeks. Though her hair was chestnut brown like our mother's, her green eyes matched my own, the tears pouring.

I finally let her go and climbed the stairs to gather my things. Loading my carpetbag on top of my small trunk, I carried them into the hall. Pausing at the top of the stairs, I turned to look one last time at my parents' bedchamber door. Such a mingling of hurt, sorrow, and longing filled my heart that I thought I would be crushed. The promise I'd made to my father was an added weight pressing down on my already over-loaded mind, and his words filled my ears as I descended the stairs.

"Cairstin, lass! Ya must marry! Promise me!"

A few moments later the three of us were standing outside on the street in the stark cold of morning, under the swinging sign with golden letters, "Hamish Blackwood, Tailor," squeaking on its hinges.

Mr. Oldcorn dismounted from his wagon to help me up.

"Thank you ever so much, Mr. Oldcorn, for taking Cairstin to Penrith with you. Promise me you will deliver her in one piece, by your own hand, to Mr. Arnison at his shop." Mother's voice was strained and pleading.

The old furniture maker returned to his seat beside me and took up the reins. "Don't ye worry, Mrs. Blackwood. As promise to take her to the man and see her safe with me own eyes, eh?"

"Thank you, Mr. Oldcorn. Goodbye, my sweet girl, and don't forget to write as soon as you can."

"Goodbye, Mam. I promise," I choked out, my throat caught by the frigid air. "Bye, my Rosie. You be a help to Mam, now."

All Rose could do was shiver in Mother's arms and nod at me, her tears still flowing.

I willed my head to turn forward as we pulled away across the bridge onto The Sands. My long-brimmed bonnet shut my loved ones from my sight, and only my future lay before me.

Chapter Two

My pulse rushed so loudly in my ears it nearly drowned out the sounds of the town as we reached the outskirts of Penrith. Mr. Oldcorn slowed the wagon as we made our way up Never End Road. I could barely contain myself, the pain of unspent tears pressing hard at the back of my eyes. I shivered and gripped the handle of Mother's basket on my lap so hard I feared I might never let it go. It had become a connection to her I had not anticipated.

I heard a church bell ring out the hour of eleven as we drove past the busy shops. Mr. Oldcorn was adept at coaxing his horse through the traffic of wagons and carriages, and I caught a whiff of freshly baked bread mingling with the scent of coal smoke. Nothing I saw on the bustling street would allow my gaze to rest. All was new and strange and foreign.

I had been to Penrith before, the few times when my father saw fit for me to attend him on his business trips there, but it had always been someplace far enough away not to matter to me.

Now Penrith mattered in a way I was still trying to comprehend.

Mr. Oldcorn drove the wagon through the broad, thronging Market Square and up the wide mouth of Devonshire Street. He came to a halt in front of a stalwart gray stone building abruptly in the path of those who would wish to continue northward, forcing travelers to take the narrow lanes on either side.

I sat gaping in front of the stately, beautifully dressed display windows of a three-story building. Above the windows were signs in gold letters, framed in blue molding and encased in glass, reading "Drapers, Costumiers, and Milliners." My eyes were then drawn above to the huge scrolling, molded white letters of "N. Arnison and Sons."

I could hardly breathe.

To my right was an enormous red stone building. The golden letters of "The George Hotel" were blazoned on a huge black sign, and the old king's portrait swung above its revolving door. To my left was another four-story giant, built in the same gray stone as Arnison's, with several shops tucked into its first floor. But they were not alone. There were more shops, vendor carts, massive banks, printers, and tradesmen, as behind me other streets turned off the square in different directions.

"All right, lass. Arnison 'tis a barie bloke and will nay hurt thee, eh? Let us help thee down." I hadn't noticed Mr. Oldcorn was standing beside the wagon and offering me his hand. He had barely spoken a word the entire trip.

I painfully forced my fingers to un-clutch the basket handle to take his. "Yes, thank you, Mr. Oldcorn." My voice whispered a curl of chilly air before my face.

Alighting on the cobblestones, I looked up, my head bent as far back as possible. The place was enormous to my country-girl eyes. Three stories of huge gray stones, colorful displays on the main floor, elaborately stone-framed windows on the second story, and smaller ones on the third, with a sprawling cornice and great quoin blocks up the corners. I never felt so small in my life, and my heart slid down to my frozen booted feet.

Mr. Oldcorn carried my small trunk and nodded. "Aye, lass. 'Twill be a change for thee, but not t'worry. As promised your mam to deliver thee t'Arnison and nay just hoy thee on the side o' the road. Come now, let's be about it."

I swallowed hard and nodded. Gripping my basket and carpetbag, I followed Mr. Oldcorn inside the glazed door.

A bell rang over our heads, and my eyes needed a moment to adjust from the brilliance of the daylight outside. Mr. Oldcorn walked toward the formidable sales counter to the right of the high-ceilinged space, paneled in rich dark oak and ornately carved window frames. Surrounded by volumes of cloth, displays, and glass-topped cases, with a burst of colors, the shop was a delicious feast for the eyes, though I did not indulge myself in more than a scanning glance.

Behind the counter stood a tall young man in a dark-gray closely fitted frock coat, with a dazzlingly white shirt and black cravat. His appearance was immaculate, but the whole effect was marred by his lack of a noticeable chin. He looked up from his writing to greet us cheerfully, then changed his tone when he took in the sight of us.

"Hmm, yes, and what can we do for you sir, and, uh, miss?" The suspicion in his voice was unmistakable, and it rattled my insides.

"Me name is Oldcorn, sir, and this is Miss Blackwood, here for Mr. Arnison, who's given her a position here."

Mr. Oldcorn motioned for me to come closer, and I scrambled to pull from my pocket the letter Father had given me from Mr. Arnison. I hadn't thought to read it on the way, and now I wish I had.

The man took the letter and scanned it. "Hmmmm, yes, I see. But you should have come to the delivery door instead of coming into the drapery."

His tone was scolding, and my cheeks grew hot. "I am sorry, sir. We weren't told, and . . ."

"Just go out the way you came and around the right side of the building. You'll see the door." He returned the letter and motioned us back out the way we came.

Mr. Oldcorn gave me a toothy side smile as we exited and walked around the building. To my surprise, this side of the structure did not go straight back but angled out from the front to the back. It looked as if this triangular-like portion had been added on to the original building, and it was sided in cream-colored stucco. The windows were trimmed in blue paint, and when we reached the side, we saw the large double doors with an arched transit, where the delivery of long fabric bolts was being made as we approached.

I was startled by a boy near to Rosie's age who winked at me as he helped to take the bolts and boxes inside.

"Eh, lad," Mr. Oldcorn called to him. "Away with thee and find Mr. Arnison, eh?"

"Mr. Arnison's just here in his office. Come and find him theeself."

Every nerve in my body stood on edge as I tried to dodge the workers unloading the goods from a wagon and was relieved when Mr. Oldcorn jerked his head toward the door and forged a way for us to enter.

The high-ceilinged hall was a bit dark, but the lad thumbed toward the first door on the left, just inside the entry, then went about his business.

Mr. Oldcorn nodded encouragingly, so I straightened my shoulders and knocked.

"Yes," a firm tenor voice said from within. "Come in."

Blowing out a quick breath, I reached up for the latch and pushed open the large wooden door.

To my surprise the room was bright and filled with light from the large arched windows. It was painted a bright yellow, which added to its cheerful aspect. It was not as neat and tidy as I might have expected, as there were many ledgers and boxes and stacks of this and that about, the glass cupboards on the wall were filled with mismatched items, and the desk was a whirl of papers.

The man who rose from the chair was of average height and slender build, with one graying curl of hair encircling his head and accentuating his long, oval face. His eyes were sharp but not harsh, and his silver sideburns curved around his jaw, touching the starched high collar of his white shirt. His thick black necktie was expertly bowed, and the silk damask waistcoat under his black frock coat was a bird's-egg blue, which matched his clear eyes.

"Ah yes," he said as I timidly approached and curtsied. "You must be Miss Blackwood. You have your father's ginger hair."

His manner was businesslike, but he held out his hand and gave mine a kind tug, then turned his attention to my companion.

"Ah, Mr. Oldcorn, and how are you? Thank you for delivering Miss Blackwood safely."

"As in grand fettle, Mr. Arnison. 'Twas no bother a tall. Shall As be taken this upstairs, sir?" Mr. Oldcorn knocked the side of my trunk.

"Uh, no. Actually, the lady apprentices do not keep their lodgings here, Mr. Oldcorn. But you can put that down, and I will have one of the lads deliver it to Miss Blackwood's room, just near here in Sutton Yard."

Mr. Oldcorn placed the trunk near the door and bowed politely to Mr. Arnison. When Mr. Oldcorn turned to me, he held a curious softness in his hooded eyes.

I gave him my hand. "Thank you ever so much, Mr. Oldcorn. I shall never forget your kindness toward me and my family."

"Aw, t'wasn't a bother, lass. And As be sure to tell thee mam thee's in safe hands now." And with that he touched the brim of his hat and went out the still-open door.

"You must take after your mother with that lovely accent of yours, Miss Blackwood. It will serve you well here at the shop. Customers from the South will feel more comfortable dealing with someone they can comprehend better than the local folk."

"Oh, I thank you, Mr. Arnison. My mother felt it might be an asset to me someday, and I suppose that day has come."

Mr. Arnison regained his desk chair and sat looking me over thoughtfully. "Indeed. I understand your father is gravely ill. I am most sorry to hear that. We were not close friends, but I always respected his work and determination when we apprenticed here together. I hope his illness will not last long."

I was still holding my bag and basket, my palms clammy inside my gloves. "Thank you for your kindness, Mr. Arnison." My voice came out wispy and soft. "My father is terribly ill, and there is little hope now that he will recover. I don't know what my family would do if you hadn't offered me a position here—"

Mr. Arnison raised his hand. "Ah, Miss Blackwood, tut tut. I am very sorry to hear your father is not improving. I was happy to take on an experienced girl, and I know your father was always a forthright man. I believe you are as good as he stated in his letter, and we are happy to have the extra hands. Have you heard the news about the new railway due to arrive in Penrith next month?"

My head swam at his description of my father's recommendation, so I completely missed his question. "I'm sorry, Mr. Arnison—did you say railway?"

"Yes. My goodness, you must have been exceedingly entrenched in your crisis at home not to have heard such news."

Mr. Arnison's calm face was now animated. "The Lancaster to Carlisle Line. Yes! And we are anticipating all the people from the south of England to come flocking to Penrith as the gateway to the Lake District. We have already seen an increase in customers, as the local folk are getting ready for all the excitement when the trains from Lancaster to the south and Carlisle to the north will arrive simultaneously at our new station."

I was bewildered by this news but glad to see that Mr. Arnison was so pleased by it. "I see. Well, that is good news, isn't it, sir?"

"The best news Penrith has had in years, Miss Blackwood. Just imagine—the little town of Penrith will be the stopping place for all the London folk on their way to their holidays. It may be the end of 1846, my dear, but 1847 will be a banner year for Arnison and Sons! Mark my words! And that is why I was more than happy to have another set of capable hands here."

The man rubbed his hands together with anticipation. My attempt to mirror his enthusiasm probably fell short, for he paused and looked at me carefully, and I heard a bell ring somewhere in the building.

"Ah, but I can see you must be hungry after so long a journey, and it is time for dinner." He rose and motioned me toward the door. "Leave your things here with your trunk, and I will have someone take you up to the staff room."

Just then, a round-cheeked girl in a plain brown dress, around my own age, walked past, and Mr. Arnison called to her. "Ah, Miss Ainslie, this is Miss Blackwood, our new girl. She'll be working with you and Mrs. Fallowfield upstairs. Will you please take her with you to dinner?"

The girl smiled cheerfully down at me, for she was a good head taller, with chestnut-brown hair and dancing hazel eyes. "Oh! Hello and welcome, Miss Blackwood. I am Annabel Ainslie, and I'm so pleased you're finally here. Come—let us go up, and we can get to know each other as we climb the stairs."

I looked back to find Mr. Arnison nodding with a small smile on his lips, then Miss Ainslie whisked me down the hall.

~

The wooden employee staircase traversed back and forth up the triangular side of the building and was well lit by the tall windows on each floor.

By the time we reached the second floor, I was a bit winded, not from the climb but by my escort's endless, Northern-laced chatter. Evidently word had gotten around about my coming and why.

"Here's the staff tearoom, as we call it. We have all our meals here except on Sundays." Miss Ainslie opened the door to a large room, brightly lit by the sunlight streaming through the windows to the right, facing the square. It was painted a welcoming cream color, and the fire on the hearth burned warmly. A group of more than twenty people—men, ladies, and boys of varying ages—were seating themselves.

Miss Ainslie guided me to the table near the windows and

found me a chair. "This is our table. Everyone sits according to their status in the company. The tables nearest the fire are for the heads o' the departments and the best salesmen."

All I did was nod and try to take it in. Soon the tables were full of chatting employees, and a few old women brought in steaming bowls of savory soup and platters of bread. My stomach rumbled at the smell of food—I hadn't realized how hungry I was. The bowls were filled and the tea poured.

Miss Ainslie passed my bowl to me, and I noticed the man from the front counter downstairs watching me doubtfully over his teacup. It was as I feared. I had made a fool of myself with him already.

"Now, ladies, let me introduce ya to our new dressmaker, Miss Blackwood." Miss Ainslie looked as pleased as a cat with a mouse as she set my soup before me. "Miss Blackwood, ya already know, has traveled all the way from Appleby this morning to join us."

I tried to smile at the others but wasn't sure the attempt was successful. My mind felt dull and slow.

"This is Miss Susan Dykes—she has the top seat, as she's been here the longest." Miss Ainslie nodded toward a thin blond girl of perhaps twenty-three, with intelligent pale-blue eyes.

"Welcome to Arnison's, Miss Blackwood." She nodded and smiled, revealing some, sadly, crooked teeth.

"And this is Miss Eliza Salkeld, who is simply marvelous with a fan bodice." Miss Ainslie's nose crinkled as she winked at Miss Salkeld and laughed into her tea.

"Miss Ainslie, how you do tease! Good afternoon, Miss Blackwood," said the not-so-amused girl, who looked to be close to my age, with a turned-up nose and high forehead. Her hair was a dark chestnut, with thick lashes and brows to match. Her eyes were fixed on something on my neck, and I reflexively reached up to cover Mother's tiny emerald.

Miss Ainslie continued. "Miss Dykes and Miss Salkeld are second cousins, though ya wouldn't know to look at them, would ya?"

"No indeed. It is a great pleasure to meet you both," I said. "I hope I will be a great help to you all—" My voice trailed off, as I could not think of anything else to say.

They all chimed in with pleasantries, how glad they were I had come and how sorry they were for my family's troubles.

"Thank you. My father is very poorly, but I will do my best to make my family proud."

I could hear the exhaustion in my voice, as well as feel it in my bones.

"And this must be Miss Blackwood." The long, low voice of a woman came from just above my head.

The girls all stood to attention. I stood with alarm and turned to find a tall, hawkish-looking woman standing over me, her black-and-silver-streaked hair parted severely in the middle of her high forehead, her rather pointed nose sticking out from under her small wire-framed spectacles, her dark eyes looking me up and down appraisingly.

I curtsied to her. "Yes, ma'am."

"I am Mrs. Fallowfield, your supervisor. I wish to speak to you after the meal, if you please." Her manner was prim and her voice firm.

"Yes, Mrs. Fallowfield. I am at your service, ma'am." I curtsied again, sure she could hear the terror in my tone.

Mrs. Fallowfield nodded and returned to her place near the fire at the head table as we took our seats again.

"She's not as frightening as she first appears, Miss Blackwood," Miss Dykes offered. "She's curt and sharp sometimes, but she doesn't bite."

The girls sniggered and exchanged teasing glances.

"Indeed not," Miss Ainslie chimed in. "We all jump when she says to, and her looks are regrettable, but she really is an even-handed woman—you'll see."

I breathed a sigh of relief and finished my salty lentil soup and coarse bread. The others took up the dishes and headed out of the room, but I stayed where I was, as Miss Ainslie advised.

I stood and curtsied as Mrs. Fallowfield approached and sat. She motioned to my chair. "I understand your father is a tailor and an acquaintance of Mr. Arnison, Miss Blackwood. I want you to know that you have my sympathies, but I will expect you to work up to the standards of this establishment and not allow yourself to dwell on your personal problems."

"I will endeavor to work hard for you, Mrs. Fallowfield, and not squander the opportunity Mr. Arnison has given me."

"I am glad to hear it."

I detected a slight foreign accent in the woman's speech and wondered if she might have come from France, but *Fallowfield* was hardly a French name.

"You will follow me now to the dressmakers' sewing room and begin immediately. After the workday ends, you will be taken to your quarters with the others. Mr. Arnison will see to it that your things are taken there."

Mrs. Fallowfield stood to go, as did I, but I remembered something.

"Mrs. Fallowfield." My voice shook with uncertainty.

"Yes, what is it?"

I hesitated but blundered on. "May I . . . You see, I have my own scissors and needles and such in my bag downstairs. Would it be all right if I fetched them before joining you?"

Mrs. Fallowfield's eyes softened, and she lifted her pointy chin. "I like a girl who has her own tools. Yes. I will see you in the room at the back of the hall to the left, on the top floor."

I forgot to say thank you as I dashed by her and tripped down the stairs.

The rest of the afternoon I was given the simple but laborious task of sewing a strip of stiff wool into the hem of a voluminous dress skirt of fine purple-plaid silk. I had never done such a thing but knew the addition of the stiff strip would help the garment hem withstand wear and aid in maximizing the volume of the skirt at the bottom. Practical as well as stylish.

The ladies' sewing room was at the front far corner of the third floor and was thankfully well lit by the window overlooking the main square. Below us we could see the stalls of the egg and butter sellers and other vendors, and busy traffic of wagons and carriages. Miss Ainslie informed me that every Tuesday and Saturday were market days, when the square was quite busy with all kinds of business.

Whenever Mrs. Fallowfield left her intricate finish work and was gone from the room, the others would speak softly but freely, asking me many questions, some of which I hardly knew how to answer.

There was talk of the Queen and Prince Albert. Miss Ainslie seemed especially enamored with them. Also, the new railway, the other staff members—especially the younger men—but when the subject of church was brought up, my interest finally piqued.

"Oh, Miss Blackwood, ya must come with us to church on Sunday. There's a new minister in town. He has been here just the last nine months and has begun a new congregational church in the upper room of The Gloucester Arms," Miss Ainslie said enthusiastically.

"Yes, ya must, Miss Blackwood!" Miss Salkeld added, her

dark eyes dancing. "He is a marvelous preacher, and all the young people in town are going to hear him. He has even been nicknamed the 'Charismatic Vicar'!"

"And has a select group of young men he calls his disciples." Miss Dykes giggled into the blue silk in her hands. "It's a very exclusive group of bachelors that every girl in church has her eyes on!"

"What kind of church did ya attend in Appleby, Miss Blackwood?" Miss Ainslie asked.

"I went to St. Lawrence's with my family. It's the only church I have ever attended," I answered wistfully.

"Oh, a parish church." The girls eyed one another as Miss Ainslie raised her brows.

"Then ya must come to see Reverend Thomas. Ya'll be enthralled by his sermons. I've never heard any so good!" Miss Dykes smiled broadly, but it faded instantly when Mrs. Fallowfield entered.

Silence reigned once again.

The thought of a "Charismatic Vicar" was intriguing. When I thought of our dear old vicar at St. Lawrence's, charismatic was hardly a word I would use to describe him.

A small meal was served to the staff at six o'clock, then we were back in our candlelit sewing room until the church bells struck nine. By the time we walked the short distance to Sutton Yard, just behind a group of shops on the west side of Long Front Street, a plan was made on my behalf. The girls would take me with them on Sunday to the Bible Church, as it was called, then they would walk me up the hill to see the new railway station and the Penrith Castle ruins.

I was also invited to join the girls in addressing one another by our Christian names when we were just the four of us together. I took note of their friendliness and was exceedingly grateful for it. Things would have been much harder if they had not been so kindly.

Our diminutive flat was on the second floor of a building on the right, just inside Sutton Yard. I shivered as we entered. Annabel informed me that our allotment of coal for the tiny stove, standing in the little hall between the two bedchambers, was barely enough to take the chill off in the evenings, and they never bothered to light it in the mornings, preferring to dress quickly and get to work, where the fires were not so scarce.

The lack of privacy in our small rooms was no bother to me, being used to sharing a room with my sister. I was not in the least afraid, especially knowing that the company cooks slept in the rooms under ours on the first floor. Evidently they were to look out that we behaved properly and no gentlemen came to visit.

When I dropped my ice-cold body onto the straw mattress on the tiny bed assigned to me, the weariness dripped from my frame. Everything felt so foreign. The scratch of the sheets, the smell of the pillow, the sounds of the house creaking, and the girls sighs all irritated my raw nerves.

All day I'd held at bay a desperate ache from the surface of my conscience, but now that all was dark and I was finally alone with my thoughts, loneliness surrounded me like thick black mist.

Chapter Three

I never knew someone as weary as I might not fall asleep for an entire night. All I did from the time I lay down was toss and turn until the town bell ringer walked by on the street below, calling out the hour of five o'clock. I was completely overtaken by what I supposed to be the agony of homesickness. And as if my loneliness were not enough, my father's ragged voice would call to me out of the shadows.

The next few days and nights were much the same. I would rise at five o'clock in the morning with the others, share a quick breakfast with the staff, and begin each day at six, checking Mrs. Fallowfield's calendar on the sewing room wall and taking up my latest assignment. Mrs. Fallowfield examined my work, and each task she gave me was more difficult than the last.

Before dismissing us each day, she would ceremoniously cross off the day on the calendar, then give us a curt nod and bid us good night. Despite my exhaustion and grief, by God' grace I was able to keep up.

Susan Dykes, having seniority, was always the girl Mrs. Fallowfield chose to accompany her when a lady came into the shop for a fitting or to be measured for a new dress. Susan always returned from these sessions with a proud tilt to her chin and full of gossip for us, which helped the time pass during our long hours.

Whenever a second girl was needed to assist at these times, Eliza was the next girl chosen. I learned that Susan had secured her cousin her position at Arnison's, and I could see she felt responsible for her.

Only four days had been crossed off Mrs. Fallowfield's calendar when she summoned Susan to the lady's fitting room, then, to my surprise, hastily motioned for me to follow. I looked at Eliza, who seemed just as shocked.

"Eliza," Mrs. Fallowfield explained, "since you are working to finish Mrs. Tibbon's gown, which is due tomorrow, I want you to stay with your work. Come, ladies."

We followed her breathlessly to the second floor. "We have two ladies to assist at present, girls. Mrs. Murphy has come, and right after her, Mrs. Kirkbride." Turning abruptly, she looked us over, as if making a decision.

"Miss Dykes, I believe you are capable of handling Mrs. Kirkbride. Miss Blackwood, you will assist with Mrs. Murphy's measurements, and I will go between both ladies. Shoulders straight now!" She led us into the ladies' fitting room and clapped her hands.

I was motioned toward a kindly looking woman with streaks of gray in her fashionably coifed hair. Mrs. Fallowfield took the measuring tape hanging from her neck and handed it to me as she escorted Mrs. Murphy to a small dais and took up a ledger.

I helped Mrs. Murphy remove her gown and petticoats, until she was in a suitable state of undress for proper measurements. I thought it odd, though, that she insisted on retaining her shawl over her shoulders and arms.

When Mrs. Fallowfield gave her a questioning look, she said, "It is a bit chilly in here."

Out of the corner of my eye, I watched Susan. I knew well how to measure a man for a suit and had measured my mother and sister, as well as myself, often enough, but I was unsure my method would be acceptable.

I proceeded with my measurements, and as Susan had started with Mrs. Kirkbride's shoulders, then neck to waist, I moved confidently and told the measurements to Mrs. Fallowfield, who wrote them down. However, Mrs. Murphy seemed uncomfortable about the whole affair. I looked to Mrs. Fallowfield to see if she might give me any clues as to what I was doing wrong, but she gave me no indication.

As I raised the droop of Mrs. Murphy's shawl from her shoulder to measure the length of her arm, I halted, my fragile confidence shattered by a terrible discovery. Mrs. Murphy's upper arms were badly bruised, and only in a manner that would have resulted from large hands gripping her violently.

I glanced up at Mrs. Murphy in horror, but she only smiled nervously at me. "Go on, my dear. I should like to get this over with so I might have Mrs. Fallowfield's assistance in choosing fabrics for my dresses. I need them delivered directly, as I plan on wearing them for my sister's visit in a fortnight."

I looked up at Mrs. Fallowfield, who frowned at me with impatience. With shaking hands, I carefully measured Mrs. Murphy's arm, keeping the shawl in a position so as not to reveal her secret to anyone else in the room.

When I was finished, I assisted her back into her things, noticing now the obviously painful face she made as she raised her arms over her head. I was as gentle as possible, and when all was finished, she gave me a meaningful look and nod of thanks. My chest ached for her.

~

Mrs. Fallowfield nodded for me to attend her and Mrs. Murphy as they went down the curving customer stairs to the first floor, and we entered the drapery inside the main entrance. All around were bolts of fabrics, laces, and trimmings, some draping from the high ceiling all the way down in colorful cascades of silk, linen, and printed cottons. The light from the tall display windows caught on the shimmering fabrics and gave the place a magical atmosphere.

Mrs. Fallowfield assisted Mrs. Murphy in choosing several beautiful bolts. I carefully recorded each choice in Mrs. Fallowfield's ledger and stacked each bolt on the display table nearest the door. I was amazed at Mrs. Murphy's light and carefree manner as she walked about, as if nothing in the world were wrong. It gave me a strangely dark feeling in the pit of my stomach.

The main-floor drapery was Mr. Bell's territory, and I could feel him glaring at me and Mrs. Fallowfield from behind the counter. Obviously he felt his domain was being invaded, and I knew he was as annoyed with Mrs. Fallowfield as he was by my presence. I tried to ignore him and focus on the task at hand, and gladly found assisting Mrs. Fallowfield unexpectedly reassuring.

After escorting Mrs. Murphy out of the shop, Mrs. Fallowfield returned. "Miss Blackwood, please gather Mrs. Murphy's fabrics and follow me to the cutting room."

"Yes, ma'am." I gathered the heavy bolts in my practiced arms, when the door opened and the bell above it sounded a sturdy jingle.

Mrs. Fallowfield turned to greet the new customer with her usual professionalism, but she swiftly warmed into a friendly smile as she gasped, "Why, Mr. Dalton! Is it you? Back after all this time!"

I took a few steps away with my awkward load and peered over the stack of bolts to see a young man, something around four and twenty, gleaming down from his tolerable height on the surprised Mrs. Fallowfield, who clearly displayed a measure of affection toward him I hadn't thought her capable of.

"I am very happy to see you again, Mrs. Fallowfield. Here I am to present myself for inspection. Is Mr. Arnison here? I've heard only good reports about Penrith and Arnison's since I've been away, and I hope the Arnisons have had only the same of me."

The man was well dressed, but not at all in a dapper sort of way. Everything from his black top hat to his black Huntington boots was tasteful to my trained eyes, but my gaze was drawn to his face, and there it remained.

"Mr. Bell, Would you be so kind as to inform Mr. Arnison that Mr. Dalton has returned from London and wishes to see him?"

Mr. Bell nodded a dour greeting to Mr. Dalton, then did as he was bid.

Mrs. Fallowfield continued to smile at the man. "My, Mr. Dalton, how the Arnisons will be delighted to see you. Please, do come—"

"Well, if it isn't Mr. Gabriel Dalton himself. How happy I am to see you, and looking so well, young man. So very well indeed, I must say!" Mr. Arnison shook the man's hand enthusiastically, with a few congenial slaps on the shoulder for added emphasis.

I stood as still as I could under the weight of my burden, which was now getting the better of my sweating hands. As I watched this unexpected reunion with curiosity, I couldn't help but study Mr. Dalton's face. He did not strike me as particularly handsome. No, that was not what fascinated me. It must be the genuine warmth in his smile.

"Well, what am I doing now, Mr. Dalton? We cannot keep you standing inside the shop door. Let us retire to the office and call for tea."

The reunited friends did not turn toward the office but continued their genial conversation, and I stared at Mr. Dalton from my hidden vantage, enjoying the view. But I was soon distracted by the ache in my arms and did my best to shift my load, as I could feel my strength waning.

I looked around for any means to ease my burden. I was on the other side of the chatting men from the table, and there was nothing else but the high counter, where I might put the bolts for a moment, but it was too far away and too high for me to hope that my failing arms would be able to hoist the bolts upon it. Besides, there stood the dubious Mr. Bell with his nose ceilingward, and I would rather fall through the floor than let him see my weakness.

I was jolted from my distress by Mrs. Fallowfield. "Miss Blackwood! Where is she now? Oh! I'd entirely forgotten you."

Mrs. Fallowfield took a step backward and whirled around, knocking her elbow at the end of the uppermost bolt I held. It was too much. Unable to rebalance the bolts and handle the weight, they flew off my outstretched arms and tumbled end over end onto the wooden floor with a muffled clatter. The unfurling fabrics reminded me of the colorful dancing gypsy girls at the Appleby New Horse Fair.

"Oh no! I am so sorry!" I pressed my damp hands to my reddening face, then plunged into the fray to gather up the bolts.

"My goodness!" Mrs. Fallowfield exclaimed. "How long have I left you standing there with this heavy load? Mr. Bell!"

To my great relief, no accusatory tone edged my mistress's voice. Indeed, I might have even detected a note of sympathy, had I not been frantically trying to make sense of the mess I'd made. I knelt and used my skirt as a place to layer the bolts to get them up off the floorboards, when I noticed a pair of gentlemen's boots walking about me and a man's soothing voice above my head. They were all decidedly not Mr. Bell's.

"Here, let me help you," Mr. Dalton said as he placed the bolts I couldn't reach onto the pile and flashed me a reassuring smile.

"Oh!" was all I could say as my face flushed anew, and I felt my heart flip over in my chest. "Oh!" I said again, this time finding more words. "No, sir, I can manage. I just need a moment to—"

"It is nothing, Miss Blackwood. I am happy to be of assistance."

"Now, now, Dalton," Mr. Arnison protested. "The staff can take care of this, and you shall come back to my office and tell me all about your adventures in London—"

But Mr. Dalton did not take his cue to follow Mr. Arnison. The bolts were put in order again, and I gathered them into my arms, then found it quite impossible to stand under their weight. Another surge of hot blood rushed to my neck and cheeks as I felt everyone's eyes upon me.

I wanted to lie down on top of those blasted bolts and cry. But before I was able to give in to the temptation, I felt the bolts lifted off my arms and saw a hand extend down toward me.

Looking up, I saw Mr. Bell with armloads of bolts and Mr. Dalton's smiling face, offering me his hand. I was stunned for a moment by his kind gesture, but especially the gentle strength in his eyes. Not pity or charity but a genuine goodness I had never seen in the eyes of any man.

I was overcome by a strange mixture of shyness and gladness. He reached his hand closer to me, and as I laid my own in it, I felt a foreign rush of warmth tingle through my body. I stifled a gasp as he pulled me to my feet.

"Thank you, sir," I said breathlessly, and curtsied.

Mr. Dalton bowed respectfully, and when he released my hand, I felt the disconnection acutely. He turned to Mrs. Fallowfield, who stood motionless in shock just behind him, and gestured toward me. "May I have the pleasure of being introduced to—"

Mrs. Fallowfield started, her eyes bulging, but she took a step closer and said curtly, "Miss Blackwood, may I present Mr. Gabriel Dalton, a longtime family friend of the Arnisons and newly returned from London. Mr. Dalton, this is Miss Blackwood, lately of Appleby, in Westmorland. She is our newest apprentice."

"I am delighted to make your acquaintance, Miss Blackwood. I hope you are fully recovered from this, uh, incident." Mr. Dalton flashed an impish smile at me, as though we were in on a joke together.

"I am fully recovered, Mr. Dalton, and am very pleased to meet you. Thank you for your kindness, sir." I listened to myself address him as if I were a lady and had the right to.

"It was my pleasure. Good afternoon, Miss Blackwood." He flashed me another smile, then turned to follow Mr. Arnison to his office.

Mrs. Fallowfield interrupted my awestruck stare and led me up to the cutting room.

~

We were paid that evening, and feeling those cold coins in my hand gave my weary soul a deep sense of relief, though I wished it had been more. I was grateful that the company bookkeeper would take charge of sending most of the money to Mother, as he did for many of the younger employees. I only kept what I absolutely needed to get by for myself.

I was so excited I could hardly close my eyes to sleep. Still, the sight of Mrs. Murphy's arms haunted me, while the memory of Mr. Dalton made me blush in the dark.

Sunday morning was clear, and the sky a crystal blue as seagulls cried out overhead. I followed the girls down the street past Arnison's, taking the shortcut through Little Dockray, then up Corn Market Street, crossed the mostly empty Corn Market Square and entered The Gloucester Arms. It was a large building covered in white stucco, with many lovely gabled roofs. The pub on the main floor, covered in rich, dark paneling with a cheery fire, was nearly empty as we passed through and up the stairs to a large hall where rows of chairs had been placed facing a wooden lectern at the front.

The room buzzed with activity. People of all ages and walks of life were gathered in little groups of lively discussion.

I was introduced to some of Annabel's friends, Miss Charlotte Barnes and Mr. Gerald Pitt, who were engaged to be married in the spring, and Mr. Robert Nixon, a tall, burley man with an infectious smile and quiet manner. There was also Mr. William Soulier, a short man dressed fashionably in a bottle-green frock coat and blue trousers. His clashing ensemble was a bit loud for my taste. His round face and dark complexion were not offensive, but unremarkable. Mr. Pitt, Mr. Nixon, and Mr. Soulier had the honor of being some of the reverend's personal disciples, a fact I was expected to be impressed with.

When it was time for the service to begin, I joined the girls in their accustomed row at the back and looked around with great curiosity, not only at all the interesting people but also at how this makeshift church was completely different from what I was accustomed to. It was nothing like going to a real church,

I thought, as I compared it to my dear old St. Lawrence's in Appleby. There were no "paid" and "free" distinctions between the seats, no stained glass, no organ, no monuments, no candles, not even a hint of solemnity.

A young man passed songbooks down each row and then sat at a piano to play. Everyone seemed to know instinctively which song to turn to, but the melody and words were new to me, as was the great enthusiasm with which the congregation sang. Such vigor and harmonies, and at such a volume as to almost drown out the piano entirely.

At last a tall, robust-looking man in a black suit and white clerical collar came smiling to the lectern and bid the congregation to sit down.

"That's him!" Annabel whispered and patted my knee. "The Charismatic Vicar!"

I nodded and turned my full attention to the speaker. The text of his sermon was taken from the book of Genesis and the story of Adam and Eve. Reverend Thomas had a square face with a reddish bulb-shaped nose, a wide mouth with thick lips, and a barrel-like frame that reminded me of the butcher back home. His resonate baritone voice projected energetically, even dramatically at times, as though he were an actor in a play.

"I shall say it again," he shouted, making me jump. "It is not good that man should be alone!"

Goodness, Vicar Hayes would never have shouted at his congregation so.

"All right then!" he continued, stepping in front of the lectern and scanning his audience with fire in his eyes. "Now I am looking all around, and I see you, you young gents, who think you are so very smart and independent that you have put off taking a wife until you are too old to do the Lord any good. I see you, and I know who you are."

How grateful I was that I was not a young, unmarried man. Sinking down in my chair, I hardly knew what to expect next.

Reverend Thomas walked back behind the lectern and glared out from under his bushy brows. "It is not good that man should be alone, so then, what is good? It is good that a man should take a wife, that's what! And why is it good, you may ask? Because the Good Lord has spoken it, that's why!"

At this, the man slammed closed his Bible and began to pray. "Oh God in heaven, help us to overcome the evils of the flesh and rise above the influences of Satan in this fallen world. It is in your blessed power and calling that you have placed upon me to shepherd these poor lost souls and bring them to a place of repentance and obedience for thy name's sake. Amen!"

The young man at the piano struck up a lively tune, and the congregation rose to its feet, singing out with all their might.

I stood in the midst of the singers, physically shaken.

The service ended and Reverend Thomas stood at the top of the stairs, greeting his congregants as they left the hall. Annabel, Susan, and Eliza gathered around me with eager faces.

"Let us introduce ya to Reverend Thomas, Cairstin. He is very amiable and will be so glad we have brought ya to church." Annabel was eager to make sure I met everyone.

"Oh, I don't know. I don't want to bother him—"

"It's no bother. See, he is saying goodbye to everyone. He takes a great interest in all his followers." Annabel took me by the arm, and they escorted me to the line waiting to greet the minister.

I fiddled with Mother's pendant uncomfortably as we approached, not at all sure I wanted to be introduced to such an important and imposing man. But there was only one way out of the hall and that was to pass in front of him and be subjected to his inspection, like everyone else.

When our turn came, I noticed a large wooden box with a slot in the top on a table near him, with a sign reading "Building Fund."

"Well well!" Reverend Thomas said, his abundant brows raised in appraisal. "If it isn't Mr. Arnison's little brood of dress-makers, and who is this fair young thing? Have you added to your number?"

The man took a step closer and loomed over me, larger than life. It felt as if he were looking right through me to my backbone.

"Please allow me to introduce our new colleague, Reverend Thomas," Annabel said. "This is Miss Blackwood, lately of Appleby. Her father is a tailor there but has taken ill, and Miss Blackwood has come to help support her family."

I was aghast at how much personal information Annabel so freely expounded upon in the hearing of so many strangers. The reverend now seemed even more interested than before. He turned narrowed eyes on me and nodded.

"I see, I see." He pushed up his full bottom lip and raised his shaven chin. "Well, it is a great pleasure to meet you, Miss Blackwood. I am very glad your friends have brought you into our humble fold. I will be sure to add your father to the list of invalids I pray for, and I will pray for you as well, my dear. You must be feeling vulnerable in a new town and a new position, surrounded by so many strangers."

"I am pleased to meet you, Reverend Thomas. I am . . . that is, I appreciate your prayers for my father. He—"

"I can see that you must be a great comfort to your family, Miss Blackwood. Willing to take on such a responsibility is noble and one that God will credit you for." Reverend Thomas touched my arm and smiled with satisfaction. "Be sure to come back to us, and I promise to help you in any way I can. Now, ladies, thank you for coming, and have a restful Sabbath."

With that, he turned to the next set of people in line. The girls all dropped a few coins into the Building Fund box and rushed me down the stairs. As we reached the pub, they turned on me with delight.

"My goodness, Cairstin! The reverend did take to ya so!" Annabel exclaimed.

"I knew he would," Susan said breathlessly. "How could he not? Cairstin is such a beauty, and so demur!"

"Ya've made a great impression on him already," Eliza added, a twinge of jealously lacing her tone.

"I-I-" I stammered. "I don't know what to say."

"Come, let's sit near the fire and give Cairstin a moment to catch her breath. Shall we order tea, girls?"

Tea was ordered, and not long after we were joined by Annabel's friends Miss Barnes and Mr. Pitt, then Mr. Soulier pulled up a chair as well. Mr. Nixon could not join us, as he had to return to work.

The next half an hour was spent drinking tea and consuming biscuits as I listened to the others prattle on about my introduction to the reverend, his impressive sermon, the glorious singing, and the various people they had seen. I was mostly silent as I sipped my tea, grateful for the time to calm my nerves and smooth over my embarrassment.

All the while I could not help but observe the somewhat reserved Mr. Soulier. He seemed eager to join the conversation at times, but at others would sit back in his chair, looking from one girl to the next, as if assessing which filly among a lot to buy. He also looked frequently at a rather beautiful gold watch on a chain, which he tucked into the pocket of his waistcoat with an important air.

He made me uncomfortable, though I wasn't sure why, for he was neither rude nor overly engaging. He laughed when we all laughed and frowned when everyone frowned, but there was something about his eyes I couldn't put my finger on. Soulier sounded like a French name, but nothing about Mr. Soulier seemed French. Not that I had met many French people in Appleby to compare him with.

Miss Barnes was cordial, and Mr. Pitt was polite enough but conducted himself with an elite air, often quoting Bible verses to back up his statements about this and that. It made me feel my lack of discipline in studying my own Bible, which was sitting unread in the bottom of my trunk.

~

The others bid us goodbye as we stepped out of The Gloucester Arms, and the girls made good on their plan to take me up the hill on Castlegate to see the new train station and the ruins of Penrith Castle. I was glad to be out in the air on a rare sunny day in late November. There were end-to-end shops, pubs, and houses along the way, and the road was steep enough that I could feel the lack of use in my legs. The exercise felt good, and I was able to shake off the events of the morning.

I was curious about the railway and the first trains due to arrive in just a few weeks' time, on December 15. Being so long cooped up in my father's shop, without much news of the outside world, I felt my ignorance of such things keenly. Everyone's excited anticipation of its arrival, including Mr. Arnison's, was contagious, and I was eager to see what all the talk was about.

As we summited the hill, the crown opened up and I saw the shiny new rail station on the right, built in red stone, with tall gabled roofs and lighter-red quoins on the corners. The doors were painted a vibrant red and the large windows trimmed in white. Across the broad roadway to the left stood the ancient red ruins of an old castle on a knoll, surrounded by lawns of brown grass, with footpaths leading up to it.

All was quiet now, as it was Sunday and the railway workers were not there, but we took a look around the station building and saw the tracks leading from the north to the south behind the station, and the platforms being finished on either side. I could imagine the hustle and bustle of the area when the workers were there, and I wandered off a bit from the group as I studied the never-ending tracks, wondering about the far-off places they led to.

"Well, hello there, Miss Blackwood," said a strangely familiar voice coming from behind me.

I whirled around to find Mr. Dalton walking toward me. My heart flooded with gladness to see him again, then quickly checked itself, keenly aware of the smile it had brought to my face, which I tried to subdue but failed.

"Oh! Mr. Dalton! It is a pleasure to see you again, sir." I was struck by how gallantly I was able to speak to this man, as if he were able to draw out of me a part of myself I had never known.

"And you as well, Miss Blackwood." He lifted his hat as I curtsied. "I see you have an interest in the coming railway. I have just been admiring the work myself. An exciting prospect for Penrith, is it not?"

His amiable demeanor and friendly smile put me at ease quickly. "Yes, Mr. Dalton. I must admit, I know very little about it, but everyone seems to be on pins and needles waiting for its arrival."

"Indeed!" Mr. Dalton replied lightly. "You have come with friends, I see."

My associates had seen me conversing with a gentleman,

and curiosity oozed from their wide eyes as they wandered over to inspect the stranger.

"Why yes, Mr. Dalton. May I introduce you to my colleagues Miss Dykes, Miss Ainslie, and Miss Salkeld. We all work for Mr. Arnison in the dressmakers' department, under Mrs. Fallowfield's supervision, of course."

All the proper pleasantries were exchanged, and I felt the eyes of the admiring girls glancing from me to Mr. Dalton and back again.

"Well, Mr. Dalton, we shouldn't be keeping you," I said. "We were just on our way to see the castle ruins. I have never seen them before, and my friends have been kind enough to bring me here."

"Splendid." Mr. Dalton clasped his gloved hands and bowed slightly. "Would you ladies mind if I joined you? I was just heading over there myself. You see, I grew up in Penrith and have been away for a long while, and I wanted to reacquaint myself with the place."

"Oh, please do join us, Mr. Dalton," Annabel said. "We'd be most glad of your company, wouldn't we, girls?"

It was agreed, and Mr. Dalton joined our humble group as we trekked back to the street and crossed to the path.

I walked as if in a dream while Mr. Dalton strolled beside me, chatting politely about the beauty of the day. The other girls happily joined the conversation, and I went back to my usual quiet observations.

What kind of a man was this, who spoke so easily and freely with young ladies who were obviously below his station? I wondered what kind of studies he had been at in London and why he'd returned to a small town like Penrith.

Mr. Dalton remained by my side, and though he was polite to the others, most of his comments about the ancient castle were directed toward me. I smiled and nodded with genuine interest but was keenly aware of his specific attentions.

Mr. Dalton, as it turned out, was a marvelous tour guide and gave our little group an animated education about Penrith Castle and the moat, now dry, that surrounded it. I found the place mysterious, especially the way Mr. Dalton brought it all to life with his colorful descriptions and stories of lords and ladies, knights and kings. We also learned that Mr. Dalton was a newly licensed solicitor and barrister and intended to set up his office in town.

All too soon the tour was over, and we walked back down the path to the street.

"Well, ladies, thank you ever so much for your company and for allowing me to prattle on about my favorite spot in Penrith. I hope I did not bore you with my overabundance of detail."

"Oh no, sir!"

"Indeed not, Mr. Dalton."

The girls thanked him profusely for his time and attention.

"And you, Miss Blackwood. What do you think of the old castle?" Mr. Dalton leaned slightly toward me, genuine interest in his cheerful brown eyes.

"I found it enchanting, Mr. Dalton. We are all grateful, I'm sure, for the time you have taken from your day to treat us to your expert guidance. Thank you very much, sir."

He leaned back, looking at me with satisfaction from under the brim of his top hat, and pressed his lips into a smile. "It was my great pleasure, ladies." And though he addressed us all, his eyes never left mine. "Well, I should be getting home to my supper, I suppose. My housekeeper, Mrs. Trimble, is always hurt when I am not at the table on time. I bid you good day," and with another knowing smile, he bowed his head, then strolled down the hill by a different lane.

"Well! Cairstin Blackwood! Who would ever have guessed that ya were acquainted with such a wonderful gentleman as Mr. Dalton of Penrith," Annabel gushed. "And what other secret acquaintances might you have, pray tell?"

The heat rose on my neck, and I turned to walk down Castlegate. "Oh, Annabel. I only just met Mr. Dalton yesterday by accident in the drapery room. He was only being kind to us, as he probably knows how cooped up we are all week, and was feeling charitable. That's all."

"Well, I would most certainly not say that charity was his only motivation." Susan stepped in front of me and blocked my way. "I do believe Mr. Dalton finds ya very appealing, Cairstin. Ya have to admit that at least."

Annabel joined her, as did Eliza, and I could see a hint of envy in Eliza's sharp blue eyes. I knew Annabel would not let this go.

"Ya know, girls," she chided, "I do believe our dear Miss Blackwood is completely oblivious to how truly attractive she is. Cairstin, why shouldn't Mr. Dalton have eyes for ya? You're a lovely girl and must learn to believe in yourself more, don't you agree, lasses?"

I grew increasingly uncomfortable and impatient with their ridiculous flattery.

"It is nothing," I persisted in a whisper. "If there is anything obvious, it is that Mr. Dalton is a kind gentleman who takes pity on poor working girls like us. Now, let us move on and stop making a scene on the side of the street."

I pushed past them, marching quickly down the hill and all the way back to the passage into Sutton Yard, not stopping until I was tucked safely behind the door of our flat.

Chapter Four

My second week of work became easier as I grew more familiar with the staff and Mrs. Fallowfield's expectations. Sleep was improving, though I still struggled with racing thoughts and homesickness.

Friday morning I awoke with my mother's voice cautioning me. *"You look out for yourself, my love. There is a great, wide world out there you are flying off to, and not everyone will be someone to trust."*

As I arose to dress with the others, I could feel a draft of coolness from Eliza. It seemed to grow as the days went on, and though I made a conscience effort to be friendly and helpful to her, the chill continued.

We were all working diligently in our sewing room that morning, when Mr. Arnison himself came in the door in a flurry of frustration. We stood to attention, as did Mrs. Fallowfield, who looked surprised.

"Mr. Arnison! What can we do for you, sir?" Mrs. Fallowfield stepped toward him, but he moved past her and came directly to me.

"Miss Blackwood, I am sorry to interrupt, but I am in need of your unique services. Will you help?"

"Oh, of course, Mr. Arnison. How can I help you, sir?" I answered, aware of the others' eyes upon me.

"There is some kind of illness spreading amongst the tailors, and they have all taken to their beds. Mr. Bell thinks it was a bad bit of beef they all shared last night, for he is the only one who did not partake of it and he is as fine as a fiddle."

"I'm terribly sorry, Mr. Arnison. Do you wish me to tend to them—"

"Indeed not, my dear. I wish you to tailor!"

With this, Mr. Arnison marched out of the room. Mrs. Fallowfield motioned urgently for me to follow, and I closed the door on my gaping colleagues.

Mr. Arnison strode quickly down the hall to the tailors' sewing room and opened the door. It was empty except for Mr. Bell, whose face fell at the sight of me.

"But, sir," he blurted, "I assure you I am quite capable of finishing Mr. Stockdale's tailcoat, and I—"

"Thank you, Mr. Bell. Everything is in hand." Mr. Arnison motioned me to a table where a handsome black tailcoat lay unfinished. "You may go back to your drapery now, Mr. Bell."

Mr. Bell's ears grew red. He strode sharply toward the door, but just before he reached it, he turned and shot me a hot glare.

"You see, Miss Blackwood, Mr. Stockdale is a very important client, a representative of the railway, who has been staying in Penrith to inspect the work on the station, and he requires this tailcoat for an important meeting with the rest of the investors this evening." Mr. Arnison looked me in the eye, and his tone became even more serious. "Can you finish it, Miss Blackwood? Answer me as honestly as you can."

I took a good look at the coat, noted what was necessary to complete it, and calculated the time it would take.

"At what time will Mr. Stockdale be arriving to pick up his coat, Mr. Arnison, or will it be delivered?" My voice was calmer than I felt.

"It is to be delivered by four o'clock this afternoon. He will try it on at his hotel, and any adjustments necessary will need to be made on the spot if it isn't perfect."

I took a fortifying breath and nodded. "Leave it to me, Mr. Arnison. It will be ready."

Mr. Arnison nodded back. "Thank you, Miss Blackwood. I would do the work myself, but it has been quite a while since I held a needle, and I fear I would not have the speed necessary, considering the time constraint."

"Of course, Mr. Arnison. I will just go and fetch my tools from the ladies' sewing room and get started."

Mr. Arnison escorted me back and told Mrs. Fallowfield I would be otherwise engaged for the rest of the day. Then I dashed back to the tailcoat, my mother's voice whispering in my ear, *"You are more than you know, Cairstin Blackwood. More than you know."*

~

When Mr. Arnison returned at half past three, the tailcoat was pressed and ready. Mr. Arnison placed it carefully in a black box, had me collect my bonnet and coat, then led me down to the drapery. Mr. Bell held the door open for us as we stepped out into the busy street, and Mr. Arnison guided me to the next building on the left of the square, to the revolving door of The George Hotel.

My heart pounded like a galloping horse, and I gripped my mother's basket with one hand, which held my sewing tools, and her little pendant with the other. Mr. Arnison said little, and it was difficult to read his face as he walked briskly beside me and up the carpeted staircase. I caught fleeting glances of elegant ladies taking tea by blazing hearths and men in gray uniforms carrying luggage, and I almost tripped on my way up because of the rich, opulent decor that distracted me.

I had never been inside a hotel, and the little I had seen of The George was to steal glances in the windows of the main floor as I passed by. I never dreamed I would one day go inside such a grand place.

I breathed a sigh of relief when Mr. Arnison went into Mr. Stockdale's rooms alone and did all the dressing and inspecting. I stood in the carpeted hall and studied a beautiful landscape framed in gold until Mr. Arnison emerged.

Mr. Stockdale joined him. "Very satisfactory work, Miss Blackwood. Mr. Arnison, good evening to you."

And with that I was whisked back down the staircase and out the revolving door.

Before opening the door to his shop, Mr. Arnison stopped and leaned down to me.

"You have proven to be a godsend today, Miss Blackwood. I thank you and want you to know I shall not forget your stepping up to the challenge and making a good show of it."

Heat spread over my face, and I wished I could bury my face in Mr. Arnison's shoulder and cry my heart out. "Oh, thank you, Mr. Arnison. It was nothing, I was only happy I could be of help to you, sir."

"Hmmm, indeed you were, my dear," Mr. Arnison said with a smile. When he turned to open the door, we saw Mr. Bell inside the display window, obviously spying.

"Don't worry about him, Miss Blackwood. He is as territorial as a dog but usually never bites."

I almost laughed at Mr. Arnison's jest and couldn't help but smile knowingly at Mr. Bell when we passed.

Mr. Arnison instructed me to rest in the staff room until supper, which was only half an hour away, before rejoining my work in the ladies' sewing room. It was quiet there, except for the cooks preparing the meal, and I took my usual seat at the dressmakers' table.

For just a moment, I rested my head on my arms and thought about all that had happened since morning. I recalled Mr. Arnison's kind words of thanks, and again tears stung my eyes. Why had it been so hard for my father to say such things to me?

I was glad to have a few still moments to myself to reflect, but soon enough I was interrupted.

"Pardon, miss, but there's a letter come for thee."

I jerked my head up to find Toby, the errand boy who'd winked at me the first day, his grimy hand holding a letter.

"Oh! Thank you."

He scurried away as I looked over the address—*Miss Cairstin Blackwood, c/o Mr. Arnison, Devonshire Street, Penrith*—written in my mother's hand.

Glancing at the clock, I had but five minutes before the room would fill with curious eyes, so I tucked my precious letter into my pocket to read it in privacy, after the others were asleep that night.

After an exhaustive evening of work and all the girls had retired, I lit a candle by the window and opened my letter.

Dearest Cairy,

Thank you for your letter telling me you are working hard and for sending me your first pay. I am so sorry to have to write you about your father, who has grown much worse since you left. The doctor doesn't think it will be long now.

Your sister and I are fine for now. Your father's savings has not run out yet, and we are being ever so careful.

Dearest, your father has told me he wants you to make good on your promise to him as soon as possible. What promise is that, my love?

We are very grateful to you for working so hard and being so brave. You are always in my prayers.

Write soon,

Mother

Hot tears ran down my cheeks unchecked. I laughed a little thinking about my promise. Who on earth would want to marry a poor working girl like me?

A flash of Mr. Dalton's face came to mind, but that was ridiculous. I wasn't even sure I would ever see the man again, let alone be an object of his interest. A girl didn't just walk up to any finely dressed man on the street and propose to him.

~

A bit of gossip flittered about the staff that Saturday, about my coming to Mr. Arnison's rescue. Mr. Bell was as cold as ever, but I expected nothing more from him. I hardly saw Mr. Arnison for a while, as he was busy elsewhere and rarely came to the third floor.

Once again Mrs. Fallowfield crossed off the last day of the workweek, December 5, on her calendar, and we were paid our wages before we left the building at the end of the Saturday shift. As I waited in line, I noticed Eliza whispering and laughing with Mr. Bell as they stole side glances my way. I was sad our relationship was going sideways even before we'd had a real chance to know each other. Now that she was talking to Mr. Bell, I felt even more helpless to change the course.

Sunday morning dawned gray and cold. We walked out of Sutton Yard and made our way quickly to The Gloucester Arms for church. This time I was less anxious and, after greeting the few people I'd been introduced to, went over to find my seat on the back row and look over the songbook that was passed to me.

"So, Miss Blackwood, you have returned to us, I see." My skin prickled as I recognized Reverend Thomas's voice just behind me.

I stood, embarrassed to have been singled out of the gathering crowd for the reverend's particular attentions. "Good morning, Reverend Thomas. Uh, yes, I have come back with my friends."

Annabel joined me and leaped into the conversation. "Good morning, Reverend! We're so eager to hear your sermon today, aren't we, Miss Blackwood?"

"Why yes, the last one was most, uh, most edifying," I stammered, trying to find something appropriate to say.

Reverend Thomas held his hand over his heart. "Praise God, dear children. Praise God. And I hope you will find today's sermon equally so. I had you ladies in mind as I wrote it out this week, you know."

Once again his eyes bored through me, and I wished I were invisible.

"Ah, here you are, Mr. Soulier. Just the man I was looking for." Reverend Thomas turned to greet the man walking past, and put his arm around his shoulder. He steered Mr. Soulier to face us and nodded toward me. "Here is one of my special boys. You see, ladies, he is attending my discipleship meetings for a select group of young men I have my eye on to expand my ministry here in Penrith. Mr. Soulier, have you had the pleasure of meeting our new member, Miss Blackwood of Appleby?"

My heart seized as Mr. Soulier bowed to me and smiled broadly. "I have indeed had the pleasure, Reverend. I was fortunate enough to join Miss Blackwood with her companions for tea last Sunday after church. I hope you are well, Miss Blackwood?"

Mr. Soulier's sudden interest took me aback. "I am very well, Mr. Soulier, and I hope the same for you, sir."

"I am well, thank you. Do you mind if I sit with you and your friends today, Miss Blackwood? I see that Mr. Pitt is already sitting with Miss Barnes nearer the front, but I believe the acoustics of the room are better from here, don't you?"

"Well! That sounds like a very nice arrangement to me." Reverend Thomas grinned from Mr. Soulier and back to me. "Indeed, you know, Miss Blackwood, Mr. Soulier is a clerk at Barclays Bank just on the corner of the main square, near Arnison's. He has a great career ahead of him, don't you, Soulier. Ah, but I must be getting to my seat—it is time to begin."

I had no time to think of a response as the piano rang out. Mr. Soulier took the seat next to me and began to sing with the congregation.

To my surprise, he had a fair voice and knew all the words by heart. When the sermon began, he withdrew a small Bible from his coat pocket and opened it to Genesis.

Reverend Thomas picked up where he'd left off the week before. His emphasis was on God's creation of Eve to be a "helpmeet" to her husband, Adam. "And what is a helpmeet, you may ask? Well, I will tell you. A helpmeet is someone who serves, someone who is a help to another. God knew that it was not good for man to be alone, because a man simply cannot accomplish all that God has for him to do on this earth without the assistance of someone who is always ready and willing to help him succeed."

This time I was more prepared for the dynamics in volume Reverend Thomas seemed so fond of using.

"There is a divine, created duty that God Almighty has placed on all of womankind. That of surrendering her own wishes in order to serve and submit to her husband so he is free to accomplish all that God has called him to do."

The room hushed as the reverend bent over his lectern and whispered loudly. "And now, I am looking out at all the ladies here today." His volume increased as he stepped forward and continued forcefully. "There are some of you who have become lazy in your activities, too eager for leisure and ease, too tempted by gossip and fashion to be of any use to your husband, and therefore any use to God Himself!"

I sat transfixed until I noticed Mr. Soulier nodding in firm agreement and whispering "Amen" under his breath.

A flush of goose bumps pricked my skin.

Reverend Thomas walked back behind the lectern, shaking his head. "It is time, my dear sisters, for you to take God seriously and start serving your husbands as the Scripture demands. May God help you to repent of your sloth and do what is right in the eyes of the Lord."

Pop! His Bible sounded off as he closed it forcefully and bowed his head. "Let us pray."

The lively piano music brought everyone to their feet, and once again Mr. Soulier's clear voice joined in with great conviction singing, "Let Your People Faithful Be!"

~

I made the excuse of writing to my mother so I could leave the others to their tea in the pub. Mr. Soulier, who was now hovering around me like a bee to honey, offered to walk me home, but I put him off as politely as I could, then escaped, first in the direction of Sutton Yard but then taking a turn into a lane, following the steep grade up the hill in the opposite direction. Weaving my way through the side streets, I finally found myself at the crown of the hill overlooking the town and took the path toward the castle ruins.

I stopped to catch my breath and calm my nerves, sitting on one of the ancient stones, which made a perfect bench. It was smooth from this common use, and I looked up at the cloud-covered sky, sending my urgent questions to the heavens.

The crunch of boots on the gravel path disturbed my prayer, and I stood. If only there were a place in Penrith where I could gather my thoughts and rest my mind, as the River Eden was far from my reach now.

Starting down the path to leave, I looked up and found the amiable Mr. Dalton approaching.

My heart skipped a beat, but I schooled myself to simply greet him politely and be on my way.

"Good morning, Mr. Dalton. It is nice to see you again." I tried hard not to look directly into his eyes as I curtsied.

"And a very good morning to you too, Miss Blackwood. I am pleasantly surprised to meet you here again so soon."

I couldn't help but smile at his genial manner. "I was just on my way home, sir. I have a letter to write I mustn't keep waiting. Good day."

"Oh, leaving so soon. What a shame. I hope everything is all right." His sincerity was irresistible.

"Well, you see . . ." I hesitated while the blood rushed to my face. "My father is poorly, and I must write to my mother, and—"

"I am very sorry to hear that, Miss Blackwood." He bent a bit to catch my downcast eyes. "Pardon my asking, but is it serious?"

"Well yes, Mr. Dalton, it is." My voice faltered, knowing I'd said too much.

"But that is grave news, Miss Blackwood. You have my deepest sympathies. Is your father in Appleby?"

Goodness, he had paid such close attention during our introduction he even remembered where I was from. "Yes, with my mother and sister. I . . . I shouldn't be keeping you, sir. I—"

"Not at all, Miss Blackwood. It is I who should not be keeping you." He stepped aside and bowed, touching his hat.

I curtsied and was about to say goodbye, but a thought struck me. "Mr. Dalton, are you inclined to attend church?" The question escaped me before I could restrain it.

"Why yes, Miss Blackwood. I have been attending St. Andrew's. It is the church I grew up in." His slight smile seemed full of happy memories.

"Oh yes, of course. Perhaps I will have a chance to visit there myself someday."

"And you, Miss Blackwood? Are you attending a church here in Penrith?"

I was suddenly embarrassed to tell him. "Oh yes, I have been attending the new Bible Church meeting at The Gloucester Arms, only these last two Sundays."

"Ah." He dipped his chin. "I have heard interesting things about Reverend Thomas. Seems he is quite a passionate preacher, with a personality to match. Have you found him so?"

I couldn't help but chuckle. "He is indeed, Mr. Dalton."

"Well, I shall have to visit next Sunday and see this phenomenon for myself. Perhaps I shall see you there?"

"Oh, it would be a pleasure to have you, Mr. Dalton. I'm sure my colleagues would be happy to see you again as well."

"Then I shall make it my plan. Now, we mustn't keep your letter waiting any longer. Miss Blackwood. Good day."

I bid Mr. Dalton farewell and nearly skipped down Castlegate. As I passed The Gloucester Arms, I saw Mr. Soulier with all the others exiting the pub, instantly regretting I had not thought to return another way.

"Well, Miss Blackwood," Annabel chided, "Where have ya been?"

"Yes, Miss Blackwood, we missed your lovely presence at tea," Mr. Soulier scolded.

"Oh! I just wanted to get some air before, and uh, well, I thought I would come back by here and walk home with you all —" I regretted what came out of my mouth as soon as I said it.

"Then allow me to escort you home, Miss Blackwood."

It was more of a command than an invitation. Mr. Soulier took my elbow and steered me across Corn Market Square, while the others fell slightly behind, whispering.

Chapter Five

During the course of my third week in Penrith, I fought at times to stay focused on my work. My thoughts were constantly on Mr. Dalton and Mr. Soulier, and I often forced myself to think of my family as an antidote to my wandering imagination.

The tailors had recovered from their bad beef the Friday before, and I was not called again to come to the rescue. But on Saturday Mr. Arnison sent a boy to fetch me from the ladies' sewing room, an hour before the close of the day.

"Good evening, Miss Blackwood. Thank you for coming." Mr. Arnison stood and strode to the door, closing it almost all the way. Then he returned to his desk chair and took up a sealed envelope, handing it to me.

"This is for you, Miss Blackwood, but it is something I would like to keep between the two of us. It's a small token of my appreciation for helping me with Mr. Stockdale's tailcoat. I'm sorry I didn't get it to you sooner, but I've been rather busy with other pressing matters of late."

I was struck dumb. "Oh, but, Mr. Arnison, I—"

"Tut tut, Miss Blackwood," he continued, standing. "I am sure you and your family can do with all the help you can get just now."

He motioned me toward the door, and I turned, but stopped to face him. "I am so very grateful to you, Mr. Arnison. I will send it to my mother right away—"

"Yes, of course. I admire a girl as resourceful as you, Miss Blackwood. Good day."

I left Mr. Arnison's office and tucked my envelope into my pocket.

"Thank you, God in heaven!" I whispered to the ceiling and twirled around like a child.

"Ahem."

I froze. Clearly I was not alone in the hall, as I had thought.

Mr. Bell came slinking out of the shadow at the back of the stairway and glowered at me over his cravat. Folding his arms importantly over his chest, he looked at the office door, then again at me.

"Don't you have something you should be doing, Miss Blackwood, other than dancing in the hall?"

"Oh, I was just on my way back upstairs, Mr. Bell. Good evening."

I tripped past him and took the stairs as fast as I could, hoping beyond hope that perhaps I would not have to force myself to marry after all.

Sunday morning dawned cloudy and cold, and snow covered the streets of Penrith as we four emerged from our flat and made our way to The Gloucester Arms. The others had complained about going at all, but when I told them Mr.

Dalton might be in attendance, their curiosity had given them the impetus to dress warmly and venture out.

We entered the upper hall, where I was approached by Mr. Soulier.

"Good morning, Miss Blackwood." Mr. Soulier's teeth were not the best, which marred what would have otherwise passed as a nice smile.

"Good morning, Mr. Soulier. I hope you are well." I was too distracted by my search for Mr. Dalton to overly engage in conversation with him.

"I am well, thank you. And you, Miss Blackwood? I hope you did not find the walk to church too cold."

"Oh, no, it was nothing. I am used to walking in the snow, as Appleby seems to get more snowstorms than Penrith." I smiled politely, then moved into the room, Mr. Soulier close behind.

"Are you looking for someone, Miss Blackwood? I didn't know you knew many people in Penrith."

I tried not to let his persistence annoy me. "Why yes, Mr. Soulier. I am looking for a Mr. Dalton, an acquaintance who told me he might come to visit. I want to be sure to greet him."

At that, Mr. Soulier stiffened and cast his eyes warily around the room.

"I see. Well, you should be sure to introduce me to him if he comes. We are always happy to warmly welcome guests here at the Bible Church. Reverend Thomas will be glad to know him too, I'm sure."

"Oh! Here he is now." I passed Mr. Soulier and motioned to Annabel, who was chatting with Miss Barnes.

We met Mr. Dalton near the top of the stairs. He was properly attired in gray woolen trousers, a black woolen coat, a navy-blue waistcoat, and top hat, which he removed upon seeing us.

"Good morning, Mr. Dalton. We are so glad you decided to brave the snow and come," I said brightly. "You remember my friend Miss Ainslie?"

"Of course, Miss Ainslie, how lovely to see you again. And you as well, Miss Blackwood."

Just then, Susan and Eliza joined us, followed by Mr. Pitt, Miss Barnes, Mr. Nixon, and the expressionless Mr. Soulier.

Mr. Dalton was most polite to everyone, and I invited him to sit with our group. The service was about to start, so we took to our row in the back and passed around the songbooks. I noticed Mr. Soulier sizing up Mr. Dalton, who was unaware of his scrutiny. Mr. Dalton placed himself between me and Annabel and held the songbook for us as the music began.

I couldn't help but hear Mr. Soulier's voice singing a bit too loudly and felt a little embarrassed for him. Could it really be that he was jealous?

I put the thought from my mind as nonsense and concentrated on the words of the song.

Reverend Thomas's nose looked redder than usual when he took his place behind the lectern. I stole a glance at Mr. Dalton, who returned it with raised eyebrows. I hid my smile behind my gloves.

"Listen, my little flock, and train up your hearts to obedience, for the Lord will not bless those who close their ears to Him."

It wasn't long before the reverend got his steam up. "If it is not good that man should be alone, and if a woman was created to serve her husband so that he may carry out God's will on the earth, then why, I ask!? Why are some of you still walking in disobedience?"

Slamming his hand down on the lectern, Reverend Thomas's face lit up to match his nose, and his eyes bulged in anger. "God will not be mocked!" he shouted. Then as if realizing he was crescendoing too soon, he turned to the side and waved his hand, regathering his thoughts.

Mr. Dalton gave me a quick look, which I returned. He rubbed his hands on the legs of his trousers and seemed uncomfortable, as was I. I clasped Mother's pendant and braced myself for what might come next.

"Dear ones," began the reverend again, in a fatherly tone. "I am indeed troubled by the state of this world of darkness, this world of sin and godlessness. God has given us His guidance, His very Word to inform us of his will in this, His plan to use those who obey Him to shine His holy light. And what is that plan, you ask?"

I clutched my hands together, as I could feel another outburst coming.

"It is as plain as the nose on your face! Be fruitful and multiply," he shouted. "The only way to save the lost of this world is to do our part. Stop wasting God's precious time and find yourself a wife!"

Slam went the closing of the Bible, and the piano burst into a mighty anthem.

I wanted to drop through the floor and disappear forever.

After the hymn was over and the congregation stirred, I remained frozen in my chair. Mr. Dalton, ever polite, stood and offered me his hand to rise. I took it but found it exceedingly hard to meet his eyes.

"Well, Reverend Thomas's reputation does not disappoint, does it?" he asked, but the twinkle in his eyes had faded.

"Yes, I'm rather . . . that is, I am not quite sure. I mean . . ." I stumbled.

"Well, Mr. Dalton, and what did you think of our service today?" Mr. Soulier interrupted. His presence didn't make me feel any better.

"It was remarkable, Mr. Soulier, truly remarkable," he answered, with half a smile.

Mr. Soulier gleamed knowingly. "I am very pleased to hear it, sir. And you, Miss Blackwood? What are your thoughts on the reverend's sermon?"

What was it about Mr. Soulier's attention that made me feel less confident in myself? "Well, it was, er, very passionate, Mr. Soulier."

"Indeed! And worthy of taking to heart, I believe. Mr. Dalton, will you be joining our group for tea downstairs, sir? I am sure we would all be glad to know you better, if you are so inclined."

Mr. Soulier stepped to my side possessively and checked his gold watch, as if he had an appointment and I was somehow involved.

I looked up helplessly at Mr. Dalton, embarrassment running fast through my veins. "Forgive me, Mr. Dalton, Mr. Soulier," I said quickly, "but I will not be able to take tea with everyone today. I have some work I need to do for Mr. Arnison this afternoon, and it cannot wait."

The awkwardness could not be more.

"Ah." Mr. Dalton dipped his head slightly. "I am afraid I shall have to pass on your kind invitation as well, Mr. Soulier. I have plans for this afternoon and will need to run along."

Mr. Dalton took my coat from the back of my chair and helped me into it. "Miss Blackwood, may I see you to the door?"

"Why yes, thank you, Mr. Dalton. Good day, Mr. Soulier."

I took advantage of the invitation to make a speedy exit. Slipping past the people waiting to greet the reverend, I took the stairs ahead of Mr. Dalton. I could feel Mr. Soulier's eyes burning through my back. What a mess.

"Well, Miss Blackwood, this has been an educational morning, I should say," Mr. Dalton said after we passed out of the inn.

"I feel I should apologize to you, Mr. Dalton. I am new to this town and this church, and—"

"No, no apologies necessary, Miss Blackwood. I was not offended in any way by the service. On the contrary. It was interesting to see how very different this church is from the more typical Church of England, like St. Andrew's. Perhaps I shall come again some Sunday if my time permits."

Though he was as polite as ever, I could tell he was disappointed, and it broke my heart. "I was just thinking, Mr. Dalton, that I might be interested in attending services at St. Andrew's. I'm not quite sure if the Bible Church is really my cup of tea."

At this his demeanor lightened. "Well, Miss Blackwood, if you decide to come, I would be delighted to show you the kind hospitality you have shown me today. May I have the pleasure of walking you to your next destination?"

"Oh, I would be honored, Mr. Dalton, but I assure you I can find my own way home. Besides, you have pressing plans to get to yourself, sir, so I will not detain you."

"Very well, if you are certain you are able to arrive safely. Let me see your boots, Miss Blackwood."

"What? Oh!" I raised my skirts just enough for him to see my half-calf boots.

"Hmm, they seem tolerably sturdy, but if you are unsure at all, you had best take my arm and allow me to—"

It was all too much. "No, thank you kindly, sir. I am well acquainted with walking in the snow." I smiled at him confidently, though I did not feel so.

"All right then, if you are quite sure. I will bid you good day, Miss Blackwood."

"Thank you again, Mr. Dalton. I hope you have a pleasant afternoon."

I sat shivering, covered in a blanket of shame at the little table by the window, sewing small scraps of fabric and ribbon into rosettes and leaves. They were given to me by Mrs. Fallowfield after I asked if there were any small tasks I might do on my afternoons off. The pieces were to be given to the milliners down the hall to decorate ladies' bonnets, and I was to be paid by the piece.

Every now and then a tear would roll off the end of my nose and drop onto my frozen hands. I was glad the others had not come home yet so I could sniffle and wallow in self-pity in peace. My reaction to Mr. Dalton's disappointment was only proof my silly heart had been forming an attachment to him, and I felt ridiculous.

Back in Appleby, the only men I was exposed to were my father's clients, whose temperaments varied, but they had all, even the younger ones, kept their distance from me. I was beneath them, and besides that, my father's gruff demeanor kept away any man, gentleman or not, from having any interest in his dutiful daughter.

Why hadn't I thought it through before inviting Mr. Dalton to the Bible Church? In fact, should I even be attending such a place myself? Was it really the kind of church my mother would approve of and where I could grow closer to God?

Annabel blew in from the wintery day and called to me as she shook the snow from her skirts. "Cairstin? Oh, there ya are, workin' away."

"Yes. I am very grateful to have the extra work. I only hope I can earn enough to keep my mother and sister—" I bit my lip.

Goodness, I was in a bad state to be sharing my private matters so freely.

"Dear, dear." Annabel removed her bonnet and came to stand over me. "I came home before the others to check on ya. Ya have the weight of the world on your shoulders, don't ya, Cairstin?"

I melted under her sympathies as she placed a friendly hand on my shoulder. "I just need to do everything I can, that's all." Then to my dismay, a fresh tear ran down my cheek.

"There, there, now," Annabel cooed as she knelt beside me and gathered my hands in hers. "I'm sorry. I do know what it's like, ya know."

"You do?" I lifted my head and sought her eyes. "Oh, Annabel, I am so sorry. I didn't know."

"No, of course not." She pulled a stool over to sit close and handed me her handkerchief. "'Twas a few years ago when my parents both came down ill and I was forced to begin working. They passed away nearly on the same day, and I've been on my own ever since." Her hazel eyes misted over.

I felt ashamed of myself all over again. "Oh, Annabel. I would never have guessed you had gone through such a tragedy. You are always so cheerful, so full of life—"

She smiled sweetly and dashed at her eyes. "Well, I made a decision after they died, to live as happily as I can and always be grateful for the love I knew as a child. My parents taught me to look for the blessings in life. And they taught me to trust in God, so I try my best to, though some times are harder than others."

Annabel was only a few years my senior. How wise she was for her age. "Yes, my mother has a very deep faith as well."

"She must be lonely for ya, Cairstin. Is your father too ill to be brought here to Penrith so ya might be able to look after them while you work at Arnison's?"

Her question startled me, but I knew it was impossible. "It is too late to bring my father here. He is gravely ill, and besides, he would never leave his shop in Appleby, not until he had no more to say in the matter." A fresh wave of bitter grief washed over me, and I bowed my head. "Oh, Annabel. I am so afraid I will never make enough to keep my mother and sister out of the workhouse."

She gently rubbed my back in a motherly way. "There, there," she soothed. "God will help ya, Cairstin. I know He will. He will make a way."

I blew my nose and turned to see her looking wistfully at me. "Thank you, Annabel. I am so grateful. You don't know how much I have needed someone to talk to."

"I am glad to know ya, Cairstin Blackwood. You're a brave girl and a hard worker, and I can see ya love your family very much. Don't lose hope."

Arnison's was humming with anticipation the next Wednesday morning as the town of Penrith made its preparations for the coming of the famed Lancaster to Carlisle Railway. Everyone was in a holiday mood, especially when it was announced that Mr. Arnison decided to close the shop at half past nine in the morning for the occasion, to allow the staff a chance to join the rest of the town in greeting the new trains, one set to arrive from Lancaster to the south, and one to arrive at the same time from Carlisle to the north.

I could not help being caught up in the excitement, and my humiliation from the Sunday before finally gave way to it. Even Mrs. Fallowfield had a spring in her step as she tried to keep us all focused on our work.

The next day, December 15, dawned bright and beautiful,

as if God Himself were pleased with what was about to happen. The streets of Penrith were never so bustling as the townsfolk and visitors hurried about in their best clothes, gathering Union flags on little sticks to wave at the oncoming steam engines.

"I wonder if they will be terribly noisy," I commented when Mrs. Fallowfield left the workroom for a moment.

"I have heard they are indeed, and that they have a rather pungent smell when they pass by," Annabel replied gleefully. "Something like a dragon, they say."

"Yes," Susan offered. "But I've heard it's the whistle that's able to wake the dead!"

"I'm ever so glad Mr. Arnison is allowing us to go see them!" Eliza chimed. "I can hardly wait till the bell rings!"

I was fortunate to be sitting nearest the window that day, as I was working on a mourning dress of black crepe and needed the extra light. I would look out and catch glimpses of the main square teeming with life and wished with all my heart that Mother and Rose were there to see the spectacle.

It seemed an age passed, but at last the bell was rung in the hall. We left our work and hurried down the stairs with the other staff, pouring out the side door of N. Arnison and Sons as if a dam had broken.

The girls and I planned to find a place near the station to the south, on the northbound platform, and if that was too full, to work our way southward near the tracks to wait and watch. The trains were due at ten o'clock sharp, and we joined the crowds making their way up Castlegate toward the top of the hill above the town.

The little station was already full to bursting when we arrived, so we moved south and squeezed ourselves into a space at the far end of the platform. I was prompted to stand in front of the others, as I was shorter than the rest.

I had never seen so many people together in my life. A band played lively marches, and I could see a stand decorated in blue, red, and white in the middle of the opposite platform, where the dignitaries were seated, all in their finest array. Joy and anticipation lit every face, and the mass of colors and fluttering flags sent my heart soaring.

The crowd grew as the time drew nearer, pressing me ever closer to the edge of the platform as the townspeople crushed in to see the spectacle. I lost sight of Annabel and Susan, who were carried farther south by the surge. Eliza was the only one still within view, but even she was not behind me anymore.

In the last few moments, a hush fell over the crowd as everyone kept one eye on the tracks and the other on the station clock. Just one minute to go. I could hear my pulse in my ears, everyone listening as one for something, something . . .

There it was! Two furious whistles in the distance, growing louder and louder with the roaring of the crowd.

I shook, both from the excitement of the moment and the fear of being pushed onto the tracks by the force of the throng.

When I saw the cloud of steam billowing from the black dragon barreling toward me, the world spun. The deafening shouts and the shrieking whistle, the surging of bodies pushing me ever forward, and then the engine was upon us! The screeching of metal, the spinning of wheels and choking clouds of smoke . . .

I screamed as my foot left the platform—

Just then, a firm hand grabbed my arm and jerked me backward. Strong arms enfolded me, and I buried my face in a gray-coated chest, holding on for dear life. Trembling from head to toe, I could not let go, but clung to this solid refuge, grateful beyond words, beyond hope, to be held safely there.

Moments later, when my trembling lessened and I could feel my feet under me again, I loosened my grip and leaned back to see in whose embrace I was in. My heart flooded with joy, then dismay, to find myself in the arms of Mr. Gabriel Dalton, my savior.

He said something, but I could not hear. All I could think of was how wonderful he was, how dear to me he was, but that I should not be here, that I had no right, that he . . . that I . . .

I shook my head and implored him with my eyes to forgive me. Then as quickly as he'd saved me, I darted away through the masses and ran to Sutton Yard as fast as my feet would carry me.

Chapter Six

It was Annabel who coaxed me from my retreat in the flat to come back outside and join her and the others in the main square. I was still quaking inside from my brush with death and Mr. Dalton's actions, but I thought the others would think me silly for not enjoying this momentous occasion with the rest of the town.

Music sounded from the bandstand, and people danced on a wide platform beside it. Vendors called out, selling all sorts of this and that, ale was being poured, and the scent of savory pies, sausages, and sweets filled the air. My stomach growled, and I could not help lingering beside Tatty Tim's Potato Stand. Usually I went without much food on my days off so I could send more money home.

"May I treat you to a spud, Miss Blackwood?"

I jumped to find Mr. Soulier at my side, smiling widely, a glint of knowing in his amber-brown eyes.

"I'll take two, please," he said to the vendor, and handed him the coins for payment before I could stop him.

"Oh, that's very kind of you, Mr. Soulier, but you needn't—"

"Nonsense, Miss Blackwood. I am happy to buy you dinner. I'll wager you haven't had a bite since the trains came in. Am I right?"

He handed me a newspaper-wrapped hot potato filled with salt and butter, grinning at me in satisfaction.

"Well, thank you, Mr. Soulier. I am obliged to you, I'm sure."

"Not at all, Miss Blackwood. Ah, and here is Miss Ainslie. Would you care for a potato, Miss Ainslie?"

Annabel looked at my potato with wide eyes. "Why, thank ye kindly, Mr. Soulier. I don't mind if I do."

The three of us strolled around the square, taking buttery bites, stopping to note a gypsy juggling tankards, a little puppet show, and various colorful amusements. I was just finishing my potato when I caught sight of Eliza, Susan, Miss Barnes, and Mr. Pitt all chatting with Reverend Thomas across the square.

I stopped short when they turned together to look straight at me, then quickly looked the other way, aware they had been caught. Once again I wanted to flee the crowds and hide myself away.

Mr. Soulier spotted the reverend and steered us across to him, much to my dismay.

"Ah! And hear is the lady herself," Reverend Thomas said magnanimously. "What is this I hear, Miss Blackwood?" The man looked down his bulbish nose and eyed me.

I flushed and averted my eyes. "I am sorry, Reverend Thomas. I do not know of what you are speaking."

"Well of course, Miss Blackwood. I have just heard about your friend Mr. Dalton, whom I did not have the pleasure of meeting in person on Sunday, and how he saved you from impending doom today."

Something patronizing fringed his tone. I looked at Susan and Eliza, mortified they had spoken to the reverend and seemed to have painted the incident in a misleading light.

"Oh, you see, I was—" I stammered.

"She nearly lost her life today!" Eliza exclaimed with a catty smile. "But Mr. Dalton came to her rescue and caught her before she fell in front o' the train, isn't that so, Miss Blackwood?"

"Well, well, how very chivalrous of him, Miss Blackwood," Reverend Thomas said, his tone sarcastic. "We are all so very happy you emerged unscathed by such an ordeal."

"Oh no, but Mr. Dalton, he . . . you see . . . I was . . . I was pushed—"

"No need to explain yourself, Miss Blackwood," Mr. Soulier chimed unexpectedly. "I can see that we all need to take better care of you, being as vulnerable as you are—"

"Vulnerable?" I said incredulously. "But I was pushed—"

"Yes, yes, Miss Blackwood, we can all see how upset you are by it." Reverend Thomas laid his large, fleshy hand on my shoulder. "I want you to know I am here for you if you should ever need assistance of any kind. In fact, I should like to speak with you after the service this Sunday, as I may have found a way of helping you and your family in your time of need. Shall I count on you?"

All eyes were fixed on me, and I shriveled inside. Even Annabel, though she said nothing, avoided my eyes when I looked to her for support. All I could do was nod my agreement in the face of so much pressure.

"Very well then! Off with you, my young flock, and enjoy yourselves. I am going to find Mrs. Thomas and treat her to tea at The George."

The group dispersed, and Mr. Soulier took me by the

elbow, steering me through the square and past Arnison's to the entrance of Sutton Yard.

"I can see you are in need of some rest, Miss Blackwood." He put on an air of thoughtfulness and protection.

"I thank you, Mr. Soulier. I do feel a bit tired."

I didn't stay to hear his response but dashed through the entrance, glad to be alone again with so many troubling thoughts to sort through.

I was unusually reserved the rest of the week as Mrs. Fallowfield slowly crossed off the days. My shock at being misrepresented and misjudged rocked my already fragile sense of security. I found myself avoiding anything more than polite conversation and thought twice about what came out of my mouth.

Being in Eliza's presence was especially uncomfortable, with her condescension poisoning the air around me.

On top of it all, Mr. Soulier was showing up occasionally at the close of work and walking us all to the entrance of the yard. He didn't seem to give me any special attention, but the others would look from him to me with a strange anticipation.

How I wished all the nonsense would cease. And now there was the new presence of the train whistles, as the steam engines would roll into the station several times a day. Every time I heard them, my heart would jolt as I again felt my foot slipping from the platform.

Another letter from Mother came. She informed me she thought Father's savings would carry them, with my further assistance, until the end of January. My heart broke at the news, but perhaps I still had enough time to find some rooms for them in Penrith so I could have them with me after Father passed. It was torture waiting for the inevitable.

I dreaded Sunday and tried to think of a way to get out of meeting with Reverend Thomas after the service. It was horrifying to be seen as manipulative by anyone, especially a reverend. I wish I had never agreed to meet him.

By the end of Saturday, I made up my mind. I would not go to the service at the Bible Church that Sunday or ever again. I would go to St. Andrew's and make myself as invisible as possible. I wouldn't even speak to Mr. Dalton, except to thank him for helping me.

After an exhausting mental debate, I decided to keep my appointment with Reverend Thomas after the service at St. Andrew's if only to spare Annabel any embarrassment and try to put the whole matter to rest once and for all. I'd tell him I decided to attend the parish church, which my parents would find more akin to St. Lawrence's back home.

It was a weak argument, but what could the man say? He could not order me to attend his church, and besides, I no longer felt comfortable in the company of my peers there. Let them judge me—hadn't they already?

It was a relief to discover the St. Andrew's service started a half an hour before the Bible Church. On Sunday morning I surprised the others when I announced I was going to St. Andrew's but would keep my appointment with Reverend Thomas afterward. Eliza's face was full of suspicion, but I lifted my chin and left them all speechless.

It felt good to walk in solitude the short distance to St. Andrew's, behind Barclays Bank, as the bells calling the faithful rang overhead. I caught my breath at the beauty of the church as I entered the stately nave. The soaring ceiling and two-storied columns took my breath away. It spoke of reverence and wonder. I slipped into the back row to the side, my heart overcome with homesickness at the sound of the organ and the smell of candle wax.

The service was familiar and comforting. I knew the hymns by heart, and the vicar never once raised his voice, allowing the content and quality of his words and the Scriptures to influence his listeners, rather than the forceful blasts of hot air Reverend Thomas employed to get his point across.

I couldn't help being curious if Mr. Dalton was in attendance, but though I studied the other congregants in the pews, I did not find his familiar profile among them.

The service ended, and I was the first one to exit. Filling my lungs with the crisp winter air, I turned my steps toward Corn Market Square. With each footfall, I felt like I was walking to my execution, but I fought off the thought.

Reaching the inn just as the closing song was finishing, I walked to the back of the room and made sure Reverend Thomas saw I was present. I wanted to vomit but clenched my teeth and hands to keep myself steady.

The service ended, but I was not approached by my acquaintances, who only looked at me scornfully, except for Annabel, who gave me a smile and reassuring nod. Mr. Soulier tipped his hat to me but followed the others down the steps without looking back.

At last Reverend Thomas shook the last congregant's hand and moved toward me, his face somber.

"Thank you for keeping our appointment, Miss Blackwood. Why don't we sit here and have a little chat, shall we?"

I sent up an internal plea for help, then took the chair he turned for me. He sat directly across and folded his arms over his broad chest importantly. "I noticed your chair was empty this morning, Miss Blackwood. I hope you are not ill."

"I am fine, thank you, Reverend. I attended St. Andrew's service—"

"Ah! So you went to St. Andrew's!" He raised his brows. "And did you happen to meet your friend Mr. Dalton there? I am sure he was very happy to see you—"

"Mr. Dalton was not in attendance today, that I saw anyway." A fact I was glad to be able to admit.

He nodded. "Hmm, I see. Well, Miss Blackwood, it has been brought to my attention by those who are concerned for you, who have your best interests at heart, that you have become rather, how did they say it, well acquainted with Mr. Dalton."

I opened my mouth to protest, but the reverend raised his hand and continued. "I wonder, my dear, if you are aware of Mr. Dalton's history, of his family and so on. Are you?"

I froze. What did I know about him, besides the kindness he had shown me personally?

It didn't seem to be any of the reverend's business, but I said, "I am not well acquainted with Mr. Dalton or his history, nor his family, but—"

"Ah, I see," he interrupted again. "And so you are perhaps not familiar with anything about his personal past or any of his dealings with other people in Penrith?"

Did Reverend Thomas know something about Mr. Dalton that was unsavory? I thought a moment. "I am only aware that he is a close family friend to the Arnisons, Reverend, and that is all—"

He smirked. "Ah, yes, Mr. Arnison. Hmmm, well, that does not seem to be enough to recommend him as—"

My anger caught flame at his insinuations. "He need not be recommended to me in any way, Reverend Thomas, for I am not interested in Mr. Dalton's past, nor his personal affairs. He was only recently introduced to me—"

"So!" Reverend Thomas pounced. "You have no interest in Mr. Dalton. Well, I declare, that is good news, Miss Blackwood. Good news indeed. And shall I tell you why?"

The man rubbed his large hands on his knees and smiled at me in a fatherly way. "Miss Blackwood, I'm aware of your plight, my dear, and have been praying that God would show me a way to help you and your family in this terrible struggle of yours—"

"But I assure you, Reverend, that neither I nor my family—"

"But of course"—he waved his hand—"you are embarrassed by your situation. An understandable reaction considering the circumstances, but you need not rebuff my generosity because of pride, Miss Blackwood. We all must beware of pride, for pride goeth before the fall, says the Lord."

How was I to say anything when the man constantly interrupted me and used the Bible to back up his words?

"I beg you to listen to your pastor, my dear, the one whom God has placed in authority over you to teach you and guide you in all of his ways."

There was nothing for it but to sit in silence before him and let him have his say. I felt my resolve melting. Who was I to decide how God will help me and by whom? I sighed and nodded.

He did not hesitate to continue. "Ah, there, now, you see, God blesses those who have ears to hear."

He adjusted his weight in his seat, and I braced myself.

"As I say, I've been praying for you, and God has answered my prayers." He leaned forward, looking at me as if I were a child. "He has brought it to my mind that it would be best for a young lady in your position to marry, Miss Blackwood, but not to marry just anyone, oh no. But to marry a man whose heart is firmly committed to the will and kingdom of God, my dear."

He paused to let his words sink in. If only he knew my own father felt the same. But I would never give him the satisfaction of knowing so.

"And do you know, Miss Blackwood, I prayed that God would show me just the right man to marry you? Yes, I did! And that man has become known to me."

I was aghast. Could this man know exactly who I was to marry without my having so much as an inkling?

"You know, Miss Blackwood, I have been discipling a special group of young men these past six months and have come to know each of them personally. But there is one man, in particular, who came to mind in my conversations with the Almighty, and that man you already know, my dear—it is Mr. William Soulier."

His eyes danced with the thought as I sat frozen in dismay. "And the man himself has confirmed to me that he has great affection for you and has asked my permission to court you. What do you think of that, my dear? Isn't it wonderful?"

I stared at him, dumbstruck.

The reverend was waiting for my reply. I hardly knew what to say. "Well, Mr. Soulier is a fine young man, but—"

He raised his fat hand again. "I knew you would be reticent, my child, and I am willing to give you all the time you need to think it over. I will have faith for you when your faith is weak, my dear. And so . . ." At this he rose and offered me his hand. I took it and stood, but he kept ahold of me and bent over to smile in my face.

"Now, Miss Blackwood, you have a lot to think and pray about. I will wait until you have given me permission to tell Mr. Soulier that you are amiable to his courtship. In the meantime, you must promise me you will carefully consider your options and not do anything to compromise your or your family's future. Will you promise?"

Oh dear. Another promise. "I'll do my best, Reverend. Good day."

Christmas was the next Friday, and I loathed its coming. Everyone who attended the Bible Church was invited to a Christmas Eve service and celebration on Thursday, but I could not think of anything I would like to attend less. How I wished I could find a way to run back to Appleby and forget all about Penrith, Mr. Dalton, Mr. Soulier, and the rest. I felt like a cornered animal with no hope of escape.

As I entered the delivery door of Arnison's Monday morning, I overheard Mr. Arnison speaking to Mrs. Fallowfield in the office and halted near the door when I heard Mr. Dalton's name.

"Yes, Mr. Dalton left yesterday and will be gone for quite some time while he takes care of his cousin's affairs in Carlisle. So he will not be able to join us for Christmas dinner, I'm afraid." Mr. Arnison sounded disappointed

Then Mrs. Fallowfield spoke up. "It is a pity he will not be there, but I am grateful to Mrs. Arnison for her kind invitation, sir, and will be most honored to attend."

I didn't pause longer to hear the rest of the conversation, but just before I turned down the hall to the foot of the stairs, I caught a glimpse of the drapery through the open door. There stood Mr. Bell, whispering something into Eliza's ear that made her face light up with a scandalous smile as they looked over a piece of paper together. It made me blush to see it. I ascended quickly, and by the time I reached the third floor, I felt unusually winded.

There, Cairy, I said to myself. *There you have it. And now you need to move on.*

Mr. Arnison was correct in his predictions that the coming of the railway would bring more business to N. Arnison and Sons. He wandered the shop and hallways with a satisfied smile and congratulated everyone on keeping up the pace. He also promised to reward us all with half of Christmas Eve off, all of Christmas Day, and the Saturday and Sunday afterward.

Some of the staff, such as myself, were not as pleased as others to hear of this reduction in work hours, as many of us would feel the pinch in our wages.

Christmas Eve came on Thursday, and everyone was busy preparing, when not working, for parties and family visits. I was more distressed than before, knowing I had the time to visit my family but not the means. All I had to look forward to was a dark cloud of homesickness, which grew thicker by the hour.

Annabel, who had no family, was staying at our flat for the holiday as well. I was grateful I wouldn't be completely alone. She tried ever so hard to convince me to join her in going to the Bible Church Christmas Eve Service, but I kept putting her off.

The bell from the St. Andrew's tower struck four o'clock, and once again the employees of N. Arnison and Sons spilled out into the frosty air of Devonshire Street. Annabel walked with me, and when we caught a few notes of music in the air, we were drawn to the bay window on the main floor of The George. Peering in from a polite distance, we could see the beautiful, brightly lit room filled with brilliantly dressed guests, champagne in their gloved hands as they greeted one another with smiles and holiday wishes.

For a moment I was caught up in the magic of the sight, like a scene from a novel or play. Then Annabel nudged me out of my trance, and we walked around Arnison's and paused before entering Sutton Yard.

"Won't ya please come with me this evening for the service and party? I'll be so grieved to know your here all alone. Please, Cairstin?" The sweet pleading in Annabel's voice tipped my lonely heart over the edge.

"Yes, Annabel, I will go, if it pleases you."

"I'm very pleased. Now, let us go and dress up in our finest and be happy we have each other." She winked and took my hand, and we made the best of the time before we stepped out of our flat as resplendent as two working girls could be.

~

The Gloucester Arms was not available for the church to celebrate Christmas Eve, so we were all invited to Reverend Thomas's home for the service and celebration. Annabel and I made our way to Lowther Street, which sloped gently up between several grand brick and stone houses. When we came to a house called Lockholm, Annabel paused.

"Oh, this is Mr. Arnison's house! I heard it was an impressive place, and here it is! I have never come this way to see it before."

We lingered and gazed in awe over the low brick fence at the grand house, glowing from within with golden candlelight in every room, and we could smell roasted meats and spicy puddings. The notes of a pianoforte reached us, with voices young and old singing Christmas hymns, sprinkled with the laughter of children from the upper floors. So warm, so full, so perfect.

Annabel drew my arm into hers, and we continued until we found the address. Standing in front of another large brick house, we joined the other guests arriving at the home of Reverend and Mrs. Thomas. It, too, teemed with life.

As we entered, Reverend Thomas took my gloved hand in his and patted it. "I knew you would come, Miss Blackwood." He looked down on me with self-confidence. "Come in, and Happy Christmas!"

After a servant took our cloaks and bonnets, we ventured farther into the spacious house and made our way into the large, inviting parlor. The house was nothing like the parsonage Vicar Hayes lived in near St. Lawrence's. The furnishings looked new and expensive to my untrained eye. The colors were bold and a bit garish for my taste, but what did I know of such things? The one thing I did know was the reverend must be doing rather well if donors to the church could allow him to live in such splendor, or he was independently wealthy to begin with.

We were greeted by Miss Barnes and Mr. Pitt, who immediately took Annabel under their wing. I was left to linger like a wallflower, wondering why I had come, until the sight of Mr. Soulier looking at his gold watch sent me to the darkest corner.

He had yet to see me when Reverend Thomas entered briskly with his wife, his face oddly grave. He held a message and scanned for someone. When his eyes fixed on mine, I wished I could melt into the wood paneling.

"Ah, Miss Blackwood, this has arrived for you by special messenger. I hope it is nothing unpleasant. Would you like to go into the sitting room to read it?"

The room hushed, but my focus was on the envelope he gave me, my name upon it in my mother's hand. He and Mrs. Thomas escorted me into their smaller sitting room, where a fireplace blazed with a yule log, and offered me a chair beside it. Mr. Soulier and Annabel had followed us, and I was reluctant to open the letter with so little privacy.

"Well, my dear," Reverend Thomas explained, "the messenger seemed rather urgent to find you. Said he had gone to your flat, but when you weren't there, the lady downstairs told him where you had gone."

"Perhaps we should leave Miss Blackwood to her letter," Mrs. Thomas said, for which I was grateful. "We will just be in the hall if you should need us." And with that, the room was emptied and the door closed.

I stared for a moment at the paper, then swallowed hard and broke the seal.

> Dearest Daughter.
>
> You father has passed. We will lay him to rest in the churchyard on Christmas Day. Come if you can, but only if you do not have to spend any of your precious wages.
>
> We love you,
>
> Mother.

I clutched Mother's necklace and let a tear escape, not as much for my father's sake, for I was only glad his suffering was over, but for my poor beloved mother and sister, so vulnerable and helpless, and for myself, that I could not be with them in this dark hour to comfort them.

Before long, the door cracked open and Annabel entered with Mr. Soulier, who offered me his handkerchief. Annabel sat beside me and put her arm around my shoulders.

Then the reverend and his wife entered. "Ah, it is as we feared. You have our deepest condolences, Miss Blackwood."

I nodded, drying my eyes. "Thank you, Reverend Thomas, Mrs. Thomas. I hope you will understand if I do not stay for your party—"

"Of course, my dear, of course." The reverend seemed truly sympathetic, but then I noticed him raise his chin at Mr.

Soulier, who stood off to the side. "I am sure you will be wanting to go home to Appleby to be with your family, Miss Blackwood, which is only right and proper."

"Yes, sir, I dearly want to be with my mother and sister, but I do not have the means to—"

"Uh, I will take you, Miss Blackwood, if you will allow me," Mr. Soulier said, his voice full of solemnity. "Reverend Thomas has offered his curricle, and I can drive you to Appleby tonight, if that is what you wish." He finished his speech, then looked up at Reverend Thomas, as if seeking his approval.

"Yes, Miss Blackwood, Mr. Soulier has assured me he is capable of driving you to Appleby in the dark, and with the side lanterns and the weather clearing, you should have no trouble at all."

I could not believe my ears.

Annabel took my hands. "And I've volunteered to go as chaperone, Cairstin. So, ya see, it's all been arranged."

"And now, it is time to be off. I have already sent for the carriage, and Mrs. Thomas is having the cook make up a basket of provisions. I must say, Miss Blackwood, that the Lord has provided, in His everlasting kindness, for you in your hour of need. And now, my children, we must acknowledge the mercies of God and offer Him our thanks."

With this, the reverend offered up a short prayer, and I was hurried out to the waiting carriage before I had even breathed a word of thanks to the reverend and his wife.

Chapter Seven

It did not seem real to me. There I sat beside the stoic Mr. Soulier, with Annabel in the back, in Reverend Thomas's curricle, my father dead, on my way home to Mother and Rose. We three seldom spoke on the dark drive, except when Mr. Soulier or Annabel thought of some practical matter to discuss.

It was agreed that Mr. Soulier would take us to my home only long enough to deliver me, then he and Annabel would go to the nearby King's Head Inn to take rooms for the night and have the horses cared for. When I expressed my despair at the expense, Mr. Soulier assured me that it was of no consequence, as everything had already been provided for.

I was beyond grateful for everything and endeavored to impress it upon them.

When we turned onto The Sands, my heart both soared and plunged to be back in my Appleby. Shortly we turned onto the bridge crossing the river. I saw my father's shop sign swaying in the frigid breeze and nearly leaped from the carriage but controlled myself until Mr. Soulier dismounted and helped me descend.

He and Annabel waited with me at the door as I anxiously rang the bell, knowing Mother would hear it in the residence behind the shop. It was just after midnight. I could not guess if she would be asleep or not.

A moment or two passed and I reached for the bellpull again, but the door opened and Mother's alarmed face peered out.

"Mother!" I flung myself through the door and into her arms. "I am here, Mother. I have come."

She held me tight. "My girl, my dear, dear girl!"

I pulled back and motioned the others to come in. "Mother, this is Mr. Soulier and this is Miss Ainslie, who have brought me all the way from Penrith. I cannot thank them enough for their kindness—"

Mother was breathless. "Goodness, I am completely in your debt. I—"

"No, no, Mrs. Blackwood." Mr. Soulier bowed respectfully. "It is God's wish that we bear one another's burdens in times of distress."

"Yes, Mrs. Blackwood," Annabel seconded. "And now Mr. Soulier and I'll leave ya to yourselves and come back to bring ya breakfast in the morning."

"Oh, but—" Mother protested.

Mr. Soulier raised his hand. "No, no, we must insist, Mrs. Blackwood. Annabel?"

Mr. Soulier took Annabel back out to the carriage, and I closed the door. Just then, little Rose descended the stairs and flew into my arms.

Reunion with my mother and sister was more precious to me than all the gold in the world. I told them how I had been able to come, of Reverend and Mrs. Thomas's generosity and how quickly Mr. Soulier and Annabel had rushed to my aid. Our affections for one another were never ending, but Mother made us retire to bed, for the morning would bring with it much work and sorrow.

I held on to my sister, and we cried together, tears mingled with sadness and fear, until we both drifted off. Morning came all too soon, and Mother called to rouse us before either of us were ready to take on the day. Christmas Day.

We were dressed and talking over Mother's plans, when Mr. Soulier and Annabel rang the bell.

They came with armloads of bread and sausages, cakes, and puddings, and we all ate a solemn Christmas breakfast in our humble little kitchen. I was impressed with Mr. Soulier's practical questions and willingness to be of service, and Annabel took over the kitchen as if it were her own.

Mother had been instructed by Reverend Hayes to come to the church after the Christmas morning service at ten o'clock, and we all walked together out the front door of the shop, down the street and through the cloisters into the churchyard. It felt all too familiar as we neared the place where my brothers lay, and I saw the plain wooden box that held my father's body.

There were a few friends there, including Mr. Oldcorn, and they stood by in silence as Reverend Hayes greeted us tenderly and motioned for the box to be lowered into the gaping earth prepared for it. I held my mother and sister on each side as we wept, and the reverend spoke the words of interment. Then we each took a handful of dirt and dropped it down, saying our last goodbyes.

It was all over so quickly. The finality of it struck me like a blow to the chest. He was gone and only the dark, uncertain future remained.

We received the condolences of the townsfolk, and Mother and Rose clung to me as we walked the short distance back to the shop. Mr. Soulier expressed his deepest sympathies, then checked his watch and excused himself, as he wished to see about something—I didn't hear what. Annabel's empathetic heart was a welcome gift to us, and she insisted we not lift a finger.

Mr. Soulier returned in time for a light supper, then he and Annabel made their way back to the inn for the evening. We were to leave the next morning in order to return the carriage and horses to Reverend Thomas, who would be in need of them.

That night, Mother and I sat at the kitchen table until after midnight talking about our future.

"Mother, I think it would be best for you and Rose to move with me to some small place in Penrith so we can be together and I can look out for you."

"I think it is a possibility only if we can manage to sell what we can here and find a way there without too much expense. The landlord will not want his shop empty for long. Reverend Hayes told me he will make inquiries about us possibly taking a room at St. Anne's Almshouses, but I am not certain they allow widows with children to live there. It will be hard to leave your brothers and father behind."

Mother's tears began anew, and I wrapped my arm around her thin shoulder. "I know, Mam, but we will be together, and that would be much better than worrying about each other from a distance."

"You are right, Cairy. My, how much you have grown up since you left us only a month ago, my love. Your father would be proud."

I kept silent at these words, wondering if he had ever been proud of me in his life.

It was even more unbearable than before to tear myself away from my mother, Rose, and Appleby and return to Penrith with Mr. Soulier and Annabel. I thought my heart would burst the bones in my chest with its grief. Never had I imagined myself capable of such sorrow.

Reverend Thomas and his wife were tender to me upon our return, and I could not find enough words to thank them for their generosity.

"Give yourself some time to recover from your ordeal, Miss Blackwood," the reverend said. "We will not find it improper if you refrain from attending church for a few weeks, my dear."

"Thank you, Reverend." My voice was frail and weak.

"And you can depend on Mr. Soulier to help if you should need any assistance, am I right, Soulier?"

The man bowed his obedience, then after saying our good-byes, he escorted Annabel and me to Sutton Yard. Annabel stepped through the entrance ahead of us, and Mr. Soulier turned to me.

My heart beat like a drum. Just then, I heard the train whistle in the distance and shivered.

"I am available at Barclays Bank on the corner of the square, should you require any assistance, Miss Blackwood, and my residence is just over the entrance into White Hart Yard on Corn Market Street, near The Gloucester Arms. You have only to send a message and I will be at your service." An inkling of satisfaction glinted in his eyes as he gazed into mine.

"I cannot thank you enough, Mr. Soulier, for all you have done. I have not even had my wits about me these last few days, and perhaps you have a family you have been neglecting on my behalf?"

"I have no family to neglect, I assure you, Miss Blackwood.

But it is a station in life I wish to alter if the Lord wills. Good day."

He bowed solemnly and strode away as I turned into the yard, his last words echoing in my ears.

Mother had given me one of her mourning dresses from when my brothers passed away, so I spent Sunday in my room making adjustments and replacing the lace collar. Since my mother and I were so similar in height and frame, little alteration was necessary.

That evening Susan and Eliza returned from their family visits and heard the news of my father passing, and though Susan was most sympathetic and affectionate to me, Eliza remained politely aloof. I set it aside, as I had much more pressing matters to worry about.

Father's savings would run out in a month's time. I planned to speak to Mr. Arnison, Mrs. Fallowfield, and anyone else I could at the shop to find some small place for the three of us I could afford on my wages. Mother was willing to do any kind of work she could to help, as was Rose, but my mother's handicap limited the kind of work she could take on, and who would hire her?

My short time in Penrith, along with most of my waking hours spent working, had not afforded me time to get to know much of the town. But I was aware there were pockets of cramped, poorly ventilated rooms for the working class and unemployed, which might be our only option. The thought of taking my mother and sister to live in a place of squalor repulsed me, but it was not as terrifying as the workhouse.

Mother decided to sell anything she could spare. All Father's fabrics, except what might be used to keep us in modest clothing, were to be sold, along with any furnishings that were not truly necessary. I grieved over the loss of her china cabinet, a beautiful piece made of rich mahogany that she'd inherited from my great-aunt. It was one among many items of sentimental attachment that would soon be parted with.

Mr. Arnison promised he would keep our case in mind should he come across news of any suitable accommodations and that he would apply my housing allowance to my wages should I move out of the dressmakers' quarters in Sutton Yard. This was a boon to me, as I had not taken it into consideration, and any addition to our meager income was welcome.

On Thursday, New Year's Eve, Mr. Arnison sent me a note with the address of rooms for let in the southern part of Penrith on Town End. Immediately after work, which ended at six o'clock that day, Annabel agreed to walk there with me. It was indeed near the town's end to the west and behind the main road, still not too far to walk to Arnison's, though not nearly as convenient as Sutton Yard.

When we turned down the narrow lane, the pungent smell of fermenting grain accosted our senses. When we rounded the bend in the road, we found the source of the offense to be a large brewery. It was impossible to get away from the oppressive smell.

We checked the numbers on the buildings, finally finding the one we searched for. Annabel nodded at me to ring the bell, but I could see the misgiving in her eyes. I tugged the handle, and soon an old woman in a tattered shawl, whose own odor could be noted above the hops, came to the door.

"Well, what thee's here for, eh?" she said impatiently as she held her hand behind her ear to hear the reply.

"I . . . I have come to see about some rooms to let, ma'am. I was sent by Mr. Nathan Arnison." I wasn't sure what that would mean to the old thing but mentioned the connection anyway.

"What? Oh. Thee's wanting a room, eh? Well, come in and As takes thee's upstairs." She held the door, then locked it tight behind us. I could hear a baby crying pitifully and people arguing through the thin walls as we followed the bent woman up a dark set of dilapidated stairs to the third floor, passing by several doors, some shut, others open, exposing the dismal abodes of the tenants, most with several dirty children looking at us with sallow faces and hungry eyes.

"Here 'tis. Have a gander."

I stepped in holding my handkerchief over my nose and mouth. Added to the smell of fermenting hops and unwashed woman was the distinct smell of urine. The fireplace was covered in black, greasy soot from the floor to the ceiling, the walls were stained, the floorboards damaged, and the meager furniture more broken than not.

My eyes watered both from the stench and the assault to my sensibilities. I ventured as far as the door to the second room, then turned sharply away, seeing a rat scurry across one of the filthy beds.

"No thank you, ma'am," I choked out as I grasped Annabel by the arm and hurried her back down the stairs, fighting down vicious waves of nausea. We nearly ran to the main road. I was glad to breathe in the air tainted only with coal smoke when we got there, and paused to gather myself.

"Oh no, Annabel! What will I do? How can I ever bring my mother and sister into such a place! God help me! I am desperate, but that was unthinkable."

"I know, Cairstin, 'tis a terrible situation, but ya may not have much choice." Annabel took my arm and guided me back toward the main square. "But don't lose hope. Ya must keep looking, and God will provide if ya trust Him."

"I will try, Annabel. I must try."

New Year's Day came and went. I spent the time working as fast as I could on my little projects and piecework and prayed with every stitch.

That night I had great difficulty sleeping and woke the next morning with a jolt from a terrible dream, my body soaked in clammy sweat, despite the chill in the room.

I dreamed I was wading in the River Eden. My shoes and stockings lay on the bank, and I held my skirts up over the surface of the clear, slow-moving water. It was a hot summer day. The water was cool, and the smooth stones under my feet were slippery. I heard a man's voice call to me from the other side.

"Cairstin, lass, ya must marry! Promise me! Promise me now!"

I whirled around to find my father but lost my footing and fell backward with a great splash. I was tangled in my dress and petticoats as they weighed me down, and I thrashed about, trying to keep my head above the water.

Suddenly I saw Mr. Soulier standing over me as my head went under. He reached for me and took hold of my collar, but still, I could not breathe.

That was when I woke to the sound of a train whistle in the distance. How I wished the sound did not plague me each time I heard it. I always felt a bolt of panic strike my heart, and then a flash of Mr. Dalton's face would cross my mind and fill me with regret that left me rebuking myself.

I was slower than usual to make my toilet and prepare for work that Monday. I tried to focus on my tasks but could not shake the frightening feeling the dream had left in me, and my head ached from thinking about it.

To add to the pressure, that afternoon Reverend Thomas paid me a visit at Arnison's and spoke with me and Mr. Arnison in his office. The reverend seemed pleased with himself for coming to check in on me, though thankfully did not stay long.

"Well, I had best not keep you from your dinner," he said importantly. "I'm sure you need all the strength you can get to face these trying times, Miss Blackwood. Just remember there is still an option that you may consider for your future, and now that your father has passed, it may be wiser for you to make your decision sooner rather than later."

My face flushed hot to my ears, and I looked at Mr. Arnison, abashed that the reverend would discuss such personal concerns in front of my employer, but I recovered my composure quickly. "Yes, Reverend, I remember and will keep it in mind. Thank you for your visit, sir. I think I should hurry upstairs now. If you'll excuse me."

"Of course, Miss Blackwood, run along now."

I curtsied and dashed up the stairs with so many conflicting thoughts and feelings I could hardly touch my food once I got to the table.

Later that night, while the others were peacefully asleep, I rolled out of my bed, knelt beside it, and begged God to help me.

It was all I could do to drag myself through the rest of the workweek. I did not attend church again on Sunday, as fear, grief, tears, and sleep demanded their way with me, and the end of January loomed one week closer. Desperate, at last I gave up the useless fight and sat down at the little desk to write a simple note to Reverend Thomas.

I will consent to being courted by Mr. Soulier. Please give him my regards and ask him to write me as to how he would like to proceed.

Cairstin Blackwood.

I laughed a dry little laugh as I sealed it. It was the most pathetic and unromantic thing I had ever seen or heard of.

Chapter Eight

I received a cordial letter from Mr. Soulier two days later. He was adequate in his addresses, but there was a flat quality to his words. I resigned myself to the fact that he was obviously not a romantic sort.

And so on January 4 of the new year, 1847, it began.

Our first courtship encounter was to meet at the Bible Church on Sunday, where we sat together and shared a songbook. He stood close to me and stayed with me as we greeted Reverend Thomas on our way out. The reverend was more than pleased to see us together, making it abundantly clear by his overly boisterous farewell. I noticed Mr. Soulier toss an impressive coin into the Building Fund box before he took me down the stairs.

We did not join the others for tea in the pub, as Mr. Soulier said he had a surprise for me. As we stepped out into Corn Market Square, I shuddered at the whistle of the train on the hill above us but shook off the sensation as Mr. Soulier escorted me down Corn Market Street to the main square, then up

Devonshire and straight into the revolving glass doors of The George Hotel!

I was beside myself and awash with embarrassment, feeling inadequately dressed and unprepared to be in such a grand establishment.

Mr. Soulier smiled at me with pleasure. "Are you surprised, Miss Blackwood? I can see that you are, and I am very happy."

My heart galloped as he addressed the attendant, and we were taken to the table just inside the beautiful bay window, the one I had so often looked into with great curiosity as I'd left Arnison's, whose stalwart face of windows and gray stone I could see only a few steps outside to the right.

Mr. Soulier helped me with my chair, then seated himself opposite with polished grace. He smiled again, knowing he had succeeded in giving me quite the shock. I was not sure I was pleased with his surprise yet but admitted to myself it was an impressive move.

He ordered tea and sandwiches, followed by cakes and sweets, and my eyes feasted on the sumptuous decor while my stomach rumbled in anticipation. Once the tea was poured, Mr. Soulier engaged me in conversation.

"I wish to offer you my deepest condolences once again, Miss Blackwood, and to thank you for your kind consideration in allowing my courtship to commence, even if the timing is not ideal."

"I thank you, Mr. Soulier, and want to express again how grateful I am for your kind assistance to me and my family in our hour of need."

He sipped his tea elegantly, then pressed his napkin delicately to the corners of his pursed full lips. "I was hoping you would agree to dispense with formalities and call me William, if you don't mind. And I would be ever so grateful for the privilege of calling you by your Christian name as well, Cairstin."

"Well, I have no objections, William, though you must forgive me—it may take some getting used to."

"Certainly, my dear. I am curious about where your lovely name came from, Cairstin. It is Scottish, I believe."

"Yes, my father was Scottish, as you know, and he named me after his grandmother."

"Yes, of course, very appropriate. But now, Cairstin, if it would also be suitable for you, I would like to be able to speak with you regarding some rather personal matters, which I think are very pressing, due to your recent bereavement. I do not wish to seem impertinent, but I know that time is of the essence, and I have only your best interests at heart."

The sandwiches arrived, and before we partook, William bowed his head and commenced with a prayer of thanksgiving, loud enough for those at the next table to take notice. I awkwardly bowed my head and closed my eyes, and upon opening them found Reverend and Mrs. Thomas standing beside the table, joining in the amen.

"Well, well! Imagine finding the two of you here, where we are in the habit of taking tea after service every Sunday."

William rose and shook the reverend's hand. I felt mute for a moment but finally found my voice as I focused on Mrs. Thomas. "Good afternoon, Mrs. Thomas. It is lovely to see you" was all I could say before Reverend Thomas noticed something on the table.

"Ah! I see you are having a spiritual conversation, good, good. I admire a man who takes the edification of his wife on biblical matters seriously. Good show, Soulier!"

I was confused, as I had not seen William produce his Bible. He must have done so during his prayer. It made me uneasy, especially that the reverend referred to me as William's wife, but I said nothing.

The Thomases excused themselves and were seated at a

table across the room, thankfully out of earshot. I looked down at my plate, uncomfortably warm.

"How nice to see the reverend and his wife, don't you agree, Cairstin?" William offered, oblivious to my embarrassment.

"Oh yes, very nice." I poured more tea, not knowing what else to do or say.

"So as I was saying before we were so pleasantly interrupted, I would like to speak with you about matters that may seem too personal, in light of how short our acquaintance has been, but feel an urgency to do all I can to be of assistance to you and your family under the circumstances. So with your permission . . ."

He paused, waiting for my consent. The atmosphere between us was thick, but I nodded and braced myself.

"Thank you, my dear. Now, I am well aware that your mother and sister are in a very precarious position and I'm guessing will be needing financial assistance very soon—am I correct?"

I could have crawled under the table. "Well, Mr. Soulier, I mean William, I am doing all I can to provide for them and have been searching for a place here in Penrith to bring them to so that we can be together—"

"Yes, I know," he interrupted, and held up his hand. "And that is precisely what I wish to speak to you about today. You see, Cairstin"—he leaned forward with a slight hint of condescension in his tone—"I have been praying that God would make things clear to me regarding us and the future of our combined relations and have thought of a plan."

I hardly knew what to think. I sat aghast that William had thought everything through already without me, but I was at his mercy to hear him out.

"God has blessed me with an adequate position as a second

clerk at Barclays Bank. A position that allows me to earn enough money to live in a modicum of comfort, with some to spare. It is my deepest wish, as I am already deeply attached to you, Cairstin, that I use the blessings God has bestowed upon me to make you happy and able to live without the terrible burden of providing everything for your mother's and sister's needs."

The man hardly took a breath in his monologue, giving me no opportunity to interject.

"And so, while we were in Appleby, I made arrangements with your mother's current landlord to allow her and your sister to stay in their home behind the shop and only rent out the front of the space to a new tenant. Thereby reducing the rent required each month and making it possible that between your wages and mine, we might be able to support them together to remain in the home they love so much."

His speech finally came to an end, and he smiled at me smugly. I sat staring at him, mystified. Was he already so attached to me and ardent in his feelings that he would be willing to help me support my family before he even proposed?

I looked out the window and tried to find the proper response. "Well, William, I don't know quite what to say. I am exceedingly surprised at your offer, but don't you think it is too soon in our . . . our courtship to be mentioning anything about financial support—"

"Indeed," he interrupted, "it may be a bit early, but the circumstances have necessitated urgent action. Don't you agree, my dear?"

I was overcome and found it difficult to focus my thoughts while sitting in a lavish setting, hearing him call me Cairstin and "my dear," the reverend and his wife watching us, and having such a generous offer laid at my feet that sounded too good to be true.

Besides, I had set my heart on having Mother and Rose near me, that we would be together and I would have my mother's council to guide me through all the life-altering decisions that had been placed on my young shoulders.

But on the other hand, hadn't I been fervently praying for God's assistance and direction? Should I refuse God's help if He was so blatantly answering my plea?

But what did I really know of William's character, his opinions and manner, and if we were compatible in a way that would last a lifetime? Oh, things were moving much too quickly, and yet wasn't it an urgent state of affairs, as William said?

"I would like to take at least a day or two to think about your most generous offer, William. It is a lot for you to take on, and you really barely know me—"

"Oh, but I know enough, my dear, to know that you are the most beautiful woman I have ever seen, and the way you have sacrificed for your family is a great testimony to the goodness of your nature and the quality of your character. Besides, the Lord has pressed upon me His will in this matter, and I mustn't refuse to follow His leading."

I felt both flattered and cornered as I sipped my delicious tea from a delicate bone-china cup and wondered what I had gotten myself into. How could I argue against someone who claimed to be called to such a mission by God Himself?

"Well, that may be so, William, but I should like some time to pray, and to write to Mother, and to seek the Lord's wisdom on this matter for myself, which is only fitting, don't you think?"

He sat back in his chair and looked slightly hurt, but he soon rallied and leaned forward again. "If that is what you wish, my dear, of course you must take some time to pray, but you will see that I am right in the end, I am sure."

With that, he asked for the bill and for the leftover cake and biscuits to be packed up for me. I was staggered when I saw the cost, which for me was half a week's wages. He politely paid the waiter, then helped me on with my coat and led me to the Thomases' table.

"We bid you a pleasant afternoon, Reverend, Mrs. Thomas. We have had a stimulating conversation with our tea." He gestured with his Bible in his hand, then placed it into his pocket. "Goodbye."

I said nothing, as William took it upon himself to speak for us both, and he led me out of The George's revolving door and onto the street, where the snow had just begun to fall.

William checked the time on his watch. "Well, Cairstin. I will walk you home now so you will waste no time in committing yourself to prayer, and when I come to walk you home from work tomorrow evening, I trust that you will wholeheartedly agree to allow me to help you and your family in your hour of need."

We reached the entrance to Sutton Yard, and he turned to me. "Please, my dear, do not deny me the pleasure of serving you in this way. As I hope you can see, I am already so devoted to you that I will not hesitate to be of service."

He took my hand from his arm and bowed over it. "Good afternoon, Cairstin. I look forward to seeing you soon." He smiled, and I noticed a distinct glint in his amber eyes that sent a shaft of hope piercing my heavily guarded heart.

"Good afternoon, William, and thank you for the lovely tea."

On Monday evening William was waiting for me across the narrow lane from the delivery door. He bowed politely, then without a word took my elbow with a smile and slowly walked me around Arnison's to the entrance of Sutton Yard, where he took me aside.

"How was your day, Cairstin? You must be exceedingly tired. I will not keep you long, my dear, but I am anxious to know if you have thought about my offer and sought the Lord's will in the matter." His tone was most kind, but he was proving to be a man who liked to get right to the point.

"Yes, I have, William, b—"

"Yes?! You will accept? Oh, Cairstin, you do not know how happy I am! I—"

I was greatly alarmed by his passionate response. "No! William, I only meant that I had considered it and have prayed about it, but—"

"But what? What or who could be of more assistance to you? Is there anyone else in your sphere of relations that I am not aware of? Some inheritance, perhaps, that you have not disclosed to anyone?" His voice now had a twinge of hurt and suspicion.

"Oh goodness no! I just wanted to ask you for a little more time to consider and to pray, for I have not come to a decision . . . yet, that is."

"Oh," he said with obvious disappointment. "Well, of course I do not mean to rush you. It is a very important decision, and I want to make you completely comfortable, my dear. If you do not trust me yet, that must be natural, I suppose."

"I am sorry, William," I pleaded. "I mean no offense, to be sure. It's just that I would like to wait and hear back from Mother regarding her feelings on the matter, because she must be agreeable to your plan as well, you know. I would greatly appreciate your patience—"

"Yes, yes, of course. You must forgive me. It is only that I am zealous to see the burden lifted from your frail shoulders that I am so eager to have this matter settled." He regained his friendly demeanor, and his smile returned.

"It is really too bad that we both work such long hours and our time to get to know each other is so limited. I have so many things I would like to discuss with you. But we must content ourselves with what the Lord has given us and look forward to a day when that circumstance may alter."

I warmed at his earnestness and gave him a sweet smile. "Yes, it is unfortunate. Will I see you again tomorrow evening, William?"

He took my hand in his and bowed. "Of course, my dear. I am already looking forward to it. May God bless you with a restful night, beautiful Cairstin."

At last, on Friday a letter from Mother was delivered to me at Arnison's, but I waited to read it and kept it in my pocket until after William walked me home, lest he pressure me to read it and answer him before saying good night.

> My dear daughter,
>
> I am surprised, astonished really, at Mr. Soulier's offer. But I cannot advise you to accept it, my dear. We cannot take advantage of a near stranger, no matter how desperate our situation is or how generous the gentleman.
>
> Reverend Hayes has informed me that there are no rooms available at the Almshouses, which is as I feared. I have spoken to our landlord myself, who has made me the same offer to let the shop and allow us to stay in the residence as long as we are able to pay. I believe, if I can take in some kind of work, we will just be able to make it, at least for

another month or two, until another situation may be found for us in Penrith.

As to your courtship with Mr. Soulier, I have conflicting emotions. First, I wish you had consulted me before consenting to his request, but I am not ignorant that if you were to marry, at least your future would greatly benefit from such a situation. It is good I had a chance to meet Mr. Soulier and found nothing in him during that brief visit to give me alarm, as he was very polite and kind to us in our grief.

Thank him for me, for his generosity and goodwill, but tell him that your association with him has not been long enough for us to consider his financial assistance at this time. And in the meantime, Cairstin, keep looking out for a place for us in Penrith. Rose and I are willing to live anywhere, under any conditions, as long as we three are together.

With much love,

Mother

A rush of relief poured over me as I read her words and clung to her little emerald. Though I knew her answer would not please William, he would have to agree with Mother's reasoning.

Saturday evening, when I exited the shop to find him waiting for me, I was glad to tell him I had heard from Mother and had an answer for him. We stood to the side of the entrance to Sutton Yard.

"She says to thank you very much for your kindness and goodwill but that my association with you has not been long enough for us to consider such an offer at this time. And it has been very brief, you must agree, William—don't you?" I was as cordial and delicate in my manner as I could be, but his face fell, and a hint of anger pinched at his dark brows. It took me by surprise.

"Well, I suppose, that is, of course your mother has declined, but she also hinted that there may be some time in the future where she might be more accepting, and that is what I will set my hopes on." Then with a nod, as if he had made an internal note, he gave me a small smile, which relieved me.

"Well, my dear, tomorrow I shall come and walk you to church, and afterward, if the weather is fine, I should like to take a walk after tea so we can have a good chat. Would that suit you?"

"Of course, William." I thought about my piecework that would help me earn more money with that time, but I dearly longed to breathe some fresh air and have an opportunity to get to know my suitor better.

"Then we shall go. Now, Cairstin, I like to arrive at church well before the service and shall be waiting for you right here at half past nine o'clock sharp." He looked at me sideways with narrowed eyes, as if reprimanding a child.

"Oh yes, I will be ready, I promise." I laughed at his jest but stopped myself short when his frown deepened.

"I am rather serious. I do not wish the Lord, or the reverend, to be annoyed by tardiness. I believe it shows a deliberate lack of regard, don't you agree?"

"Why, of course, William. I have never been late to church—"

"No, but you have been known to wander astray to another, I have observed." His tone was almost patronizing, and I felt the heat prickle in my cheeks.

"I will be ready on time tomorrow, as promised, William," I said quietly, then tried to lighten the air. "I hope the weather will not spoil our plans."

His face softened and his smile returned. "Don't worry, my dear. I shall take it up with the Lord this evening and put in a good word. We are very well acquainted, you see." That warm glimmer touched his eyes as before, and I found it almost charming. "Good evening, Cairstin."

"Good evening, William."

As I readied for church the next morning, part of my heart was sorry not to be returning to St. Andrews. It now felt like a forgone conclusion that I might never return there again, and I was surprisingly sorrowed by the thought.

William was pleased I was waiting for him with the other girls, but his affect was dull as we exchanged pleasantries on the way to The Gloucester Arms. I could not decide the cause of his lack of felicity. Perhaps he was just tired, as was I, from another long week of hard work.

Reverend and Mrs. Thomas greeted us cheerfully, and I was relieved when William smiled brightly on them and me and continued to be cordial and amiable, in his quiet way. He sat between me and Annabel and did great justice to the songs before the sermon, then sat almost on the edge of his chair, intently listening to the reverend's sermon on the destructive vice of a gossiping tongue.

"For who can tame the tongue, I ask you?" Reverend Thomas asked the congregation. "Can you? Are you resisting the devil when you so eagerly run from this person to that with what you just heard about so and so? And you, ladies! Is it any of your neighbor's business if you have a disagreement with your husband? No!" he slapped the lectern and leaned his barrel chest upon it.

"Difficulties in marriage are a natural occurrence and are to be expected, considering that one sinner is married to another, but you must not add to the sin by spreading word of it to everyone whose ears are tickled by such things. Wives, you dishonor your husbands, whom you have been commanded to respect and obey, when you run to your mother or sister every time you have a misunderstanding at home."

I secretly snatched a look at William just then and found him nodding in wholehearted agreement.

"Keep your minds and your hearts from being corrupted by the world, and do not be tempted to add to the world's corruption by your own sinful deeds. May God help us all if we do!"

Slam went the Bible, and up stood the congregation for the final song. William smiled with great satisfaction, but not at me, then sang with gusto, "Make Us Wholly Thine."

We said our goodbyes and greeted Reverend Thomas on our way down the stairs.

"Ah, and here is a wholesome sight. It is good to see the two of you, Mr. Soulier. And, Miss Blackwood, I hope that you are feeling the comfort of the Lord during your recent bereavement."

The reverend's smile seemed genuine, but an added hint of pride edged his tone, and I couldn't help but notice the knowing look he exchanged with my companion.

"Thank you, Reverend Thomas. I appreciate your prayers for me and my family."

The thought of Mother and my sister brought on such a wave of grief I felt suddenly weak. I was glad when William picked up the rest of the farewell and led me down the stairs.

I held on to the bottom of the banister and touched my aching forehead. William must have noticed, for he took me directly out of the inn and looked at me soberly.

"Cairstin, I am concerned for you. You are overworked, especially after your recent loss. Your tireless efforts to provide for your mother and sister are commendable, but if anything should happen to you, where would that leave them?"

"I . . . I am only a bit tired, William. It has been rather hard for me to keep up my spirits lately, but I am—"

"Yes, I have noticed. I will take you home immediately, though I must admit I am disappointed we are able to spend so little time together." He looked across the street, obviously hurt.

"I'm so sorry, William. I feel the same way, as I am anxious to get to know you better, but—"

"Then we shall just have to walk slowly, and you shall ask me anything you would like to know." Once again his smile returned, but I was not warmed by it.

We walked slowly down Corn Market and onto Little Dockray. The wind picked up, and the chill went right through me as a train whistle sounded in the distance.

"What would you like to know about me, Cairstin? Ask me anything and I will gladly answer."

"Well, I would like to know things like where you were born, and about your family. Everything, really."

At this he brightened. "I was born in Oxford. My mother was a beautiful woman, the daughter of a wealthy accountant, and my father's father was French but left the continent after the war to work at the university. My parents had high hopes for me to one day study at Oxford, but"—he looked down at the cobblestones pensively—"alas, they were both killed when I was only eight years old, and I was raised by my uncle, my mother's brother, in London."

I stopped in the middle of the street, shocked and equally

bewildered at how casually he shared this heartbreaking information.

"Oh, William! I am so very sorry! I had no idea—"

"No, no, of course not. I am very private about my personal history and have not shared it with many people in Penrith."

"I understand," I whispered, and felt terrible about the shallow ambivalence I'd felt toward him. "I am stunned by your story and so very sorry for your loss." My heart swelled with compassion, as I now saw him in a completely different light. "I would never have guessed."

As he steered me on, his eyes shone with that peculiar glint I found so intriguing. "Thank you, my dear. My life has been full of many challenges, to be sure. I have been hindered time and time again in my struggle to realize my full potential, but perhaps those stories should wait until you are feeling better."

We reached Sutton Yard and stood within the sheltering walls of the entrance.

William took my hand in his. "I want you to promise me you will take this precious time away from me to rest. I do not like the little dark circles that are starting to appear under your lovely green eyes."

The heat rose in my cheeks despite the cold. "I promise to rest as much as I can, William. Thank you for your understanding."

He bowed over my hand and bid me good afternoon, then watched as I wearily mounted the steps to my humble dwelling.

Just then, I remembered something and whirled to find William still watching, though his warm smile had turned to something cold and leering. It startled him when I saw him, and the warmth instantly returned.

I let it pass, and leaning over the iron railing, I called to him. "William, would you be willing to help me find a place for my mother and sister here in Penrith next Sunday? Would you know of any?"

He frowned for a moment but rallied quickly. "Of course, my dear. I am your servant." He bowed just as a train whistle blew, his brown overcoat billowing around him in the wind as he stepped out of the entrance and onto the street.

Chapter Nine

Mrs. Fallowfield, who scrutinized my work to see if my state of mourning was affecting my performance adversely, gave me the task of making a complete evening gown for an important lady from town, Mrs. Langley. It was to have a fan bodice with sloping shoulders and a revealing neckline, made in a rich brown silk that shimmered with hints of gold.

I straightened my shoulders and took a deep breath as I stood at the cutting room table and commenced with cutting out the precious fabric, knowing if I made a mistake, I would pay for it out of my wages. I measured carefully and double-checked every mark before applying my scissors. I was down to the last piece when I was startled by Eliza, who cried out in pain, having burned herself with an iron.

I turned around to find her sucking her finger and looking at me pitifully.

"Are you all right, Eliza? Shall I get you a bandage?" I offered to look at her finger, but she jerked away from me.

"No, I think it is only a little burn," she said sweetly, and went directly back to her task.

I returned to my table and looked down in dismay, as my scissors had jerked at the sound of her cry and made an irreversible gash in the fabric that would require me to cut an entirely new piece at my expense.

My heart sank as Mrs. Fallowfield entered the cutting room, but I screwed up my courage and went to her straight away. "I have made a cutting error, Mrs. Fallowfield, and will require another half yard of the brown silk for Mrs. Langley's dress. I am sorry and know that the expense must come out of my wages."

"That is too bad, Miss Blackwood, but you knew the rules. Go to the drapery and have Mr. Bell get you the bolt, if you please." Her black eyes searched me as she spoke, and she left the cutting room with me.

She paused in the hall and looked down her beaked nose at me through her little round spectacles. "Miss Blackwood, it isn't like you to make such a costly mistake. Are you quite all right?"

My heart was pricked open by her kind words. "Oh, yes, Mrs. Fallowfield. I am very well, and I promise not to make the same mistake again." I chose not to make the excuse of Eliza's outburst, and forced a smile to my lips, avoiding her gaze.

She pushed up her bottom lip, unconvinced, but didn't pry more. "Very well, Miss Blackwood. I will depend on you to keep your promise. Run along to the drapery."

I dashed down the stairs to face the humiliation that Mr. Bell would certainly heap on my head for my mishap with the scissors.

As I made my way back up to the cutting room with my new piece of silk, my face insisted on remaining hot and flushed with embarrassment. I hated having anyone displeased with me, and Mr. Bell was able to express his displeasure without saying a word.

I entered the cutting room as Eliza was taking her pressed pieces up to the sewing room.

"How is your burn, Eliza?" I asked with genuine concern. "Is your finger very painful?"

She gave me a quizzical look. "What burn, Cairstin? I'm sure I have no idea what you're talking about."

~

That evening when I walked out of Arnison's, I was surprised to find William speaking animatedly with Annabel, who laughed at something he said.

"Cairstin, Mr. Soulier was just telling me that he wishes he could sew ladies' dresses so he could be with us in our sewing room all day—can you just picture it?"

I couldn't help but smile at the image that came to mind. "That would indeed be a sight to see, Mr. Soulier. Shall I teach you?"

William chuckled and waved a hand. "No, no thank you, Miss Blackwood. I will stick to counting money. But perhaps I should teach you how to keep accounts so you could work all day with me at the bank instead."

The three of us laughed together, and it felt so good. I couldn't remember the last time I'd laughed.

"Now there's a pretty sight." William tucked my hand into his arm. "I am glad to see that lovely smile at last, Cairstin. I knew it was hiding somewhere all along."

I breathed in deep draughts of the crisp night air as we three walked to Sutton Yard and felt some of the harshness of the day fade away. Annabel gave me a knowing smile as she left us in the entry and went up to our rooms. I leaned my tired back against the stone wall and smiled shyly at William. How good it was to see him in such fine humor as well.

William stepped back from me and looked me over. I blushed under his appraising gaze and looked down at the cobblestones.

"I long for the day when you will be out of your mourning black, Cairstin. It doesn't suit you at all. I picture you in a green silk plaid, to set off your lovely red hair."

"Oh, William, it will be quite some time before I can think of such things." My voice was husky with the cold, and I was flustered by his compliments.

He sighed. "I am only glad that—" He shook his head, checking the watch from his waistcoat pocket. "No, it is not the time to discuss such things. You must be off to your bed now."

"Only glad that what, William? You cannot think I will be able to sleep with such a mystery hanging in the air." It felt daring to ask, but I couldn't help myself.

"No, no, I misspoke, my dear. We can discuss it another time." His eyes did not match his words, which urged me to try him again.

I felt foolish for coaxing him. "Please, William, won't you tell me now?"

"Oh, all right then, if you insist." He looked at his shoes and kicked at a pebble. "I was just about to say that I am so very glad you look nothing like my—"

He paused again and peeked at me from under his hat brim. My pulse quickened and my lightheartedness faded.

"Nothing like whom, William?" I urged.

He looked sheepishly at the ground again, then drew a breath. "I am very relieved you look nothing like my former fiancée, Lydia Netherwood."

I physically flinched at his words. "Your . . . your former fiancée?" I could not hide my shock and dismay.

"Uh, well, yes. You see, I told you it was an inappropriate time to discuss such a matter—"

Stunned, I could hardly think. "I didn't know you were engaged to be married before. Reverend Thomas never told me—"

"I asked him not to, as I wanted to explain it to you myself." Now he came nearer and reached for my hand, which I reluctantly gave him.

"You see, I was tricked into proposing to her by her father, who was my superior in the bank I worked at in London, and I want you to know that I never had any regard for her like I have for you, Cairstin. It was all just a terrible mistake, and it is over. Now, I have found my true soul mate." He moved very close, and my back pressed into the cold stone wall.

I could feel his warm breath on my face, and panic struck my heart. "I see," I said weakly. "I think we should discuss this further, William, but I am rather tired, and—"

"Yes, yes, we can discuss it another time, my dear. I will let you go now." He kissed my gloved hand and turned abruptly into the street without saying goodbye.

Tuesday morning, I arose with a terrible headache. When the memory of the conversation with William resurfaced, I had a difficult time pushing it to the back of my conscience to focus on Mrs. Langley's evening dress.

When I took up where I left off the evening before, I found that all the perfect little gathers I'd made for the fan bodice the day before had been cut here and there, leaving all that intricate work ruined. My heart sank as my alarm rose, and I looked over to where Eliza sat near the window, working on a blue day dress.

She did not look up at me, but I saw the tiniest twitching of the corners of her mouth as she swayed slightly from side to side. I knew she had done it.

I sat still as a great debate ran back and forth through my thoughts. I should go directly to Mrs. Fallowfield and show her this, but if I did, then who would I say I suspect would do such a thing? And when I said Eliza, then she would ask me if I had any proof, and I would be humiliated, because I had none.

And so I decided not to tell Mrs. Fallowfield, but I did lean over to Annabel and showed the broken threads to her in silence.

Her eyes grew wide, and she shook her head slightly, but I only gave her a knowing look, glanced toward Eliza, then went about re-stitching the gathers, wondering what I had ever done to the girl to deserve her hatred.

Just then a train whistle blew.

Chapter Ten

I could not even look at Eliza for the rest of the day, but as I crossed the hallway to leave that evening, I once again spied her and Mr. Bell through the drapery door, having an amusing and intimate conversation.

When I saw William waiting across the street for me with a bright smile on his round face, I stopped short, not prepared to speak to him again after all I was dealing with in the ladies' sewing room.

He came to me, tucking my hand into his arm possessively and escorting me around the buildings to the right instead of our usual path around the front of the shop. Then instead of taking me to the entrance of Sutton Yard, he walked past it. My heart pounded and I wanted to object, but by the time I found my voice, we were already stepping into Queen's Street, going the opposite direction.

I finally stopped and pulled my hand from his tightly held arm. "William, where are we going?" I whispered, aware that other working-class people were making their way home as well.

"I just want to find a place where we can sit and talk for a while. You need to understand my former unfortunate circumstances, my dear, for I fear I gave you quite a shock last night."

He took my hand and began to walk on, but I hesitated.

"Come now, Cairstin, don't be angry with me," he said sheepishly. "I meant to tell you when the time was right, believe me."

"I suppose I believe you, but . . . but . . ." I couldn't put my words together properly.

"I know, I know," he coaxed, and once again I found myself being led along, not at all sure I wanted to be.

I paused again, but he held tightly to my hand. "Please, Cairstin," he said earnestly, "I promise everything will be all right and I'll take you home soon. Don't you trust me, my dear?"

Nodding in agreement, I allowed him to guide me farther onto Stricklandgate to Corney Place, a strangely shaped intersection with a short stone-wall median in the middle. There William took me and bade me to sit down. There was not much traffic that evening, but it felt odd to be sitting there in the middle of the converging lanes. What a conspicuous place to have a serious conversation, I thought, rather embarrassed.

"You see," William said, "I have brought you to a safe, public place where you needn't be afraid for your reputation. I know it is a bit awkward, but I will be as brief as I can."

He smiled reassuringly as he sat beside me, not too close but near enough to speak without having to raise our voices.

"I'm listening, William" was all I could manage.

"Cairstin, my dear, I have been in agony all day thinking about what you must think of me after what I revealed to you last evening. I simply must clear myself before I have another sleepless night."

He took my hand in both of his and held it gently. "You

must understand, I was placed in a terrible position. The managing officer of the bank where I worked in London had his eye on me, as I am a hard worker. I am excellent with numbers, and I was the best employee he had ever supervised. He even said so."

The amber gleam in his eyes caught the light of the streetlamp as he spoke. It was such a bewitching look and almost made up for his otherwise unremarkable countenance. My hand warmed in his, and he was so earnest in his tone and manner that I could not help but listen with a great desire that he should have a good explanation.

"You see, I was up for a promotion and an increase in my salary, but Mr. Netherwood dragged his feet on giving me my due. Instead, he convinced me to court his daughter, Lydia, all the while dangling my promotion like a bait just out of my reach. He even hinted that if I became his son-in-law, he would be able to give me a much higher position with an even greater salary."

I shifted on my cold, stony seat but said nothing.

"Well, I was young and foolish then and very determined to better myself and my situation, and Lydia was tolerably pretty. Not as pretty as you, of course, but she had rather good manners and hair as black as night, all ringlets and—"

He caught himself and stumbled on. "Well, she could be very charming in the beginning, and I thought, what harm would it do to propose to her and get my promotion. Then I would prove to her father that I was worthy of it, and if I married Lydia, we would be set up for a brilliant future together."

William paused and looked at me out of the corner of his eye, but I stayed as stoic as possible.

"So you see, I did propose, and she accepted, but her father wouldn't grant me my promotion until after the wedding. But

Lydia's character changed completely after our engagement was announced. She became intolerable, and her true character showed its ugly head. She would tell the most vicious lies about me and even became violent toward me on occasions when we disagreed on some trivial matter. So I decided that no promotion or any amount of money was worth marrying such a wicked woman, especially since I was truly coming to know God and that He had great plans for my life."

He finally took a breath, then moved closer to me and looked intently into my eyes. "Won't you please forgive me, my dearest Cairstin, for being a young fool? I have had so many struggles in my life to overcome, with no mother or father to guide me, but I promise you I have changed and matured since then. I will not be able to live with myself if you will not forgive me."

He let go of my hands and turned his face away, obviously in deep pain. I tenderly touched his chin and turned his eyes back to mine. "Of course, William. We all make mistakes, and I can forgive you for this. Only, please don't keep secrets from me, William. It breaks my heart—"

He eagerly took my arm, and we stood, that amber glint in his eyes flashing with relief. "Oh, thank you, my dear. Thank you! I am so happy to have your trust and confidence. Besides, Lydia Netherwood is nothing compared to you, my dear."

We hurried down Long Front Street to Sutton Yard. I hardly said a word as he went on about how he was struggling again with an unjust manager who was reluctant to give him the salary he deserved but would never be tempted to marry again for money.

I was quite aware it would not be the case if he married me. If William proposed, it would not be for money.

When we parted, he glanced at his watch, then held my hands and smiled. "I was just telling Reverend Thomas at cur discipleship meeting this morning about how blessed I am to have you in my life, Cairstin Blackwood. May you have a pleasant rest, and I will be waiting for you tomorrow, as always."

~

On Wednesday morning I determined to keep a closer eye on Eliza and always asked Mrs. Fallowfield to inspect my work upon the completion of every section. I even considered approaching Susan about Eliza's behavior but thought it best not to stir the pot.

At breakfast, Toby, the errand boy, delivered a letter to me, and I was grateful it came at an opportune time so I could read it right away.

> Dearest Daughter,
>
> Thank you, my brave girl, for sending your wages again in such a timely fashion. We are so very grateful to you for your hard work and for supporting us, my love.
>
> Your sister and I are well and have been able to find some temporary work at the Crown and Cushion, cleaning rooms after their overnight guests leave on the post. It isn't much, and Mrs. Morland—you will remember her—is a bit frustrated I cannot carry as much as the other maids, but the little we are paid is enough for me to buy some necessary items, such as the paper I am writing you on.
>
> Have you had any luck in finding a place for us in Penrith? Remember, child, that we do not need much, and we can make do with anything you can find.
>
> I am anxious for any word you can share about how things are progressing with Mr. Soulier. I was greatly surprised to receive his note asking me how we are faring

and offering his sincerest apology for not speaking to me before commencing with your courtship. But do not worry. He did not pressure me about the offer he made you, which was most sensible.

We always long to hear from you, so write as often as you can.

You are always in my prayers. Much love from both of us,

Mother

William had written to Mother and apologized? I was mystified and absently played with her pendant. It seemed an appropriate gesture, but why had he not spoken of it to me? Perhaps he was waiting to sort things out with me about his former engagement.

I made up my mind to think of his actions in a positive light and to try to give him the benefit of the doubt more often. Besides, he was an orphan, raised by what sounded like a disinterested uncle, and had perhaps not learned how to conduct himself with greater decorum.

Perhaps William's great esteem for Reverend Thomas stemmed from his need for a father figure in his life. The thought warmed my heart, and I recalled what William had said about having no family and wishing to rectify that situation soon.

That was it! William was a lonely man without the experience of a warm family life to smooth off his awkward edges. Perhaps that is why God had seen fit to put us together. William to help us in our hour of trouble, and us to surround him with the kind of support money could never buy.

William had promised me that he would take me to a couple of rooms for rent after church on Sunday, and I was anxious to find something that would suffice.

Both Eliza and Susan were escorted home by Mr. Bell that evening. Eliza was all smiles and giggles, but Susan looked uncomfortable. William, not wanting to be overheard by them as they stood conversing in the entryway, ventured to take me into Sutton Yard as far as the bottom of the stairs, and I noticed the face of Mrs. Tweedle, one of Arnison's cooks, watching us through the crack in the curtain of the flat under ours.

"Who is that with Eliza? He certainly doesn't strike me as the type of man who would be to her taste." William eyed the couple with a slight curl to his upper lip.

"I am surprised as well, but I have seen them whispering together on occasion. His name is Mr. Bell, and he is the draper. They seem very similar in character to me."

William leaned closer to me. "What do you mean, Cairstin? Do you know much about him?"

"Actually no, but he has made it very obvious that I do not impress him." I half giggled into my gloved hand.

"Not impressed with you, my dear? But how can that be—you are the most beautiful lady in Penrith."

Before he could say more, I faced him. "William, why didn't you tell me you wrote to my mother? I received a letter from her today saying you did."

The corners of his mouth drew up, and his eyes narrowed. "Wasn't it right for me to write her and apologize for my oversight? Don't you approve?"

"Oh, I think it was a very noble thing to do. I just wondered why you hadn't mentioned it to me—"

"Now, Cairstin"—he turned slightly away, as though hurt by my question. "When will you ever begin to trust me? Have I ever done anything to deserve your distrust?"

I was startled. "No, William, never, I just thought—"

"There, you see, then why must I always feel that you do not trust me? Surely you can tell by now how devoted I am to you."

"I am sorry, William. I meant no offense, truly—"

"That's all right, my dear." He finally turned toward me and took my hand. "I am not offended, knowing that you still need time to know me better. And now"—he set me loose as Eliza came to mount the stairs—"you should be getting some rest, my dear. I'm sure you will see everything in a clearer light in the morning."

He looked at his watch and bid me good night.

I stood puzzled by his words, but I climbed the stairs after Eliza, who looked back at me with a cattish grin.

When we entered our quarters and took off our bonnets, she faced me. "What's the matter, Cairstin? Mr. Bell says ya've been looking a bit peaked lately."

"Nothing is the matter, Eliza. But it looks like you and Mr. Bell are getting along quite well."

"Indeed we are! In fact, he took me to the post today and mailed a letter to my dah asking if he could court me, all official like. Isn't that romantic? Too bad things didn't work out for you with Mr. Dalton, eh?" She tossed her head as she spun away.

~

The end of another week was crossed off Mrs. Fallowfield's calendar on Saturday, January 23. Snow lay heavy and wet on the streets of Penrith that Sunday morning. William walked ahead of me so I might follow in his footsteps on our way to church, and Annabel came behind me.

Susan wasn't feeling well and stayed in bed, while Eliza said she had plans to meet Mr. Bell, much to my relief. Living in such close quarters with someone who distinctly did not like me had become a torture. At least Mr. Bell seemed to be enough of a distraction to keep her from attempting any more sabotage.

The upper hall of The Gloucester Arms was only half-full when Reverend Thomas rose to preach. My head and shoulders ached from weariness, and I took a deep breath, anticipating the usual Sunday morning barrage. William gave me a smile before turning his full attention to the reverend.

I'd never seen the reverend so downcast before, and he began his message bemoaning the lack of attendance. He sighed heavily and stroked the Bible on the lectern. "Does not your heart yearn with mine to be in a sanctified, holy house?

"But how shall that ever be, especially when the people of this dear fellowship do not brave a little bad weather to assemble together? Not only to bring glory to God but also to bring our tithes of financial offerings, which keep near the hope of soon being able to worship him in a place we dedicate to Him?"

Reverend Thomas passed his beefy hand over his large forehead. "Perhaps it is some failing of my own that is to blame. I scatter the seed of the word as faithfully as I can and labor in the fields, but where is the fruit, my friends? Where is the fruit?!"

His face was now its familiar red, and he stormed behind the lectern. "My children, we must put aside our own comfort to suffer with Christ! We must sacrifice our all and build the Lord a house!"

Slam went the Bible, and the ragged congregation rose to sing the closing song. William sang with great gusto, and I tried my best to enter in, but a pang of guilt seeped through my chest as I chastised myself for never putting a penny into the Building Fund box.

Annabel greeted the reverend with us, and I fished a few

precious coins from my thin reticule. William saw, and he smiled on me approvingly as I quietly slipped my coins into the lid of the box on the table.

"I am very proud of you, Cairstin," he whispered as we descended.

Annabel planned to have tea with Miss Barnes and Mr. Pitt, who invited us to join.

"Oh, thank you kindly, but no," I said, "William has promised to take me to see some rooms to let—"

"I did?" William interrupted.

My heart fell to the floor. "Well yes, you said you had some addresses—"

"I'm so sorry, my dear. I think you must have misunderstood me. I never promised to take you to see rooms for let, only that someday, if I had found out any, we would go together to inspect them."

"Oh, but you said just the other day that—"

William smiled but shook his head. To the others he said, "Well, I think Miss Blackwood is a bit tired. We would be very happy to join you, as some tea and biscuits might do her good—shall we?"

I was dumbfounded. He led me speechless to a table and pulled out a chair for me, but I stood staring at him in disbelief. His smile vanished, and he looked me over doubtfully. "Or perhaps I should take you home straight away, my dear. You are looking very pale indeed."

"No, no, I am all right, just disappointed, that's all." I sat, not knowing what else to do.

"Well, I am sorry to disappoint you, my dear, but since I made no such promise, I can hardly see why you are so vexed with me—"

"No, never mind, William. I suppose I did misunderstand, and I am all right now, truly."

A sickening knot tightened my throat, and I could only pretend to listen to the conversation around the table. Had I misheard him? Surely not. I distinctly remembered and could even recall exactly where we were standing in Sutton Yard and that a train whistle blew as he spoke.

Chapter Eleven

As we walked home after tea, I debated on whether to confront William about not keeping his promise, but he preempted me.

"You know, Cairstin," he said with an imploring look, "that my offer still stands to send money to your mother and sister and enable them to stay in Appleby, in the home they already know and love."

"Oh, I thank you, William, for your very generous offer, but I have already told you how Mother feels—"

"Yes, I know, and I respect her reasoning concerning the matter, but what about what is best for her, for your sister? Surely you can't see them living in squalor in some filthy place in the poorer parts of Penrith when they enjoy such comfort and beauty around them in Appleby."

"But it is such a great expense, William, and I really do want to be with them to watch over them—"

He sighed with exasperation, "Ah, Cairstin, have you considered that your motives for bringing them here are of a selfish nature? You wouldn't want them to suffer because you are not feeling mature enough to face life without your mother near you, would you?"

I paused my steps and faced him, desperate to know. "Do you think I'm selfish, William? Tell me, truthfully."

My heart galloped against my ribs, and the cold air caught in my throat. Was I truly a selfish person?

William lifted his chin and looked upon me appraisingly, the corners of his mouth lifted strangely. "No, Cairstin, you are not any more selfish than the average girl your age who is in a difficult situation." He gathered my hand in his arm and continued to walk slowly. "But you must do as God would wish and think of others more highly than yourself, as we all should."

His answer was not reassuring. "Then I am selfish," I said defeatedly.

"We must all fight our natural, sinful tendencies toward selfishness, and you, my dear, though you are the most remarkable woman I have ever met, and your motives to help your mother and sister are all from good intentions, are no less susceptible to temptation than anyone else."

I was silent the rest of the walk home as I contemplated all William had said. When we reached Sutton Yard, Annabel had already gone up to the flat. I heard a train whistle as William checked his pocket watch, then came close to me with a wide smile as we stood in the shelter of the entrance. I leaned my back against the solidness of the cold wall.

"William," I asked shyly, "will you let me look at your lovely watch? I have never looked at it closely."

He flinched, which I found curious, but pulled it back out of his pocket. "Certainly, my dear, but the clasp is a little tricky, so I ask you not to open it."

I held its weight in my hands and marveled at its smooth cold casing. Holding it nearer my face, I noticed an inscription. "W. E. S.," I read aloud.

William smiled and held out his hand. "Yes, it stands for William Edward Soulier." I placed it in his hand, and he quickly tucked it away.

"I have some good news, my dear. I am up for a promotion at the bank. I have been eager to be alone with you to tell you." His amber eyes glinted with anticipation.

"I am so happy for you, William!" I said with genuine pleasure. "And your supervisor, Mr. Florence, he is no longer standing in your way?"

"Well, he is still digging in his heels, but I ran into the president of the bank himself, and he said he had his eye on me for a new position as his second secretary because he knew I had proven myself to be brilliant with numbers."

William stood proud and self-satisfied. "So that means I will not only be able to assist your family but will also be able to support a wife, who will no longer have to be a working girl but will be a kept lady."

My pulse surged in my ears as he stepped closer still and clasped my hands to his chest.

"Now, what do you think about that, my dear Cairstin?"

His face was so close I could feel his warm breath and his weight pressing me against the wall. I could hardly breathe but managed to whisper, "I . . . I'm not sure, William—what does it all mean?"

He stepped back and laughed. "It means that I intend to write another letter to your mother. That's what it means."

He bowed gallantly and touched his hat, then whirled away back into the street, leaving me breathless.

Just then, as I tried to gather my wits about me, I heard a voice I had not heard for a while. *"Cairstin, lass! Ya must marry! Promise me! Promise me now!"*

I walked around Arnison's on Monday in a kind of trance. So William was about to propose. I would be able to fulfill my promise to my father and see my mother and sister cared for, but I was not elated. In fact, I was terrified. But wasn't it what I wanted? Wasn't it what was best for me and my family?

I tried to rally, but my heart would not have it. If I were honest, I felt little warmth of affection for William Soulier, though I was grateful for the help he had given me when Father died. Still, the face of Gabriel Dalton would flash before me, adding further torture to my confused heart, and I prayed fervently for deliverance from my wickedness.

Plenty of people married for money, I told myself, and God did not seem displeased when they did. I had to face the fact I was indeed a selfish person to want to feel loved and to love in return.

Pushing aside these debates, I concentrated on finishing Mrs. Langley's dress, as she was due for her fitting that afternoon. I was glad I had chosen to bother Mrs. Fallowfield for her inspection every step of the way, and now as I finished the last touches on the ruffles on the sleeves, I took the dress to her table and smiled.

"Here I am, Mrs. Fallowfield, with Mrs. Langley's dress all finished for her fitting this afternoon."

"Hmm, yes." She eyed the intricate stitching and checked to make sure the ruffles were evenly placed. "This is fine work, Miss Blackwood. Take it down to the cutting room and give it a last pressing, then hang it in the ladies fitting room. After that you can assist Miss Dykes for a while, until Mrs. Langley comes for her appointment."

"Yes, ma'am." I curtsied, then gathering up the shimmering gown in my arms, took it down a flight of stairs to the cutting room.

I smiled with satisfaction over my work and hoped with all

my heart that Mrs. Langley would be pleased. It was the most beautiful dress I had created by far, and I wished Mother could see it.

Eliza hovered over a cutting table when I entered. She briefly looked up, then went on with her work as I lay the dress over the ironing board and heated an iron. It was the habit of most of the sewing staff to spit on the iron to test its temperature, but I found it a vulgar practice, so I dipped my fingers in a pitcher of water to flick at the hot black surface.

When Eliza left the room, I breathed a sigh of relief. Since her courtship with Mr. Bell had begun, she seemed less interested in harassing me, and I was grateful.

The dress pressed and hung up in the ladies' fitting room, I rejoined the others in the sewing room and sat down at the table across from Susan, whose eyes were rimmed with red, and she scratched at her hands from time to time. When I looked down on the garment she was making, something hit me like I had slammed into a brick wall.

Green wool. The fabric of the dress she was making was the exact green wool my father had been working on to make the mayor's green woolen coat when my father's illness had begun, his initial symptoms being red-rimmed eyes and irritated hands.

I looked up at Susan, my mouth gaping.

"What's the matter, Cairstin? What's gotten into ya?" Susan asked in a harsh whisper.

"Susan, how long have you been working on this dress?"

"Oh, I don't know, about a week, I guess."

"And how long have you been feeling ill?" I pressed.

"Well, just the last few days. Why?"

Mrs. Fallowfield cleared her throat, annoyed we were talking, but I just couldn't help myself. I stood and went to Mrs.

Fallowfield. "I'm sorry, Mrs. Fallowfield, but may I please speak to you privately for a moment?"

I could feel the other girls' eyes on me as Mrs. Fallowfield looked at me in irritation but rose and went out into the hall.

"What is it, Miss Blackwood? Why are you delaying your work?"

"Please, Mrs. Fallowfield, I have something to say that may be important—will you allow me to explain?"

"All right, but let us not tarry too long."

"Thank you, ma'am. You see, Miss Dykes has not been feeling well these past few days, and I wonder if you have noticed the redness around her eyes and the skin of her hands?"

"Hmm, yes, I did notice, but she has said nothing to me."

"No, of course not—she would never want to disappoint you, ma'am. It's just that, you see, my father, who passed away at Christmas, was a tailor, as you know, and his illness began in exactly the same way."

Mrs. Fallowfield looked at the sewing room door, then turned back to me, her knit brows carving great creases in her high forehead. "Go on, Miss Blackwood."

"Yes, ma'am, and I have just discovered that the dress Susan is working on is the exact same green wool that my father was using when his symptoms first appeared. A vivid green wool."

She pressed her lips together thoughtfully. "Are you saying that you believe there is something about this fabric that made your father sick and may be making Miss Dykes ill as well?"

"I am not entirely sure, ma'am, but it does seem to be more than a coincidence." My voice fell flat as I realized how implausible it all sounded.

Mrs. Fallowfield pursed her lips again, then nodded slowly. "Thank you, Miss Blackwood, for your concern. I will investigate the matter. In the meantime, I ask you to go about your business and say nothing more to Miss Dykes until I have a chance to discuss this with Mr. Arnison."

I curtsied and thanked her as she led me back into the sewing room. I sat down across from Susan and asked her how I could help, loath to touch the green wool on the table.

Mrs. Langley arrived, and I followed Mrs. Fallowfield to the fitting room. We assisted her with undressing, then I brought the gown out of the closet for her to see.

"Oh, it is very lovely, Mrs. Fallowfield. Exactly what I pictured it would be," Mrs. Langley gushed, and my cheeks flushed with pleasure.

Mrs. Fallowfield gave me a pert nod and assisted me with lifting the dress over Mrs. Langley's head. Once the bodice and sleeves were in position, I went around her to begin hooking the back of the bodice together.

Just as I reached the top of the row of hooks above Mrs. Langley's corset, she jerked away.

"Ouch! Oh, that hurts! Ouch! Oh! Take it off! Take it off!" she screeched, and I obeyed. As I unhooked the back of the dress, to my horror I saw little scratches on Mrs. Langley's upper back, with little drops of blood dripping onto the dress.

"Oh dear! Mrs. Langley, I am terribly sorry," Mrs. Fallowfield cried as she came around and helped me lift the dress off again with a whoosh.

The dress was left in a heap on the floor as I ripped my handkerchief from the cuff of my sleeve and began dabbing at the little scratches. I was mortified.

Mrs. Langley whipped around and pierced me with a look of indignation and hurt. "Well, I have never in my life been subjected to such abuse in a ladies' fitting room. What on earth are you trying to do to me?"

"I'm so very sorry, Mrs. Langley. I can't imagine—"

By that time, the fitting room attendant had come in, and Mrs. Fallowfield escorted Mrs. Langley to a chair. I dashed to the dress on the floor and examined the back opening, and there, tucked into the seam beside the hooks was a needle, its sharp tip barely visible where it stuck out of the tight stitching.

My mind whirled with confusion. I would never have left a needle inside a seam like this. Never!

Dread squeezed my heart as Mrs. Fallowfield came over and I showed her the needle in the seam. Her eyes widened, her brows furrowed, and her thin lips pressed together. She gave me a scathing look, then heaped the dress into my arms.

"Miss Blackwood, you are dismissed. Take this dress into the hall and wait for me there."

Utterly dismayed, I turned to Mrs. Langley.

"I am deeply sorry, Mrs. Langley—"

"That will be all, Miss Blackwood." Mrs. Fallowfield nodded toward the door, and I left the room.

Shame washed over me, with flashes of anger and suspicion. I leaned my back against the wall of the employee hallway and heard the scuffling sound of someone quickly descending the stairs below me. Rushing to lean over the rail, I just caught sight of Mr. Bell dashing away toward the drapery.

I was livid. I ran down the stairs with the heaping dress in my arms, flew into the drapery and right up to the counter, where Mr. Bell stood as if he had been there all day. Laying the dress on the counter, I held up the seam where the needle still protruded to Mr. Bell's whitening face.

"Do you know anything about this, Mr. Bell? Why would you do such a thing?" I cried, tears flowing unchecked.

"Miss Blackwood? What is all of this?" I heard Mr. Arnison's indignant voice say behind me.

My heart withered as Mr. Bell smiled and I turned around to find Mr. Arnison and a gentleman customer standing among the fabric displays.

My chest heaved and I gathered up the dress as fast as I could. "I beg your pardon, Mr. Arnison, I . . . please forgive me —" I fled from the drapery and up to the second-floor hall.

Realizing my position was in jeopardy, I swallowed hard and faced Mrs. Fallowfield when she came into the hall, pointed at the crumpled dress, then motioned toward the stairs.

I followed her back down to the first floor and into Mr. Arnison's office, where he was waiting for us.

"Well, Miss Blackwood, I hope you have a very good explanation for your conduct today. I have never been so embarrassed by an employee, not with one customer but with two." His light-blue eyes flashed, and he looked down his thin nose at me.

"I am terribly sorry, Mr. Arnison, sir. I swear that I did not leave a needle in this dress. I am exceedingly careful and even had Mrs. Fallowfield inspect every stitch I made, sir. Isn't that true, Mrs. Fallowfield?" I turned pleading eyes on her.

She took a deep breath before answering. "It is true, Mr. Arnison. Miss Blackwood was extremely conscientious in having me inspect every part of the dress along the way. I must admit that I never noticed a needle in the seam myself, but as you can see, it is very well hidden."

Taking the dress from my arms, Mrs. Fallowfield brought it over to Mr. Arnison for his inspection.

"Good heavens! This is completely unacceptable, Mrs. Fallowfield. I expect you to—"

"Please, Mr. Arnison," I interrupted in despair. "It was not

Mrs. Fallowfield's fault. I think I know who placed the needle in the seam."

Fear struck my heart at my own brazenness, but I couldn't let Mrs. Fallowfield take any blame for this.

They both stared at me. "Do you mean to say you believe someone placed this needle here on purpose?" Mr. Arnison's words cut me like a knife, but I had set my course now and would have to see it through.

"Yes, sir," I whispered, then swallowed hard. "I am certain."

Mr. Arnison still brimmed with incredulity as he stepped closer.

"Then who is it, Miss Blackwood, and why would they do such a thing?"

I licked my dry lips and tried to control my inner shaking. "It was Miss Salkeld and Mr. Bell, sir."

They both blanched.

"Mr. Bell and Miss Salkeld? But how can you be sure? Did you see them do this?" Mr. Arnison's tone hardened even more.

"Well, no, sir, I would have taken the needle out if I had known—" Oh dear, this was going from bad to worse.

"Then how to you know it was them that did this?"

"Well, you see sir, I have been having some issues with Miss Salkeld trying to make trouble for me and my work."

"Trouble? What kind of trouble? Why did you not come to me, Miss Blackwood, if anyone was causing you trouble?" Mrs. Fallowfield demanded.

"She has been sabotaging my work, ma'am, snipping threads, making me cut something wrong. You will remember the piece I had to pay to replace—"

"Do you have any proof of this behavior, Miss Blackwood?"

I could hear a softening in his voice and pressed on. "I'm not sure how I could prove it, Mr. Arnison, but . . . but—"

"But why would they do such a thing? What would they

possibly have against you to treat you so? And to actually plot to hurt a client! It is unimaginable!"

I faltered. "I am not quite sure, Mr. Arnison. I suppose Eliza is jealous of me somehow." My voice drifted off, and I looked at the floor, a tear dripping onto my folded hands.

Mr. Arnison sighed and wiped his hand over his tired face. He sat in his desk chair and looked up at Mrs. Fallowfield, still holding the offending dress.

"It is a beautiful dress, Mrs. Fallowfield, and I am inclined to wonder why on earth Miss Blackwood would have done such a thing on purpose. Perhaps it was an oversight—"

Mrs. Fallowfield opened her mouth to speak, but Mr. Arnison raised his hand. "No, no, I am not blaming you either, Mrs. Fallowfield, but this is indeed a tragedy. We have wounded a very prominent lady in Penrith society and probably lost a customer for life, as well as embarrassed ourselves in front of Mr. Jones."

My face flushed hot, and I looked up, but again, Mr. Arnison held up his hand.

"Yes, Miss Blackwood, I understand now that you felt justified in confronting Mr. Bell if you indeed suspected him of this treachery, but you should have taken more care and controlled yourself before barging in as you did."

I nodded sorrowfully. "Yes, sir. I am so very sorry, and I will do anything you ask to make up for my behavior. Anything."

"Ah, well, I shall need to put some thought into how to remedy the situation." Mr. Arnison stood and motioned toward the door. "In the meantime, Mrs. Fallowfield, I expect you to make a thorough investigation into this matter, and Miss Blackwood, I am putting you on leave until this is all sorted out. You may collect your things and go now."

I silently gathered my things from the sewing room, stealing glances at Eliza, whose mouth twitched with the urge to smile, then descended the stairs. As I crossed the hall to the employee exit to leave, Toby crossed my path.

"Letter for thee, miss." He handed me an envelope and quickly disappeared into the storage room.

It was from Mother. The lump in my throat nearly suffocated me as I almost ran to Sutton Yard and entered the flat. Ripping off my bonnet and coat, I flung myself on my bed and tore open the seal.

Dearest Cairstin,

I am loath to send you such news, but the landlord has just informed me that he is raising the rent. I fear we will not be able to afford to stay past the end of the month and must find a place to move to by then. I have sold everything I dare to, not knowing what we will need when we can no longer afford to stay here, but it is inevitable.

I also regret to say that I have been dismissed from the Crown and Cushion, as I had an accident with a bedpan, but Rose is still bravely working there in the kitchen. I am trying to take on some cleaning, but you know what I am up against.

I know how desperately busy you are with work and that your hours are making it difficult for you to find us a place. I have spoken to Mr. Oldcorn, to see if he might be able to do some searching for us when he takes his furniture for delivery to Penrith, and he has agreed to try. He will come to Arnison's to find you if he is successful.

We must not lose hope, child. Trust in the Lord. Write soon.

Mother

A wave of nauseous agony washed over me. I had never known such cruelty in my life. What would possess people to be so spiteful?

I had no solace in that moment but that I was alone to hold Mother's pendant and cry my heart out. At some point I must have fallen asleep, for I was awakened by Annabel, who had come to check on me during the dinner break.

"Oh, Cairstin, I'm so sorry. What a frightfully mean thing to do. I could just give that Eliza Salkeld a good slap in the face!"

"I could as well, Annabel, but I have no way of proving that she or Mr. Bell placed that needle in the dress. But I know for a fact it was not there when I hung it in the dressing room closet —of that I'm sure."

"And now she is sitting pretty as a flower, still working, and ya may not even get paid for all the work ya did on that lovely dress."

"What?" I couldn't believe my ears! "How do you know?"

"Well, I'm not sure, but it's the word going round. They say Mr. Arnison is considering giving the dress to Mrs. Langley for free, just to smooth things over with her."

"Oh, Annabel! What will I do? Mother has just written to say the landlord is increasing the rent. Oh, God, what is to become of us?"

"We must pray, Cairstin." Annabel kissed my forehead. "I have to go. I'll try and sneak ya a piece o' bread from supper."

After she left, I knelt by my bed and cried aloud, "Dear God, please show me what to do! I'm desperate, Lord. Help me, please!"

Chapter Twelve

The next morning I lay in bed pretending to sleep as the others prepared and left for work. I was glad when they were gone so I could be alone in my cold bed with my even colder thoughts.

Why were Eliza and Mr. Bell out to ruin me?

I was sure William had learned some version of yesterday's events, and since I had not even received a note from him, I assumed he was appalled. Perhaps it was just as well.

I held mother's pendant. The thought had come to me several times that I might sell it, but I wouldn't think of it until it was the very last resort.

It appeared I had the whole day free and needed to make good use of it. I left the flat with a determination to find a room somewhere in Penrith where I could bring my family, and I hoped our combined efforts would provide us with enough to survive on.

But where to look? Whom to ask?

Walking deeper into Sutton Yard, I checked the rubbish

bins for old newspapers until at last I found a whole paper from two days before, the outer pages covered in cooking oil but still legible.

I found the advertisement page for rooms to let and smiled hopefully. Why had I not thought of this before? Back home, only my father read the paper, then afterward used it to make patterns for cutting fabric.

Throwing off my sullenness, I marched to the first place whose street name I recognized. I made my way past Arnison's without a look, sailed across the main square, continued down Netherend, and turned left on Barkhouse Lane.

I was affronted by the odorous air of the ironworks, whose aroma was then mingled and overtaken by something decaying I had never smelled before. I followed the lane as it turned right, then realized I could not find the address. The people in this area of town were mainly laborers, mostly men, but I caught the eye of a young woman wearing a dress in desperate need of washing, and I smiled.

"Excuse me, would you be able to direct me to the Barkhouse Lodge?" I asked.

"Aye!" she said warily. Her brows raised high as she looked me over.

"Ower yonder, lass, down t'alley." She pointed to an alleyway on the right, then hurried on her way.

"Thank you kindly!" I shouted after her and saw her head bob.

I entered the alley with my heart in my throat. It was shadowed by the buildings on each side, and the smell of barnyard animals mixed with other foul scents I didn't recognize grew as I walked farther in. Then I understood the terrible stench and its origin, as I could see through a break in the buildings to a large sign rising above them on my right: Penrith Tannery.

Only a few more yards and on the left hand I found my destination, Barkhouse Lodge. It was a large square building with many small windows filled with lines of drying clothes. I could not imagine wearing anything dried in such foul air but mustered up my courage to pass by the dirty children playing near its entrance.

The inside was not as dark as I had anticipated, and I stood looking at the squares of stairs winding their way up the three-storied building. A sign over the door inside the entrance said "Manager," and I knocked. I could hear voices inside speaking gruffly, and a man's cackling laughter grew louder as it approached the door.

The door opened, and a man in a shabby, ill-fitting purple frock coat stood just inside and looked me over from head to toe before speaking, making the blood rush in my ears. He was no taller than I, with long, greasy hair slicked back over his rather flat skull.

"Well, well, look who's come to pay us a visit, eh? And what can we do for ya, miss?" His breath reached me like a green cloud, and I reflexively stepped back.

"I have come to see about some rooms you have for let," I said softly and motioned to the newspaper I still held firmly in my gloved hand.

"Ah!" He smiled like a dog who had just found a bone. "Aye, we've got a couple o' empty ones just now." He leaned back to take a large set of rattling keys on a ring from the wall inside the door and stepped out. "I can show ya. Right this way, miss."

He swung the ring around his wrist with a practiced motion, then led the way up the stairs. When we reached the second floor, he turned down a hall to the left. It was dark but for the light that drifted in from the occasional open door, where I glanced in to find much the same as the rooms near the brewery, scarcity screaming silently from the walls.

My escort stopped before a door at the end of the hall and unlocked it with a flourish, his yellowed smile forcing the apples of his unshaven cheeks toward his milky eyes. He motioned for me to enter, and I passed through the door to find a bare room with no furniture save a small table and two unmatched chairs.

A small fireplace was framed by empty shelves on each side, and dirty windows lacking coverings. Determined not to be so easily repulsed, I walked into the bedchamber and found one bed and two rolls of straw-filled mats against the wall. There were no bed linens, but it did have a small window allowing in a thin beam of light.

I returned to the other room, and the landlord, or whoever this man was, stood between me and the now closed door, twirling his rattling key ring. I did not like the look in his eyes but gathered my courage. "How much for these rooms?"

"Well, that all depends, eh? I could tell ya the price in coin, or I could tell ya the price in—" At this he once again looked me over and licked his lips.

I was sure the look on my face was more than indignation, for the man chuckled, low and soft at first, then he cackled and slapped his knees, until I made a move toward the door.

He beat me to it and stood before it, wiping his mouth with the back of his hand.

"I will leave now, sir," I said as strongly as I could, and tried to reach around him to the handle.

I cried out when he grabbed my wrist hard and pushed me against the adjoining wall, pressing his filthy body up against mine. I tried to scream, but he covered my mouth with his callused hand and chortled.

I slammed my fists against him and tried to push him off

me, but he only dropped the key ring and wrapped his now free arm tight around my waist. Fighting for air, panic shot through my core.

Trying to turn my head, he held me fast. "Shhh, lassie. I'll not hurt thee. All I want is one little kiss, as a down payment for the rooms, eh?"

Something inside me snapped, and a wild instinct surged through me. I raised my foot high against the wall behind me and shoved the man's chest and face as hard as I could. He gripped me tight but could not keep his balance and took me with him as he fell backward onto the filthy floor.

Not stopping to think, I rolled off him and reached for the doorknob, pulling myself up as I threw open the door and ran for my life down the stairs. I ran out the building and back the way I had come until I was nearly to the main square.

Hiding myself in the tiny space between buildings, I gasped for air. Though I was relieved not to be followed, I could not suppress the tears that stung my eyes. I looked across the square only to see N. Arnison and Sons standing in solid mockery, daring me to pass its beautiful windows to find refuge in Sutton Yard. A refuge that might not long exist for me.

I sat in wallowing misery at the little table in the flat, trying to summon up the courage to venture out and search for another place, but the morning's incident had knocked out all the courage I had. My dignity as well. My stomach gnawed, but I could not even think of making myself a cup of tea, as that would mean lighting the stove, and I dared not use any of our communal coal ration to help myself.

I started when the door burst open and Annabel came rushing in.

"It's a letter for ya, Cairstin. I think it's from your mam." I could tell she had run all the way from Arnison's, and impulsively I embraced her.

"Thank you, Annabel. You have no idea how good it is to see you just now."

"Are ya all right, Cairstin? Oh! I almost forgot!" She reached into the pocket of her coat and brought out a folded piece of buttered bread wrapped in her handkerchief.

"God bless you, my dear friend!" I took the bread and hugged her again.

"I must run back now. Do not lose hope. I've spoken to Mrs. Fallowfield, and there's a chance ya may not lose your place!" And off she went.

I sat down to eat and look at the letter. *Thank you, God*, my heart whispered as I licked my fingers and opened the seal.

My Dearest Cairstin,

I am daring the expense to write you this letter because I have something to share with you I feel it is time you should know.

Your father and I were introduced by my late aunt Eunice when he visited her friend's family in Luton, which you know is where I grew up. I lived with her most of my life because my parents had all but abandoned me after I was born deformed. I will forever be grateful she took me in, and though she was warm and kind to me, she was also a practical woman and raised me to not be ashamed of my defect but to understand my limitations.

When I met your dah, Aunt Eunice was old and sickly, and she probably knew she would not live long. She also knew I would not survive well on my own, so she practically forced me onto your father, offering him a small dowry if he would take me as his wife. It was all arranged without much say from me, and in such a businesslike fashion that love was never a thought.

We were married at my parish church only weeks after meeting. I said farewell to my dying aunt and traveled with my new husband north to Appleby, where he determined to set himself up as a tailor.

Cairstin, I did not love your father when we married, but I was grateful to him for taking care of me, and he never once made me feel ashamed of myself. As the years passed, I grew to love him, even with his rough manners and cross ways, as he was always faithful to me and worked hard to provide for us.

Marriage is not always roses and romance. Sometimes it is a partnership for survival, but God, in His mercy, can sew love into the seams.

May God give you wisdom and strength. Write soon.

Love,

Mother

I stared at the letter in my hands. "Oh, Dah," I cried. "Why have I never understood this before?"

That evening I found myself sitting mutely across a table from William in the Gray Goat Pub. He had heard all the news but waited until we were served a steak and ale pie and mash before asking me anything.

His demeanor was rather more dispassionate than usual, and I could not tell if he was angry or simply ready to end our courtship. Either would be understandable, and I had already braced myself for more disgrace. I debated about telling him of my experience that day, but if we were to part ways, what was the use?

William sat in prim silence as we ate. I was almost too hungry to care. At least he was kind enough not to end our courtship with me starving.

The plates were finally cleared. Subdued, I sat with my hands folded in my lap, looking at the table while William checked the time on his watch.

"Thank you, William, for supper. It has been a while since I've eaten," I offered meekly.

He took a deep breath and let it out, studying me. "I am most sorry to hear that, my dear. I wish you would have sent word to me right away about what happened. Why didn't you?"

"Well, to be honest, I never thought to. I didn't want to subject you to any embarrassment." I looked up to find him almost smiling at me. "I want you to know, William, that I have done nothing wrong, but I completely understand if you choose not to associate with me—"

He held up his hand and leaned forward. "Cairstin, why would you think such a thing? I have told you before how devoted I am to you and how I believe with all my heart that God Himself has brought us together."

That strange amber glow filled his eyes, and my heart let down its guard a bit.

"Oh, thank you, William. I was afraid—"

"No need to fear, my dear." He grinned casually and leaned back in his chair. "I am sure what happened at Arnison's was all an accident, but it does not matter. Annabel has apprised me of everything, including the landlord raising the rent on your mother and sister. Terrible man."

He clicked his tongue and shook his head. I wasn't especially encouraged by his tone, but at least he seemed to be taking my tragedy at Arnison's in stride.

"Now, it is not clear whether your position with Arnison's will be restored, and without your assistance, your mother and sister are doomed to be displaced. This puts you in a very desperate position, my dear."

I did not need his reminder. I started to speak, but he held up his hand again. "Please allow me to finish."

I bit my lip, then nodded for him to continue.

"I have some exceedingly good news to share with you tonight. I have received my promotion at the bank and am now in a position not only to support a wife but her family as well."

He smiled broadly and stood, then bowed to me deeply and went down on one knee.

My heart fluttered with sudden confusion. I was not prepared for this.

"Miss Cairstin Blackwood, may I have the great honor of having your hand in marriage?"

I gasped. William reached for my hand, and I heard other people in the pub give a smattering of applause.

It was all so sudden. I couldn't feel my heart. Could this be happening?

He knelt there smiling like a cat with a mouse, and I hesitated. Was this what I truly wanted? Should I forever tie myself to this man for the rest of my life?

William noticed my hesitation.

"I had a feeling you would be hesitant, my dear." He regained his chair and held my hand across the table. "I have something else to show you to help you make up your mind."

Reaching into his inner pocket, he produced a letter, and I noticed immediately my mother's handwriting.

I gaped at him as I took it. Opening it, I found a short message.

Dear Mr. Soulier,

Thank you for doing me the honor of consulting me and asking for my permission to marry my daughter.

I hear by give you that permission, based solely on my daughter's consent. If she accepts you, then I will wish you both all happiness and pray that God will bless your union.

Sincerely,

Jessica Blackwood

I sat in astonishment. When I finally found the strength to look up, William still smiled at me knowingly, the embers of his eyes glowing.

Finally I found my voice. "I . . . I am . . . that is, this is a complete surprise, William. I was not expecting this after what has happened."

Leaning over the table, he looked into my eyes and spoke quietly. "Come now, Cairstin. Have I not made myself clear to you? Besides, God is making a way for you and your family to escape your toil and suffering. Why would you even hesitate?"

At this, I sat back in my chair and took a deep breath. He was right. I should be overjoyed that God was rescuing me in this way. Not only me, but Mother and Rose as well. How could I say no to God's help?

I looked down at Mother's letter once more, than back up at William's round smiling face. "Yes, William, I will marry you."

Dear Mother,

I have accepted Mr. Soulier's proposal of marriage, and he wishes for a quick wedding. I will write to you as soon as we know the date. William has promised to send for you and Rose to attend the service, which will be officiated by

Reverend Thomas and Reverend Stuart at St. Andrew's, the parish church in Penrith.

The wages you will find with this letter are not all mine. Something regretful has happened. I will write you about it later. Fortunately, William has just been given a promotion and raise in his salary, so what you have received is from our combined efforts.

William says I shall discontinue working at Arnison's as soon as we are married, as he can support me as his wife, and you and Rose as well, which is incredibly generous of him. I must tell you that a great weight has been lifted off my shoulders since his proposal.

Please don't worry anymore about the rent, Mother, for William has promised he will be able to pay it out of his salary for now and says when we are able to find a suitable place for all of us, he will gladly move you to Penrith. In the meantime, we will be living in his rooms above White Hart Yard.

God has answered our prayers.

Your loving daughter,

Cairstin

I posted my letter during the noonday meal, then returned to my temporary purgatory in the cutting room. Mr. Arnison decided to keep me on probation but insisted I prove my trustworthiness again outside the ladies' sewing room in order to appease Mrs. Langley, who was demanding I be dismissed. I didn't mind really, as it kept me mostly away from Eliza and Mr. Bell. The most difficult parts of the day were in the mornings and evenings, when I must put up with her feigned innocence.

She seemed to be especially irritated when I announced my engagement to Mr. Soulier, something I couldn't understand at all. Wasn't she being courted by her beloved partner in crime, Mr. Bell?

Susan, on the other hand, was glad for me, and Annabel was overjoyed.

"I'm so happy for ya, Cairstin, I could cry!" And she did.

"Will you stand up for me, Annabel? I would be so honored if you would."

She threw her arms around me and hugged me tight. "O' course I will, my friend, and proud to!"

The next few days passed by quickly, and my heart felt lighter than it had since I could remember. William, ever faithful, was there to walk me home each evening, but there was something sweeter in his presence as he tucked my arm around his, walking slowly to Sutton Yard, as much to avoid Mr. Bell and Eliza as to speak of our plans for the wedding and my moving in with him.

"I want you to be aware, my dear, that I live in quite a bachelor's way," he told me. "I have not had need of more than the scantest furniture and would rather wait until we settle somewhere more comfortable to invest in much more. You will have to learn to get by with the mere basics until we find a place suitable for all of us."

"Oh, William, I don't mind at all. I can get by with next to nothing so long as we can one day move together with Mother and Rose."

"Hmmm, yes, I am very proud of your fortitude, my dear."

William smiled at me with those amber eyes, and I actually felt my heart flutter in my chest.

"Reverend Thomas asked if he could announce our engagement at church this Sunday. I told him it was a fine idea."

The blood rushed to my face at the thought of so much attention, but I couldn't find a reason not to agree.

Kissing both of my hands, William bid me good night and

watched me mount the stairs to the flat. I smiled down on him and waved as he turned to go, my heart daring to give way to a little joyful excitement.

Eliza was waiting for me just inside the door.

"Well, look at those roses in your cheeks, Cairstin Blackwood. Ya would almost think the man was in love with ya."

Before I could respond, she dashed into her room and shut the door.

Chapter Thirteen

My concern over Susan's illness increased by the day. I thought of telling her my suspicions about the green wool but did not want to go against Mrs. Fallowfield's request not to mention it to her until she had spoken to Mr. Arnison. At this point I could not expect any more communication regarding such a delicate matter from her, as my reputation for being overreactive was growing amongst the staff.

It was just as well I was getting married and would no longer be the subject of their gossip. The more time I spent at Arnison's, the less welcome I felt. I was grieved my employment there was ending on such a sour note. I was proud of my work and still held a high regard for Mr. Arnison, but it couldn't be helped. William told me not to mention my leaving to anyone until after the wedding, as he did not wish them to dismiss me any earlier.

William asked me to dress very particularly and be extremely prompt that Sunday morning. He greeted me and Annabel at the entrance to Sutton Yard, looking very well, and gave me a formal bow. Once again Susan felt too ill to attend and Eliza had plans with Mr. Bell.

"Good morning, Miss Ainslie. Good morning, my dear. I am glad to see you looking so pretty. I am honored to escort the loveliest girl in Penrith to church and let the whole world know that she is mine."

Annabel and I giggled at his flattery. "Oh, William, you should lower your voice. What will the neighbors think?" I whispered loudly.

He laughed and took my arm. Annabel fell a little behind, as was her way, and my heart soared to a place it had never been before as we walked to The Gloucester Arms. What was this elated feeling? Was I falling in love with my fiancé?

I marveled at the thought as we mounted the stairs to the hall and were greeted magnanimously by Reverend and Mrs. Thomas, while Annabel slipped past.

"And here is the happy couple"—the reverend beamed—"all smiles and sunshine. May the Lord bless you both, my dear children."

"Thank you, Reverend, Mrs. Thomas. May I present to you my betrothed, Miss Cairstin Blackwood."

I was struck shy by William's grandiosity, but Reverend Thomas laid his beefy hand on my shoulder, bent, and gave me a knowing look. "There, there, Miss Blackwood, do not be overcome. Mr. Soulier is a very blessed man, and I have told him so myself."

My face burned, and I was grateful when William whisked me away to where Annabel stood with Miss Barnes, Mr. Pitt, and Mr. Nixon.

Though I was terribly preoccupied with my own thoughts, I happened to notice, out of the corner of my eye, tall Mr. Nixon smiling down on Annabel as he handed her a songbook. Annabel blushed crimson but did not object when Mr.

Nixon asked if he could sit with her and turn the pages for her.

Once again my heart took flight with happiness for my friend. Mr. Nixon seemed an affable, sturdy fellow, and though Annabel was a bit tall, he was taller by far. I liked the look of them sitting together and fervently wished for my friend to find happiness of her own.

Just as the service was about to start, I caught sight of a familiar top hat making its way to the top of the stairs. My heart plummeted from its lofty height. Mr. Gabriel Dalton.

My chest pounded as he spied me standing in the back row beside William, and he smiled warmly. The world came crashing to a halt.

Mr. Dalton made his way to the other side of the hall and found an empty chair, far enough ahead of me that I could see his profile as he took up a songbook as the piano began the first hymn.

I snatched a look at William, who had obviously spotted Mr. Dalton. He was staring at him with smoldering eyes, but when he noticed me looking at him, his demeanor changed in an instant back to a wide smile, and he patted my hand.

I did not even know Mr. Dalton had returned to Penrith. Why had he come to the Bible Church instead of going to St. Andrew's? The questions darted through my head as quickly as my pulse through my veins. How I wish he hadn't come.

I barely sang a note of the songs before the sermon, hardly aware of anything but the battle ensuing in my head, and to my dismay, my heart also. *Stop it, you little fool! It has nothing to do with you*, I told myself. But a hidden piece of my soul screamed, *He loves you! He loves you! And you love him!*

I was glad when we took our seats, for I was feeling faint. How could I be sitting next to my fiancé and still have my heart so moved by a man I hardly know?

It was all I could manage to endure Reverend Thomas's sermon. I could not even remember what he said. I prayed fervently I would not succumb to my own wickedness and flee from the hall. From William, from Mr. Dalton.

After the sermon, instead of the usual triumphant piano playing the last song, Reverend Thomas smiled brightly upon the congregation, and William pulled me to my feet.

"And now, dear ones, we have a very special announcement to make today. Mr. Soulier and Miss Blackwood are engaged to be married!"

I couldn't breathe. My gaze shot to Mr. Dalton's profile, and my greatest fear was realized. When he turned his head slightly, I saw the light drain from his face, to be replaced by confused embarrassment. His cheeks flushed, and he swallowed hard, looking down at his hat in his hands.

All of this I saw in an instant as the congregation applauded and cheered. I felt William tug at my arm and tried to snap out of my trance, smiling and nodding mindlessly as I watched Mr. Dalton from the corner of my eye.

After the closing song, William took me firmly by the arm as we received the congratulations of the congregation. I heard my mouth saying thank you and my head bobbed appropriately, but my insides were ice.

Mr. Dalton approached, and William's grip on my arm tightened so much it almost hurt.

"Well, Miss Blackwood, Mr. Soulier, I see that I return to Penrith to find a pleasant surprise. Congratulations and many happy returns to you both!" He smiled kindly and reached to shake William's hand.

I noticed William's hesitation, but he shook Mr. Dalton's hand firmly, with a knowing smile, then looked at me. "Thank you, Mr. Dalton. My fiancée and I are very happy indeed, aren't we, my dear?"

"Oh yes, yes, of course. Thank you, Mr. Dalton. Have you been back long?" I said without truly meeting his eyes. Those warm, kind eyes I would love to get lost in.

"I only arrived last night, Miss Blackwood. My cousin's charity is now legally established in Carlisle, and I am free to finally set up shop here in Penrith," he said lightly. "Well, it was a pleasure to see you both again, and I wish you all happiness. I must be off."

With a touch to his hat and slight bow, he was gone. How I wished I could drop through the floor. After saying goodbye to the gushing reverend and Mrs. Thomas, William took me downstairs to the pub.

We were surrounded by the young people of the church and took tea with them. I was often timid at such gatherings, so perhaps I did not seem unusually quiet to the casual observer, and even William didn't seem to notice. But once we were outside and passing by his lodgings on the other side of Corn Market Square, he paused and took me aside in the White Hart Yard entryway.

"Cairstin, I am most disappointed in you. What did you mean making eyes with that man, Mr. Dalton?"

He was clearly angry, and I stepped away from him with my back against the wall.

"What can you mean, William? I would never do such a thing—never!" Or had I? I wasn't sure of myself at all.

"Well, he has heard of our engagement and can sulk for all I care. You must never have anything to do with him again, Cairstin, is that clear?"

I was appalled at William's frightful tone but could not even be sure I didn't deserve it.

I nodded and swallowed hard. "Yes, William, perfectly clear."

"Well, I am glad to hear it," he said in a quieter tone. "I will take you home now, but I shall call on you later to take you for supper. We will discuss this further then."

I sat at the little table and looked out the window, seeing nothing. I was sick at heart, shame laying over me in a blanket of pain.

William had seen, or at least I had revealed, something on my face about my duplicity, and now he was hurt and angry, and rightfully so. How I hated having anyone angry with me. It was like having my moorings cut and I was adrift, my soul flailing about, searching for any means of recovering the security I'd lost. Then my mother's letter to me about my father flew up before me and redoubled my guilt.

Mr. Dalton's disappointment played itself over and over without my bidding. Surely there was something in the falling of his demeanor that meant he was displeased by the announcement.

If I had only known. And now it was too late.

I lay down in defeat and awoke sometime later, my pillow wet from tears. I must decide now. I must choose to either give my whole heart to William or ruin my family's lives by telling him my heart longed for another man, a man who most certainly would no longer consider having me.

It had to be William, no matter what my heart screamed to the contrary.

I waited on pins and needles the whole afternoon until William came to take me for supper at the Gray Goat. Watching him closely, I tried to gauge the temperature of his mood, relieved to find it calmer than when he left me. I was emotionally exhausted but tried my best to be considerate of him.

After ordering pie and mash for the two of us, William smiled thinly. "Well, my dear, it is time for us to settle on a date for our wedding. I spent the afternoon discussing it with Reverend Thomas, and we have agreed I should apply for a special license, thereby forgoing the need for a reading of the banns, which makes it possible for the wedding to take place sooner."

"Oh?" was my weak response, noting that I had been left out of this discussion.

"Yes. We looked at the calendar and have decided it should be Sunday after next, on February 14, St. Valentine's Day. We can have a simple ceremony after the church service, and the whole church will be invited to come over to St. Andrew's for it. I think that should do nicely, don't you?"

His mood lifted as he spoke, and he patted my hand. Not waiting for my reply, he flagged the waiter and asked for a bottle of wine.

"We must celebrate, Cairstin, and say a toast to our upcoming nuptials."

Before I could protest, the food was set before us. William reached for my hand and closed his eyes. "Lord, for that which we are about to receive, make us truly thankful. Amen."

"Amen," I repeated awkwardly.

As William took a bite of his potatoes, I ventured to speak.

"William, I am not much used to wine, you know. I would not want you to waste your money on buying it for me." I smiled as sweetly as I could and waited for him to finish chewing.

"Ah, I greatly admire your temperance, but you will not refuse me the honor of tasting just a little with me, will you?" His eyes flickered with amber, and my cheeks grew hot.

"Well no, of course not, if that is what you wish."

He touched the tip of his napkin to the corner of his pursed lips and smiled contentedly. "I do wish it, my dear."

Then he sat back and watched me eat for a moment and sighed. "I know I should not say it, Cairstin, but I am exceedingly glad you do not put on airs like Lydia did. It is not right for a woman to think of herself too highly, especially a good Christian woman such as yourself."

My fork froze in midair. Such a mixture of emotions stirred through me. I had no idea what to say to such a statement.

"Well, as I said," he continued, "I shouldn't have mentioned it. I am only relieved to be betrothed to such a lovely, demure lady as yourself. You cannot imagine how tiresome it is to be in close company with a person who speaks only of herself all the time."

The heat from my cheeks spread up to my forehead. Was I supposed to be flattered by such comments? Would Mr. Dalton have ever spoken to me this way?

Stop! I screamed inside my mind and forced my heart to refocus. "I am glad that you feel more comfortable in my presence, William."

"Thank you, my dear," he said with satisfaction and resumed eating.

The wine came and was poured. William lifted his glass and motioned for me to do so as well.

"Here's to us, the soon to be Mr. and Mrs. Soulier. May God bless our union and show us how to honor Him in all we say and do."

I nodded and took a small sip with him, the sour flavor striking my tongue, the alcohol burning down my throat. I stifled a cough, and William laughed heartily.

"My my! You do have virgin lips, I daresay!" He chortled some more.

I wanted to crawl under the table as a vision of the man at Barkhouse Lodge flashed before me. I felt his hand over my mouth and heard his oily voice close to my ear saying, *"All I want is one little kiss, as a down payment for the rooms, eh?"*

"Please, William, please," I whispered, as tears ached behind my eyes.

He finished a last chuckle, took another long draft of wine, then leaned over to take my hand. "You are a simple little thing, Cairstin Blackwood, but do not worry. I am here to teach you and protect you. Even if everyone else in the world should abandon you, I will always be by your side."

~

I was wading in the softly flowing water of the River Eden. I could feel the cool, slick stones under my feet as I carefully inched farther and farther toward the middle of the stream. I held my skirts in a bundle above the water's surface and smiled at my reflection, the blue sky framing my young face.

I could hear children laughing somewhere and the summer birds calling to one another from the densely leafed trees. The air smelled of honeysuckle and wet earth, and my heart was bathed in sunshine.

"It is lovely to see you again, Miss Blackwood," a familiar and dear voice called to me from the opposite side, and I whirled around to see Mr. Gabriel Dalton smiling broadly as he stood on the grassy bank.

Suddenly my foot slipped, and I fell with a cry backward into the water with a great splash. My skirts and petticoats billowed around me, weighing me down as I gasped for air. My face went under just as William reached for me, taking me by the collar. I thought he would lift me up above the surface, but he seemed to hesitate, smiling at me as the sun glared behind him, piercing my sight.

Then I woke up.

It was sometime before dawn Monday morning. I sat up straight in my little bed, my chest heaving painfully. *What does it mean?*

I lay back down holding tight to Mother's pendant but found it impossible to shake the foreboding in my bones. My head ached from my attempts to interpret the dream, so like the one before. *Am I in danger?*

I could not stand my interior battle and rose from my bed well before the others, determined to forget the dream altogether.

Dressing quietly, I sat down at the table to try and finish a silk flower or two before departing for work with the others. I had barely started when I heard sounds of distress coming from Susan and Eliza's room.

I just reached the hall when their door was flung open and Eliza ran out, her face aghast.

"Susan has wretched, and I feel I might as well!" She flew out the door to heave over the railing.

Annabel rushed and grabbed Eliza's coat, taking it to her outside in stockinged feet while I dashed in to find poor Susan, her head hanging over her bed and a pool of vomit on the floor beneath.

"Oh, Susan, you poor dear!" I cried. "Here, let me help you."

She allowed me to help her back onto the bed. Then I ran to fetch a bowl of water and a rag.

Susan moaned as Annabel walked Eliza back inside. "I can't go in there," she whimpered. "It smells worse than—"

Before she could finish, Annabel took her into our room as I gently wiped Susan's face, then mopped up the floor.

The cleaning up finished, Annabel joined me as we looked Susan over carefully, and my heart sank at what we found. She had terrible open sores on her fingers and under her nails, with green and yellow streaks under the skin. Her mouth was dry, lips cracked and puffy, and her eyes were swollen and red.

"Susan, will you take some water, dear?" I motioned for Annabel to fetch a cup of water from the kettle.

"I'm so thirsty," she whispered weakly. "I can never drink enough."

Annabel and I exchanged fearful glances. She dashed to the hall, calling over her shoulder, "I'll fetch the doctor!"

If only Mrs. Fallowfield had listened to me sooner.

Chapter Fourteen

Old Dr. Briggs listened carefully to my suspicions about the green wool and the green plaid silk of the newest dress Susan was in the process of finishing when she became too ill to work. When he heard about my father's death and the similarities with Susan's symptoms, he took down notes and said he would do some investigating.

Susan's family was sent word to come and take her home, and on Wednesday Annabel and I saw her tucked in as comfortably as possible in her father's farm wagon. We said a tearful goodbye and promised to pray for her full recovery, while Eliza stood aloof, afraid what Susan had was contagious.

I slipped Susan's father a letter after he took his place and reached for the reins. He gave me a grave nod and tucked it into his pocket before guiding his horse out onto Long Front Street. Once the wagon was out of sight, we three made our way to Arnison's and slowly took the stairs to the third-floor ladies' sewing room, where Mrs. Fallowfield waited for us.

"Miss Dyke's illness is most unfortunate. I am grateful that her family is able to care for her. But now it is time for us to get back to our work. I have spoken to Mr. Arnison regarding which one of you will take Miss Dykes' place as head dressmakers' apprentice."

I glanced at Eliza, who had seniority but was not as fast or as capable as Annabel. My heart sank at the thought of Eliza holding any authority over me, but I reminded myself I would soon be married and not subject to her schemes any longer. I wished Annabel might be promoted, as the slight raise in salary would help her, and I believed she deserved the title.

"First, you should know that Miss Mary Hodgson is being promoted from the cutting room and will join us this afternoon. She will be taking up lodgings with you in Sutton Yard this evening."

I had met Miss Hodgson before. She was an older woman in her late thirties and as homely as a duck. I couldn't help a slight smile when I thought of Eliza having to share a room with her.

"Mr. Arnison and I have discussed this thoroughly, and he has decided that Miss Blackwood will be promoted to head dressmaker."

My heart stopped beating. *Me?*

"But, Mrs. Fallowfield, I do not—" I began.

She raised her slender hand and continued. "Yes, I know, Miss Blackwood. It is usual that we give the position to the woman with the most seniority. However, Miss Salkeld is still learning, and she and Miss Ainslie have yet to gain the amount of knowledge you have acquired under your father's tutelage."

My mouth gaped, and I looked askance at Eliza, whose face was red. She gave me a scathing look but kept her tongue.

"Miss Salkeld"—Mrs. Fallowfield turned to Eliza, looking through her little round spectacles down her long nose—"you must understand that Mr. Arnison wants only what is best for our clients, and I am sure you will agree that your knowledge and skill is still developing. Perhaps you will benefit from Miss Blackwood's tutelage."

Eliza blanched, and she finally found her voice. "But what about Miss Blackwood's making a mess with Mrs. Langley's dress? Shouldn't she still be in the cutting room?"

Mrs. Fallowfield stiffened, straightening to her full height. "It is not for us to question Mr. Arnison's reasoning or decisions. This is his shop, and it will be run according to his wishes."

Eliza withered under her scorching gaze.

"I insist that those under my watch will take this change in stride and in a professional manner." Mrs. Fallowfield looked the three of us over judiciously. "There is much catching up to do. We have several dresses that need to be finished by the end of the week, and we will meet this deadline come what may."

She clapped her hands, and we scattered. I reflexively went to my table, but Mrs. Fallowfield raised her hand, then pointed to Susan's table closest to the window. I nodded and took a seat.

There on Susan's table lay the unfinished green plaid dress I was now doomed to finish.

As usual, William was waiting for me after work, and I introduced him to Miss Hodgson, who had joined us in the ladies' sewing room after the noonday meal. I found her a welcome addition to our little group, as she was quite amiable and determined to establish herself as a seamstress.

William raised his brows but was cordial to her. As Annabel led her toward Sutton Yard, with Eliza on Mr. Bell's arm, William and I held back and followed more slowly.

"William," I began timidly, "the most extraordinary thing has happened today, and I—"

"Yes, my dear, but wait until I tell you my news!"

His interruption frustrated me, but I bit my tongue and nodded.

"Reverend Thomas has asked me to join his Married Men's Committee. He told me since I am so brilliant with numbers, he wants me to assist in managing the church Building Fund and help raise money for it."

"That's wonderful news, William. The reverend must have great trust in you for him to give you such an important task." I was truly happy for him and proud the reverend had such a high regard for my intended.

"Yes, he is very impressed with me and my new position at the bank, and my status with the men at the church will improve immensely once I'm a married man." He gave me a knowing look, the amber embers in his eyes sparking to life. "It looks as though I am finally gaining the recognition I deserve for my efforts, in spite of all the obstacles I've had to overcome."

"I am proud of you, William." I smiled and gave his arm an affectionate squeeze.

"Thank you, my dear. I live only to please you." He lifted his chin with satisfaction.

"I need to discuss with you something that happened today," I ventured.

"Yes, yes." William sighed with irritation. "Susan's family came to take her home. How is she faring?"

"Well, I am glad she will be in good care, but, William, I was promoted today by Mr. Arnison and Mrs. Fallowfield to take her place as head dressmaker's apprentice—"

He stopped and turned to me, his smile gone in an instant. "But I told you that you were going to quit your job and I would take care of you. I thought we agreed—"

"Yes, of course, but I promise you I had nothing to do with

it. You see, I thought that Eliza would be given the position, as she has seniority, and I was as surprised as everyone that—"

"Then it is no matter." His posture softened, and he resumed walking. "You will still leave just after the wedding, though I am sure they will miss you, I daresay."

"Yes, William, but there is something else I would like to talk to you about." This time it was my turn to stop walking and face him. "It is the matter of the green wood dress Susan was working on when she became too ill to work that troubles me. I feel so strongly that there is something about the green in these fabrics that made her ill, just like my father—"

"Oh, Cairstin," William interrupted impatiently. "What could possibly be in fabric that would cause such sickness and death? You must not overact, my dear, which is something I notice you have a tendency to. Besides, you will soon be out of Mr. Arnison's shop and taking care of your husband."

I was hurt by his dismissal but thought in the end he was right. I gave up the topic and changed the subject. "I wish I had the money and the time to make myself a proper wedding dress. How I would love to see the surprise on your face when I walk down the aisle to you."

"Yes, yes, you are a sentimental girl," he said with a patronizing tone and patted my hand. "But we mustn't indulge ourselves in needless expenses like wedding dresses. I would marry you in a potato sack if that was all you had in the world."

I chuckled at the thought and paused with him in the entrance to the yard.

"Now, let's have no further talk about dresses," he continued. "I want you to send this to your mother and ask her to hire two seats on the evening post to Penrith on the Saturday before the wedding. I will arrange a room for them at The Gloucester Arms for the night so they will be able to attend church and our wedding the next day."

He placed a generous number of coins in my gloved hand with a flourish and looked smug indeed.

"Oh, William! I can't thank you enough!" Impulsively I threw my arms around his neck and kissed his cheek.

"All right, all right, that's enough now!" He held me back from him awkwardly. "I am glad you are pleased, but we mustn't make such public displays of affection."

I blushed. "I'm sorry. I am just so excited to see my mother and sister again."

He took my hands and smiled. "I know, but you must be off to your bed now. I will see you tomorrow evening."

It was the habit of women who sew to place the end of the thread in their mouth to moisten it and make it more cooperative when threading a needle. I'd done it myself countless times since I was a child, but the green thread I was now forced to use to finish the dress on my work table gave me a sick feeling in the pit of my stomach. On Tuesday I placed a small cup of water on the windowsill near me so I could dip my fingers in it to moisten the thread. By the end of the day, the water and my fingers were green.

As I descended the stairs at the end of the day, I asked Annabel if she would stay with me, as I had something to ask Mr. Bell.

"O' course, but what on earth would ya want to do with him?" she asked doubtfully.

"Just come with me. You'll see."

Mr. Bell was just leaving the drapery as we approached, and he glared at us in suspicion.

"Mr. Bell," I began, ignoring his scorn. "I would like to

know what is used in the dye to make green fabric. Would you happen to know?"

He snorted. "Why? Dyes are a very complicated scientific process. I'm sure you would not understand such things."

I would not let him off with his insulting remark. "I might surprise you, Mr. Bell. Try me."

He sighed impatiently and crossed his arms over his chest. Just then, Eliza dismounted the stairs and came to stand by him.

"What do you two want? Are they bothering ya, Mr. Bell?" she asked with heat in her voice.

"It's no bother, Miss Salkeld." He smiled down at her, his weak chin nearly disappearing.

"If you are speaking of the vivacious and fashionable Scheele's green, Miss Blackwood, you might find information on Dr. Scheele's formula in a scientific journal at the library. I cannot be expected to know all the chemical formulations for every color used to dye fabric, as I have the more important duty of providing Mr. Arnison's customers with only the best products money can buy."

With that, he took Eliza by the elbow and pushed past us to the exit.

"Scheele's green," I repeated, half to myself, half to Annabel. "Very helpful, Mr. Bell, very helpful indeed."

~

Remaining extra cautious, I washed my hands frequently during the day and was careful not to let any part of the fabric or thread touch my face or mouth, hoping that would be enough to keep me free from harm until I gave my notice to Mr. Arnison.

The thought of leaving Arnison's filled me with unexpected sadness. To my surprise, I was enjoying having the responsibility of being the head seamstress and the one the others, even Eliza, would come to when Mrs. Fallowfield was not available to advise them.

I finished with the green plaid dress in a matter of days, sustaining only mild soreness under my fingernails and some headaches. It was a relief to have it off my table, though I worried yet again when I thought of the lady who would wear it and somehow be harmed by it unaware.

What could I do to prove my theory? The library was out of the question, for it was never open during my free hours, but I was encouraged by the thought that I might go there after the wedding sometime and try to find out more about Scheele's green, a color that now gave me a shudder when I saw it.

That Thursday morning Mrs. Fallowfield beckoned me to the fitting room for the new owner of the plaid green dress, a Miss Gleeson, the daughter of a prominent Penrith banker. Miss Gleeson left pleased with her new dress and how the color set off her creamy complexion.

I sat in the staff room with the others as the noon meal was served, wallowing in guilt.

Time with William after work was always too brief, and I was increasingly frustrated we had so little time to talk, especially with our wedding approaching so rapidly. When I asked him whether it wouldn't be better for me to remain working for a while longer, so we could save my wages toward our move, he was annoyed and stated emphatically that he preferred his wife not to work outside the home. Once again he gave me a handful of coins and told me to use the money for anything I needed to prepare for our marriage, but not to waste it on a wedding dress.

That night the same dream appeared to me, with me wading in the river, Mr. Dalton on the shore calling to me, and me falling into the water, this time with a wedding dress billowing around me when William came to take hold of me.

I awoke in such distress I could not possibly remain in bed. It was Friday morning, and I dressed quietly and made my way out into the foggy morning. Perhaps a walk before work would help clear my head.

The clanging of the town bell ringer passed me in the mist on Devonshire Street near Arnison's. "Five o'clock an' all's well," he called.

The other girls would soon be emerging from their beds.

I reached the lower part of the main square, then I thought I should turn back and tell Annabel I was all right, when something caught my eye. A man exited Sutton Yard and headed the other direction up Long Front Street, dressed in a long brown overcoat with a matching top hat. William.

What on earth was he doing in Sutton Yard at such an early hour? He was too far ahead for me to call to him, but I quickened my pace and entered the yard soon after. The cooks were just leaving their rooms below ours, but I rushed past them and dashed up the stairs, where a light shone in the window of our flat.

"Hello! What are ya up so early for, Cairstin? I was worried for ya." Annabel was just pinning up her hair when I entered the little hall between the bedchambers. I had a flashing thought and instinctively put a finger to my lips and pled with my eyes for her to keep quiet.

I did not take off my outer things but removed the glove from one hand. I felt the others' coats that hung there. When my hand rested on Eliza's, it was colder than the others and slightly damp, as if it had just been worn outside.

My head reeled. What could this mean? Was it only my imagination? Why would William be meeting Eliza in the yard so early on a winter's morning?

Annabel tiptoed into the hall, and I motioned her close.

"Feel the coats, Annabel. Does one feel colder than the rest?"

She looked at me as if I uttered gibberish, but I motioned toward the coats, and she obeyed. First she felt her own brown wool cloak, next Mary's gray, then when she felt Eliza's dark green, her eyes widened. "Has Eliza already been out?" she whispered. "But why?"

I took her by the hand, and we retreated to our room and closed the door.

"I just saw William leaving the yard," I told her, panic striking my heart. "Why would he be speaking with Eliza at a time like this?"

Annabel shook her head. "I cannot understand it. Are ya sure t'was William?"

I sat on the edge of my bed and shook my head as well. "No, I suppose it might not have been. I wasn't close enough to know for certain."

Annabel sat beside me and took my hand. "Perhaps you're just nervous about the wedding, Cairstin. I can tell ya've not been sleeping well."

"I haven't," I admitted. "I know I should be as happy as a queen, but there are so many things I feel unsettled about, Annabel. If only my mam was close and could advise me. I have so little time to discuss things with William. Everything is going so fast."

Annabel took my hand and patted it affectionately. "I can feel for ya. All this, and then you've been given a promotion—"

"Oh, Annabel." I nearly sobbed. "I must tell you something, but you must promise not to tell anyone else, as William would be most displeased with me."

"No, Cairstin," she scolded gently. "Ya mustn't tell me if he doesn't want ya to. It's all right. I'll understand, whatever it is."

I nodded slowly and thanked her for her wisdom and friendship, then said no more.

When the noonday meal came around, Toby came in and handed me a package. It was from Mother, and as much as I would love to open it there, I knew it would be best to do so in private.

I tucked the package safely under my worktable and picked up where I left off on a luscious cranberry satin dress for a young lady's engagement party. She had given me license to embellish it as I saw fit, and I looked forward to designing something lovely.

A knock came at the sewing room door, and Toby entered, tipping his hat. "Miss Blackwood, Master Arnison wants thee."

I rose, looking first to Mrs. Fallowfield, who looked bewildered, then to Eliza, who kept her eyes firmly on her work but could not completely suppress the smile twitching at the corners of her pink lips.

When I arrived at Mr. Arnison's office, he sat facing me in his desk chair, his hands folded across his stomach and a grave look on his face. My heart sped up when he sighed with disappointment.

"I have been made aware, Miss Blackwood, that you intend to leave our service within the next fortnight after your wedding. Is this true?"

Horrified, I could not speak. When I finally found my voice, I swallowed hard and barely spoke above a whisper.

"Yes, Mr. Arnison. It is true. But I intended to inform you myself at an appropriate time. You see—"

"I do see, Miss Blackwood," he interrupted, and sighed again. "I must say I am exceedingly disappointed at such news. I was hoping we had a better understanding—"

"Please, Mr. Arnison, my fiancé has just been given a fine promotion at Barclays Bank, and he would prefer I no longer work outside the home—" I ended weakly, but I regained my footing quickly. "I was going to inform you myself, sir, and give you ample notice. Please believe me."

Mr. Arnison raised his hand and rose from his chair. "Yes, yes, I believe you, but now I must make some other arrangements. I am sorry to lose you, Miss Blackwood, but these things happen."

My chest throbbed as he motioned me out of the office. I stopped with one last bold question. "Please, Mr. Arnison, will you tell me who preempted me and told you? I am very grieved to have you think less of me because someone else spoke out of turn."

He pressed his bottom lip upwards and lifted his chin. "I suppose you have a right to know. It was Miss Salkeld."

"Thank you, Mr. Arnison. I want you to know how much it has meant to me that you gave me a chance and believed in my work. I will never forget your kindness to me, sir."

He gave me a half a smile and patted my shoulder. "I am glad you have found a young man to care for you and your family, my dear. I wish you only the best."

With that, I found myself in the hall, Mr. Bell peeking at me from the drapery doorway.

Chapter Fifteen

Every fiber of my being drooped with humiliation seared with anger as I ascended the stairs to the third floor. I never knew myself capable of such emotion. Up to now my life had been so simple, so predictable, passionless, but now I found myself riding helplessly on a wild ride of feelings I'd never felt, much less imagined I would ever have a reason to experience.

Did William tell Eliza of our plans?

I stopped still before the closed door of the sewing room, trying to regain my composure, and clutched Mother's pendant, deciding whether to confront Eliza or not.

I smoothed back my hair and straightened my shoulders. Entering, I went to my table without a word and took up where I left off and did not look up until the bell rang for the evening meal. I remained in my chair while the others left. Once alone, I laid my head on my folded arms on the table and wept bitterly. Surely the pain of betrayal was the worst of all pains.

Just then, I remembered my mother's package under the table and removed it. My hands trembled as I untied the string and opened the box. I gasped when I folded back the thin paper and saw the beautiful white lace and ribbons of an exquisite nightdress made of white gauze. A letter was tucked into its folds, and I removed it, carefully replacing the paper and tying on the lid.

I secured the letter in my dress pocket to open after Annabel was asleep. Somehow the presence of the box at my feet gave me the strength to finish the day. Annabel walked beside me as I carried my package down the stairs, but she was unusually quiet.

As we exited the building with the other employees, I took her arm and guided her aside. "I suppose Eliza has told you about my intentions to leave Arnison's."

She smiled sadly and nodded. "I cannot say as I blame ya, Cairstin. It's only that I'll miss ya something fierce."

William crossed the narrow street to join us, and I gave him a beseeching look. "Oh, William, Eliza has spoiled everything, and now everyone knows I am leaving Arnison's."

His smile quickly left, and his brows furrowed. "What's this? Why did you tell her of your plans?"

Suddenly I was put on the defensive. "But I didn't, William. You must believe me."

His tone did not soften. "But how else could she have known? I certainly didn't tell her."

I looked helplessly at Annabel, who said, "I'll let the two of ya sort this out," and she hurried away.

William gestured toward the package under my arm. "What's this? Not a wedding dress, I hope."

His tone was sarcastic, crushing my spirit even further. "No, no. It is a very kind gift from Mother. I would not go against your wishes like that, William."

"Really? It seems you already have by telling Eliza about leaving your position. That, or you must have told Annabel and didn't realize she was listening. Either way, you have hurt me deeply by betraying my trust."

"But I didn't tell Annabel either. I cannot understand how Eliza knew."

William took my elbow and steered me toward Sutton Yard in silence. When we reached the entrance, he held out his hands. "Let me see what is in the box, Cairstin."

I was shocked at his condescension. "But, William, it is a surprise for you. You mustn't see it now. It will spoil it."

"I am not in the mood for any more surprises this evening. Now, Cairstin, show me what's in that box."

Quick hot tears welled up in my eyes. "But, William, wouldn't you rather wait until our wedding night? Please, please believe me. It is not a wedding dress, I promise you."

Could my heart be any lower?

He put his hands on his hips. "Well, I certainly hope it is what you say, but you must not play games with my trust any further."

A train whistle blew in the distance like a night beast searching for prey.

"I have never thought to do so, William, as God is my witness."

"Well, let's not carry things too far. I will be here at the usual time to escort you to church in the morning. Be ready."

Mother's package included her lovely wedding nightgown, a set of blue garters, her best pair of white kid gloves, and a penny for my shoe. I cried over her thoughtfulness and began to feel a little like a real bride-to-be.

In the note she included some intimate advice for my wedding night, which both horrified and enlightened me. I couldn't imagine William doing such things to me or that I would enjoy it. What would it be like to have him touch me, hold me, kiss me passionately?

Since the wedding was to be such a simple affair, there wasn't much to be done, but I made good use of the money William gave me to prepare for making my home with him. Fortunately, Arnison's not only sold clothing but also household linens, and I purchased some nice bedsheets and two new pillows, as well as some simple white cotton for any other necessities that might come up.

By Thursday William's mood became more somber, but he told me not to worry. It was only his way of acknowledging the seriousness of the vows he was about to take and that he was working extra volunteer hours for the church Building Fund.

On Friday I felt what Annabel called "wedding jitters" and was as nervous as a cat. I soothed myself with thoughts of seeing Mother and Rose the next day, but in the staff room at the noon meal, I heard a terrible piece of news that rattled my core.

"Mrs. Murphy was found dead by her housekeeper this very morning!" Annabel told us as we filled our teacups. "Isn't that just terrible?"

I felt the earth shake under my chair.

Eliza snatched at the news. "How did she die? Did she fall down the stairs?"

Annabel's usually cheerful face was pale as she answered. "Yes, but the constable is not so sure it t'was an accident!"

My stomach knotted. I couldn't speak. But shouldn't I? Shouldn't I tell about the bruises I saw on her arms not so long ago?

Standing, I moved slowly around the back edge of the room. The girls' eyes followed me, full of questions, but I ignored them. I made my way to the door and waited to catch

Mrs. Fallowfield's eye. When our eyes met, I motioned to the door with my hand over my heart, and she nodded slightly, then stood.

I stepped out into the hall and waited, my hands sweating and pulse racing.

"Yes, Miss Blackwood?"

Mrs. Fallowfield's tone was slightly impatient, but I had made up my mind. "Mrs. Fallowfield, I have information about Mrs. Murphy."

She jerked her chin up and studied me gravely. Nodding once, she motioned for me to follow her. We descended the stairs, then she knocked on Mr. Arnison's office door.

"Come in," said the voice inside, and we entered. To my shock, Mr. Dalton was sitting with Mr. Arnison, having tea.

The gentlemen stood. Mr. Dalton barely looked at me.

"This is an unusual time for you to visit my office, Mrs. Fallowfield." Mr. Arnison looked at me uncomfortably.

Mrs. Fallowfield turned to me. "Miss Blackwood has some information regarding Mrs. Murphy, sir."

She gestured for me to step forward. I did so and curtsied. "Yes, Mr. Arnison, Mr. Dalton. There is something I think I should mention now that I have just heard about Mrs. Murphy, sir." I kept my voice as steady as possible.

Mr. Dalton's eyes sprang to mine. "You know something that may be helpful, Miss Blackwood? Please, tell us."

I nodded. "You see, Mrs. Murphy came in for a fitting some weeks ago." Turning to Mrs. Fallowfield, I continued. "You will remember, ma'am, the day Mrs. Kirkbride came in at the same time."

"Yes, I remember." She nodded.

"You may also remember that Mrs. Murphy insisted on keeping her shawl around her shoulders while I measured her. She said it was chilly."

"Hmm, yes, I remember it seemed a bit odd," Mrs. Fallowfield acknowledged, to my relief.

"Well, I lifted her shawl up to measure her arm and was shocked to find—" Tears welled at the back of my eyes. I blinked hard and looked at Mr. Dalton. "She had bruises on her upper arms, sir, like large hands had grasped her hard."

A cloud of shame rolled over me, but I continued. "I probably should have said something sooner. If I had, perhaps . . . perhaps this wouldn't have happened." I gritted my teeth to keep the tears in check.

"Oh dear," Mr. Dalton said, while Mr. Arnison shook his head.

Mrs. Fallowfield looked at the floor somberly, her nostrils flaring.

"Thank you for notifying us, Miss Blackwood," Mr. Arnison said. "You may go back to your dinner now, and we will let you know if we need anything else from you."

Nodding, I turned to go, feeling like a defeated coward.

"Miss Blackwood," Mr. Dalton said before I reached the door. "Would you be willing to tell this to the constable if need be?"

I swallowed hard. "Of course, Mr. Dalton. I will do whatever is required."

The world seemed hazy and slow as I ascended the employee stairs, passing the second floor and heading up to the sewing room on the third. Why had I not said anything before? What if something could have been done to save poor Mrs. Murphy from a cruel death?

~

I was interviewed later that afternoon in Mr. Arnison's office by Constable Jackson, who had been brought there by Mr. Dalton.

All my foolish notions about him had vanished as the grim reality of our difference in class and intelligence was now throwing itself in my face. I was thoroughly ashamed of myself, and the seriousness of Mrs. Murphy's death weighed down my heart like a stone.

It was over quickly, and I was surprised when Mr. Dalton escorted me from the office into the hall, shutting the door.

"Thank you again, Miss Blackwood. It was very brave of you to step forward like this."

I wanted to throw myself into his arms and cry my heart out on his chest, but only shamed myself for the thought. "I should have told someone sooner, sir. I am very sorry I didn't."

"I'm sure you felt you were helping her keep a confidence," he said softly. "You mustn't blame yourself for this. In fact, this type of thing happens all too often, I'm afraid."

I looked up at him incredulously. "I didn't know. I have never heard of such a thing." I shook my head, my eyes to the floor. "You must forgive me, Mr. Dalton. I am only a simple country girl, and I—"

"There is nothing to forgive, Miss Blackwood. It is still shocking to me to find the world such a dangerous place. It can unravel the best of us to look upon evil when one has seen so little of it." His voice was full of compassion.

The door to the office opened, and Mr. Arnison came out with the constable.

I slipped away up the stairs as the three men talked and made my way back to my table without looking at the others. I took up the piece of cranberry satin I was finishing and paused when I found a slip of paper underneath.

Not letting the others see, I held my work over it and turned it over. "Thank you, Miss Blackwood. You did the right thing today. Mrs. F."

I glanced up to find Mrs. Fallowfield looking at me with

mist in her dark eyes. She gave me the slightest of nods and went back to her needle.

~

William was aghast when I told him the events of the day, especially when I mentioned seeing Mr. Dalton. He stood back from me in the shelter of Sutton Yard's entrance as the frigid wind blew down the street and over the rooftops. My heart was too sick and weary to withstand his criticism of my actions.

"What were you thinking, Cairstin? That was Mr. and Mrs. Murphy's private business, and you had no right to interfere. Besides, how do you know where she got those bruises? How do you know she was pushed down the stairs when the silly woman could have fallen over her own skirts?"

I cowered under his words, a tear spilling over my frozen cheek. "I don't know, William. I just thought it was the right thing to do. That it was my duty to say something—"

"Your duty is to me, and now you have gotten yourself all caught up in a mess that is none of our business." His words stung like sleet down upon my head. "Did you think of me at all? I demand that you have nothing further to do with this. Am I being clear?"

"Yes, William, perfectly clear."

He took a deep breath and stood closer to me. "Very well then, we shall put it behind us." He lifted my chin with his gloved hand and met my eyes. "This will not happen once we are married and you know my wishes better. God will give me the patience of a saint, and I will guide you in all His ways."

I nodded meekly.

"Now, you must turn your thoughts from all this and focus on our marriage. Your mother and sister will arrive tomorrow night, and we shall dine with them at The Gloucester Arms.

I'm sure you will be happy to see them, as will I." He checked his watch and barely looked at me. "It's time to say good night."

He kissed my hand and left me standing in the wind.

Saturday dawned bleakly as I made my way with the others, fighting a fierce wind all the way to Arnison's employee entrance. I was frozen clear through, down to the icy lump in my chest. I cursed the storm closing in on Penrith, hovering to the south, and knew Appleby was probably already in its path.

I could smell the threat of snow in the air and prayed a silent and passionate plea that it would not be so. I was desperate to see my mother and sister.

Large white snowflakes drifted by the sewing room window by nine o'clock, and by noon you could no longer see through the blowing snow to the far side of the square. There was less and less traffic on the streets, and by five o'clock there was none.

At the evening meal, Toby came to me with a note from William.

"The post from Appleby is not coming. I will still come to collect you for dinner at nine o'clock."

Annabel saw my distress and came around the table to lead me out into the hall. I dissolved into her arms.

"I know, I know," she whispered. "They're not coming."

I startled at Mrs. Fallowfield's voice behind me.

"It is sad indeed, and I feel for you, Miss Blackwood."

I dried my eyes with my handkerchief and turned to her.

"Thank you for understanding Mrs. Fallowfield. I will go up and finish my work—"

To my surprise, she laid her slender hand on my shoulder and interrupted me. "No, Miss Blackwood. I am sending you home now. We will see you bright and early on Tuesday morning after your wedding. May God bless you."

I looked into her dark eyes, softened with compassion. "Oh, Mrs. Fallowfield, thank you. Thank you so much."

"Yes, yes, and Miss Ainslie will see you home and stay with you this evening. I'm sure you can both use a good night's rest before tomorrow."

I was struck by a notion and wondered why I hadn't thought of it before. "Mrs. Fallowfield, would you do me the honor of attending my wedding tomorrow, if it isn't inconvenient for you? I would be so honored to have you there." My heart reached toward her with yearning as I spoke.

She considered for a moment. "I would be honored to attend, Miss Blackwood. What time should I be at St. Andrews?"

"That's wonderful, ma'am! The wedding will begin shortly after ten o'clock."

She pressed her lips into a thin smile. "I will do my best. Now, get your things and go."

Chapter Sixteen

Annabel and I jumped at a knock on the door of the flat. We went to answer it and found William standing at the top of the stairs, covered in snow.

"William!" I hurried him inside, not caring about decorum, and helped brush off his shoulders. "I received your note. Isn't it terrible?!"

He stomped his boots and took off his hat.

"This blasted blizzard!" He growled. "The streets are full up to my knees."

Annabel placed another lump of coal in the little stove, and I fetched him a chair to sit near it.

"I'm afraid I will not be able to take you to supper tonight as planned, my dear. It would be impossible for you to get there in your skirts."

"I understand, William. I am just disappointed that Mother and Rose are not able to come. Do you think we should postpone the wedding until next week?" My heart longed for him to agree.

"What? No, of course not. I will not cancel my wedding for anything, even a snowstorm."

Annabel retired to our room, closing the door. She probably felt in the way.

"But what if the snow doesn't stop? What if Reverend Thomas or Reverend Stuart cannot get to the church? It would only mean waiting one more week. Is that such a long time?"

His face grew grave and his eyes flashed amber. "I will not wait. The snow is bound to stop soon. Besides, Cairstin, it would be a betrayal to me and your family to postpone for a mere inconvenience. You don't want to hurt me, do you?"

I was taken aback by his vehemence. "No, of course not. I was only thinking of—"

"You were only thinking of yourself and not your husband-to-be." He rose in a huff, and I panicked.

"No, William, I swear I didn't mean it like that. Please, please sit down and let us not quarrel on the eve of our wedding."

I motioned to the chair, and he sat again, his eyes smoldering.

"You must understand how deeply I care for you, Cairstin, and how anxious I am to have you as my wife, my family." His tone was like that of a mournful child.

My heart softened, and I took his coat from the hook on the wall and held it near the heat to dry. "I'm sorry. I didn't mean to hurt you, William. I'm only so sad about this terrible storm ruining our lovely plans, that's all."

"Yes, it is a shame, but we must make the best of it." He looked at his watch and stood. "I must be going. I will pick you up here at the usual time in the morning. Come what may, tomorrow we wed."

He gave me a smile as I helped him back into his coat. "Oh." He reached into his pocket. "I almost forgot."

He brought out a half a loaf of bread and nice piece of cheese wrapped in paper. "I hope this will make up for missing our supper."

I gave him a grateful smile and took his offering. "Thank you, William. You're very kind."

I jerked awake at the sound of someone banging loudly at the door. The light of Sunday's dawn peeked into the windows of the little flat, and Annabel and I hurried into our dressing gowns and answered the door.

Eliza peeped out of her room with a scowl.

"Good morning. As t'Reverend Thomas's man and have a message for thee."

He handed me a note, and we brought the snow-covered man inside.

> Miss Blackwood,
>
> There is too much snow for us to hold church today, but never fear! Mrs. Thomas and I will meet you at St. Andrews with Reverend Stuart at noon, for by then we ought to be able to make our way there. Please ask Miss Ainslie to be sure to come and stand in as your witness.
>
> God's blessings,
>
> Reverend Thomas

"Oh my goodness! Have you been to see Mr. Soulier, sir?" I asked.

"He's the next one." The man thumbed in the direction of the Corn Market.

"Will you be sure to tell him you have seen me and I will be ready at half past eleven for him to collect me?"

"Aye, miss" was all he said and was out the door.

The deep snow on the little landing and stairs had been cleared off, and I noticed the man take up a shovel and make his way back out of the yard. The sky was a crystal blue, the morning light sparkling on the new snow like a blanket of diamonds.

Annabel lit the stove and started some tea.

I heaved a sigh. "Well, at least the snow has stopped. How considerate of Reverend Thomas to send us word."

"Yes, he has a good heart," Annabel replied with a smile. "I'm so sorry about your mam and sister, Cairstin, I know your heart must be broken, but it is your wedding day, and we will make the best of it."

I was grateful for her attempts to cheer me. "I am exceedingly disappointed. Perhaps William and I could go and see them in Appleby tomorrow on the post, if he is willing."

"Oh, Cairstin, I wouldn't ask him. Wait till after ya finish your time at Arnison's."

I nodded. "Yes, perhaps you're right."

Annabel curled my hair on the sides in a fashionable way, framing my face softly. I had on my best dress of deep-blue wool, with a white lace collar, feeling like I could set aside my black mourning dress for the occasion. My little Bible was in my reticule, and I wore Mother's good gloves and blue garters. I pinned some white silk roses I had made onto my blue bonnet and inspected myself in the little washstand mirror.

"Ya look so lovely, Cairstin," Annabel said as she fussed over me.

At half past eleven, William and Mr. Nixon came to escort us to St. Andrew's. I was so grateful for Annabel that Mr. Nixon came, and it made me smile to see them together. William looked somber but polished as he looked me over appraisingly.

"You look lovely, my dear. It's a pity your family can't see you looking so beautiful today, but we will see them all in good time."

Just then, Eliza and Mary came out of their room.

"We're coming too," Eliza cooed. "We wouldn't miss your wedding for the world."

I was greatly surprised at her desire to come and felt a niggling at the back of my mind, wondering why. I didn't want her there, but what could I say?

The six of us left Sutton Yard and walked out into the dazzling sunshine. The sky was deep blue, the snow blinding white, and though there were a few brave souls digging out here and there in the near waist-deep drifts, it was otherwise peacefully quiet.

Someone had made a path down Long Front Street to Devonshire Street, past Arnison's and The George to the narrow lane at the north of Barclays Bank, where William worked, behind to the entrance of St. Andrew's churchyard. Someone had worked very hard for hours creating such a path, and we were blessed to have it.

William kept a good hold on me as we entered the gates under the scrolling iron arches and followed the path to the door at the base of the high tower. My heart twinged with longing for my family as we entered, my eyes adjusting to the dimmer light inside, and we were greeted warmly by Reverend and Mrs. Thomas and Reverend Stuart, who was introduced to me. Eliza and Mary slipped by to take their seats.

Reverend Thomas gave me a sideways look and patted my hand. "There you see, Miss Blackwood—God in His heaven is watching over you and has made your path clear to this very day."

"Thank you, Reverend Thomas, Reverend Stuart. William and I are grateful to you for making such an effort for us, aren't we, William?" I smiled up at my groom, trying gallantly to feel like a happy bride.

"Yes, we are most grateful. And now, shall we begin?" William gave me a nod and handed me off to Mr. Nixon, who was to walk me down the aisle and stand up for William, and Annabel was to stand up for me.

Mrs. Thomas stepped forward and handed me a small bouquet of silk flowers, kissing my cheeks.

"They're lovely, Mrs. Thomas. How very thoughtful of you!"

"You are most welcome, my dear. We are so excited to hold the first wedding for the Bible Church!" She took Reverend Thomas's arm as Reverend Stuart led them down the aisle and the organ began to play.

"Oh!" I cried, as I had not been expecting anything so grand. Sentimental tears dashed to my eyes as the hymn "A Mighty Fortress Is Our God" swirled above me.

"Shall we?" Mr. Nixon offered his arm with a warm smile, and I took it. We entered the nave, the light through the stained glass windows at the opposite end above the alter glowing with color. I was overwhelmed, caught up in the moment without any chance for second thoughts. *This is it.*

William watched me solemnly, his hands held in front of him. I kept my focus on him, but the back of a lady's bonnet I did not recognize caught my eye fleetingly. William nodded as he took my hand, and we stood before the reverends. I looked into his eyes and smiled shyly.

I hardly remember the ceremony. I know I said my vows and William his, he placed a thin gold band on my finger, and we prayed, but I had the odd sensation that I was not in my own body. That I was watching myself standing in the nave going through the motions, until Reverend Thomas said, "And now I pronounce you man and wife."

Suddenly I was back inside myself as the organ rang out again, and before I knew it, we were walking back down the aisle as husband and wife.

It wasn't until we turned that I saw Mrs. Fallowfield sitting in a pew dressed in a lovely maroon satin dress and bonnet. William whisked me past her, but she met my eyes. I smiled brightly and waved at her. I was so glad she came.

The small party assembled in the entryway, and everyone congratulated us. Even Eliza, who lingered in her greeting with William longer than I liked.

Mrs. Fallowfield came to me and shook my hand. "Many happy returns to you, Mrs. Soulier. Thank you for inviting me for your special occasion."

"Oh, Mrs. Fallowfield! I am so delighted you were able to come." I was deeply sincere. "How on earth did you find out the time, and how did you make it through the snow?"

"I live very near here and spoke to Reverend Stuart when I saw him out this morning. It was no trouble. I will look for you bright and early on Tuesday morning."

"Mrs. Fallowfield, please don't leave until I've introduced you to my husband." I motioned to William to come over.

"William, this is Mrs. Fallowfield, my supervisor at Arnison's. I am so very honored she came."

William bowed to her slightly with a small smile. "Thank you for honoring us with your presence, Mrs. Fallowfield."

She eyed him through her spectacles, as if sizing him up. "Yes, Mr. Soulier. You are a very fortunate man. Good day" was her curt reply. She left before I could invite her to join us for tea.

William was unusually reserved as we gathered in the

small Coach and Horses Inn next to the church for our simple wedding breakfast of tea and cake. His stoicism worried me, and though I tried to cheer him, he remained polite but cool. Fortunately, I was distracted by the others in the small group, but soon enough it was time to leave.

Annabel and Mr. Nixon were very cordial to each other, and she blushed now and then as I watched them converse. They escorted William and me back to Sutton Yard to help us gather my things and take them the short distance through Little Dockray to Corn Market Street and into White Hart Yard. The alley was narrow, and there were people who worked at the stables at the back of the yard, still clearing away snow. The smell of hay and horses wafted around the buildings.

A rather alarmingly distorted man came limping out of a door on the ground floor of the next building. His dirty cap sat crooked on his balding head, exposing a patch of crusty skin. One of his eyes was almost shut closed from a growth on the lid, and his bright-red nose belied his love for strong drink. I was unsettled as he approached and studied me rudely with his open eye.

"Hiyop, Mr. Soulier, here's the new missus, eh? She's a bit scrawny, ain't she?"

William stepped forward and shook the man's hand. "Yes, Mr. Crick. Please allow me to introduce you to my bride, Mrs. Soulier. This is Mr. Crick, my dear. He is our landlord and has been eager to meet you."

I nodded to the man. "Pleased to meet you, Mr. Crick."

He nodded back and kept his eye on me but spoke to William. "Well, ya gone and done it now, eh? I suppose ya won't mind paying a bit more for the rent, seeing how there's two o' ya now."

The man coughed and spat, then held an open palm out to

William, who ignored him and turned toward the stairs. "I will be down to see you presently, Mr. Crick." He pulled me past the ugly man, who cursed under his breath.

William led us up a set of stairs to the third floor and entered a narrow entryway.

As soon as the door was shut, I asked, "What kind of a man is that, William? How rude he was!"

He laughed and helped me out of my coat. "Don't waste a thought on him, Cairstin. We will be done with him soon enough."

"Yes," I answered. "Thank God for that."

William dropped the subject. "Now, ladies, as I have made it quite clear that I live like a true bachelor and have a very humble dwelling. You will forgive me, I'm sure, for my lack of taste in furnishings, but I am loath to spend money unnecessarily on more suitable decor when we plan to move from here so quickly."

My nerves tingled as we stood in the dim little hall. A set of sturdy cast-iron hooks lined the wall just inside the door, and some of William's coats and hats hung there. I noticed that the hook closest to the door was bent down straight, like a spike, its sharp tip pointed dangerously at my chin. I hoped we could fix it, as it looked dangerous.

William showed me a simple closet with shelves on the right a few paces from the door, then the hall opened to a small sitting room with a fireplace, a table, and two chairs. He went over to kindle the fire, and I looked around me. It was a simple, cozy space, lacking in such fineries as pictures or trinkets or even a curtain for the window overlooking the square.

I was comforted by the snugness of the place, as its lack of practical items was made up for by its privacy.

"And here is the bedchamber." William opened a door near the hall entrance opposite the fireplace. "Remember, I warned you. It is only a mattress on the floor." William glanced at me, and the heat rose in my face.

Peering in, I saw a lone mattress, large enough for two, with a mix of bedding that looked in need of a good wash. The room also had a small high window facing the square, a row of shelving, and a washstand in the corner.

"Well, Mrs. Soulier, is it as I described? Are you brave enough to join your new husband in such a humble abode?"

I smiled quietly and nodded. "Yes, William. It is exactly how I pictured, and we will be happy here, I'm sure."

We thanked Annabel and Mr. Nixon for all their help, and they left us. A streak of panic flashed through my chest when the door was closed and I found myself married, my husband standing beside me. We were truly alone for the first time.

"I assume you would like to do some unpacking. I am going to venture out to J and J's grocery and get us some supplies." With that, he replaced his hat on his head and went out without saying goodbye.

I was taken aback but thought it made sense that we would need some provisions. Shrugging, I went into the sitting room and looked around more carefully. The place needed a good cleaning, and I went about searching for serviceable items, the kettle, a water vessel, a broom, some rags, but there was not much to be found.

I hung up a few of my things in the bedchamber, blushing the entire time. What would it be like with William tonight?

A train whistle blew and made me jump. It sounded louder here than it did in Sutton Yard. How strange to think I would never sleep there again.

My heart sank with homesickness, and I sat down to write Mother a letter. William still hadn't returned by the time I signed and sealed it.

By five o'clock I was truly worried.

I changed out of my best dress and put on my mourning dress again, donning my coat and black bonnet. The sun was setting, and the light would be gone soon. Careful of the ice and snow, I hurried out of White Hart Yard and down Corn Market Street, the short distance to the grocer, but found the shop was closed and my groom nowhere to be found.

Where else should I look? All the shops I could see in the main square were closed. Only the dim light in a few pub windows shone into the growing gloom, and my mind raced. I stood helpless in the bitter cold, turning around in circles, until I heard someone call to me.

"Cairstin! What the devil are you doing out here? I thought I told you to stay home!" William came out of nowhere and was decidedly angry.

"Oh, thank goodness. I was so worried about you, William. You've been gone so long, and I thought something had happened to you."

He quickly took my arm and turned up the street. "I am quite all right. You should not be out in the streets alone at a time like this." He was firm in his tone and manner, but my relief that he was safe helped me to brush it off.

"I'm so glad you're not hurt. I thought you might have fallen on the ice."

He said nothing but whisked me into the yard and up the stairs, locking the door behind us.

"I am quite fine, as you can see." He took my coat and hung it beside his.

I found myself having to be careful not to run into the unbent hook and followed William into the sitting area, where he laid a few packages on the table.

"Where have you been, William? I looked for you at the grocers, but they had closed. Did you bring anything for me to make for supper? Have you had some tea?"

He glared at me and gestured toward the packages, then sat down to take off his boots. He said nothing, so I went to the table and looked through the packages. There was a loaf of bread, badly squashed, a large chunk of cheese, and a bottle of wine, which I looked at with suspicion. It was half-empty.

"I've been trying to do a bit of cleaning while you were away. We will need a few things so I can do a better job," I said casually as I reached on the shelves near the fireplace for the only two plates in the flat. "We'll need a broom and some rags and such."

I watched him out of the corner of my eye as he rose and took a glass from the shelves. I continued as he pulled the cork from the wine and poured himself a generous amount. "William, do you have a bucket for collecting water from the pump in the yard?"

He pulled a chair closer to the fire and sat down with a huff. "I only use the pitcher from the washstand" was his monotone reply.

"Oh, I see. I will fix you some bread and cheese and go fetch some for tea."

He said nothing when I handed him his plate. I left with the pitcher, careful not to slip on the icy steps, and went to the pump. My heart shuddered, not from the cold but from William's coolness toward me.

Just then I caught sight of Mr. Crick's twisted face watching me from his window, and I hurried up the stairs. I didn't care for having him as a neighbor.

Returning with the water, I found William's empty plate on the table. I filled the kettle and swung it on the hook over the fire. "William, are you angry? Have I done something wrong?"

His amber eyes glowed as they reflected the light from the fire, unblinking. Why wouldn't he look at me?

After a long pause, he finally said, "There's nothing wrong, Cairstin. Now eat your supper and go to bed."

I blanched.

Not sure I heard him correctly, I pulled over the other chair next to his and ate my meal in silence, occasionally glancing his way. He was like a statue, except for the times he raised his glass to his lips.

Laying my plate on the table, I lit a candle and went to the bedchamber, closing the door behind me. My heart was in my throat, and I found it hard to breathe as I undressed and donned my mother's beautiful lacy nightgown. I looked in the washstand mirror at my naked body just visible through the sheer gauzy fabric, my long red hair falling in waves around me, and trembled both from cold and fear.

Leaving the candle on the washstand, I silently walked across the room and stood next to the fireplace, presenting myself to my new husband, trembling.

He glanced up and looked me over briefly, then his eyes returned to the fire, emotionless. "Go to bed, Cairstin" was all he said.

I did as he bid. He never joined me.

Chapter Seventeen

I awoke to find myself alone in a strange room. I lay on a cold mattress on the colder floor and could feel the ache in my eyes and head from shedding many tears. My marriage had not been consummated.

I dressed and tended to my hair, washing my face and eyes with the icy water at the bowl. Staring at my pale face in the little mirror, I fought back another onslaught of tears and jerked myself away.

The flat was empty, and William's coat and boots were gone. I went to light the fire and looked out the window at Corn Market Square. Snow still clogged the walkways and streets, but many people were doing their best to get where they were going. There was no sign of William.

I made myself some tea and toast and did what I could to tidy up, but soon found myself at a loss. Sitting before the fire, I held my head in my hands and pled with God.

What have I done wrong? Why is William so angry with me? He must be repulsed by me. I could just die!

I paced the floor and prayed. I sat by the fire and prayed. I lay down and prayed . . . All with no answer. I awoke to the sound of someone in the hall and shot off the mattress to the door.

"Hello, William. Are you all right?"

He glanced at me with a nod. "I am well, and you?"

I was baffled by his casual reply. "I am well."

He went into the little closet in the hall and emerged with a leather satchel. Tucking it under his arm, he turned to go.

"Are you leaving again? Have you had any dinner?" I was desperate to get him to speak more than two words to me.

"I have. I left you something on the table. I must go out. Stay here." He was out the door before I could say anything more.

There were a few rolls and a lump of butter on the table, with a package of tea and another bottle of wine, unopened. I ate my dinner in deafening quiet, the only sound coming from the street below. I moved my chair by the window and watched for what seemed like hours, when a familiar man strode by.

Mr. Gabriel Dalton made his way across the square, unlocked the door of a small storefront, and entered. My heart leaped in my aching chest. There was no sign over the door, and the place looked like it had been unoccupied for some time. Staring at the door intently, I wondered if he would reappear. He did not.

I resolved to go out, against William's wishes and my better judgment. What was I to do? I couldn't even clean my own home without a few rags, and I determined to go and find some and to post my letter to Mother. I was out on Corn Market Street in a few minutes and made my way toward the shops on the upper edge of the square near The Gloucester Arms. A secondhand shop there might have the items I needed.

I was successful in purchasing a small bag of rags, but that was as far as my scant funds would go. I couldn't possibly afford a broom, so I went directly to the post around the corner, then back to our flat, where I was able to keep myself busy cleaning.

William did not return until after sunset. I greeted him as cheerfully as I could and took off his coat. "I've been cleaning the flat today, William. I hope you will be pleased."

"Hmmm" was his stingy reply.

I made him a plate of bread and cheese while he opened the wine and poured himself a glass. We ate at the table in tense silence, then he moved his chair in front of the fire as before.

I sat beside him and said as calmly and respectfully as I could muster, "William, you are very quiet. Please, will you speak to me and tell me what's bothering you?"

He sipped his wine, eyes half-closed, staring at the flames. At last he sighed with irritation. "There's nothing on my mind, Cairstin. Perhaps you should retire."

Again, my heart felt as if it had been stabbed. "Will you come with me, William?"

His nostrils flared and his eyes narrowed more. "I'm not tired. Now go to bed."

I sat dumbfounded but stood soon after and did as he bid.

~

I rose early on Tuesday morning after little sleep and dressed for work. Emerging from the bedchamber, I found William pulling on his coat.

He glanced at me, then took his hat from its hook. "What are you doing up so early?"

Puzzled by his question, I stated the obvious. "I am going to work. I assume you are as well." My flat tone matched his.

He paused and shook his head. "No, you're not. I have informed Mr. Arnison you will not be returning."

I gasped and wavered, touching the wall for support. "What? But why, William? I thought we agreed that—"

"I changed my mind. I want you to stay put, Cairstin. Is that understood?" He growled, startling me more.

"Yes, William, but—"

He turned swiftly and approached me like an angry dog. "You are my wife, and you will obey me. There are no buts about it!" He seethed.

My back pressed against the closet door. "Yes, William, of course." My knees quaked. He stood eye to eye with me, flashing contempt and breathing heavily.

"That's better." He stepped back and was out the door without another word.

I shook from head to toe and could not move for a full minute. Finally I went to stand by the cold fireplace in fear and confusion.

I stooped to find there was not enough coal to heat the flat for the entire day. Wrapping myself in a blanket from the bed, I sat at the table with my head in my hands, weeping bitterly. No more Arnison's. I didn't even get a chance to say goodbye.

There was little food left, but I trusted that William would bring more, as I'd promised to stay home and had no money to buy any. The hours crept by as I sat by the window and watched. Mr. Dalton came to and from the little shop a few times, but my heart was so broken I could not care.

Desperate for some occupation, I brought my Bible and sat by the light of the window and tried to find something that would comfort my bleeding heart, but the words were dry and only made me question God about why He had put me in a marriage with a man who detested me. What happened to the man who had courted me with so much attentiveness and told me how devoted he was to me?

William came in at half past ten, well after his shift at the bank had ended.

I could smell the liquor on his breath before he came close to me. He had no food or coal, and when he found only a tiny fire in the hearth and the room was cold, he turned on me with an icy glare.

"Why is there no coal?" he said in a disturbingly hushed voice.

I didn't know what to say. "There wasn't much when you left today. I saved it until I could bear the chill no more. I only just lit the fire half an hour ago."

His eyes smoldered and his fists clenched.

I stepped back from him.

"I will go and get us some coal in the morning, William, if you will leave me a few coins—"

"Haven't I made myself clear enough?" he whispered harshly. "I don't want you stepping a foot outside that door, do you hear?"

He stormed toward me, backing me against the wall. My soul rocked with fear, and I clutched my hands. "Yes, William, I hear you. That is why I didn't leave to get coal today, I . . . I don't have any money and—"

"Good." His voice was deathly quiet. "Go to bed, Cairstin."

He turned quickly and left, leaving me to sink down on the floor, trembling.

William did not come home that night or the morning either. I hardly slept, afraid he would come back and blame me again for there being no fire, but what was I to do? I huddled in blankets to keep from freezing, and my stomach growled with hunger, as the food was gone. I sipped some water and watched the world go by in ignorant bliss below me, unaware of the destitute bride who watched them from above.

I thought about Mother and Rose and what they would think of my condition. Perhaps this was the price I would have to pay for keeping them safe with food and a roof over their heads. I thought about Mr. Arnison and wondered if he would even care now that I had broken my word to him. Humiliation seeped through me and seared my conscience.

How I longed to see Annabel's cheerful, loving face and pour out my heart to her. But she would not listen, for I would be revealing my marital issues out of turn, and Reverend Thomas would be most displeased to know I shared such confidences outside of my home. What would Reverend Thomas think about William's treatment of me? Was this what he had in mind when he taught that wives should obey their husbands?

That afternoon Mr. Dalton came with two laborers to the shop, where I now assumed he was setting up his practice. I watched numbly as the men hung a sign above the door as he directed. "Mr. Gabriel Dalton, Solicitor."

Some corner of my tortured heart was happy for him. I saw him step back with his hands on his hips, admiring his accomplishment. Then to my surprise, William entered the square and walked to him. How I wish I could hear what they said to each other as they shook hands. Then, Mr. Dalton bowed and went inside his office, and William turned, facing White Hart Yard. He looked up to find me looking at him from the window.

I jerked back in fear.

Before I knew it, he came in and looked at me standing by the table in deadly silence. He slowly removed his gloves and hat and threw them on the table.

"So I see your friend Mr. Dalton has taken an office just across the square. How very convenient. Did you tell him to set up shop there so you could watch him every day from the window?"

I shivered from the lifelessness of his tone, so unfeeling. "Of course not, William. I have barely spoken to Mr. Dalton since the day I told him and Mr. Arnison about Mrs. Murphy." I kept my voice as calm as I could, but my insides quivered.

He walked into the bedchamber, then reemerged with one of the brand-new bedsheets I had made up the mattress with for our wedding night.

He took a knife from the table and cut it, then ripped it in two, handing me the pieces.

"Now, my little seamstress, you will make a curtain for that window, and I will never find you looking out of it again. Get to work."

I jumped when he stabbed the knife into the wood of the table and swept up his coat with a flourish.

"I swear, William, I didn't know Mr. Dalton would set up his shop there. Don't you believe me?" I should have left it alone, but I was desperate for him to know, to understand.

"Believe you? A woman who shuns her new husband from her bed? Why should I believe anyone as wicked as you?" he spat, taking up his hat and gloves and storming out again.

~

The next three days passed much the same. William nailed the curtain over the window all the way around, with only a slit down the middle, which would be obvious to see someone pulling apart from the street below.

His stone-cold silence persisted. Still, he did not bring any more food and only enough coal to have an evening fire when he came home late. He must have been eating and drinking before he came home, and his cruelness in keeping me starved was the worst. I was too terrified to ask him for something to eat.

By Friday I was desperate. William left early that morning, and I went about the flat searching everywhere for a coin, something I could purchase even a slice of bread with. I remembered how Father would hide his money in a box under the floorboards, and I even went around trying to pry up any loose boards with the cooking knife.

At last, on my knees in the hall under the hooks, I found a coin lodged between the floorboard and the wall. It was enough. I dressed and calmly went to the water pump, the only place I could safely go, but when I found the yard empty, I rushed into the back alley that led to Little Dockray and joined the people on the street, trying to be invisible.

I made my way, at the risk of being seen by someone in Barclays Bank, across the main square to Tatty Tim's Potato Cart. I could barely speak but held out my money to him, which he took with a smile. In a moment I held a large hot potato dripping with butter in a newspaper wrapper.

My mouth watered, and I took a bite, closing my misting eyes. *Thank you, God. Thank you.*

Turning to go back the way I came, I jumped at the sight of Eliza and Mr. Bell heading my way. Eliza stopped and stared at me, her eyes wide. I sped away the other direction and made my way to the flat by the back alleys. There I sat shivering in my coat, wolfing down the rest of my potato and weeping.

When I finished, I unfolded the newspaper and looked it over. There were the usual advertisements for hair oil and baby bottles, a recipe for blood pudding and such, but a small headline caught my eye. "Banker's Daughter Gravely Ill."

Most of the article had been torn away, but I gasped when I realized it was about Miss Gleeson, the lady who'd bought the green plaid dress I'd finished for Susan at Arnison's. I almost vomited the only food I'd had in days.

~

William returned earlier than usual that night. I had the tiny fire ready to light but hadn't lit it, as I was expecting him later.

"Why isn't the fire lit?" he asked patronizingly.

"I didn't know you would be home so soon. I will light it now."

I stooped to the hearth, and William continued to hurl insulting questions at me.

"Haven't I told you never to leave the flat, Cairstin?"

My spine stiffened, and I stood with my back to him. "Yes, William, you have."

"Then why has Eliza Salkeld informed me that she saw you in the main square today?"

A ripple of fear shook my heart, and I turned to him slowly. "Why have you been speaking to Eliza, William?" I tried to change the direction of the conversation.

"I will speak with whomever I wish." I could hear the contempt drip from his tongue. "Now tell me why you were in the square today."

"I was hungry, William," I answered softly.

"Hungry? Why haven't you made yourself something to eat? Are you such a glutton you have already eaten everything in the house?"

"Why do you speak to me so, William?" I asked. "You know you have not brought home any food for days." The hot tears spilled over.

"If you were an obedient wife, you would be worthy of feeding, but as you are not—"

At this he whirled and went to the bedchamber. I heard

him throwing things about, and he emerged with my few pair of shoes in his arms. Then he went to the hall and came back into the room with my boots as well.

"What, William? What are you doing?" My voice quivered, afraid of what he had in mind.

"Silence! I will teach you not to disobey me again!" he hissed, and shoved my shoes into the fire.

"No! No! How could you?" I cried. "Please, William, please don't!"

I watched in agony as my shoes caught fire, and I grabbed his arm, trying to keep him from burning my boots as well.

He shrugged me off and threw them in, then turned to hold me roughly from behind, forcing me to watch the flames destroy my sense of freedom. My knees gave way, and I sank to the floor, William kneeling behind me with his hands holding my upper arms like a vice.

His hot breath whispered in my ear as I succumbed to his cruelty. "This is what the Lord does to those whose wickedness rises up before him. Change your ways, Cairstin, or you too shall see the fire of God's wrath!"

As the last of the leather soles withered to ashes, William released me, opened a bottle of wine, and sat down before the fire with a glass. "Go to bed, Mrs. Soulier."

Chapter Eighteen

I paced the floor in the only slippers I had left, the ones I'd worn the night before. William had not thought to take them and add them to his bonfire of revenge. Perhaps he was right. Perhaps I was the most wicked woman in the world and deserved nothing better than to be starved and frozen in this godforsaken flat.

These slippers were thin and worn, and I wore them only inside as house shoes. They would never withstand the cobblestones, gravel, and snow outside. I felt like a caged animal, walking back and forth, back and forth, trying to make sense out of my life.

I sat and wrote a letter to Mother, telling her nothing of my current sufferings, for fear that William, whom I must now ask to post it, would read it and find me out. If only there was someone I could turn to, but if I did, I would be in more trouble because of it. I must endure. I must, for my family's sake.

I thought of Reverend Thomas, but if I went to him, would he believe me? I was certain he would find my claims I was being frozen and starved preposterous. No one from the Bible

Church would believe me. In fact, I was sure they would condemn me for speaking of it at all.

Rubbing my sore shoulders, Mrs. Murphy's face passed before me, and I saw again the bruises on her arms. Was this how it was for her? She had ended up dead at the bottom of her staircase. Was William capable of such violence?

It was my fault. He would never have hurt me or burned my shoes if I had obeyed him and never left the flat. I was wicked. No matter how hungry I was, I'd still disobeyed my husband.

Another part of my mind stood up to argue that it was wrong of him to treat me this way. But then I thought my very thoughts were proving my wickedness.

My agitation grew and grew, as did the ache in my belly. The walls of the flat felt more and more like a prison, until I could take it no longer. *I must get out of this place! I must or I will go mad!*

I threw on my coat and bonnet and pulled on my gloves as I picked my slippered steps down the stairs and out the back of the yard. Heading up the steep grade through the alleys and back lanes toward the top of the hill, I heard a train whistle blow, like a craven spirit urging me on.

Not stopping, I hurried across the broad street toward the castle ruins. My foot slipped on the icy stones, and I fell forward hard on gravel on my stockinged knees and gloved hands. Pain surged up my arms and legs. A passerby offered me a hand up, but I refused, regaining my feet and running recklessly toward the ancient stones.

I entered the vacant, broken walls and cowered under a low, covered section, like a shallow cave. Sitting on a large red stone, I held my wounded hands over my mouth, trying to muffle my sobs, which echoed against the rock walls. I gasped as someone came into view. I turned my head, trying not to be noticed, which I knew was futile. The crunch of the man's boots grew louder, and I huddled closer to the wall, praying he would pass by.

"Mrs. Soulier? Are you all right?"

My heart lurched as I recognized the voice of Gabriel Dalton. I raised my hand to hold him off, hiding my face from him.

"Please, Mr. Dalton, please do not trouble yourself—"

He ignored my plea, ducking his head and coming slowly closer. "Forgive my intrusion, Mrs. Soulier, but I can see that your hands are bleeding through your gloves. I saw you fall from a distance and came to see if I can be of any assistance."

"No, no, I am all right, Mr. Dalton." I was terrified that someone would see us together. "Please, sir. I only need a moment to collect myself."

He did not leave but crouched down against the wall opposite me. I was sure our echoing voices would be heard by someone and wanted with all my being to be back in the flat, where I should have stayed.

"Please, Mrs. Soulier," he said gently. "You are in deep distress, and you are injured. May I take a look at your hands?"

Reflexively, I clasped my hands and held them tightly to my chest, shaking my head.

"All right, but I now see drops of blood near your feet. Are your legs injured as well?"

His kind words touched the raw wounds in my heart. I shook my head again and whispered, "No. Please, Mr. Dalton, you must leave me." With that, I laid my head on my lap and clasped my aching knees to my chest.

He did not leave.

"Would you like for me to take you home, Mrs. Soulier? Or can I take you to a doctor or to Mr. Soulier?"

My head snapped up at the name, and I rose in a panic.

"No, no. Thank you, Mr. Dalton. I must go home now. I must—"

I tried to step out, but my foot slipped from under me again and I was forced back to my frozen seat with a jolt. At this, Mr. Dalton crossed the distance and sat down beside me, steadying me with his hand on my shoulder.

"Mrs. Soulier, these slippers are much too dangerous to wear on the ice. Where are your sturdy boots?"

The thought of my burned boots nearly stopped my heart. And here I was again, out of the flat, speaking with Mr. Dalton and doubly disobeying my husband. *I am wicked to the core.*

Mr. Dalton removed his coat in an instant and drew it over my shoulders.

"You're frozen through. Please allow me to take you to my home, Mrs. Soulier. It is not far from here."

I shook my head violently, but he would not take no for an answer. He put his arm around me and lifted me to my feet, then before I knew what was happening, took me up in his arms and out of the little shelter.

He ignored my pleas to put me down and carried me over to West Lane, a way I had never been before. I was exhausted and could not begin to physically extract myself from his strong arms. Though I was sure that God no longer listened to my prayers, I still prayed no one had seen us.

At last I hushed as he soon entered the gate at the back of a large townhouse on the left, not far from the rear of The Gloucester Arms.

Mr. Dalton kicked at the back door gently until someone answered.

"Mrs. Trimble, I have an injured lady here. Make sure the

fire in the sitting room is roaring and bring some water and bandages."

He whisked me down a long hall into a warm sitting room and laid me on a red settee. Bewildered, I struggled yet again to get to my feet and flee.

"No, Mrs. Soulier. You are not going anywhere until we've had a look at your injuries." He turned. "Thank you, Miss Ainslie."

My mind caught the name, and I looked up to find Annabel hovering over me, aghast.

"Cairstin! What's happened to ya?!"

"Oh, Annabel!" I whispered in disbelief as she knelt beside me. I couldn't be gladder to see her dear face.

"Mrs. Soulier fell on the ice and has been hurt," Mr. Dalton explained. "Here, let me take off your glove, Miss Ainslie. Can you manage the other?"

I looked from one to the other, then noticed a large bandage completely covering Annabel's left hand in a white ball.

"Annabel! What happened to your hand?" My concern for my friend helped slow my spinning thoughts.

"We can talk about that later. Let's see about you first," Mr. Dalton interjected.

My gloves came off painfully, as the blood had dried them to the raw skin underneath. Despite my gloves, my right palm had a deep cut.

"Thank goodness you had your gloves on, or these would be much worse."

Mrs. Trimble joined the others from behind the couch, and between the three of them my hands were cleaned and embalmed with bandages.

Mr. Dalton stood and stepped back. "Please attend to Mrs. Soulier's legs. I think perhaps her knees are hurt as well."

He left the room, but I could hear him pacing in the hall as Annabel and Mrs. Trimble removed my slippers and stockings.

"But, Cairstin, where are your boots, lass?" Annabel asked. "Why were ya out and about with these thin things?"

I winced as Mrs. Trimble cleaned the cuts on my knees and didn't answer. Once my knees were tended to, Mrs. Trimble had a maid fetch me clean stockings from her own room.

"Oh, no, please, I can manage without. I must be going." I attempted to stand, but Annabel pushed me back down and sat beside me.

Mr. Dalton entered once my legs were covered, and I was given a sturdy pair of shoes to borrow, only a bit too large for m. Annabel gave me her gloves, promising to clean and mend mine and return them.

Drawing a chair closer, Mr. Dalton sat in front of me, his brows knotted over his kind brown eyes. I looked from him to Annabel, and my cheeks grew warm. "I really must go back to the flat now. William will be most unhappy I am not there."

"We shall take you home presently, Mrs. Soulier, but first I would like to see you take some tea."

I was given tea and biscuits, finding it difficult to restrain myself from wolfing them down in my hunger. My limbs finally thawed, and I could feel my toes again. My hands and knees throbbed, as did my head.

Seeing Annabel's hand, I asked again, "Annabel, please tell me what has happened to you."

She gave Mrs. Trimble a glance, then Mr. Dalton, and swallowed. "It happened on Monday after your wedding. I was about to test the heat of an iron and thought I was flicking water on it, but it t'was oil. It lit up and caught my hand on fire." Her face clouded over in pain, and she rubbed her wrist. "I'll never sew again."

My heart wrenched, and I threw my arms around her. "Oh,

Annabel, I am so very sorry!" Holding her shoulders lightly, I looked into her eyes. "How on earth did oil get into the cutting room?"

She bit her lips a moment as tears welled up. "I think perhaps it was put there on purpose."

My mouth gaped. "Eliza?" I was incredulous. "My God, how could she do such a thing?"

"Now, ladies, we must not speculate until we have more proof," Mr. Dalton said in a professional tone.

"Mr. Arnison was very sorry for me but had to let me go," she said sadly. "Mr. Nixon's sister works in the kitchen for Mr. Dalton, and I'm working for him now. He's been ever so kind to me, and Mr. Nixon has asked to court me." She gave a shy smile and looked down at her wounded hand.

"My poor friend. I am happy for you and Mr. Nixon, but shouldn't something be done about Miss Salkeld, Mr. Dalton?"

He sighed and placed his teacup on a side table. "It will be hard to prove, but I am in conversation with Mr. Arnison about the matter. We shall see."

A grandfather clock standing next to a landscape painting chimed out the hour of five o'clock, and I startled and stood uneasily. "Oh no! I must be getting back. I really must."

Mr. Dalton stood and steadied me. "Miss Ainslie and I will take you home in my curricle. It will be ready shortly."

He left the room with Mrs. Trimble, and Annabel turned to me. She took me by the shoulders, and I winced unwittingly. Shock struck her face, and she took my elbows instead.

"Cairstin, did ya hurt your shoulders in the fall as well?"

"Oh yes, I suppose so. I am only outraged about what has happened to you, my friend, and that I have only learned of your injury just now." Did William know about this?

Annabel sighed. "I must admit, I am quite upset about it myself. Something must be done about that girl."

Mr. Dalton came in and gingerly helped me into my coat. "We are ready. Lean on my arm, Mrs. Soulier."

Before he assisted me up to the seat in the rig, I turned to him and asked awkwardly, "Mr. Dalton, do you mind driving the back way to White Hart Yard? I would prefer no one sees—"

He nodded slowly. "Of course," he said gravely, and handed me up beside Annabel.

I insisted they drop me off at the stables. Praying no one would notice me, I walked stiffly through the yard and up the stairs, relieved to find the flat empty. There was no trace of William having been there, and I scurried about trying to find a good hiding place for my borrowed shoes. I rolled them up in one of my dresses and tucked it back in my trunk, hoping William would have no reason to look for anything there.

Lighting the fire around half past nine, I took myself to bed, praying he would leave me alone when he came, as I did not want him to question me about my bandages. I lay awake pretending to sleep when I heard him enter and open the bedchamber door. He muttered something under his breath and shut the door again. I breathed a sigh of relief and tried to get comfortable with all my sore limbs and finally dozed off.

He was gone before I woke the next morning, cold as ever. My stiff joints protested loudly as I rose from the mattress, and I found it difficult to get up without kneeling on my scraped knees. My breath misted in front of my face as I looked out the bedchamber window at the sky, which was all I could see from there, as the window was small and high on the wall.

My mind felt clearer, and though my heart still beat painfully in my chest, I sat down at the table and tried to gather my thoughts. Was this it? Was this how I was doomed to exist until the day I died? My only solace was that William was supporting my mother and Rose. How else could I bear it?

The day drew on lonely, cold, and hungry. I thought I should try the same method that evening and be in bed before William came home. Perhaps it would make things more bearable if we simply didn't see each other.

Where was the polite man who called me "my dear" and told me he thought I was the most beautiful woman in Penrith? If only he would return. I wish I knew how to draw him back to me.

I lit the fire and went to bed as the night before, but this time William came barging into the bedchamber and drug me out by my arm.

I cried out, but he pushed me against the hall wall and covered my mouth with his hand violently.

My heart raced in terror as he pushed his weight against me, crushing me against the wall.

"You will say nothing. You will not cry out or make a sound. Is that clear?"

I could hardly breathe but nodded, staring at his altered face. I hardly recognized him. He adjusted his grip on my jaw and held it between his thumb and fingers like a vice. His other hand gripped my arm fiercely, and I stifled another cry.

"Who do you think you are, Cairstin Soulier, to disobey me yet again?" His grip tightened, and my eyes watered from the streak of pain shooting through my head.

His voice never rose above a harsh, hissing whisper. "I know who you were with yesterday, you slut. You were with him, weren't you?"

I remained still, his insult ringing in my ears.

"So you won't service your own husband, but you'll spread your legs for Gabriel Dalton, won't you."

I tried to shake my head.

He grabbed my throat with both hands and squeezed. "I told you not to have anything more to do with him, and now this!"

I tried to pull his arms, but he squeezed harder, pushing me against the wall with all his strength. I couldn't breathe as my vision darkened, and I feared he would crush my windpipe, when suddenly he thrust me onto the floor.

I landed sideways, wheezing, desperate to get air into my lungs. Then he kicked me in the ribs and walked past.

I coughed and struggled to breathe, every breath stabbing like a knife in my ribs. Something was broken.

I lay on the cold hard floor in agony. The pain from my throat encompassed my whole head. The sharp stabbing in my ribs renewed each time I tried to fill my lungs. I no longer noticed the ache in my scraped knees and hands as I pulled myself onto all fours, stifling the moans that threatened to reawaken William's anger.

Hold fast, Cairy. Hold fast! My whole body shook with weakness as I reached out to clutch the doorjamb of the closet and slowly pulled myself to my feet. Using the wall for support, I reached the bedchamber door, only to find William leaning on the wall, watching me with a smirk on his face.

I flinched and stepped back in horror. "Please, William, I'm sorry. I will never go out again, I promise," I said in ragged breaths, tears finally spilling over. There was no way for me to fight him off in my weakened state.

He laughed. He laughed and laughed until he was bent over slapping his thighs.

My blood ran cold as I watched him. Who was this man? How could he enjoy torturing me like this?

His fit of hysterics subsided, and he opened the bedchamber door.

"Oh, Cairstin, my dear, if only you would not provoke me so, we would be such a happy couple. But here, let me help you to bed and I will forgive you."

He came toward me, and I shrank against the wall. "Now, now. It hurts me that you don't trust me. I am your husband and only want what is best for you. Come now." And he picked me up in his arms gently and laid me on the mattress, as tenderly as a mother would a child.

I awoke to the blare of a train whistle and groaned. Every inch of my body was racked in pain, and I shivered both from the cold and weakness, my mind clouded with disbelief.

I heard William enter the flat whistling cheerfully. The sound grated my raw nerves. Such a strange thing to hear in contrast to the events of the evening before. My vacant stomach clenched with hunger, and I barely had the strength to sit up on the mattress.

The cuts on my hands had reopened in my struggles, and dried blood caked my palms. But by far the worst was the never-ending piercing in my ribs.

I startled when William opened the door and greeted me cheerfully.

"Good morning, my dear. I have brought you a surprise this morning. We will have a fine breakfast before we are off to church." His smile was wide, and he came to me, offering his hand. "It is time to be up and about, lazy bones!" He took me under my arm and dragged me to my feet, and I bit my lip, trying not to cry out. I didn't breathe a word for fear of how he would react.

He brought me to the table and sat me down. It was covered with bread and rolls, butter and cheese, cold ham, and a jar of preserves, even a pot of steaming-hot tea. The smell made me dizzy, and I looked up at William with suspicion.

"You see! This is all for you, my dear, and you are to eat your fill." Sitting across the table, he passed me a roll with a grin. "These are as fresh as they can be—still warm!"

I cautiously took the roll and held it over my plate. My mouth watered at the yeasty aroma as it warmed my cold hand. The fire was lit, and I could feel my limbs thawing.

William bowed his head and prayed. "Lord, for that which we are about to receive, may you make us truly thankful. Amen."

"Amen," I whispered, though my fearful heart did not feel a morsel of thanks.

"Eat, eat, Cairstin. We mustn't dally, or we'll be late for church, and you know I like to be punctual." His manner was jovial, but I now perceived a hollowness to his speech I'd never noticed before.

I buttered my bread and took a bite. Hot unbidden tears rolled down my cheeks, and I no longer cared what William thought. My hunger took over, and I ate all I could with abandon.

William eyed me from across the table, smirking now and then with a snort. "Careful not to eat so quickly, my dear. You'll get a stomachache."

How ironic that he should be concerned about that now, I thought miserably, but slowed my ravenous bites all the same. I must not upset him again.

Finished, William went to the bedchamber to change and left me to clean up. The broken bones of my corset poked through my chemise and tore at my skin as I moved, but I bit my lips and did my best, storing the leftover food carefully in a box on the shelf.

William emerged dressed in his Sunday best, his dark-brown hair combed to perfection. "Hurry and dress now, Cairstin. I don't want to be late, and be sure to cover up your unsightly neck. I don't want you to be embarrassed by your need for correction."

My need for correction? His words echoed through my soul with dread.

"Please, William, perhaps you should go to church without me today. I am not feeling well and—"

"Nonsense! What you need is some fresh air and a good sermon. Move along now." He motioned toward the bedchamber.

When I hesitated, he sighed impatiently. "You don't want to embarrass me in front of the reverend, do you? What would your mother think if she knew you refused to go to church with your new husband?" His tone was laced with warning, and I hurried to obey.

It was with great difficulty that I undressed, only to find the cuts from the bones of my corset to be bleeding and the bruising on my side severe. How could I be expected to go out in this condition? The only thing different was my belly was full and no longer screaming for food.

I ripped a strip of white cotton from my store of fabrics and bound up my torso as well as I could. Then I quickly tacked a folded scrap of stiff corduroy to the inside of my damaged corset and hoped it would do until I could make some real repairs.

Tying a gray ribbon around my neck, I hid the red-and-blue fingerprints that were tender to the touch.

"Come along now, Cairstin, for God's sake. It's time to go!" William called from the hall.

I emerged dressed in my gray plaid, my mourning dress in too bad a condition to be seen in, and dared not put on my borrowed shoes

"It's about time." William checked his watch. I caught a groan in my sore throat as he helped me on with my coat. He held my arm tightly as we made our way out of the yard and across Corn Market Square to The Gloucester Arms. I leaned on him heavily but wished bitterly I didn't need his assistance in my weakened state, my slippers hardly protecting my feet from the ice.

Reverend Thomas greeted us but gave me an odd look, though I did my best to smile. I let William do all the talking, as I was barely able to breathe, let alone speak. I watched him in disbelief as he greeted everyone as if nothing had happened. He was a completely different person.

Mr. Nixon appeared at the top of the stairs, escorting Annabel, her wounded hand still covered in bandages. The sight both warmed my numb heart and lit it with anger.

Just then, Eliza came up the stairs with Mary Hodgson. If I were not so terribly spent, I might have confronted her there and then. William directed me to a row near the front, as we were married now and expected to socialize with other married couples.

I could hardly stand the pain in my ribs. I held Mother's pendant as Reverend Thomas preached a sermon about overcoming the evil desires of a disobedient heart. He was as blustery as ever. William nodded in agreement from time to time and even grunted his ascent. I sat in agony and dismay as the reverend's words about wives obeying their husbands in all things condemned and convicted me.

Chapter Nineteen

After the service, William offered his hand to help me stand, but my body had stiffened from sitting so long and forced out a whimper.

He leaned over to me. "Stop faking it, Cairstin," he whispered harshly, but his smile never left his face.

I was indignant. "You know I'm not, William," I whispered back in anger, regretting it as it came out of my mouth.

William's smile never flinched, but he squeezed my right hand hard, and I felt the blood from my cut palm warm and wet in my glove. Annabel and Mr. Nixon came over to greet us, and I averted my eyes, afraid Annabel would read the pain on my face.

"I found a pair of your gloves under your old bed, Cairstin." She gave me my gloves, clean and mended. But how could I return hers, now bloody, without raising suspicions?

Swallowing back tears, I nodded and smiled. "Thank you, Annabel. How is your hand? Is it very painful?"

William hardly let her answer and brushed them off

quickly, almost rudely, as he turned us toward an older couple near us.

"Good morning, Mr. and Mrs. Drinkwater. It is a pleasure to see you. May I introduce my wife, Mrs. Soulier?" His tone was confident and friendly. I could not believe this was the same man who'd attacked me in the flat the night before.

"It is a pleasure to meet your new bride, Soulier. May we congratulate you both on your recent nuptials." The man looked me over, his high forehead crinkled with raised white brows. He offered his hand, and I faltered, then gave him my left. His wife was a demure woman dressed severely in dark-gray silk up to her chin. She smiled at me quietly with a nod, which I returned.

The blood from my hand was seeping through my glove. I tried to concentrate on William's conversation with the man but panicked that someone might notice.

"Mr. Drinkwater is the head of the Building Fund Committee, and we have been raising quite a tidy sum this week, Cairstin. It is difficult, as my work hours limit my time to canvas, but I am pleased so far with our efforts." He beamed down on me, and I felt some sense of relief knowing what he was doing after work before coming home so late at night.

"Indeed. You would be very proud of your new husband, Mrs. Soulier. He is most faithful in his work for the Lord, and it will not be long before we will be able to purchase the land for our new church."

I fumbled to respond, but William preempted me. "I look forward to meeting with you and the other married men at the reverend's house this afternoon. Mrs. Drinkwater, will you be going, to visit with Mrs. Thomas?"

Her husband patted her hand and answered for her. "Mrs. Drinkwater will be visiting her mother this afternoon in Appleby, won't you, dear?"

Appleby?

The mild woman smiled slightly and nodded.

"Who is your mother, Mrs. Drinkwater? I am from Appleby, and perhaps I know her?" My frail voice was so soft I feared she might not have heard the question.

William crushed my fingers, but I was unmoved.

"My mother-in-law's name is—" Mr. Drinkwater began, but William pulled the watch from his pocket.

"Dear me, look at the time!" he exclaimed. Bowing to the Drinkwaters, he quickly excused us, steering me toward the stairs. He paused at the Building Fund box and dropped in a few coins and momentarily let go of my hand on his arm. I pulled it away, making a fist, but the edges of the bright-red bloodstain were still visible, as was the blood that had seeped onto William's coat sleeve, which he took note of in an instant.

I shoved my hand into my pocket and whispered pathetically, "William, that lady might know Mother and Rose. Why wouldn't you let me speak to her?"

His light smile never faded while he took my elbow and rushed me down the stairs, and before I could say more, I was hurried across the square and up to our rooms.

William unlocked the door impatiently and nearly threw me inside. I crashed into the hall wall and cried out as my ribs shot hot streaks of pain through my chest.

"Look what you've done to my coat!" he spat. "How could you be so careless?"

I struggled to get air back into my lungs, holding my bloody gloved hand behind my back and grasping my rib cage with my left.

"I . . . I'm sorry. I didn't mean to—" I wheezed, bracing myself for what he would do next.

He ripped off his coat and flung it on the floor at my feet.

"You better have this fixed by the time I come home," he said in a low growl, his amber eyes flashing.

I nodded furiously. "I will, I promise. It will be fine."

A train whistle blew as he checked his watch. Without another word he took his other coat from the wall and left me cowering in the hall.

I shook from the cold and pain as I tried to pump water into the pitcher in the yard. Each pull and push of the handle were excruciating. A plump woman in an apron with a bucket came out of the flat under ours and waddled to the pump.

"Hiyop." She looked at me curiously. "Thee's the new bride upstairs, eh?"

I nodded, my face flushed with exertion despite the chill that caused my breath to mist before my face. Continuing my efforts, I hoped she would not notice I was being rather rude in not speaking to her.

"Having trouble there?" She looked me over, and seeing my bandaged hands, her worn face dawned with pity. "Here, let As have a go."

Setting down her bucket, she waved me off and pumped, filling the pitcher in seconds, then she lifted it carefully.

"I thank you kindly." I reached for it.

"Hang on, now—let As carry it for thee." Before I knew it, she nodded me toward the stairs.

"Oh, thank you, but I can manage—"

"As daresay thee can't," she insisted.

I was too weak and frightened to argue. Taking the stairs before her, I opened the door and turned to take the pitcher with the best smile I could muster.

She tried to look past me into the hall but paused. "As

Mrs. Merryman, living under thee there." She pointed to her door under ours. "Thee needs anything, just come and knock, eh?"

My guarded heart softened at her kindness. "Thank you, Mrs. Merryman. I am Mrs. Soulier, and I am pleased to meet you."

Before she turned to go, she looked into my eyes. "Pardon, Mrs. Soulier, but what happened to thee hands?" She pointed her chin to my hands under the pitcher, which was now almost too much for me to hold.

"Oh, it's nothing. I fell, that's all. Good day, Mrs. Merryman."

Before she could say more, I turned and pushed the door closed with a parting smile.

I spent the afternoon carefully working the bloodstains out of William's coat, Annabel's gloves, and whatever else I could manage to clean with no bucket or means of properly washing clothes.

I lay the laundry over the chairs to dry, then endured the agony of laying myself down on the mattress. I dozed off from exhaustion. The pain in my ribs did not let me sleep long. Rising carefully, I made myself a meal of bread and cheese, then braved the cold and undressed to attempt some repair to my corset.

I sat mending at the table in my dressing gown, wrapped in blankets, when William came in, his face lit with malice. My heart seized.

He threw his hat and gloves on the table and leaned on his fists.

"I can't trust you for a moment, can I, Cairstin?" he hissed, then paused, waiting for a reply.

My stomach quivered and fingers trembled. "I don't know what you mean, William. All I have done all afternoon is—"

"Keeping company with Mrs. Merryman!" He shoved a chair, spilling the clean clothes on the floor.

I rose slowly and shook my head. "No, William. I only met her at the pump, that is all. I needed water to clean your coat, and I—"

He came around the table, and I braced myself. Grabbing my chin, he eyed me fiercely. "No more water. Do you hear me? You are never to set foot out of this place again!" he whispered harshly. "If I catch you disobeying my wishes one more time, I shall cut off your mother and sister and make sure they are kicked out into the street."

Before I knew it, he spun me around. Taking a tight grip of my upper arms, he kneed me in my backside as hard as he could several times, then flung me onto my chair.

My spine cried out from the bottom to the top. Even my head felt split open. I did not cry out but managed the thinnest of whispers through my ragged breath. "Why? Why?"

He stood behind me, and I could feel his silent, menacing presence. I felt his warm breath on my ear. "Because you are a wicked woman and don't deserve to live."

~

He left and was gone until well after dark. His words haunted me the rest of the day. I could do nothing more than groan on the cold mattress and wish I could die. When I rose hours later, I found myself locked in the flat.

The next five days went by in an aching blur. I hardly saw William, which was better than seeing him. By the end of Wednesday, the food and water ran out, and I lay dreaming of Mother and Rose, Annabel and Mr. Nixon, Mr. Dalton, my father, even Eliza and Mr. Bell. Between my hunger and pain, the worst part of my isolation was the fear that kept my every nerve alarmed and waiting for the next time my husband walked in the door.

He rarely did. He opened the bedchamber door only long enough to see that I was still there, then shuffled about in the sitting room or closet and left again.

By Friday, though my thirst drove me close to madness, I had recovered enough to sit at the table for short periods, with a pillow on the chair. I opened my Bible and tried to read but found it impossible. The words lay lifeless on the page, and my heart was dead to them. Still, something in me felt that they must have meaning, and I took to reading them out loud in dry, whispered tones. Perhaps speaking them would somehow dispel the evil in my prison.

"'The Lord is my shepherd; I shall not want.'" I choked out the lines of the psalm until I reached, "'Yea, though I walk through the valley of the shadow of death, I will fear no evil: for thou art with me; thy rod and thy staff they comfort me.'"

I laid my head on my arm, destitute. *God! Where is your comfort? If you are going to take my life, Lord, take it swiftly. I cannot bear this thirst!*

I rummaged around the room for the twentieth time, desperate for anything to ease my dry tongue. I carefully searched through all of William's things on the shelves in the closet, even his shoes. At last I tipped over his best pair of Huntington boots and heard a thud. Reaching in, I pulled out a hidden bottle of wine.

Taking it to the table, I sat gazing at it in a delirium. What would he do to me if he found I had opened it and helped myself? It was torture to my very soul, this cruel dilemma, having to choose between dying of thirst and dying at the hands of my husband.

Resolved to face the certain consequences, I opened the bottle and drank deeply. The alcohol burned down my throat and sat like fire in my belly, but I tipped the bottle to my lips and drank more.

With a sick irony, I held the bottle in one hand and held up my Bible in the other, continuing to read the psalm aloud.

"'Thou preparest a table before me in the presence of mine enemies: thou anointest my head with oil; my cup runneth over.'"

I couldn't help but give a short, dry chuckle and raised the bottle to the ceiling. "My cup runneth over!"

Taking another swig, I finished my reading.

"'Surely goodness and mercy shall follow me all the days of my life: and I will dwell in the house of the Lord forever.'"

~

Dizzy, I tucked the remainder of the bottle back into William's boot and stumbled to the mattress. If only I could sleep and regain a modicum of strength before he came home and found his latest reason to torture me.

Hours later, when I heard him unlock the door and rummage in the closet, I got to my feet and crept to the door, listening, waiting for him to barge in to drag me from the mattress. When I heard him back out in the hall murmuring to himself, I cracked the door open.

In the dim light of twilight, I could see him reaching for the unbent iron hook just beside the closed front door. He pushed up hard on the hook, and I heard a slight click but could not see what he did with something above it on the wall. I heard the soft sound of paper fluttering to the floor, and William said an oath under his breath as he stooped to pick up what had fallen.

I closed the door.

Shaking, I thought it would be best to be found asleep

instead of spying, so I lay painfully on the mattress and closed my eyes, my heart beating rapidly against my aching ribs.

Did William have some kind of hiding place?

When I heard him leave and lock the door, I waited until I was sure he would not return, then pulled my protesting body off the mattress and went out. Everything seemed the same. I shuffled to the fireplace and lit the last of the coal on the grate, then lit a candle.

With my limbs shaking, I took a chair to the hall. I went back and retrieved the candle to examine the wall near the straightened hook, its tip pointing at my throat accusingly. Since William and I matched in height, I knew whatever I was looking for was not far up the wall.

I saw nothing unusual, then felt with my fingertips around the edges of the wood paneling. Still I found nothing remarkable. Setting the candle on the chair, I stood trembling before the hook and grasped it with both bandaged hands and pushed up with all the strength I could give it.

I heard something click and move, and to my amazement the board above the hook was now ajar, a dark opening behind the slit at the bottom.

My energy renewed and my pulse surged in my ears as I hurried to retrieve the other chair. Setting the candle on one and using the other to stand on precariously, I pried open the panel and removed the board, then took up the candle and peered into the dark space.

It was only a few inches deep, but it ran the entire length of the board I removed. It was empty. Frustrated, I pulled at the boards beside it, only to find them securely attached to the wall. Then I pushed on the other hooks, but none of them produced the same clicking sound and no more panels opened.

Sighing heavily, I raised the loose panel to replace it, when a speck of white at the bottom of the space caught my eye. I set the board back down and stood again on the chair, the warmth of the candle close to my face. The speck was so tiny and lodged in the crevice between boards I could not pick it out with my fingernail.

I sat on the chair and rested, grateful that the chill in the air was lessening from the heat of the fire. A few minutes later I went to arm myself with a needle. Picking at the white speck with the tip proved helpful, as the corner of a slip of paper emerged.

Eventually I was able to carefully pull the whole page out with my fingers. In my hands I held a ten-pound note. I stared at it in disbelief. It was more money than I had ever dreamed of touching. Why did William have such riches hidden in the wall? Were the other pages he'd taken out notes as well? If so, it would have amounted to quite a fortune.

Chapter Twenty

I waded in the River Eden, my skirts bundled in my arms above the slowly moving surface of the water, and I smiled down at my reflection. The birds darted in the trees and called sweetly to one another, and bees buzzed around the cherry blossoms on the branches of a tree nearby. I could smell the mossy-scented air floating over me from the dense grove on the far side.

"Cairy! Cairy! Come quickly!" my mother's urgent voice cried, and I looked up to find her and Rose reaching toward me from the bank, fear etched on their dear faces. "You must live, Cairy! You must live for our sakes! Come quickly!"

"Mother!" I called, but my feet slid on the slippery stones, and I went down, thrashing to keep my head above water. My wet skirts weighed me down, and my hair came loose, matting over my face and catching in my mouth as I tried to surface for air. I was choking, drowning, the panic causing me to sink farther, farther down.

Then William appeared over me, his hands around my

throat, squeezing the life out of me. I could hear the muffled screams of my family through the deepening water.

I gasped awake in a cold sweat, my heart racing, and I knew. The message of the dream was finally clear. Holding Mother's pendant in my trembling fingers and lying still, I thanked God and listened. *He is not here, and I will not stay in this prison another day.*

Rising slowly, I dressed to the best of my ability, the ten-pound note securely tucked in my corset. I retrieved the borrowed shoes from their hiding place and put them on. The wine was gone, but I was not as thirsty as before. I felt weak as a kitten, but a new anger burned within my bones, which steadied me.

Checking the front door, I found it locked as expected. I spent some time sitting on the floor with my sewing tools, trying to pick the lock. That failing, I went to the large covered window in the sitting room and could hear the busy market below. Considering, I left it alone and took a chair instead to the bedchamber and stood upon it. I could see most of the square from this height and nearly burst into tears when I sighted a light in the window under Mr. Dalton's sign. He was there.

Now, I would wait for an opportunity. For a sign from heaven.

My weakened muscles objected strongly to standing for long periods on the chair, and before long I was sitting on it in frustration.

Rigging the other chair under my trunk and bracing it with the washstand, I was finally seated on the top chair, like a bird on a perch with an almost ideal view.

Once I saw Mr. Dalton exit his office, I waved and pounded on the window, but he did not see my shadowed face behind the glass. I watched him walk up toward his home past The

Gloucester Arms but hoped he would return after the dinner hour and look my way again.

I carefully climbed down and went to pounding on the floor, hoping perhaps Mrs. Merryman might hear, but soon lost the strength to make a loud enough noise. *I must keep trying. I must live for Mother and Rose.*

Again I spotted Mr. Dalton returning to the square, and I pounded on the glass, even attempting to scream, but my dry throat could only produce a thin cry. When he entered his office, I gave up for a time, sinking onto the mattress in exhaustion.

It was hours later when I awoke and climbed up to the window. It was suppertime and perhaps Mr. Dalton would emerge again.

As I sat staring at his door, a familiar figure caught the corner of my eye. Mr. Oldcorn. *If only he would see me!*

Renewing my pounding and waving, I watched him pull his wagon near my side of the square and dismount. My heart started when he removed his hat and looked right up at the building. I waved for all I was worth, but my hopes were dashed when he replaced his hat and adjusted his horse's harness.

Please Mr. Oldcorn! See me!

Mr. Oldcorn straightened, and I froze when I saw William coming up from the main square below.

Recognition dawned on William's face when he saw Mr. Oldcorn and tried to avoid him, but it was too late. Mr. Oldcorn blocked his way and spoke to him in an urgent manner, moving his arms and pointing now and then. *Was something wrong with Mother? With Rose?*

Then Mr. Oldcorn handed William a letter and tipped his hat. I held my breath as I watched William tuck the letter in his inner coat pocket and extend his hand. Mr. Oldcorn shook it briefly and mounted his wagon, then William turned in directly under me.

I was down from the window like a shot.

I shoved things back in order as fast as I could move. When William turned the key in the lock, I was sitting panting at the table, my Bible in my trembling hands.

He stopped in the hall to hang his hat and coat, then strode into the sitting room with a wide smile.

"Now there's a proper sight. My dear, sweet little wife sitting quietly reading the Scriptures. And what passage are you reading, my dear?"

I swallowed hard and tried to calm my voice. "I am reading the psalms, William. Psalm 23, to be exact."

My stomach churned at the sight of him. A newfound hatred had taken the place of my fear, a loathing that masked the pain in my body.

"Awe, yes," he mocked. "'The LORD is my shepherd.'" He chuckled low and long, then sang a line from the song we sang often at the Bible Church. "The Lord is my shepherd, I shall not want."

I remained as motionless as possible, steeling myself for an attack, but the rest of my mind was on that letter and how I would get my hands on it.

William sat opposite me and casually put his feet up on the table, stretching his arms up and lacing his fingers behind his head. This was something new. I took note of his position and watched him from the corner of my eye as I pretended to read.

"I forgot my bottle of wine on the floor by my boots, Cairstin," he whined, like a little boy. "Go and fetch it for me."

I only glanced at him before laying the Bible down and rising slowly to my feet.

"Feeling any better, my dear?" he tossed out sarcastically as I passed by him on my way to the hall.

He grabbed my hand, and I stiffened. If I could only see what was in his coat pocket.

"How is your little hand, Cairstin?" he asked with a sneer and ripped the bandage off.

I caught my breath but managed not to wince.

"Oh, it is much better, much, much better." He patted it harshly and gave my fingers a rough squeeze. "Good for you."

Letting me go, he set his feet back on the floor, and I went to the hall, trying not to look in too great a hurry. I silently felt in his coat pockets, devastated to find them all empty, but his top hat hung oddly from the next hook, and I reached for it.

"Hurry up, wife—your husband is thirsty and has much to celebrate. Perhaps you will join me for a toast."

My hand darted into the hat and came out with a letter, which I swiftly shoved into my pocket while picking the wine bottle up off the floor. I was back in the sitting room before he could say anything more.

Setting the bottle on the table, I went to the shelves and brought back two glasses, then took my chair.

"What do you have to celebrate, William?" I dared to ask quietly as he opened the cork and filled the glasses, sniggering.

He pushed a glass my way and lifted his. "Here's to me, Cairstin. The greatest and cleverest husband to ever live!" He laughed out loud and swallowed half the glass, slamming it down on the table, making me jump despite my efforts to keep still. When he saw it, his laugh grew louder, and tears winked in his amber eyes.

I wanted to scream, but while he was so gleefully distracted, I slipped the letter from my pocket and held it in my lap under the table. I looked down demurely and saw my name in my Mother's hand. My heart lurched as my suspicions were confirmed. I slipped the letter back into my pocket and stood.

"William, will you take me for a walk?" I asked calmly.

His merriment died, and he looked up at me in confusion. "For a walk? Are you out of your mind?" His laughter renewed. I strode quietly to the hall and donned my coat. By the time he got up from the table, my bonnet was in place, and I was fitting my sore hands into my gloves.

William leaned on the hallway wall and crossed his arms over his chest, still smiling. "Well, Mrs. Soulier, where do you think you're going?"

"Home," I said flatly, my voice hoarse and brittle. "Unlock the door, William." I turned and faced the door, waiting.

His chuckling ceased. "Why should I? You are my property to do with as I wish." He slid his shoulder down the wall and came closer. I could feel his leering eyes penetrate the back of my skull. "Besides, Cairstin, there is nowhere for you to go. No one cares for you anymore. Not even your own mother. She hasn't written you a word since our wedding day. She must be glad to be rid of you."

He was close now, and I could feel his moist, hot breath breathing down my neck. I turned and looked him in the eye, holding the letter in front of his detestable face.

Catching my wrist, he wrenched it from me. Pulling me close, he snarled in my face, "Where did you get this, slut?"

"You know where," I whispered, never moving my eyes from his.

He tossed the letter onto the floor and in a flash had my back against the wall, his hands around my throat. I tried to pull them away. I struck at his face, but he only smiled, his amber eyes aflame. Hard against the wall he forced me, the searing pain gripping my neck and head like a vice. No air, no air.

"Cairy, you must live!" cried my mother. *"You must live for us!"*

I felt the little chain of mother's necklace break and slide off my neck. I moved my hands from William's wrists to his chest and face, one foot against the wall, and just as my vision grew dim, I pushed with all the rage within me in one violent motion. There was a sickening crack as William's head hit the opposite wall and his hands let go.

I fell to the floor, fighting for breath. My lungs searing and wheezing, my throat whooping with every effort. My body shook like thunder from my spent rage and exertion. No thought came into my mind for some moments, no emotion to my heart. I felt as though I were under water, my eyes foggy and my hearing muffled. The only sound was the heavy thumping of my heart against my ribs and my breath wheezing in and out.

Finally rising on all fours, the air came easier. My head cleared, and I jerked back, seeing William's boots and that he still stood over me. Terror bolted through me once again, and I looked, my hands held over my head defensively. Then I saw.

Blood dripped from William's gaping mouth onto his sparkling white necktie. His amber eyes were bulging but no longer lit from an inner evil, and his arms hung limp at his sides. I could just see the tip of the straight cast-iron spike supporting his weight from the roof of his mouth.

He was dead.

Chapter Twenty-One

I scrambled back in horror, a scream catching in my flaming throat. His lifeless eyes stared at me, mocking. *You see, you are a wicked woman, and I am the proof.*

In sheer panic I ran to the sitting room and tore the curtains from their nails. I pounded wildly on the glass. No one on the darkening street below looked up. Then I saw the glow from Mr. Dalton's window and screamed again like a rasping wraith.

Daring to witness his dead state again, I held down my terror and went to the door beside William's hanging body and tried it. Still locked. I was trapped inside with him.

I leaned back on the wall and closed my eyes to keep him from looking at me. I must get out of here.

Think, Cairstin, think . . . The key. Where is the key? His pockets, somewhere in his pockets.

Keeping my eyes low, I reached toward him, hands trembling. I could feel the lingering warmth of his body as I rifled through his pockets. His gold watch fell out of the waistcoat pocket and hung on its chain. I drew out some small papers, letting them fall to the floor. The key was in his trouser pocket, with two others, which dropped to the floor. I thrust the door key into the lock.

Flinging it open, the wind burst cold against my hot face. Without hesitation I closed the door and stumbled down the first flight of stairs, my heart pounding. I saw Mrs. Merryman at the pump. Steadying myself on the rail, I reached helplessly toward her.

My voice rasped. "Help me! Please! Help me!"

She left her bucket mid pump and hurried up to me. "Mrs. Soulier, thee mustn't be out. Thee's husband told As!"

I collapsed at her feet when she came near and grasped at her skirts. "Please, help me!"

Bending her face to mine, her eyes filled with alarm. "George! George!" she shouted at her door.

A stout man with a weathered face rushed out of their door. "George! She's out," Mrs. Merryman cried again, trying to pull me to my feet.

Her husband joined her, and they pushed me forcefully back up the steps. I tried to resist, my crackling voice sounding like a wild crow, but they were stronger and determined.

"Thee must not be out, Mrs. Soulier. It's not safe for thee." I couldn't understand what they were saying. I shook my head, desperate for them to comprehend.

"No! No! I cannot go back! I cannot go back there!" I croaked, but they would not let me go.

The door flung open, and the Merrymans forced me inside and I fell to the floor in the hall. They bent over me, patronizing and talking over me as if I were a child. I shook my head, thrashing in panic, when Mrs. Merryman stood and turned toward the door. She let out a bloodcurdling scream that surely pierced the walls of the building and reached the street below.

I cried out myself, then curled into a ball and cried hysterically into my knees, still terrified of making too much noise with William staring down upon me with his vacant eyes.

Before I knew what was happening, the flat was filled with men all shouting and talking at once. Then I heard the voice of Mr. Crick and his hobbled step inside the door.

"What's this? What's happened here?" His grating voice spat as he pushed his weight around and stood over me, his stinking mass casting a cloud over my cowered form.

"Take a look at this, Crick," a voice said, and I raised my head in time to see him turn and find my dead husband's body hanging behind the open door.

"Bloody hell, that!" he growled. Turning to me, he pointed at William and shouted, "You do that, eh? Hardworking man there come home to his supper and you hang him up like a pig on a hook, eh? All 'cause he wouldn't keep you in fine clothes and feed ya your favorite cakes, eh? Ya little priggish murderer!"

"NO!" I rasped. "No, no! I didn't mean to kill him! He was choking me, and I—"

"Ah! He was choking you, eh? Then how'd he wind up up there? Ha! He was choking ya, all right! And ya think the constable's going to believe that, is he?"

"Now, Mr. Crick, maybe what the lass is saying is true. Me and me wife both heard the scuttling above us from downstairs just afore—"

I was nearly trampled under the men's boots as more joined them, and I recognized Constable Jackson from the gaps between the crowd of legs surrounding me.

His attention was immediately directed by Mr. Crick to William's body, who's blood was still trickling from his gaping mouth down his chin and chest. Every inch of my body was ablaze with pain and fear, but I stayed huddled on the floor, pressing my back against the wall, wishing with all my soul that I could pass into it and not live another moment.

I was not afforded another instant to reflect as Constable Jackson took the three steps to stand over me with his hands on his hips, pursing his lips, as if considering what to do.

"I didn't mean to kill him, Constable, I swear it." I could hardly get the words to leave my mouth. "He was choking me. I couldn't breathe. I—"

"Ya don't need any more proof than this, do ya, Jackson? Here he is, hanging on the wall like a slab a bait, and no yan else was here to do it than she," Mr. Crick hollered, pointing his thick finger at William, then me. "The whole town knows how crazy she is. Soulier's been telling me and others since they wed how she has a razzie and flies at him like a mad witch, eh?"

"What? No, no! It isn't true," I croaked in disbelief. "I have never once—"

"Merryman!" Crick yelled. "T'weren't you and I just having a crack t'other day about poor Soulier having to put up with such a miserable lass, eh? Wasn't you t'was saying how odd she was?"

My head swirled at these revelations. William had convinced everyone I was out of my mind?

Constable Jackson, who had been conferring with the men in the room, bent over me and took my upper arm, pulling me to my feet. "I shall have to take you with me, lass," and saying no more, he compelled me toward the door. I took one last horrified look at William on the wall. God only knew what more harm that man had done to me outside of the walls of this cursed place.

A crowd waited in the yard around the bottom of the stairs, but Constable Jackson steered me through the rabble and out to the street, where still more people had gathered. They looked at me with accusing eyes and pointed, shouting about the mad bride and tapped dressmaker.

"No! No! I am not!" My whimpered cries were useless as the constable pushed through the mob into Corn Market Square. My heart was failing, crushed under the weight of my guilt and the horror of the shame being hurled at me from every side.

I stumbled and fell just as Gabriel Dalton fought his way to my side and caught me.

"Mrs. Soulier! What has happened?" he shouted above the mob.

Before I could answer, the world went black.

~

I could hear people talking in hurried, hushed tones but could not make out their words. My head was under water, the sounds muted and swirling. I tried to open my eyes, but my lids felt like lead, too heavy to lift. My body was being touched, and the pain drew out hoarse moans, but they were muffled and weak, no more than whispers in the dark. I felt like a lifeless stone, sinking, sinking.

Something warm and wet was spooned into my mouth. Swallowing was torture, but it drew me closer to the light, closer to the air. A soft, tender hand brushed my face and lifted my head to drink again.

Then a young woman's voice called to me from above. "Cairstin, poor Cairstin."

Yes, poor Cairstin. She is lost. She is finished. She is not enough.

My eyes fluttered open, and I saw an angel before me. Her familiar face and loving smile warmed my soul and brought life back into my veins. "Annabel," I whispered harshly, my dry, cracked lips hardly moving. The tears rolled down her round cheeks, and she kissed my forehead.

"Oh, Cairstin! What has he done to ya?"

Terror split through me like a knife, and a vision of William hanging from the hook forced my hazy mind back to reality. The sudden realization that I was in a gaol cell tore my soul. I cried out, my every breath condemning me.

"What have I done? God forgive me! What have I done?" My voice burned as if fiery embers had been poured down my throat. My heart burst with the agony of my shame. "What have I done!?'"

Annabel clung to me, but I was inconsolable. William's face, his eyes, the blood from his yawning mouth all screamed at me in judgment of my hideous crime. *"You are wicked, and you don't deserve to live."*

I heard manly voices around us as I buried my face in Annabel's lap, weeping, too ashamed to look up and see who was there.

Annabel held my face and looked into my eyes, speaking softly. "It's all right now, Cairstin. He cannot hurt ya anymore. You're safe now. Don't be afraid."

I stared at her precious face and tried to slow my racing thoughts. But when I thought of her innocence, her clean, kind heart and how black mine had become, I buried my face again.

"Mrs. Soulier, please, you are with friends now. Don't be afraid." I heard Mr. Dalton's voice next to me and realized he sat near me on one side, then found old Dr. Briggs on the other.

Gradually I became aware of being dressed, but without my corset. I was on a crude wooden bed, and I lay my head back on the smelly straw mat, weeping bitterly. "Let me die. Please let me die."

"Hush now, lass." The doctor's voice was full of compassionate authority. "Just breathe in and breathe out now. That's it. In and out."

I followed his slow commands, then looked into Annabel's eyes pleadingly, lips trembling, "I didn't mean to kill him. I swear it. As God is my witness, I meant him no harm."

"I know, my dear. I know. T'was an accident, I'm sure of it." She stroked my hair, the smooth motions like the brush of angels' wings.

After some time my sobbing slowed. Annabel dried my tears and helped me to sit up, my back against the rough stone wall.

It was cold in the cell, and I hugged my knees to my chest. I could hear the voices of someone speaking with Constable Jackson outside the door with the barred window but could not make out what they were saying. I was glad. I didn't want to hear any more. I couldn't stand what they said to me, what they said about me.

I couldn't look at Mr. Dalton but asked Annabel, "How could he tell so many lies about me? How could all these people believe him? My reputation has been torn to shreds!" I covered my face with my hands.

"There, there now, lass. You mustn't be so ashamed." The doctor stood over me. "I've taken a good look at you, and I must say, you've been through it. That you lived to see this day is a miracle from God."

Mr. Dalton bent over me as well. He laid his hand on my shoulder, his voice thick with pity. "Yes, Mrs. Soulier. Thank God you are still with us."

I shook my head, a wave of nausea passing over me. "Please don't call me by that name—I cannot stand it."

"Of course, Cairstin. We will forgo it." He drew his stool closer and took my hand. "Look at me, Cairstin. Look at me please."

I shook my head. "I cannot. I am wretched. I am nothing."

"No, no," he coaxed. "You are certainly not. You are a brave and strong woman who has done nothing more than defend her life."

I could hardly believe he could still show me any pity now.

"Now please, let me see your eyes. I want you to look at me."

He shook my hand slightly, and I emerged, still hanging my head in shame. At last I met his eyes, the eyes I had once wished to get lost in. They were full of compassion, full of, dare I say . . . love?

"That's it," he coaxed. "Now, listen to me, for I am telling you what I know to be true from the bottom of my heart. Are you listening carefully?"

I sniffed and nodded, feeling like a child.

"Good." He bent closer. "This is what I know. That you have done nothing wrong in the eyes of God. The evidence is clear. A man tried to strangle you, and you fought back, as anyone has the right to—do you hear?"

I hung my head again. "I want to believe you, sir, but my husband is dead and at my hands. It will not matter what he did to me. I am a woman. I was his property to do with as he wished. He told me so himself."

"You must not think such things, Cairstin. He hurt you, more than once by the looks of it. The doctor says you are covered in bruises and have not eaten in days."

I raised my eyes to his. "Why?" I whispered. "Why did he stop bringing me food? What did I do to make him hate me so?" I shook my head in disbelief. "And now I have proven what he said about me, that I am wicked and deserve to die. Oh, what will become of my mother? Of Rose?"

A fresh wave of shame and grief plunged me into despair

again, but Mr. Dalton stood and took my face in his hands. I shut my eyes and would not look into his.

"He lied to you, Cairstin. I have sent for your mother and sister. Now, please look at me!"

I shuddered. My eyes closed fast. "I cannot, sir. It is because I loved you and not him that this has come upon me. God saw into my evil soul and is meting out his wrath upon my head."

Chapter Twenty-Two

"But if you felt so, why didn't you wait for me? Why didn't you write to me when I was in Carlisle?" Mr. Dalton sat near me, leaning close.

I stole a glance at him—pain lay in eyes and his light-brown wavy locks were disheveled. I puzzled over his questions. "How was I to know I should, sir? You left Penrith before Christmas without a word."

Mr. Dalton sat back as though stunned, silent.

Annabel still stood on the other side of the bed and gave me a fresh handkerchief, while Dr. Briggs mixed something in a bowl at the little table.

"Without a word?" Mr. Dalton finally said, disbelief in his tone. "But I left you a letter at Arnison's." He shook his head, his eyes wide. "Do you mean you never received it?"

"What letter?" Now I looked at him in shock. "You wrote to me before you left? But I never received it." My heart pounded anew. What was this? Some kind of cruel joke?

Mr. Dalton stood incredulous, then looked down on me

with genuine pain in his eyes. "I left it with Mr. Bell to give to you before I boarded the train. Are you saying he never gave it to you?"

A memory flashed through my mind of Mr. Bell and Eliza just before Christmas, laughing over a piece of paper and glancing at me with scorn. *A letter, my letter.*

I shook my head, my very soul torn asunder. I buried my face in my hands. "How could they? Oh God! How could they?"

"Mr. Bell and Miss Salkeld have had it in for Cairstin since the day she came to Arnison's, Mr. Dalton." Annabel's voice was hard as a stone. I had never heard her speak so. "They are cut from the same evil cloth."

Mr. Dalton stood and paced wildly. "Dear God in heaven." He then turned to me. "I am sorry, my dear. So terribly sorry." He sat again, tears in his eyes. "It is all wrong." He groaned, shaking his head. "All so very wrong."

He took my hand and bowed over it with a moan. "My God, what have I done? Can you ever forgive me?"

My heart nearly burst. How could this be? How could life be so cruel?

I slipped my legs over the side of the bed and tenderly took his hands in mine. "There is nothing to forgive, sir. Nothing," I whispered, then laid my forehead on his hands and wept.

~

Mr. Dalton and Annabel made me as comfortable as possible, and Annabel helped me eat a bowl of bread soaked in salty beef broth. Nothing had ever tasted so good. I sat against the wall, utterly exhausted, but an undercurrent of merciful peace now anchored me, and I felt less frantic. He'd sent me a letter. How different everything would be if only I had received it.

Then, fresh anger surged from my belly at Mr. Bell and Eliza Salkeld. "Why in God's name would they do this to me? To you, Mr. Dalton? What kind of people take delight in such meddling, in such cruelty? And what about Annabel?"

I reached for her bandaged hand and held it gently. "Oh, Annabel, how much you have suffered at the hands of these detestable people. I am so very sorry, my friend." I kissed it and bowed over it. "Dear God, please help my dear Annabel. Help us all."

I looked into her misted eyes and shook my head.

"Thank you, Cairstin," she said. "We must keep trusting that God will answer our prayers."

Trust God? Had He been speaking to me all along?

These thoughts were too much for me. I closed my eyes and wished only for sleep, for escape from these overwhelming revelations. Dr. Briggs approached me with a cup of something to help me rest, when Constable Jackson came in with a man of average height and a balding head, whom I had never seen before.

Mr. Dalton waved off the doctor and motioned for Annabel to leave, then leaned over me and took my hand. "Don't be afraid, my dear. The constable and the coroner only wish to speak with you and learn what has happened. I have already spoken to them and went with them to the flat and saw everything they did. Dr. Briggs has given them his report on your condition."

"Mother's letter and emerald pendant. Did you find them? Will you give them to me?" I had forgotten them in my panic and pain.

Constable Jackson stepped forward. "They were found, but they will be kept for a while as evidence."

I swallowed hard. The rasp in my voice increased the more I talked. "Evidence, Mr. Dalton? Evidence of what?"

He patted my hand comfortingly. "Evidence of what happened, dear. That is all."

Mr. Dalton stepped back. "Mrs. Soulier, this is Dr. Mark Garside, the coroner here in Penrith. Gentlemen." He was sober in his introductions but gave me a reassuring nod and stepped aside to allow the men to take the stools.

"Mrs. Soulier." Constable Jackson tucked in his chin and eyed me under his hooded brows. "Dr. Briggs has apprised us of your condition, and we have tried to delay our interview with you as long as possible, but it is time to ask you some questions."

"I am at your service, gentlemen," I answered, my voice crackling.

Constable Jackson looked to Dr. Garside, who put on some spectacles and held a clipboard with paper, his pencil poised to write. "Dr. Garside will be taking notes, Mrs. Soulier, so that everything is recorded properly. You understand?"

I nodded and took a deep breath. "I do."

"Mr. Dalton has informed us that he will be standing in as your legal counsel. That is why he is allowed to remain present."

My eyes shot to Mr. Dalton, who nodded to me again.

"Now, Mrs. Soulier, you are aware of the condition in which we found your husband, Mr. William Soulier, are you not?"

The question hit me like a bullet between the eyes. I squeezed the handkerchief in my hands and nodded. "I do, sir. He was caught on a hook on the wall, which had gone through the back of his head." I could not help the shudder that convulsed through me as I spoke the words aloud. Neither could I help the tears that welled up from the raw horror of the memory.

Constable Jackson nodded and cleared his throat uncomfortably. "Hmm, yes. And do you know how he came to be in such a state?"

I hung my head and nodded. "Yes, sir. He was strangling me in the hall next to the door, and I pushed him." Panic boiled up inside me. "But I meant him no harm, sir. I only meant to stop him from killing me."

I held the handkerchief over my face as despair washed over me. In a few moments, I looked up at Mr. Dalton to see him watching me with deep tenderness, and I regained my composure.

The men sat patiently, then continued. "I can appreciate your distress, Mrs. Soulier. Now, let us go back to the day of your wedding . . ."

The interview took well over an hour. I told them every last detail of all that had occurred in the last fortnight, including some of the events leading up to our wedding, and was about to cover the subject of Eliza and Mr. Bell, when the constable stopped me.

"Thank you, Mrs. Soulier, but I believe that discussion will need to be kept for later. In the meanwhile, I would like to ask you about some of the things we found today in your flat."

I was shown a box of all the evidence they had collected in their search, including pieces of my burned boot heels and cobbler's tacks covered with ash, some notes and receipts, a small key and a larger one, Mother's pendant and letter, which I begged to read, an empty wine bottle found in a boot, and William's gold pocket watch. To my surprise, they also produced my torn and broken corset.

They asked me if I had any knowledge about the keys and what they were for, but I told them I had no knowledge and only saw them for the first time that evening when I'd searched William's pockets for the key to the flat so I could get out.

I was handed William's watch and asked about its inscription. "Yes, the initials stand for William Edward Soulier," I offered, but when asked about the date inside, I was puzzled. "I have never looked closely at the inside. He told me that the clasp didn't work properly, and I never opened it when he showed it to me."

To my surprise, Constable Jackson clicked the latch and it opened easily, and there on the inside of the cover was a date—Feb. 4, 1845.

"I'm sorry, sir. I don't know the meaning of the date. William always told me his birthday was in September."

The watch was closed, and I took note of the date, wondering why William had not wanted me to see it before.

It wasn't until they brought out and unfolded the ten-pound note that I truly worried. I had already told them how I came to be in possession of it, but the look on Constable Jackson's face darkened as he held it in front of me.

"Can you tell us again how you came upon this, Mrs. Soulier? Explain it to me in as much detail as you can."

I retold the story of watching William from the bedchamber, all the details of how I found the secret compartment and managed to extract the bill with a sewing needle, even pointing to the little holes in the corner made by the tip.

Constable Jackson removed a small magnifying glass from his coat pocket and examined the note carefully. He gave a low grunt, then handed it and the glass over to the silent coroner. While he looked it over, the constable turned to me again.

"Mrs. Soulier, do you have any idea how this note found its way inside the paneling of your flat? Did you see Mr. Soulier put things into the compartment, or only extract them?"

"No, sir. I only saw the once when he took the papers out."

"And do you have any idea if anyone else had access to this compartment?"

"No, sir. I never saw anyone come into the flat but the day I moved there, when Miss Ainslie and Mr. Nixon helped carry my things inside. They were only there briefly."

"And this was your first time inside the flat, on the day of your wedding?"

"Yes, sir." The heat rose in my face. "We thought it would be inappropriate for me to go there beforehand."

"I see. And do you have any knowledge of how your husband came to acquire this note? It is a lot of money for a bank clerk to have on hand."

"I have no knowledge, sir. I am very curious myself to understand where it came from and how it got there. It disturbs me greatly to think my husband was doing anything he should not, sir."

"Hmmm, yes." He grunted, then took a deep breath and adjusted his seat.

"Dr. Garside, I will leave the more delicate questioning to you, sir." Constable Jackson reached over the bed and took the clipboard and pencil from the coroner, who tugged at his lapels and removed his spectacles, looking at me somberly.

"Mrs. Soulier, you have indicated to us that your husband never"—he paused awkwardly and cleared his throat—"that he never shared the bed with you, is that correct?"

"Yes, sir. Our marriage was never consummated." Somewhere inside I felt relieved, glad William had never touched me in such an intimate, violating way.

"Well," he said with a heavy sigh, "I believe that is enough for now, Constable. Mrs. Soulier, you have yet to be charged with a crime, but I believe it is in the interest of your own safety that you remain in our custody, due to the hostility being expressed toward you by the town's folk, and your counsel has agreed."

The men stood. Constable Jackson took up the box of evidence and turned to go.

I panicked. "Please, Constable, before you leave, may I read my mother's letter?"

He paused and looked at Dr. Garside, who eventually nodded. My desolate heart soared as he handed me the letter, which had been opened, then crashed to the ground as I read its brief contents.

Chapter Twenty-Three

I had no idea my agony could be any worse than it already was. Learning that William had ceased to send Mother another farthing after the wedding and that she and Rose were now utterly destitute without home or money was nearly the end of me. They had been taken in temporarily by mother's old friend Mrs. Grundy, but she and Mr. Grundy were too poor already to sustain them for long.

My heart was rent in two to read how Mother could not understand why I didn't write and why the support William had promised had not come. The fear in her words over what had become of me almost sent me over the edge.

"How could he? What have they ever done to him? He promised! He promised, and I believed him!"

Mr. Dalton took the page from my hand and read the letter out loud to the other men, while Annabel returned and took me in her arms.

He concluded his reading. "'Where are you, my dear daughter? I am desperate for word that you are safe and cared for and all of this is some unfortunate mistake. Sending my love and prayers, Mother.'"

My heart bled and my mind raced as I watched Constable Jackson taking hurried notes, then Mr. Dalton handed the letter back to him.

"I have sent my man to retrieve Mrs. Blackwood and her other daughter from Appleby only two hours ago. I hope they will be found and brought here sometime tomorrow." Mr. Dalton's voice was soft and serious.

"Hmm." The constable grunted. "I am very sorry for your distress, Mrs. Soulier. Try to rest now, and we will be back in the morning after breakfast."

Mr. Dalton saw them out, and I heard them asking to speak to Annabel. By that time it was well after midnight. Dr. Briggs made me drink his bitter-tasting sedative, and I lay back on the pillow, spent. My eyes grew heavy with the sight of Gabriel Dalton sitting beside me, his head in his hands.

For a long time, the world was warm and black, and I did not stir. My dreams ebbed and flowed like the River Eden curving its way around the town of Appleby, but altered, full of hidden dangers I had never imagined before. Everywhere I went, William was already there waiting to entrap me, or Mother was slipping off the platform in front of an oncoming train, or Rose was drowning in the river under the weight of a wedding dress twice her size. I screamed, unable to help them or myself, totally at the mercy of the man whose demeanor had gone through such an overnight alteration that I no longer knew who he was.

I was jolted awake by the voice of Constable Jackson. "Mrs. Soulier, wake up. We must speak with you." He shook my shoulder, and I started, sitting up with a head that felt as heavy as an anvil.

I rubbed my eyes. Only the light of a candle lit the cell, and Dr. Garside held it close to me. Two other men in uniform stood behind them.

"What do you know about the money missing from Barclays Bank, Mrs. Soulier?" the constable barked at me.

"What? What money, sir?" I fumbled. "I do not know what you're talking about, sir."

"What about the money missing from Mr. Arnison's till? Or the Bible Church's Building Fund box?" He threw his questions like stones at my aching head.

"I know nothing, sir! I have no knowledge of these things!" I was terrified at his tone and pushed my back against the wall. "What has happened? Where is Mr. Dalton?"

The man himself pushed his way into the room, his unshaven face gray and serious. "Constable, I would like a word with my client before you question her."

Constable Jackson hesitated but nodded slowly and motioned for the others to leave the cell.

Mr. Dalton was breathless and looked like he had not slept at all. "Have they told you that Mr. Joseph Bell has been arrested and charged with theft, Cairstin?"

My eyes grew wide. "No, sir. They asked if I knew anything about Mr. Arnison's missing money and about Barclays Bank and the church Building Fund box." My pulse raced as I tried to take it all in. "What is happening, Mr. Dalton? Why do they think I know something?"

He pulled a stool close and sat beside me, rubbing the stubble on his chin. "I am not sure, as I have no proof, but it seems that your husband has been stealing. The money missing from the bank and the church fund I can guess at, but the money from Arnison's doesn't add up, unless he had an accomplice."

I shook my head, my mind spinning. "Could it be Eliza Salkeld or Mr. Bell?"

"Possibly. He will be questioned shortly. I'll try to find out as much as I can. In the meantime, Cairstin, if you know anything about this, you must tell me. Your life depends on you being completely honest with me."

His words struck me like a hammer. My voice trembled with fear. "I promise you, sir—I know nothing about any of this. I swear it."

He nodded. "I believe you, but you must know that there are those who believe you did know and that you killed your husband for the money."

I gasped. "How can they think such a thing?"

He shook his head. "You also need to be aware of what your husband has been saying about you to all kinds of people in the town." He closed his eyes for a moment, then looked up at the ceiling, as if praying for help. "He has convinced many people that you have gone mad, that you have become a monster at home, demanding he spend all his money on expensive clothes and shoes, that you eat like a pig, and you have tried to beat him when he has not given you all you demand from him."

I sat dumbstruck. A million questions and thoughts clamored for attention, but one finally rose above all the rest. "But why? Why would he say such things, sir? What could he possibly have to gain from slandering me so?"

He sighed heavily. "That is a very good question." He sat back and searched my face. "If he has been planning to steal, then he would also be planning a way to escape with the money. My question is, why did he need to marry you in order to carry out his plan? Did he think he could use you as a scape goat?"

I could not wrap my mind around it. "But surely he knew he would be found out? I have no new dresses, and he burned all my shoes and boots. How can I be accused of killing him for money when it was him who locked me away without food and water?" A wave of anger washed over me. "I am so confused!"

Mr. Dalton patted my arm. "You must stay calm now, Cairstin. Now that they believe you are not in your right mind, you must prove them wrong every moment and remain as calm as possible."

His voice was deadly sober. I nodded with understanding. "I will try, sir. But it is so terrible to be so misunderstood and discredited." I swallowed the hard lump of fear in my tortured throat. "And now they will hang me."

I dropped my face in my hands. The realization that William was truly out to destroy me left me cold.

There was a loud jangling knock at the cell door and Constable Jackson came back in with Dr. Garside. I looked up as they entered, hearing William's laughter echoing through my mind.

Eliza Salkeld was caught at the train station trying to leave Penrith. Mr. Dalton informed me she had little money with her and denied knowing anything about Arnison's missing money. The constable had the dressmakers' flat searched and found nothing suspicious there.

"But if she had done nothing wrong, why try to secretly leave town?" I asked.

"Exactly." Mr. Dalton rubbed his hands on his trousers. "Mr. Bell claims no knowledge of the missing money at Arnison's and was very upset about his dismissal and arrest. I was in his cell when they informed him of Miss Salkeld's attempt to leave town. He seemed truly devastated."

"Do you think the missing money from Arnison's is linked to the money from the bank and the church fund? Perhaps Eliza is lying and knows where all the money is." I felt like I was grasping at straws. My mind felt muddy and slow.

"Yes. It is too much of a coincidence that all of this money should go missing all at once." Mr. Dalton stood and paced the cell.

How had it all come to this? The question was my constant companion and plagued me every waking moment.

At last he paused and turned to me. "I have spoken to Reverend Thomas."

His voice was cold and heavy and speared my soul with dread. I remained silent, waiting for him to continue.

"He is convinced you have used him and the church severely."

The dread spread through my veins. Still, I listened without a word.

"Mr. Soulier was rather thorough in his slander of you within the church leadership. They are convinced you drove him to steal for you and your family."

My eyes drifted from his face seeing nothing. My family, my poor, desolate family.

Mr. Dalton sat on the stool and took my hand. "Cairstin, you must not let these lies sink into your soul. You must find a way to fight them off from taking root in your heart and mind and remember that God sees, God hears, and God knows you are not guilty of these things."

"God? Where is God? Where was He when you gave that letter to Mr. Bell?" I lifted my eyes to him. "If he sees and hears, why has He allowed all this to happen?"

He hung his head over my hand wearily. "I cannot say. All I

know is, we must fight this until we are free of it. We cannot allow this evil to have the final say."

"We?" I whispered.

His eyes met mine. "Yes, my dear, *we*, and it's time you called me Gabriel."

I was charged with murdering William Soulier. If found guilty, I would be hung.

Gabriel was with me when Constable Jackson and Dr. Garside gave me the word. My wounds notwithstanding, I was officially arrested based on what Gabriel called *circumstantial evidence*, that being the ten-pound note found in my corset, and because of the pressure Constable Jackson was receiving from the leadership of the bank and the Bible Church. It seemed it was more important to them to have someone to blame than to pursue the identity of the real thief.

As I promised Gabriel, I was calm to a fault. I answered any and all questions as someone in their right mind and cooperated fully. My hearing, as well as Mr. Bell's, was set for the next morning at the Assembly Room of The George Hotel, above the arcade on Devonshire Street.

I was told to be thankful that the Quarter Sessions court was being held the next day, as it only happened four times a year. I would not have to wait for months in a cell to have a hearing.

Gabriel and Annabel brought me food and water, blankets, and a change of clothes. Mother and Rose had still to be brought from Appleby. Gabriel received word that Rosie was ill and would not be able to travel until morning.

My family. Look what this monster had done to my family.

I received a letter that night, just before Annabel and

Gabriel were leaving me to sleep, another glass of Dr. Briggs's sleeping draft on the table waiting for me.

It was from Reverend Thomas.

> Mrs. Soulier,
>
> I am appalled at your actions and lack of morality. These wicked deeds will not go unpunished by God. If you have any conscience left in you, you will disclose the location of my money and return it immediately.
>
> God will not bless the hands that sew such iniquity, seeking to deceive his church and ministers of His word.
>
> You have been confronted with your sin, Mrs. Soulier! Repent while you still can and may God have mercy on your soul.
>
> Reverend Herbert Thomas

I was awakened by Mr. Dalton stooping over me. "Cairstin, it is morning."

I lifted my weakened, weary frame from the straw mattress, and he helped me to stand. He stepped outside the cell, and Annabel gave me some bread and cheese, then helped me dress. Then a guard came in and clasped heavy irons on my wrists and ankles. My head ached, but that was my only sensation until the cell was unlocked and I stepped out into the narrow hall. My knees gave way, but Gabriel caught me and held on to me until we were standing outside the gaol, the cold fog weaving its searching way between the stone and brick buildings of Penrith.

He spoke gently to me and explained what was to happen, but I remained silent. I felt as though I moved through water—sights and sounds were strangely undefined, though I understood everything happening around me. I was taken by coach to the entrance of the stairs leading above the arcade to the Assembly Hall of The George Hotel, where the Sessions Court met and handed out their justice on local matters.

I struggled to mount the steps in my chains and loathed their rattling in the echoing stairwell. My whole being flooded with humiliation and shame.

The hall was full of people, and I was met with a crescendo of voices as Gabriel escorted me to a seat at the side of the makeshift "bench" where the Quarter Session justices of the peace would soon take their places. Gabriel told me they were there to tell me formally of my charges and take my plea, and the worst part to endure would be the prosecution's witnesses against me. It was a way of judging if my case was indeed valid and merited a trial by jury by the Circuit Court, held in the city of Carlisle to the north.

"The only words you need to say are 'not guilty, Your Honors,'" Gabriel coached. "And don't be afraid of anyone. They can do nothing to you here."

I took a ragged breath and could think only of Mother and Rose. It sank in that Rose was truly ill. If only they could get to Penrith. If only I could see them before . . . before—

"The court shall rise!" a man in a uniform said sternly.

The justices came in from the side door near us and took their seats in their wigs and robes, all local men with proud airs and stoic faces. A chill ran through me, and I shivered, though the room was not cold.

Mr. Bell sat near us to the left. He shot me an angry glare, then looked forward, his nostrils flaring. I was sure he thought I was to blame for the suspicions against him. Couldn't he see how impossible it was for me to steal anything from the till he guarded? I found it hard to imagine him stealing from Mr.

Arnison. As bad as he was, I still believed he had great respect for his employer.

Mr. Arnison sat with a woman I knew to be his wife from the few times I had seen her at the shop. How I longed to go and tell him everything. He was a good man with a kind and fair mind. If only I could convince him I had nothing to do with his losses.

Then there was Reverend and Mrs. Thomas. The reverend glowered at me when our eyes met. Did he truly think I had been using him and the church all along? What had William said to be so convincing? Did he have no pity for the suffering I'd endured at William's hands?

Beside them were Mr. and Mrs. Drinkwater, the couple William had introduced me to that last Sunday I went with him to church. Mr. Drinkwater would have been lied to as well by William, who worked closely with him to raise money for the Building Fund. Money that William had planned to steal. They did not meet my gaze.

Annabel sat unexpectedly with Mrs. Fallowfield, who met my eyes and gave me the slightest of nods.

The official proceedings began. There were small cases of misdemeanor charges, mostly petty theft and disorderly conduct that were tried there on the spot. This took some time to address all those on the lists, and a short recess was taken before the next round of more serious cases were to be heard.

I was allowed to stand for a moment and stretch my stiff limbs. My rattling chains condemned me, and the shackles chafed my wrists and ankles. It was then that something dawned on me. I looked back at the Drinkwaters and softly gasped.

Leaning over to Gabriel, who never left my side, I motioned for him to come near. "I finally think I understand why

William had to marry me in order to execute his crime." I spoke quietly into his ear.

He leaned back and looked me in the eye before bending forward again. "Yes, why?"

"Because only married men were put in charge of the Building Fund money. He had to be a married man to get anywhere near it." We both leaned back and eyed each other with the dawn of understanding.

The court was called to order again, and another list of charges were brought forward, but my mind was too preoccupied to pay much attention.

Gabriel scribbled a note on some paper and showed it to me. "You must be correct. He only needed you to gain the trust of the reverend and church leadership."

I nodded with a sense of relief that something was becoming clear.

Gabriel went back to scribbling, then showed me. "It makes sense now. He needed credibility, and once he had it, you were expendable."

The word echoed in my head. *Expendable.*

I met Gabriel's eyes and swallowed hard. His face set like flint, the muscles in his cheeks flexing. He bent to his paper once more."He meant to kill you, and we must find a way to prove it."

Chapter Twenty-Four

I lay in the chill of the gaol cell on the stinking straw mat, thinking about all that happened that day. The level of evil spoken against me by several witnesses, including the Merrymans, Mr. Crick, Eliza Salkeld, Mr. Bell, Reverend Thomas, Mr. Drinkwater, and a man from the bank, Mr. Noble, was beyond my comprehension. I'd been forced to stand at the wooden bar and listen to them spew lie upon lie about me, that I was mad with an insatiable craving for wealth and pleasure, and that I murdered my husband for not fulfilling my desires and giving me the money he stole at my insistence.

For some reason the worst was not being accused of planning and executing the murder of my husband but that I had fabricated my family's tragic need for assistance to deceive the church into giving me charity I never deserved.

William's slander was both strategic and effective. He'd created a caricature of me, laced with enough fragments of truth to lend his lies credibility. How could I defend myself against such deception when he had died at my hands? How in God's name was I to ever turn the tide of public opinion? It felt like the more time this wicked picture of me was allowed to fester, the more people were eager for it to be true.

I was not afforded any opportunity to speak in my own defense, nor was Gabriel allowed to present any evidence beyond Dr. Briggs's findings about the abuse I'd suffered at William's hands. In the end it was the ten-pound note found in my corset that was the fatal blow. I was charged with murder and theft and informed I would be held at the Penrith gaol until I could stand trial before the Circuit Court magistrates at the assize court in Carlisle, a month hence.

How the people cheered at my disgrace. Never in my wildest imaginings would I have thought people so eager to see the demise of a poor little dressmaker from Appleby. It was almost as if lying under the surface of the normal, everyday folk there was a slumbering hunger for scandal, for something or someone to revile and cast their unspent self-righteous wrath upon.

I was returned to the gaol, and Constable Jackson removed the shackles. Gabriel left me in the cell to seek news of my mother and sister. What did they think of me? How low I had brought them. It would have been better to die in the workhouse than die a criminal's death.

The gaoler rattled his way down the hall, and I heard the voice of Mr. Bell asking if there were any letters for him, from a cell not far from mine. He had been charged with theft and was to await a jury trial in Carlisle as well. He was curtly told there were no letters for him, and the door to my cell was opened.

"Cairy! Oh, my darling!"

I sat up in disbelief. "Mother!" I engulfed her thin frame in my embrace, wishing I could hold on forever.

I did not release her for a long time and poured out tears of sorrow, grief, and shame on her frail shoulder, as if a dam had broken. She held me tight, crying and cooing, stroking my back tenderly, as if I were a babe in her arms.

I looked up to find Gabriel standing with misty eyes near the door, his hat in his hands.

"Thank you," I whispered to him.

Finally, after many words of affection, we disengaged and I held her back from me, looking her over with great concern. "Mother, you are so thin and pale. What have I done to you? How is Rose? How can you ever forgive me?"

I sank onto the bed and hid my face in my hands.

"Hush, child. I am all right, and Rosie is getting better. You have done nothing but what you thought was right, and Mr. Dalton has told me all that has happened."

She sat on a stool and held my face in her hands. "Oh, my love. How awful! How truly terrible that man was to you. You must not blame yourself for this, do you hear?"

She lifted my chin and looked into my eyes. How blessed I was to see her beautiful, loving face again, the face I'd yearned to see for so long.

"Cairy!" she cried. "How can you ever forgive me for allowing that man to marry you? I should have known better. I should have seen what he truly was."

Her words pierced me like a sword. "No, Mam! No! It was not your fault. I should have seen for myself, I only wanted to . . . to help you and Rose so desperately."

"I know, love. I know. And how ill-used you have been for having such a pure heart. I can hardly stand to know what he did to you."

Grasping her shoulders, I pled with her. "Mother, please do not think of it. It is what you and Rose have suffered and will continue to that matters to me now."

She wrapped her arms around me again. I thought my heart

would burst with grief, with pain over what I knew I had brought upon my family.

Gabriel approached and took up the other stool, clearing his throat. "I have no words to express how deeply sorry I am to you both. I feel my own guilt in this matter keenly."

I sniffed and raised my eyes, drying my face. He sat with his head hanging, as if he somehow shared in our grief as profoundly as we.

"What can you mean, Mr. Dalton? You have done nothing but good to me since the day I met you. I can never repay you for the kindness you have shown me." I could not stand to see him in such a state any more than I could my mother.

He shook his head and sighed heavily. "No, Cairstin. You do not know what I suffer for my own cowardice and pride."

His words shocked me. "How can you think such a thing, sir? Have you not stood by me on a day when the whole world has turned against me?"

He rose and paced the tiny room, slapping his hat against his leg in agitation. "No, you do not know." He shook his head again and again. "I was a fool, an utter fool."

Stopping before us, he took his stool again and lay his hat on the table. He did not lift his eyes. "I should have listened to my own conscience." He spoke the words as if they pained him. "I should have ignored the counsel of . . . of other people—"

"Please, sir, what do you mean? What other people?" I whispered, only because I thought if he spoke the words out loud, it might relieve some of his terrible burden.

He took a long breath and finally met my eyes. "I was persuaded not to pursue my interest in you by . . . by Reverend Thomas."

I gasped.

Gabriel looked at me and nodded. "He met me the day after I

visited the Bible Church at your invitation. I was walking down Devonshire Street to leave a message for you, thanking you for the invitation and inviting you to join me at St. Andrew's the next Sunday, when he stopped me outside of Arnison's shop door."

Running his hand through his hair, he stood and paced again.

Mother sat beside me on the bed and faced him with me. I barely breathed the question, "What did he say?"

"He said that I would do better than to waste my interests on a poor dressmaker like you." He faced me, and ice ran through my heart. "That I should stick to charming ladies within my own sphere and not stoop to such a low level."

I hung my head. "He was correct, sir. Look what I have become."

Suddenly he was on his knees before me. "No, Cairy! He was entirely wrong, and his actions have proven it. He only wanted you for his special disciple, William Soulier. His success in putting the two of you together was only motivated by his own ego."

He took my hands and continued. "It took me a few days to realize that I was a fool for doubting my own heart. I only wish now that I had spoken to you in person before I was called away instead of writing you to let you know I hoped our acquaintance would continue and that I wanted to know you better."

My heart squeezed with regret at his words. *If only . . . if only . . .*

He lifted my chin to face him. "And, my dear, you need to know that I am only who I am today because my father married a beautiful little dressmaker like you."

I looked at him wide eyed and shook my head. "Oh, sir, if only—"

He took the stool again and drew it very close, looking at

Mother, his voice full of anger. "My hesitation was inexcusable. None of this would have happened if I had not been a prideful coward and listened to a meddling old man."

Turning to me with pleading eyes, he gave me a crooked little smile. "I've felt a great affection for you since the first time I saw you drop those silly fabric bolts on Mr. Arnison's floor. I don't care that my father was a successful accountant—he felt the same way when he first saw my mother in the very same drapery where Mr. Arnison was a tailor's apprentice with your father. I'm sure Mother would have known him. That's why my family have been friends of the Arnisons for all these years."

Mother sat so still beside me that I almost forgot her presence. She shifted and finally spoke. "Mr. Dalton, I believe you two need a bit of privacy to talk this out. Will you have the guard unlock the door? I will be waiting right outside."

She stood and lay her hand on my cheek. "Cairy, it is time you think for yourself and forget what anyone else has said. You must trust that God loves you enough to give you what you need to make your own decisions for your own life, especially now that it hangs in the balance."

Her words took my breath away. I always felt my own judgment was not to be trusted, but where had listening only to the voices around me and not believing I was worthy of anything better gotten me?

Gabriel called the gaoler, and Mother stepped out, standing with her back to the barred window.

"Please believe me, Cairstin." Gabriel's voice was rough with emotion. "If I had only known . . . if I had known the danger you were in, I would have been there to protect you." He bowed his head. "Can you ever forgive me?"

My arms ached to embrace him, to hold him against me and lay my head on his strong chest and pour out my love for him, but I sat frozen, lost in his words.

"There is nothing to forgive, Gabriel. You did what you thought was right, and I cannot blame you in any way. What's done is done. We have only what lies before us now." He opened his mouth to speak, but I went on. "You cannot know how much your friendship and generosity means to me. What would I do without you?"

Suddenly he stood and paced, his muscles tense and eyes flashing. "But I am too late to save you from that monster." Stopping, he faced me. "Please, I must have your forgiveness so I can be freed from this terrible guilt to serve you better." His face fell as he sat again, and my heart broke. "Cairstin, you did not deserve any of this, and you do not fully understand the danger ahead of you. If I had not allowed myself to be influenced, think of how different our lives would be."

I turned my face from him in agony. "I cannot think of it, Gabriel, for it is a torture to me. I must only think of here and now and how sorry I am for my own folly in not trusting my own heart as well. If I am to forgive you, then you must also forgive me."

He sighed and looked down at his hands. "I cannot see enough of the road ahead to speak as a man of wisdom, especially when it comes to matters of my own heart"—he met my eyes—"but if you are willing to start afresh, then I will have the hope I need to face whatever lies before us. You have my word."

"But why, sir?" I pled. "What have I ever done to deserve such a promise from you? What possible gain could there be for you in seeing me through this nightmare? You are a young man with a bright future ahead of you. Why sacrifice your reputation for my sake?"

He breathed a slight, rye chuckle. "You know, I have been

looking all my life for the chance to do something truly meaningful in the world, for some way to repay God for the blessings he has bestowed on me, which are many." He paused and swallowed hard, then locked eyes with me and took my hand. "You, Cairstin, you are my purpose. When I caught you before you fell before a train that day, I was startled by my fear for you and for how alive I felt holding you that brief moment in my arms. It was the most important thing I have ever done in my life. I cannot allow you to fall before this heinous charge without doing all I can to help you again."

I covered my face with my hands. "Oh, sir. It is too much for me. I am not worthy of your society, nor your aid. What can I ever do to repay you for saving my life once, let alone twice? I have nothing but misery to offer you in return."

"No, Cairstin. You can offer me your friendship, which I sorely need." He held out his hand to me. "Now, shall we forgive each other and agree to a new beginning?"

I fell to my knees before him and took his hand, bowing over it. "Thank God for you, Gabriel Dalton. God bless you. God bless you."

Chapter Twenty-Five

That night I lay awake on the straw mat in the blackness of my cell. Something within the core of my being had altered, and I knew I was a different person than the one who had awoken in that cell the morning before. To know that Gabriel Dalton was my friend, my true and good friend, was a gift like I had never known. And beyond that knowledge, I had a deeper understanding that somehow God placed him in my life, that his presence was more than mere coincidence or chance.

And if that was true, then God had not abandoned me or my family. And perhaps God really did care for me and all this suffering was not without meaning.

I went to sleep clinging with all my soul to these thoughts and refused to allow all the others screaming for my attention to push them out. I had a friend, and God, the real God, loved me and had tried to tell me of the danger I was in all along.

I was allowed to have my Bible back from Constable Jackson's evidence box, and I was reading a passage about the sufferings of Christ when Gabriel returned the next morning with Mother. Rose was not allowed to visit due to her young age, but mother brought me a note from her.

As I read it, I laughed through my tears. "Rose calls you a 'barie bloke,' Gabriel. She must like you very much."

It was wonderful to see a smile on his face. "She is a dear, and I will tell her I think she is a 'barie lass' when I see her this evening."

How good it felt to smile a little and have this tiny connection with my sister, to have my mother wrap her arms around me and kiss my cheeks. *God has not abandoned me.*

"I have thanked Mr. Dalton a hundred times already this morning for all he is doing for us and for you, Cairstin. What a godsend you are, sir."

Gabriel smiled down on Mother. "It gives me great joy to be of service to you all, Mrs. Blackwood." He motioned her to take a stool and for me to sit as well. Then he took the other stool and produced a packet of papers and a pencil.

"Now, ladies, we have just under a month to put together a defense, and we had best get started." He sighed and gave me a sober look. "It's going to be a long morning, Cairstin, as I have many questions for you and want you to answer them in as much detail as you possibly can, all right?"

"Of course. I am ready." I sat up straight on the edge of the bed and listened for his first question.

"Very good. Now, from what the prosecution presented as evidence yesterday, we have a pretty good idea of what they will try to bring against you at your trial in Carlisle. So our job will be to present as many facts as we can to refute their case, and to bring out any evidence that will more than prove you acted only in self-defense. We must also dig as hard and wide as we can to bring a case against your husband."

At this he shifted uneasily on his seat. "Actually, if you don't mind, I would like to refer to him as Soulier from now on, at least for our own discussions. Would that be more suitable for you?"

"Yes, of course. Thank you for your consideration, sir."

"And we can forgo the 'sir' and 'madam' as well, don't you think?" he asked with wink and with a half smile.

I returned his smile and nodded shyly.

"Splendid. Now, I want you to think back before your wedding and tell me everything you can remember about Soulier, especially the things that seemed out of place to you at the time. For instance, did he do anything out of the ordinary, or did he have any strange habits? Did he ever tell you anything that caused you alarm?"

It was a lot to think about. I rummaged through my memory, all painful to me now, and landed on one that had greatly troubled me at the time.

"Soulier told me he had been engaged to be married before but the marriage had not taken place."

Both my mother's and Gabriel's eyes shot to mine. "Cairstin, you never told me!" Mother cried.

Gabriel's brows knitted, and he made a note. "And when did he tell you this? Can you remember?"

I tried to recall and shook my head. "I don't remember which day precisely, but it was not long after our courtship began, and that was only a short time after New Year's Day. Maybe a week or so after?"

He nodded. "Close enough. Now tell me, what exactly did he say?"

"Well, I remember he walked me home from Arnison's and we were standing in the entrance to Sutton Yard. We were saying good night when, well, I suppose he misspoke, or perhaps he pretended to." A light illuminated the scene in my mind's eye. "He said he was very glad that I was nothing like

. . . and then he paused, as if he had let something slip. But now looking back on it, I think he meant to bring up the subject."

"Interesting," Gabriel mused. "Go on."

"Yes, and when I asked him to complete his thought, he spoke as if he wanted to drop the subject, but I could see in his eyes that he wanted me to pull it out of him." The memory made me queasy all over again, with an added layer of new anger on top.

"So I urged him to tell me, and he said he was glad that I was nothing like his former fiancée, Lydia Netherwood."

Gabriel went to writing, then turned back to me. "Did he say anything more about this Lydia Netherwood? Why didn't their marriage take place?"

"Yes. We didn't speak any more about it that night, but the next evening he walked me all the way to sit on the median in the middle of Corney Place so we could talk in public without anyone overhearing."

"Corney Place? Wasn't that an odd choice?" Gabriel wrinkled his nose.

"Indeed. I was terribly uncomfortable, but he insisted that it was a way of protecting my reputation." At this I moaned and shook my head. "Oh, Mother, how could I not see how ridiculous it was?"

She shook her head. "We often don't see what is right in front of our nose, my love. Now, continue. What did he have to say?"

I sighed and picked up the story. "He told me he'd had a position at a bank in London and that his supervisor was unfair to him, not giving him the promotion he deserved. When the supervisor hinted that if he would court his daughter and propose to her, he would give him a grand promotion, Soulier did so. But after his proposal, the man told him he wouldn't get his promotion until after the wedding, and he claimed that Lydia's personality changed completely—"

I paused. "But isn't that what happened with him? Soulier's personality changed completely the evening of our wedding. He was never the same again." A shiver ran through me as I recalled the stone-cold look on his face when I stood before him in my bridal nightgown and he sent me to bed without another look.

Mother smoothed her hand over my back and brought me back to the present. "It's all right, love. He will never hurt you again."

"I am sorry to have to make you relive such troubling memories, Cairstin. Can you continue?"

Blinking hard, I took a deep breath and nodded. "He told me how sorry he was, that he was young and foolish then, and how devoted he was to me . . ." I wanted to be done talking about it. "That's all I can remember, really."

Gabriel leaned back and tapped the pencil on his square jaw, then bent forward. "Did he tell you any details about these people? The name of the bank, which part of London it was?"

I shook my head. "No, nothing more specific about the bank, but he did say that Lydia was pretty and had hair as black as night. He said after their engagement she would tell vicious lies about him and even fly at him in violent rages if she didn't get her way—"

Gasping, I looked incredulously from Mother to Gabriel. "Oh no! It wasn't true! He has been telling the same lies about me. Oh dear. What if he did the same to that woman as he did to me?"

My heart raced, and I held Mother's hand, looking urgently to Gabriel. "We must find her. We must find out what he did to her."

He stood and paced the floor. "Yes, if I could find this woman, we might learn much more about Soulier from her. But where do I begin to look? He probably lied about her name, and London is far too large a city to go wandering around looking for women with black hair." He sat down, defeated. "There is also the chance that she never existed. He could have made her up to manipulate you."

"How I wish I could remember more or that he had told me more, that I had asked him more about her." I hung my head, wishing I could see then what I saw now. "I just wanted to get beyond it and have things be all right between us again, like a fool. Like a little fool."

~

We talked for hours about many things, including the incident with the manager at Barkhouse Lodge. Mother and Gabriel were terribly upset by the tale and horrified at all I went through to find them a place in Penrith.

Gabriel turned my attention to Mr. Bell, which was an irritating though easier subject to discuss. I told about seeing him and Eliza laughing over a letter in the drapery, most likely Gabriel's letter to me. He was incensed, and rightly so, and said he would have to have a word with Mr. Bell about it. The memory made me want to scream.

Then there was the episode with Eliza in the cutting room and Mrs. Langley's dress with the hidden needle. I was sure Mr. Bell was the one who'd placed it there to cause me trouble. Knowing the man, who coughed frequently, was just down the hall in a cell of his own gave me such a strange feeling. As much as I disliked him, I was confounded as to how he got himself there and told Gabriel as much.

By the time we heard church bells sounding the noon hour,

I was spent. Gabriel and Mother took their leave, and I ate the small dinner they had brought me alone.

After a short nap, I awoke to the keys rattling at the door of my cell, and Gabriel entered with Dr. Briggs.

He greeted me kindly. "Good afternoon, Mrs. Soulier. I have come to see how you are getting along."

"I am tolerably well, thank you, Doctor. Having enough to eat and drink does wonders, doesn't it?"

"Indeed, it does, my dear," he agreed. "Let me take a look at you."

He examined my neck and looked down my throat. "Your bruises are healing and the swelling is going down, but I still detect some roughness in your voice, which may or may not improve with time. Thank God the scoundrel didn't hold on to you long enough to break your larynx or your windpipe, or you wouldn't have anything more to say ever again!"

Gabriel hovered over me. "Yes! Thank God you were able to fight him off as soon as you did, Cairstin. One or two more seconds of pressure like that and you would have been killed."

Their words brought back the sensation of William's hands around my throat squeezing harder and harder. I shivered, and my pulse quickened as I clutched the side of the bed, trying to bring myself back to the present.

The men must have noticed my distress. "I'm so sorry, Cairstin. I should be more mindful of what I say." Gabriel sat beside me and took my hand.

"That goes for me as well, my dear. You have had quite a shock, and your constitution is naturally sensitive to things that bring on recollections of your distress. Might I suggest that when this happens, and your body returns to the understandable state of fear it remembers, that you do not shame yourself for feeling so. It takes time for these wounds of the soul to heal, and they heal much more slowly than the wounds of the body."

Just listening to the wisdom in the doctor's voice calmed me, and the spell passed. "Thank you, Dr. Briggs. I am blessed to have you watching over me."

"Dr. Briggs has been watching over me since I was a child. I would recommend him to anyone," Gabriel said affectionately.

My ribs were mending, though the hardness of my bed made them ache throughout the night. My hands and knees were all but healed, though I was sure the scarring would never go away.

"Dr. Briggs," I said shyly, "I was wondering if there is a way to prove . . . that is . . ." I glanced at Gabriel awkwardly. "Is there any way to prove that a woman is still, still a . . ."

"A virgin, my dear?" the doctor interjected calmly. "Well yes, there is. But it involves an intimate examination with more than one doctor present, I'm afraid."

I looked down at my hands and laced my fingers. "I think I would like such an examination, if you would also be present, doctor. It means something to me."

Dr. Briggs leaned back on his stool while I avoided looking at Gabriel.

"Hmm." The doctor grunted. "I will arrange it, madam. It may take a few days to arrange, but you may consider it done."

~

It was quickly discovered that the smaller of the two keys from William's pockets was to the lock on the Bible Church's Building Fund box. The other seemed to be for a regular door, but it matched nothing at the bank. Gabriel was certain the missing money would turn up when the matching door was found, but finding it was proving impossible.

Gabriel sent word to his connections in London to search for a dark-haired young woman named Lydia Netherwood, who had possibly been wounded or killed by her fiancé, William Soulier. It was a long shot, but it didn't hurt to ask.

The small papers I had flung onto the floor from William's pockets were another mystery. They were receipts of some kind, but the business names had been torn off, leaving only the amount paid for each.

For the next few days Gabriel, Mother, and I engaged in lengthy sessions of questions, answers, and memories, some difficult to bring to the surface. At one session, I recalled the morning I woke early after a disturbing dream and left the dressmakers' flat to walk in the mist before going to work and thought I saw William leaving Sutton Yard. It was only a few days after our engagement was announced at the Bible Church.

"I entered the little hall where we hung our coats and bonnets and felt prompted to touch the other girls' coats."

Gabriel cocked his head. "Curious. And what did you find?"

"Annabel's and Mary's coats were dry and warmer than mine, but Eliza's was damp and cold."

"So you think she was out meeting with Soulier?" Gabriel asked.

"It's the only reason I can think of why she went out." The thought of William having clandestine meetings with that girl vexed me to the core. "Later that day she went to Mr. Arnison to inform him that I intended to leave my position at the shop a fortnight after my wedding. I had said nothing to anyone of this plan, as Soulier told me not to. He had to have been the one to tell her, and now that I think of it, he probably asked her to tell Mr. Arnison ahead of me to . . . to . . ."

Mother shivered beside me. "To discredit you to Mr. Arnison. Oh, how I'd like to get my hands on that girl!"

Her words brought a smile to my face. The image of mother taking Eliza to task was both heartening and amusing.

Gabriel stood and paced with his arms folded across his chest, which he did when the wheels of his mind were turning quickly. "Sutton Yard. Sutton Yard." He repeated to himself, tapping the pencil on his chin. "I'll take a walk over there today and ask around. Perhaps someone saw them talking together."

He regained his seat and wrote some notes. Then he lifted his chin and stared into space. "Why would Eliza want to damage your reputation in such a way? Why did she and Mr. Bell sabotage your work the way they did?" His eyes met mine, and he raised his fine brows. "And why did she cause Annabel to be harmed so hideously?"

I followed his thoughts and added, "What if it wasn't purely out of spite? What if there was a greater purpose to her actions?"

Gabriel rose and went to the door, calling through the window for the gaoler, who came jingling down the hall.

"Please excuse us, Cairstin." He took up Mother's coat to help her into it. "I need to speak to Annabel immediately and take that walk up to Sutton Yard."

Mother hugged me and left with him. I stood at the door and watched as Gabriel paused before Mr. Bell's cell door. I could tell he wanted to speak to him but shook his head as he escorted Mother out of sight.

When the gaoler followed them, I screwed up my courage and called out, "Mr. Bell, will you talk to me? Mr. Bell."

I heard him cough and moan. "Mr. Bell, are you unwell?"

"I am," he answered weakly, "and all because of you."

His coughing continued, and I waited for it to subside to answer. "Please Mr. Bell. I am very sorry that you are in this position. Will you allow me to ask you a few questions?"

"Leave me alone, murderer. I have nothing to say to you."

Chapter Twenty-Six

Gabriel did not return until the next day, with Annabel instead of Mother. He reported to me about his discoveries, and the more he connected the threads of all that had happened, the more the tapestry looked like a comprehensive picture.

He interviewed Mr. Noble from Barclays Bank and found out a great deal about how William had managed to steal by skimming off small amounts from the deposits he was entrusted with, giving a correct receipt to the client but fixing the interior paperwork to reflect the deposit as being the amount he put in after taking some off the top.

William had begun his theft only a fortnight before the wedding and continued until his last day, in which he took a formidable amount from one large account, probably because he meant to escape that night or the next day.

Gabriel also spent time interviewing Reverend Thomas and Mr. Drinkwater about the church's Building Fund. Since only married men were allowed on the fundraising committee, William had only gained access to the money in the donation box and the church account at Barclays after our wedding.

This revelation shed more light on his insistence that our wedding go forward despite a blizzard. He was on a tight time schedule and wanted nothing to stand in his way.

The weight on my chest lessened with each new insight, but at the same time left me shaking my head at my own gullibility. I was deeply touched and humbled by how much work Gabriel was doing outside my cell—I noticed little gray circles under his eyes. My heart overflowed with gratitude and affection.

Annabel's hand had healed enough for her to show me the damage under the bandages. It was horrible to see. The red, yellow, and purple skin of her fingers was melted over the bones, and they were curved inward. She would never open her hand again.

I held it gently and cried over it, sorrow, anger, and compassion wringing my heart. "Oh, my friend. How could she do such a thing? What can be done?"

She gave me a wry smile. "It'll all be sorted out in the end. Besides, your mam is teaching me how to get by with one hand. She's remarkable with all she can do."

I shook my head in wonder. "How strange that you have been put together just when you needed each other."

There was more here to consider, such as how God allowed people to suffer, then provided what you needed to endure it. But these were deep and lofty thoughts I tucked away to ponder during my many vacant hours in my cell at night.

"The attack on Annabel is an important part of the mystery we are trying to unravel," Gabriel said. "I've written down the pieces of the puzzle on some cards for us to start to put together. Cairstin, will you stand and let us lay them out on the bed?"

I stood and watched as he placed many small cards out on top of the blanket.

"I am laying them in as close to chronological order as I can. Now, ladies, take a look and see if there are any cards that might tie to one another or if there is anything to add. Don't second-guess your intuition."

The task felt overwhelming, but as I read through the cards and examined the order, some things fit together, with hindsight. My eyes were drawn toward the end of the collection, where several cards in a row read "Wedding," "Wedding Night," "Annabel's Burn," "Isolating Cairstin," "Burning Shoes"—they caught my eye.

I pointed to the cards. "Look here. If indeed Soulier and Eliza were working together, there seemed to be a great need to get Annabel and me out of the way, as if we posed a threat or would have caught them in something."

"Yes." Gabriel took up the thought. "It all seems to be a progression of luring you into marriage but at the same time setting you up to be discredited or even blamed for their actions."

Annabel chimed in. "Why would she and Soulier need me out of Arnison's? If she was working with Mr. Bell ta steal from the till, they could have done that whenever they were in the drapery and I'd have never known."

Gabriel tucked in his chin and pressed his lips together, then tilted his head. "What if she didn't need you out of Arnison's but out of Sutton Yard instead?"

My anger surged, and I wanted to rip something. "Perhaps she didn't want you to find out she was sneaking around meeting Soulier there. That terrible girl!"

Gabriel nodded. "It only makes sense they were working together. Cairstin, didn't you say something about Eliza telling you that Soulier didn't love you?"

"I did." The light registered. "I think I understand now. She thought he didn't love me because he was in love with her."

Gabriel's eyes narrowed. "But why didn't he just marry her if that's all he needed to get access to the church fund?"

"I think I know," Annabel whispered. "Reverend Thomas never paid any attention to Eliza, but he took ta Cairstin from the day he met her. And Soulier helping Cairstin when her father died made him look like a mighty fine Christian. I'm sure the reverend encouraged him ta pursue Cairstin instead of Eliza."

Gabriel picked up the card reading "Wedding Night" and grunted. "I wonder what kind of promise he made her to keep her affections when he married another woman?"

My eyes turned to the cell door. "And where does that leave Mr. Bell?"

The next time Dr. Briggs visited me, he informed me I would be examined the next day by himself and Dr. Garside. I wasn't sure how I felt about Dr. Garside's presence, but knew I had little choice in the matter. At least if the coroner knew I was still a virgin, it might lend me more credibility with him, and credibility was something I desperately needed.

I asked Dr. Briggs if he would be so kind as to look in on Mr. Bell, as I could hear his coughing day and night and knew he was truly sick. He said he would ask the constable and was sure it would be all right. I couldn't help thinking Mr. Bell had been ill-used by Eliza and hoped that his stony resistance to speaking with me would start to crack.

The next day I was subjected to the most humiliating invasion of my womanly dignity I could imagine. As I lay on the cell bed holding Mother's hand, the two doctors examined my lower parts, and though they were extremely gentle, I was touched in places I had not been since I was a bairn.

I was sure my face was crimson when they allowed me to sit back up.

Dr. Briggs patted my hand reassuringly. "Well, my dear, your claim to remaining pure is confirmed. It will be duly noted in your records that your marriage was not consummated and therefore—you will be very glad to know this—is not legally binding."

The revelation stunned me. "You mean that I . . . that I'm . . . that—"

Dr. Garside stood with a chuckle. "Yes, Mrs. Soulier. You are free to ask the court to annul your marriage. Once the annulment is complete, you are no longer bound to the legal name of Soulier and can go back to your maiden name."

"Oh, Mam!" I clung to her with the first hint of joy in my soul for many, many days.

This news was a boon for my spirits and gave me a new will to fight for the chance to live beyond my trial, but my hopes were dashed when Gabriel later came with a dark look of foreboding on his dear face.

"I'm afraid I have some difficult news. Eliza Salkeld has disappeared. Now it will be harder than ever to prove her connection to Soulier and obtain any justice for Mr. Arnison or Annabel."

~

Why had it not occurred to me before that Eliza had never come to visit Mr. Bell at the gaol? Gabriel said it was only more proof that her courtship with him was nothing but a farce. That she had used him only as a means of gaining what she wanted, and he was flattered enough by her pretty attentions to go along with her designs.

My pity for the man grew, much to my surprise, and after Dr. Briggs examined him and gave him medication for his cough, I tried again that evening, while the guard was out of the hall, to coax him into conversation.

"Mr. Bell, please, will you speak to me?"

I heard a rustling in his cell but there was no reply.

I kept my voice low and gentle. "Please, Mr. Bell, I am concerned for your health. Was Dr. Briggs able to help you today?"

He coughed, and I heard him come closer to his door. "Leave me alone, Mrs. Soulier. I want nothing to do with you."

"I'm sorry you're not feeling well. Has Eliza come to see you?" I already knew the answer but wanted to try and engage him.

"That's none of your business. Now leave me alone, I tell you!"

I heard him shuffle away and nearly gave up. I wanted to ask him about why he didn't give me Gabriel's letter but knew it would only make him angry. Then another thought occurred to me. "Mr. Bell, I don't believe you stole that money from Mr. Arnison. Do you want to know who I think is the real thief?"

I waited by my window, holding my breath. At last I heard him stir.

"Why do you think it wasn't me?"

"Because you have too much respect for Mr. Arnison, and you loved your position there. You never would have done something like that to jeopardize your job," I said with genuine confidence.

"Huh, is that so? Then who do you think is the culprit?" His question was laced with sarcasm.

"I think Eliza Salkeld lied to you and used you. I think she stole the money when you weren't looking. She has left Penrith and is nowhere to be found."

Chapter Twenty-Seven

A month turned into weeks, and weeks turned into days as my extradition to Carlisle and the date of my trial loomed before me. Not much more was found out after Eliza disappeared, though Gabriel did all he could to join the pieces of the puzzle together. There remained little evidence and too much speculation about events, and without solid proof, my case looked flimsy indeed.

Gabriel kept me ignorant of public opinion against me for as long as he could, but finally told me gravely of the newspaper reports, which painted me as a deviant woman with an insatiable greed that drove my husband to steal, then I murdered him in cold blood. It was emphasized that I had prior knowledge about the hook and its exact position when I baited him into a fight and strategically placed myself in the hall in just the right position to push him to his death.

He brought only one article to the cell to show me, and that was one printed in a London paper that offered a more balanced depiction of events—that I claimed I killed William in self-defense because I was brutalized by my husband, and it cited Dr. Briggs's report on my physical state upon arrest.

Many hours I spent reading my Bible and getting to know God better for myself. In time my reading helped to replace all the nonsense that had so easily influenced me before. I came to realize that although Reverend Thomas might have been well intended, he also took his positions and his supposed authority too far.

I committed some of my favorite verses in Psalm 3 to memory and would speak them aloud in the night when the panic would overtake me to the point of madness in my damp, dark cell.

> "'*LORD, how are they increased that trouble me! many are they that rise up against me. Many there be which say of my soul, There is no help for him in God. But thou, O LORD, art a shield for me; my glory, and the lifter up of mine head.*'"

The words brought light into the darkness around me. Realizing that God had truly heard my prayers left me in awe, and I began to feel God's own presence in the cell with me. Even if I were to hang, the faith that had been growing in my heart helped me to know He would be with me even then.

Though my stay in the Penrith gaol was awful, it was graced with the blessed presence of my mother, Annabel, and Gabriel, and our friendship and affection deepened by the day.

By the time the day for my removal to Carlisle came, I had prayed all my prayers and resigned myself to whatever fate lay before me

Mother and Annabel helped me prepare for the journey, which, ironically, would be taken by rail. The trip that would have taken most of a day by coach would now take less than an hour, hurrying me toward the noose that awaited me.

Constable Jackson was in charge of my extradition, and he arrived early in the morning to clasp me in irons and lead me from the cell. The gaoler opened Mr. Bell's cell after I passed, and I met the man's eyes fleetingly, too fast to learn anything from his glance. He was made to follow us, and our chains mimicked each other, jingling up the stairs.

Gabriel joined me as I came through the door into the fresh air, squinting in the sun I hadn't seen in a month's time. Mr. Bell and I were loaded into separate carriages, and Gabriel held my hand as we ascended the hill to the Penrith Station.

I gasped at the crowd waiting for a glimpse of the murderess and breathed a sigh of relief when a gate to the side of the station opened and the coach pulled inside. There were still many people inside the station, but their mood was less mob-like, and they stood back as Gabriel handed me down.

I caught a glimpse of the castle ruins as we walked toward the station building. It felt like years since Gabriel had carried me out of the rocks with bloody hands and knees. More than years . . . a whole lifetime.

The people pushed and shoved to get a look at me. When someone in the mass of faces shouted "Murderer!" he was joined by a roar of voices overwhelming me with a torrent of hatred. I faltered, but Gabriel put his arm around my waist and kept me on my feet.

He hurried us inside and took me to a small room with two guards to wait for the train, joined by the pale and worn Mr. Bell, no longer his stiff and proper former self. There were red rings around his eyes, and his clothes were dirty and disheveled. He met my eyes briefly, then turned away and stared at the door.

My heart throbbed mercilessly in my chest as I prayed,

standing next to Mr. Bell. *Lord, how are they increased that trouble me! But thou, O Lord, art a shield for me; my glory, and the lifter up of mine head.*

Gabriel assured me that Mother, Rose, and Annabel were all waiting on the platform to board the train, as were the witnesses from Penrith who would testify at the trial. I hung my head, despising the shame I was putting my family and friends through. My chest felt the weight of the world crushing down upon it, and any ember of lingering hope was extinguished when I heard the train whistle blowing louder and louder.

Funny, I thought. *I never heard the train whistle from my cell in the basement of the gaol*. Hearing it again felt like the return of William's ghost mocking me. *"You are a wicked woman and deserve to die."*

Perhaps I truly was? Could there have been a thought lurking in the back of my mind of the spike in the hall beside the door? I honestly knew that the thought of killing William had not crossed the forefront of my mind, but was there really something evil inside me that knew all along his death was my only way of escape?

My stomach swam with nausea as the door was opened and I was escorted by Constable Jackson and Gabriel out to the waiting train. I looked desperately for a glimpse of Mother and Rose, but the choking steam wafted in my face, causing me to close my eyes. I stumbled but was caught once again by my faithful friend and passed into a car near the rear of the train, my chains jangling all the way.

I was seated beside the window opposite the station and was glad there were few people on the other platform gawking at me like vultures over a corpse. Gabriel was not allowed to be with me in the prisoners' car, and Constable Jackson sat beside me, panting.

I bowed my head, my bonnet closing off the rest of the world, but I started at the jolt of the train, and we were moving fast to the north out of the station, toward my final unraveling.

As we traveled at a dizzying speed, jostling our way through the winter-brown sheep fields with their stacked stone fences and leafless trees, I thought of my beloved Appleby and the prayer I'd prayed the night before I first left for Penrith. *Please, God. Please let me see this place again.* It was a prayer that would likely not be answered again, and I couldn't help the tears of grief that spilled over. I caught my weeping reflection in the window as the world whipped by and thought about that girl, standing in the freezing cold.

Look what has happened to you, Cairy. How far you have wandered down a path to violence and disgrace. No one would have ever guessed how low. No one.

I thought long and hard about my dreams of the River Eden. In not a one did I ever resurface from the water. Could it be a sign?

I felt like the character of some tragic novel or play, forced into a role on a stage for the world to leer at and judge. I hated the dramatics of it all, the public display. If I had to die, why couldn't I be hung quietly and tucked in a grave? Close down the theater and send the audience away.

The whistle blew as the train slowed, and I thought my heart would stop when the massive Carlisle Station came into view. There were many tracks and platforms, with people walking on bridges above them, and the ceiling was so high it took my breath away. We came to a stop, and I gaped. The steam of the engines, the massively curved iron braces, and the sounds of hissing and shouting gave the place an otherworldly quality, making me feel small and insignificant.

But thou, O Lord, art a shield for me . . .

Constable Jackson, who had been silent the entire way, helped me to my feet, and I rattled my way toward the door of the car, aware that Mr. Bell followed closely behind. A crowd had gathered on the platform there as well, but I saw Gabriel forcing his way through the people and was there to take my arm when my foot left the step.

Other constables in uniform were there, and they gathered around me, Mr. Bell, and my escorts and carved a way through the shouting horde to the exit of the building, where more people were crowded to see the murdering dressmaker of Penrith. I kept my focus on putting one foot in front of the other and not tripping on my chains, which scraped on the cobblestones.

I caught the sight of the grand square around me, the enormous buildings surrounding it and the round towers of the ancient citadel to my left. This formidable fortress was the place where my fate would be decided. A closed carriage stood before me, and I was bundled inside with Constable Jackson and Gabriel.

The door shut and I groaned, holding my face in my hands. "How can this be! How can so many people hate me so much?"

Gabriel wrapped his strong arms around me and held my head to his chest. "Try not to look at them, Cairstin. They only know what the papers have told them. They are like sheep without a shepherd."

"Huh! Indeed." The constable huffed. "I've never seen such witlessness in all my days!"

The ride to our destination took seconds, but I was glad they had not made me walk the distance in my shackles. The carriage was led under a massive Tudor stone building attached to the west tower of the citadel, into a tunnel, where we stopped. The gates closed behind us.

~

The cell I was taken to in the belly of the citadel was small and damp and smelled of mold, with only a mattress on the floor and bucket in the corner. Gabriel was barely given enough time to say goodbye before the guards forced him out and locked me in. I watched out the tiny barred window as he strode past the next cell, where Mr. Bell was being placed.

Our trials would be held back to back in the morning, mine first, then his. Since he was one of the prosecution's witnesses against me, Gabriel thought he would be given a lighter sentence in exchange for his testimony. No wonder he didn't want to speak to me.

It was nearly dark in the cell. My shackles had been left on, and I jangled awkwardly to take off my bonnet and wrap, laying them on the mattress, then I lay my weary, aching body down. This might be my last night on this earth, and I wanted to be as right with God as I knew how.

Only God knew how long I prayed, confessing every sin I could ever remember committing and asking for Christ's mercy and forgiveness. I prayed for everyone I could think of, especially those who had shown me any amount of kindness in my life. My prayers for Mother, Rose, Annabel, and Gabriel were long and the hardest of all.

Finally I whispered the words one last time to the blank blackness surrounding me, "'But thou, O Lord, art a shield for me; my glory, and the lifter up of mine head.'"

Chapter Twenty-Eight

I have no inkling of when the sun rose, but the guard opened my cell door and handed in a bowl of salty gruel and a cup of water. I bent my head and thanked God for what might be my last meal, and ate it trying not to think too far ahead. I left enough water to wash my face and hands, and when they came for me, I was ready.

Mr. Bell watched me from his cell window, but I did not meet his eyes. It was too late to appeal to him any longer. I felt numb as the guards took me down several corridors, then up a flight of stairs. As I ascended, I heard the low roar of voices above me. When the door at the top opened, the sound swept over me, and I emerged into a large courtroom teeming with people.

The noise subsided slightly, and I heard a train whistle as I was led to the side of the magistrates' bench, to the dock where I would stand for my trial. The room was paneled in dark, rich wood, with tall windows above letting in light, as well as the brass candle chandeliers hanging from the ceiling. The floor was carpeted in green, and I wondered if it was Scheele's green.

Silly thought to have in such a moment. Over my head was hung a large sheet of wood at an angle, the one Gabriel told me would allow my voice to be better heard around the room.

The shackles chafed at my wrists and my palms were sweaty, but I stood as still as possible and kept my eyes on the wooden barrier before me. Only a moment later Gabriel's face, framed by a short white wig, took that space, and he looked deeply into my eyes.

He was in a black robe and motioned for me to lean down. He spoke into my ear. "There has been a new development regarding Annabel's burn. Mrs. Fallowfield has come to testify on your behalf if need be."

I looked at him wide eyed but had no time to question him as a man in uniform came in, stood before the bench, and called out, "The court shall rise!"

My gaze followed Gabriel to the near end of a long table in front of the taller bench. The two magistrates in their long white wigs and black robes, with white linen bands tied at their necks, entered, one short and stodgy, the other tall and gray. They were joined by other dignitaries, and they took their seats on the raised platform behind the long wooden barrier with the magistrates in the middle, barely looking my way.

I dared to glance around the room and spotted Mother, Rose, and Annabel smiling encouragingly at me from the gallery. I nodded at them, then noticed Mrs. Fallowfield and Mr. Arnison sitting near them. Mrs. Fallowfield gave me a straight look and nodded, as did Mr. Arnison. What a surprise!

Next, I saw Mr. Noble from Barclays Bank, then Mr. Crick speaking to the Merrymans and another man I did not recognize. My heart jolted at the sight of Reverend Thomas standing severely next to Mr. Drinkwater and other men from the Bible Church. The reverend cast a dark look at me, then turned his face away.

How could he treat me like this? How could he spread such slander and gossip about me? It must be his way of saving his own reputation. After convincing me and the men of the Building Fund Committee that William was a trustworthy man of God, he couldn't possibly admit he had been wrong. To save his reputation he had to have a scapegoat, and I was it.

The idea made me sick, but I had no time to consider it, as the bailiff stood unfolding a parchment and faced me. The room hushed, and the short judge cleared his throat and squeaked in a high tenor, "This court will come to order. Bailiff, please read the charges."

My chest seized as the man looked at me, then the paper. "Mrs. Cairstin Rowan Soulier, lately of Penrith, you are charged with the murder of your husband, William Edward Soulier, also of Penrith, and the theft of ten pounds from the Building Fund of the Bible Church of Penrith. How do you plead?"

I found it almost comical that the money I'd hid in my corset was being claimed by Reverend Thomas, but without hesitation I answered, "Not guilty, Your Honors."

A rumbling went through the crowd, and for the first time I looked across from where I stood at the gentlemen of the jury, in whose hands my fate lie. I saw them studying me, sitting on their chairs, and leaning forward with rapt attention.

"Mr. Edgar," the short judge said. "Please proceed."

Mr. Edgar, I knew from Gabriel, was the prosecutor, known for his wit and keen intellect. Gabriel had practiced for days with me and Mother, doing his best impression of the man, leaving us all in stitches. There was no laughing now.

The man strode to address the jury with an important air. He had a Romanesque, angular face with a chiseled nose and hooded eyes. Though he was not as tall as Gabriel, his presence was commanding, and he shot me a narrowed look before pointing to me and speaking.

"Gentlemen of the jury, behold! There stands before you a murderous demon in disguise. This woman, doubly deviant, though outwardly meek and virginal, is actually a cold and vicious soul, capable of such calculated violence as men rarely have scene in this day and age of progress and enlightenment."

Goodness! Stuff and nonsense.

"She not only trapped her husband into a premature marriage but used her wicked influence upon him to steal from his own employer and church on her behalf, and once that money was procured, she killed him in cold blood by impaling the nape of his neck on a spike she knew full well was near the doorway of their home and capable of inducing death."

My heart pounded like a drum against the bones of my chest, and I struggled to keep my breathing in check. Such lies! How could any man with a conscience spew such lies against a woman trying to defend her very life?

"Oh," the man continued, his voice as thick as syrup, "she will claim that he was strangling her, trying to kill her, but I contend to you that she provoked attack at just the right time and in just the right place so she could carry out her designs to push her husband's head onto that spike and be done with him forever." He paused and strode dramatically in a circle before the bench.

"We will prove that she had more than money to motivate her heinous actions. She is also a brazen woman without conscience, who is known to throw herself at any man in order to manipulate them to her gain. She has used her beauty and womanly powers to seduce more than one man who stands in this court today."

At this, Edgar whirled around to glare at Gabriel and called for his first witness. "My lords, I call Mr. Timothy McGrady to the stand."

A lanky man mounted the short step onto the platform behind the rail. He was sworn in, and Mr. Edgar had him confirm that he was the bartender at The General Wolfe Inn on Little Dockray Street in Penrith, a place I passed by many times but had never been inside. What on earth could he have to say?

Mr. Edgar approached the man with a confident smile and began, "Mr. McGrady, tell the court how you became acquainted with the deceased, Mr. Soulier." Taking a step to the side, he motioned with a wave toward the jury.

The man was as nervous as a cat, clutching his cap in his fidgeting hands. "Well, sir, Mr. Soulier, he was a regular, ya see, and he came in quite often to have some skram and a pint, and near the end, came in almost every night."

The worn man took out a handkerchief and mopped his sweating brow. "He would often sit near the bar and have a crack, ya see, and tell me all about his betrothed, until he married her, and how much she was altered after the wedding."

"Tell us more specifically how Mr. Soulier described the change in his wife, Mr. McGrady." Mr. Edgar crossed his arms over his chest.

"Well, sir, he was troubled by how his sweet little love had turned into some kind o' awful witch, sir. That she was tapped in the head." Mr. McGrady darted a frightened glance my way, then continued. "He said she was always demanding he bring her home expensive things, like shoes and jewelry, and that she could never get enough cakes and pies."

Mr. Edgar walked to the bar and leaned his back on it. "And what did he say happened if he did not indulge her demands?" He turned his arrogant gaze on me, the corners of his lips tugging upward.

I wanted to scream but remained outwardly stoic.

"He said she would fly at him in a razzie, sir. That she would try to scratch his eyes out and wouldn't let the man sleep in his own bed."

A low rumble passed through the room. "Did Mr. Soulier ever tell you he was afraid for his life, Mr. McGrady?" Mr. Edgar turned from me.

"Aye, sir. More than once. Said he was afraid ta go home most nights cause he never knew what kind a mood she'd be in, sir."

I shook my head in disbelief. It was too much.

"Your witness, Mr. Dalton." Mr. Edgar stepped away.

Gabriel shot me a fleeting look and stood before the bar. "Mr. McGrady, have you ever met the defendant, Mrs. Soulier?" His question was curt and to the point.

"Well, no, sir." Mr. McGrady looked offended and raised his chin.

Gabriel kept up the pace. "Then you have no personal knowledge as to the character or disposition of Mrs. Soulier either before or after her marriage to Mr. Soulier, is that right?"

"Well, I suppose not, sir."

"And you have no way of proving whether Mr. Soulier's description of his wife and her actions was true or not, is that so?"

"I, well, no, I—"

"Then you also cannot possibly know whether what Mr. Soulier said about his wife was a lie told to you to discredit her in just such a moment as this, can you?" Gabriel's voice was solid as a rock, and my heart surged with love for him.

Mr. McGrady's face fell. "No, sir. It might have been a lie as much as the truth, for all I know."

Gabriel turned briskly. "Your honors, I ask that Mr. McGrady's testimony be stricken from the record as hearsay."

The taller justice nodded. "Agreed. Mr. Edgar, stick to the facts, if you please."

Gabriel glared at his opponent as he took his seat. The subdued Mr. McGrady was dismissed. Mr. Edgar shrugged, then called out, "I would now like to call Mr. Joseph Bell to the stand."

I pitied the man as he dragged his scraping chains across the floor, his once proud countenance gone as he took the oath.

"Mr. Bell," Mr. Edgar began, "now, you have known the accused for some time as a coworker at N. Arnison and Sons in Penrith, have you not?"

"Yes, sir," he answered in a thin voice and coughed, still pale. "I worked for Mr. Arnison for five years in his drapery. Mrs. Soulier joined the staff as a dressmaker in November of last year, sir."

Mr. Edgar gestured toward the bench. "Will you please tell the court your knowledge of Mrs. Soulier's character and actions during her time at Arnison's?"

After sliding me a scathing look, he turned his eyes to the magistrates. "Mrs. Soulier was a problem from the beginning. She would make mistakes in her work and blame them on other people. I once found her dancing alone in the hall, talking to God, and she has a terrible superstition about the color green. Believes it poisons those who touch it."

Sniggering murmurs filled the room.

Mr. Edgar nodded for him to continue.

"I have also heard of her faking an accident to gain the attentions of a certain man."

Mr. Edgar pounced. "And who is that man, Mr. Bell?"

"He is there, sir, sitting at the end of the table—Mr. Gabriel Dalton."

The crowd shouted, and I clenched my fists in the folds of my skirt. *How dare he!*

"And have you ever seen the accused in a fit of anger? Has she ever displayed a loss of temper in your presence?" Mr. Edgar coaxed.

I felt the blood drain from my face as Mr. Bell stole a dark glance my way. "She once left a needle in the seam of a dress, and when the lady came to have it fitted, it cut scratches in her back. Mrs. Soulier ran with the dress into the drapery, where I was in my usual position behind the sales counter, and screamed outrageous accusations at me in front of Mr. Arnison and a gentleman customer."

Mr. Edgar's face lit with satisfaction as he stepped aside and nodded at Gabriel. "Your witness, sir."

Gabriel approached slowly, his hands held behind his back. I could see he was considering carefully how to proceed.

"Mr. Bell, do you remember the evening of December 21 last year, when I came to Mr. Arnison's shop and gave you a letter to give to Mrs. Soulier, then Miss Blackwood?"

My jaw dropped at the question, but my eyes darted to Mr. Bell. What would he say?

The man behind the bar looked as if he had been struck. "Well, I faintly recall you stopping by . . ."

"Objection," Mr. Edgar shouted. "Irrelevant."

Gabriel turned toward the bench. "If it please, Your Honors, I am attempting to establish the credibility of the witness."

The short magistrate sighed. "Proceed, Mr. Dalton."

Gabriel bowed, then turned back to Mr. Bell. "Did you ever deliver the letter I gave you to Mrs. Soulier, Mr. Bell?"

The man looked around and he swallowed hard. "Well, I don't recall, I—"

"Mr. Bell, I understand you have been courting another one of Mr. Arnison's dressmakers, a Miss Eliza Salkeld, is that correct?"

The man looked down at his shoes, his pale cheeks splotched with red. "Yes, sir."

"Was she the one who convinced you not to give my letter to Mrs. Soulier?"

Mr. Bell's chains scrapped the floor as he shuffled his feet. "Well, I don't remember, I—"

His answers infuriated me.

Gabriel didn't let up. "Do you know where Miss Salkeld is and why she left Penrith suddenly after Mr. Soulier's death?"

"No, sir" was his flat reply.

Gabriel paused and paced a few steps. "Strange, don't you think, Mr. Bell, that Mr. Soulier's death would trigger your intended to run away without a word to you or anyone else? Didn't Miss Salkeld come into the drapery in the evenings at the end of your shifts to speak with you before you walked her home?"

"Sometimes."

"Then have you no suspicions that while Miss Salkeld distracted you with her charm and beauty, she dipped her hand into the till and helped herself?"

"I object, my lords," Mr. Edgar interrupted. "What does this have to do with the murder of William Soulier?"

The short magistrate glared at Gabriel. "Well, Mr. Dalton?"

"My lords, I have reason to believe that the money stolen from Mr. Arnison's till may be connected to Mr. Soulier's theft of money from Barclays Bank and the Bible Church and will have bearing on Mr. Soulier's motives to partner with Eliza Salkeld in discrediting the defendant."

The magistrates bowed their wigged heads together in consultation, then the taller one nodded to Gabriel. "You may proceed. The witness will answer the question."

A cloud of pain crossed Mr. Bell's face. "I cannot believe it, sir. She was . . . she meant the world to me." His last words trailed off as he fought back his emotions.

"I will remind you, Mr. Bell, that you are under oath and must answer truthfully." Gabriel stepped close to the bar and placed both hands on it. "Wasn't it you who placed that needle in that dress to cause trouble for the defendant?"

The hissing of whispers swirled around the gallery. Mr. Bell's neck and face turned bright red, and his lips twitched with anger as he stared down Gabriel. Gabriel stepped back and gestured toward the bench.

The short judge gave and demanded. "Answer the question, if you please."

Mr. Bell shuddered. "It was Eliza. She made me burn your letter and place the needle in the dress."

The gasps of the crowd sucked the air from the room as Gabriel stepped back from the stand. "No further questions, Your Honors."

Chapter Twenty-Nine

The sun shone directly through the tall eastern windows, blinding me and heating the backs of those in the gallery. I was relieved when the curtains were drawn, and felt the ache in my feet and lower back from standing so long. My gloves kept the shackles from cutting the skin on my wrists, but the weight was almost unbearable.

Mr. Merryman stood uncomfortably in the stand, avoiding my eyes as Mr. Edgar questioned him. "Now, Mr. Merryman, you and your wife live directly below the Souliers' flat, is that correct?"

The man sniffed. "Aye, sir."

"And you and Mr. Soulier were on speaking terms?"

"That's right."

"Will you please tell the court what Mr. Soulier told you about his wife, Mr. Merryman?"

The man nodded his nearly bald head and took a deep breath. "Mr. Soulier told me he was to be wed to a pretty, young dressmaker. That she was a good Christian girl with good manners. But after the wedding, he said she changed altogether, even before the . . . before they, er—"

"Yes, before what, sir?" Mr. Edgar pried.

"Ah, before the wedding night, sir. Said she refused to let him sleep with her in his own bed."

There was a flurry of chatter. As Gabriel called out his objection, I could not help the heat that rose in my face, aghast that William would speak of such things to people, especially when he was the one who had turned me away.

The tall magistrate slapped the bench and called for order. "No more hearsay, Mr. Edgar," he warned.

Mr. Edgar bowed and returned his attention to his witness.

"What happened the evening Mrs. Soulier came out of the flat and you had to force her back in? Tell us what happened." Mr. Edgar leaned on the jury railing, staring at me with his pale-blue eyes.

"Marion and me, we were out in the yard just after supper, and Mrs. Soulier come rushing out o' her door in a tizzy. Barely made it to our landing and sat on the step, crying and wheezing."

The ache of tears built behind my eyes at the memory.

Mr. Merryman briefly looked at his wife in the gallery and went on. "Marion and me, we was paid by Mr. Soulier to put her back in their flat if we ever saw her leave—even gave us a key so's we could lock her back up—so we took hold o' her arms and fought her back inside. It was then Marion saw Mr. Soulier hanging on the wall with the blood dripping from his mouth. He was dead all right."

The crowd reacted, and my insides rolled over as I relived that terrible moment, every word the man spoke trapping me back in that flat with William's body hanging there, condemning me.

Mr. Edgar turned dramatically to Gabriel with a wave of his arm. "Your witness, sir."

Gabriel stood and approached the stand, then looked kindly up at Mr. Merryman. "I'm sure you and Mrs. Merryman have been quite disturbed by what has happened, Mr. Merryman."

The man looked down at the cap in his hands. "Aye, sir. Never wanted my dear wife to ever see something like that. Never."

"Yes, I'm sure." There was a sincerity in Gabriel's voice that touched me. "I understand that Mrs. Merryman once helped Mrs. Soulier to operate the pump in the yard. Isn't that so?"

"Aye, sir. My wife is a dear little thing, always helping others."

Gabriel nodded. "Did you or your wife ever see her at the pump again?"

Mr. Merryman cocked his head. "I never saw her there again."

"Did Mrs. Soulier ever say anything when you saw her come out of her flat the day Mr. Soulier died?" Gabriel cocked his head.

"What? Oh." He thought for a moment. "I suppose she was saying 'Help me, help me,' though her voice was so rough and croaking—ya could hardly make sense of it."

"And you say that Mr. Soulier paid you to force Mrs. Soulier back into her flat if you ever saw her out. What was his reasoning, did he say?"

"He said she had gone touched in the head, and she was a danger to herself and others, sir."

"And how much did he pay you for such a service?" asked Gabriel.

At this, Mr. Merryman looked at his shoes. "Three guineas, sir."

The crowd collectively caught its breath, and I joined them.

"Well, Mr. Merryman, you did all right for yourself. No further questions."

Mr. Edgar called on Mr. Crick, who limped to the stand, pulling on his ill-fitting trousers and licking his yellow teeth. His hatless head was a disgusting sight, and he glared out his open eye at the magistrates, then turned it on me with a crooked grin.

"Mr. Crick," Mr. Edgar began, "Mr. Soulier was your tenant for just under a year when his wife came to join him at your property on the third floor of the building over the entrance to White Hart Yard, is that correct?"

"Aye, sir, and never was a day late on his rent," Mr. Crick answered with pride.

"I see. And he told you much the same about his fiancée, then wife, as he told Mr. Merryman, is that so?"

"Aye, sir. Caught himself a regular banshee, he did."

Laughter sprinkled through the room.

"He told me he couldn't even come home for supper, he was that afraid of her."

This time it was my turn to laugh inwardly. William afraid of me? Ludicrous.

"Can you tell us, Mr. Crick, of the time you observed Mrs. Soulier come down the stairs of their flat and nearly slip on the ice?"

My pulse quickened.

"Aye, sir. T'was only a few days after she came. I saw her from my window on the first floor. She nearly fell at the bottom o' the stairs and went racing out the back o' the yard past the stables. I thought I might keep an eye on her, for Mr. Soulier was at work in the bank."

"So you followed her. And where did she go?"

I felt like I would fall apart in a million pieces right there on the spot. He had followed me to the castle ruins.

"She went up the back alleys to the top o' the hill. I saw her fall, then get back up and run into the castle ruins."

"The castle ruins? That's a strange place for someone to go in the middle of a frigid winter's day, isn't it?" Mr. Edgar's feigned wonder made me ill.

"Aye, sir. Queer indeed." Mr. Crick licked his lips, as if he liked the taste of his words.

Mr. Edgar leaned closer to his witness, his eyes sparking. "What happened next?"

"Well, I went 'round all quiet-like and heard her weeping. Then I spies her and Mr. Dalton."

His pause gave the intended effect. The room burst with condemnation.

I felt something inside me break. *I don't care if I die. I can't let them humiliate him this way.*

Gabriel's eyes were on mine. I was certain he could see my distress, and he lifted his hand ever so slightly to me, as if to say, *It's all right. It's nothing.*

Mr. Edgar turned and looked at Gabriel, his arms folded over his chest. "And what did you see after that, Mr. Crick?"

The man smiled, his open eye gleaming. "Then I saw him pick her up in his arms and take her home with him."

This time the murmuring sounded muffled, my pulse in my ears drowning it out. I felt a pressure on my chest like a load of lead, and my unspilled tears filled my head to aching. Gabriel looked down at the papers in his hands and then met Mr. Edgar's eyes coldly.

"Very interesting, Mr. Crick. Your witness, Mr. Dalton." Mr. Edgar bowed to Gabriel with a sardonic look.

Gabriel was slow to rise from his chair. He did not look Mr. Crick in the eye when he quietly asked him, "You saw Mrs. Soulier fall at the top of the hill near the castle, did you not?"

Mr. Crick shrugged his uneven shoulders. "Aye."

"And you did not render her aid?" Gabriel looked at the gentlemen of the jury and still did not look Mr. Crick's way.

"Well, I wasn't close enough to her, and she took off afore I could offer." Mr. Crick scratched the side of his neck, then cleaned his fingernails on the collar of his coat.

"So you followed a distressed woman, watched her fall, and kept your distance until someone else offered to take her someplace safe to tend to her wounds, is that right?"

Mr. Crick's open eye bulged. "Well, how was I to know she was hurt?"

Gabriel finally turned to the man with a warning look. "Exactly," he said with a nod. "Did Mr. Soulier also pay you to keep an eye on the wife he regularly beat and tried to starve?"

The man arched his back a little. "Well, he paid me the same as the Merrymans', but I never knew anything about him beating her. I only knew he wanted her to stay locked up, is all."

"Are you sure that is all you knew about the Souliers? Remember, you have sworn an oath to testify to the whole truth, sir. That means you are to leave nothing of significance unsaid. Is there anything else you are aware of that this court needs to know, Mr. Crick?" Gabriel was on the verge of shouting.

"I know nothing more, sir. There's nothing else to say," Crick answered emphatically.

Gabriel glowered at him.

There must be something else he knows, but what?

"No further questions, my lords."

Chapter Thirty

The court was put on recess to allow the magistrates to take their dinner, and I was taken out a side door to a room with a table and chairs. The guards gave me a cup of water and a piece of bread, but I lay my head on my arms.

Moments later Gabriel and a guard entered the room with haste.

"Cairstin, my dear, are you all right?" Gabriel took a chair beside me and took my hand.

The guard took a chair and sat near the door.

I touched my forehead to Gabriel's hand. "You are a saint from God, Gabriel Dalton, an angel in disguise."

"No, no, my dear. Here now, you need to eat something to keep up your strength. I cannot imagine the torture all this has been for you, standing there listening to lie after lie." He handed me his handkerchief, and I dried my tears.

He drew from his pocket a hard-boiled egg still in its shell. "I took this from the breakfast table this morning," he said with a half grin.

I buried my face in my hands, my chains banging against the table. "You are too good, sir. Too good."

"Please, Cairstin, you must eat now. The time is very short, and I must tell you many things."

Nodding, I cracked the shell and peeled it as he spoke rapidly.

"First off, Constable Jackson took the first train back to Penrith this morning to follow a new lead. Toby—you remember Mr. Arnison's errand boy—has come forward with news, but we must confirm he is telling the truth and wait for Jackson's return before playing that card."

My mind swirled around this development. "What did Toby say?"

Gabriel shook his head. "We mustn't take the time to discuss it now. You will know all if it turns out to be true."

He patted the table and continued. "So far only the prosecution has been allowed to call witnesses. Mr. Edgar has two more I know of, Mr. Drinkwater and Reverend Thomas. I am not concerned about Mr. Drinkwater, but the reverend has been doing a lot of talking around Penrith about you, trying to save his own skin. He knows his reputation is at stake for putting all his trust in Soulier, in putting you two together, and giving Soulier access to the church's money. He will be ready to feed you to the dogs, and we must be ready for it."

I swallowed my bite of tasteless bread and looked into his eyes. "Oh, Gabriel. Who will ever believe my word against his? How will we ever prove I didn't kill William out of jealousy or greed? It seems impossible."

Gabriel patted my shoulder. "I know it looks very bleak right now, but we must keep believing that one of these people will crack under the pressure and reveal that Soulier planned to kill you on his way out of town."

I met his eyes and shook my head. "But why would they?

Even if Soulier told anyone his plan, why would they tell the court? Wouldn't it make them guilty of not preventing a murder?"

He sat still for a moment. "You are right—it is a long shot, but we must keep up the pressure as long as we can. After the witness testimonies, it will be time to question you."

He turned my chair toward him and took my shoulders. "Cairstin, no matter what happens, I want you to know that I love you. I will do everything in my power to save you. Do you believe me?"

"Oh, Gabriel, if you love me, that is all that matters. I will live or die with that knowledge and be blessed."

We fell into each other's arms and held each other tightly. *How can I ever let him go?*

The guards unlocked the door, and Gabriel released me. I saw the tears on his face and gave him back the handkerchief. "I love you, Gabriel Dalton," I whispered, as he kissed my forehead. "God bless you."

Gabriel quickly shut down the questioning of Mr. Drinkwater as hearsay when it was found he had nothing new to offer.

When Reverend Thomas took the stand, the fresh pain of betrayal sliced through my heart like a knife. *I trusted you*, I cried out to him in the silence of my mind. *I trusted you and look what has happened! And now you will try to have me hung all because you are too full of pride to admit you were wrong.*

He lay his thick hand on the Bible, tucked in his chin, and glared at me from under his bushy brows. "I swear, by Almighty God, to tell the truth, the whole truth, and nothing but the truth."

Mr. Edgar wasted no time. "Reverend Thomas, how long did you know the deceased until he met his untimely end?"

"I met Mr. William Soulier when he began attending the services of our new Bible Church in Penrith. That was some ten to eleven months ago."

"Can you explain to the court how you came to be better acquainted with him?"

"I was impressed by Mr. Soulier's dedication to the faith and his zeal for knowledge. He seemed a quiet, sturdy fellow with a promising career at Barclays Bank, so I decided to invite him to join a very special group of young men I wished to disciple in God's Word, who might be trained up to assist me in my work for the Lord."

He paused and closed his eyes and shake his head, sighing heavily, a tack I had seen him use often for dramatic affect. "What a terrible loss. To lose such a devout follower of Christ in the prime of his youth. It is a tragedy, sir, a most unnecessary and egregious tragedy." His voice was low and somber by the end, bringing all his practiced skills to bear.

Mr. Edgar locked his hands behind his back and paced. "Did you ever find anything in Mr. Soulier's character that would give you pause? Did he ever display a tendency to anger or violence?"

"Never, sir!" the reverend replied, as if injured. "I am an excellent judge of character, and I assure you the man conducted himself with the best of manners and sober judgment."

"When did Mr. Soulier first approach you with the idea of taking up a courtship with Mrs. Soulier, then Miss Blackwood?"

Reverend Thomas glanced at me with smoldering eyes. "It was just after I sent him to take Miss Blackwood home to

Appleby to be with her family at the passing of her father, at great expense to the church, I must add."

My eyes met Mother's in the gallery. I could see her tears from where I stood in the dock.

Mr. Edgar leaned on the railing of the jury. "Reverend Thomas, when and where did you first meet the accused?"

"She was introduced to me at my church the fourth Sunday in November after the service, which is currently meeting in The Gloucester Arms in Penrith."

"And what was your impression of her at that time?"

"She presented herself as a lady in distress, sir. I was told that her father, a tailor in Appleby, was dying and that she had come to take a position at Mr. Arnison's shop as a dressmaker in order to help her struggling family." He paused and gave me a sideways glance. "I promised to pray for her father and offered to help her in her time of trouble, and when her father died, as I've said, the church, my wife, and I went out of our way to be of assistance to her."

"So by the time Mr. Soulier approached you with his idea of courting her, you were agreeable to the idea?"

The reverend's nose grew a deeper shade of red and he nodded. "Regrettably."

"How long did this courtship last before the two were wed by you and Reverend Stuart at St. Andrew's in Penrith?"

"Only two weeks, sir." He paused, and a wave of surprise passed through the room. "There was a need for haste due to the fact that Mrs. Soulier's family was in dire need of financial aid, and out of the goodness of his heart, Mr. Soulier offered his hand and his wages to keep his new wife and her family living in the kind of comfort they were accustomed to."

This last pronouncement was made as if he were reading a passage of Scripture. I fought hard to keep my face from showing my revulsion.

"And when did you begin to notice a change in the couple? How did you become aware of the troubles brewing in their home?" Mr. Edgar asked, his eyes fixed on me.

"When Mr. Soulier came to my home the day after the wedding and told me that Mrs. Soulier prevented him from coming to bed with her on their wedding night."

The crowd reacted. My heart plunged at the lie.

"So Mrs. Soulier refused to consummate the marriage? Why, did he say?"

Gabriel was on his feet. "I object, Your Honors—more hearsay."

Mr. Edgar waved at the magistrates. "Forgive me, Your Honors. I will change tact."

Gabriel sat back down and Mr. Edgar paced a moment.

Suddenly he turned to the evidence box that sat in the middle of the table. Pulling out a piece of burned boot sole, he asked, "Take a look at this, Reverend. What do you think it is?"

What?

"Oh yes! It's a piece of boot sole," he said with a smug smile. "Mr. Soulier said his wife burned every pair of shoes she owned, including her winter boots, just to make him buy her new ones."

My knees buckled, and I couldn't help but reach for the rail for support.

Mr. Edgar didn't stop. "Did Mr. Soulier ever tell you that his wife was tempting him to steal for her?"

"Of course not. He was probably so under her spell by then that he could not bring himself to reach out for help."

Gabriel objected, and I felt my body jolt as if I had been struck.

The reverend caught sight of my reaction and turned on me, shaking his thick finger, the blood rushing to his fat face. "You, Cairstin Soulier! You are a fraud and a temptress! Down on your knees, you vixen, and pray God will have mercy on your mortal soul!"

The whole room was ablaze with scorn and wrath. I thought I would faint, but Gabriel's voice rang out above the fray. "I object, my lords! The witness has gone too far!"

"Order," the taller magistrate shouted in a clear baritone. "Order. The witness will refrain from such outbursts in the courtroom."

I perspired from head to toe, and my heart beat hard against my corset. My legs quivered, but I kept my feet, training my eyes to focus on the man in the room who had just confessed his love for me. I would stand for him.

"Mr. Dalton, your witness." Mr. Edgar slid back into his chair at the opposite end of the table.

Gabriel strode toward the stand, Reverend Thomas in his sites. "Reverend Thomas, do you recall intercepting me at the door of N. Arnison and Sons in the late afternoon on Monday, December 21, of last year?"

My eyes widened. It was so courageous of Gabriel to speak of that day.

"Well—" Reverend Thomas had not anticipated this question. "I . . . I suppose I do."

"You had come to tell me that I shouldn't waste my time pursuing my interest in Mrs. Soulier, then Miss Blackwood. You told me that she was beneath my station and that I should turn my attentions elsewhere, did you not?"

The gallery stirred, and the reverend shifted his feet, his nose flaming. "Well, yes, I vaguely remember—"

"But when Mr. Soulier approached you about entering into a courtship with Mrs. Soulier, you had no objections. Why?" Gabriel turned to look importantly at the jury. He wanted their full attention on the reverend's reply.

"Well I . . . I suppose I thought they were a more suitable match. I—"

"Was the reason you thought Mr. Soulier a more suitable match for her because you wanted to keep Mrs. Soulier under your personal supervision and therefore keep her from leaving your church?"

Mr. Edgar jumped to his feet. "Objection, my lords. Conjecture."

"Sustained," the short judge said.

Mr. Edgar sat with a catty smile, and Reverend Thomas puffed up his barrel chest.

"Sir, you have testified to this court that you are an excellent judge of character. If you believe so, then why did you so misjudge the character of Mrs. Soulier?"

There was a sudden hush in the room. An excellent question.

"Well, as you can see, she is very convincing in person, but she is an entirely different woman behind closed doors, as you probably know, Mr. Dalton."

Dear God, did I really just hear him say that?

Gabriel nodded with narrow eyes. "I am not on the stand just now, sir—you are," he shot back, and the gallery gasped together. "How do you know so much about Mrs. Soulier's alteration in character? How often did you see her with your own eyes after the wedding?"

The reverend paused. "Well, only the once, at the church service the Sunday after."

"And did she seem in any way different to you than she had any previous time she came to your church? Did she fly off the handle at your sermon or scratch her husband's eyes out during the singing?"

Reverend Thomas lifted his doubled chin. "Certainly not.

Mr. Soulier had her well in hand, and Mrs. Soulier knew better than to expose her true nature in such a public place."

Gabriel paced, looking at the floor. "You say that Mr. Soulier had her well in hand. Tell us why he could handle her better in public then he could in private if she were so unruly?"

All the beet-red man could do was sputter.

Gabriel kept hammering him. "Did you know, Reverend, that the night before that church service, Mr. Soulier had almost killed his wife by strangling her and kicking her in the ribs, breaking several?" He stopped still in front of the stand and looked up, waiting for the answer.

"Why, no. Mr. Soulier told me that very afternoon his wife had hurt herself the night before in one of her tirades."

Gabriel glared at the man with a fury in his eyes I'd never seen. "Since you were so insistent to oversee this couple, did you ever confront Mrs. Soulier about her behavior to her face? Surely if one of your flock had gone so astray, the shepherd in charge would never let such behavior stand without some kind of pastoral interference?" Gabriel chose his words wisely.

Pastoral interference indeed.

"Well no, though I offered my services to Mr. Soulier. He refused on the grounds he was afraid it would only exacerbate the situation, and I respected his wishes, and, I might add, his fortitude and constancy to his wedding vows."

Gabriel ignored the insinuation. "So you never actually witnessed anything Mr. Soulier said about his wife's behavior for yourself? Did you witness Mrs. Soulier burning her shoes with your own eyes?"

"Well, no," the man stammered, "but the heal of the burned boot is here as evidence."

"Can you prove that it was she and not Mr. Soulier who burned those boots, Reverend? No!" Gabriel shouted. "What you have shared with this court today is only repeating Mr. Soulier's words to you, isn't that correct?"

Reverend Thomas nostrils flared. "I, well . . . yes. That is correct." The man worked his jaw, as if he didn't like the taste in his mouth.

Gabriel was unrelenting. "I understand that your Bible Church has a policy of only allowing married men to serve in leadership that involves the handling of any money, is that right?"

"It is," the reverend answered curtly. Clearly he was growing weary of the conversation.

"So if a thief wanted to get his hands on your substantial and still-growing church Building Fund, the easiest way for him to obtain access would be to have a wife and the complete trust of the pastor, is it not?"

Gabriel cocked his head and raised his brows while my heart swelled with love and pride. *If only I will live long enough to show him.*

"Well," puffed the reverend, his chest sinking. "Yes, that would be necessary."

With another step closer, Gabriel struck again. "Then why is it so hard for you, a man of means and education, to believe that the person who took you in was not Mrs. Soulier, but Mr.?"

Reverend Thomas's face lit up like a tomato. "Look here, Dalton, all of this is due to your meddling with another man's wife!" He shook his finger in Gabriel's face, but he did not flinch. "If it hadn't been for you and that girl fraternizing behind the man's back"—at this his finger swung over to me—"she never would have convinced Soulier to steal my money and kill him off so she could run away with you!"

The gallery erupted. I nearly screamed.

"Order! Order in the court room!" rang out the magistrates, pounding on the bench.

"No, sir!" Gabriel yelled over the crowd. "It is you who are the meddler! You are the one who put pressure on this girl to marry a thief and a con man who almost took her life. You whose pride and misjudgment enabled William Soulier to steal hundreds of pounds from your own church and Barclays Bank. If not for you, sir, she never would have suffered and been locked up like a prisoner to be starved and beaten. You, sir. You are the meddler!"

"Mr. Dalton! That will be enough! Order! Order in the court!"

Chapter Thirty-One

Gabriel's eyes still blazed with anger as he glanced at me and made his way to the bench. The judges obviously took him to task, then he took his seat at the table. Our hearts beat hard together as we matched our breaths, and I felt more alive in that moment than ever before.

Someone believed me. Someone believed *in* me and was trying with all his might, with all his soul, to save me from the gallows that waited for me. *God in heaven*, I prayed, *please let me live if only to live my life thanking you through loving this man.*

There was a pause in the proceedings as the magistrates conversed, then Gabriel was asked if he wished to call any witnesses for the defense.

Gabriel stood and took up a packet of papers. "Yes, my lords. I call Dr. Samuel Briggs to the stand."

The racing of my worn heart slowed as the dear old doctor stood and repeated the oath. Finally someone to speak who knew what I'd been through.

Gabriel led Dr. Briggs through the findings in his report

methodically, and the audience was captivated by his words, including the findings from his examination with the coroner, Dr. Garside. My eyes searched the gallery, and I saw Mother as she and Rose sat weeping for me next to Annabel. Mrs. Fallowfield met my gaze as she sat with her hands folded solemnly in her lap. Somehow I read understanding in her angled face, something beyond mere sympathy.

Mr. Arnison's brow furrowed, and he stared into space as he listened, his lips drawn in a thin line. Then I caught Reverend Thomas looking at me, then turning his sober face to stare at the paneled wall behind the bench. Mr. Drinkwater shifted in his chair, and Mr. Crick patted his knees and almost smirked with a glint in his one open eye.

Dr. Briggs told everything he knew in a compassionate and professional manner, clearly the most credible witness who had yet to testify that day.

When Mr. Edgar's turn came to cross examine him, he tried his best to get Dr. Briggs to acknowledge that I could have wounded myself in a fit of rage, even throwing myself against the back of a chair to break my ribs, but the doctor easily refuted his efforts. I breathed a great sigh of relief when Mr. Edgar gave up and let the doctor leave the stand.

Gabriel's next witness was Mr. Nobel from Barclays Bank, who testified about William's position there and how he was able to skim off money from many accounts, a small amount from each over the course of time, and fixed the books brilliantly so he wasn't caught until he took one last large sum the day he died.

There wasn't really anything Mr. Edgar could get out of him besides the facts he'd already stated, and he let him go with no further questions.

The difference in the state of the gallery from the time of the prosecution's witnesses and the defense was noteworthy.

The gallery had become sedate and quiet, with no drama and nothing but facts to consider, as did the jury.

Gabriel's next witness was a complete surprise to me. "I call Mr. David Liddell to the stand, please."

Mr. Liddell was a lively man with an enormous blond mustache who worked in the travel ticket sales office in Penrith.

Gabriel went to the evidence box and removed two small slips of paper. "Mr. Liddell, can you please identify these two receipts?"

The man took the papers and looked them over. "Yes, sir. One is for a train ticket to London from Penrith, and the other is for passage on a ship from the Port of Dover to France."

A new light went on in my mind.

"And what is the date for the train ticket, sir—can you tell from the receipt without the ticket in hand?"

"Well, sir, I remember Mr. Soulier, and also the date of his departure. He was to leave Penrith on the first train out on Sunday, February 28."

"The day after his death," Gabriel confirmed. "And did he purchase a ticket for a traveling companion at the same time, Mr. Liddell?"

"No, sir. Just the one for himself."

"How did you know it was Mr. Soulier? Did he introduce himself?" Gabriel prompted.

"I knew him from Barclays Bank, sir. That's where I take the deposits from the ticket sales for the company."

"And do you know if the travel company's account was one of the ones from which money was missing at the bank?"

"Yes, sir. I was told by Mr. Nobel, the man who has already testified."

The room filled with murmured speculations as Gabriel handed off his witness to Mr. Edgar.

He did not approach the stand but turned to face the

bench. "My lords, I understand that the crime of theft has been committed and that the deceased is the most obvious suspect, but I fail to see how Mr. Soulier's wish to leave his deranged wife has anything to do with his death at her hands."

Gabriel stood and flashed, "Oh, come now, Mr. Edgar. If the man committed these crimes and planned to murder his wife before skipping town, the jury has a right to know—"

"Gentlemen, gentlemen, please," the tall judge called. "Mr. Dalton is correct, Mr. Edgar. Now, either question the witness or let him go."

Mr. Edgar glared at Gabriel, then sat down with a huff. "I have no questions, my lords."

Just when I breathed another silent sigh of relief, Constable Jackson broke into the room with two guards from the Penrith gaol carrying trunks and the satchel I'd seen William take from the closet in the flat, as well as a shallow black box just like the ones lining the shelves in the men's department of Arnison's. The constable handed a note to the bailiff, which he scanned and then gave to the magistrates.

My heart pounded.

The crowd rustled with energy, and the short judge slapped his hand down. "This court will take a ten-minute recess," and they stood to leave.

Gabriel sped right to Constable Jackson, who motioned his men to bring forth their findings. How I wished I could hear what they said, but I was taken back to the holding room, my chains clattering all the way.

It was the longest ten minutes I have ever endured. I sat and prayed with my whole being for God's mercy and to grant Gabriel the wisdom of Solomon. At last I was taken back into the court and to my place in the dock.

The court rose as the magistrates returned. "Mr. Dalton, you may proceed."

"Thank you, my lords." He cast a meaningful eye my way. "I call Toby Elliot to the stand."

I caught my breath as Mr. Arnison's errand boy was escorted in from the side door and shown to the stand, where he stood trembling, his wrists and ankles in shackles. I listened to his quivering young voice as he was sworn in. I could hardly think what he might say.

Gabriel approached him with a gentle smile. "Hello, Toby. Don't be afraid. I'm going to ask you some questions, and it is very important that you answer them truthfully, all right?"

Toby nodded, his eyes wide and stained with tears.

"Good." Gabriel leaned casually on the rail and continued. "Toby, you work as an errand boy for Mr. Arnison in his shop in Penrith, don't you?"

Toby eyed Gabriel and nodded again. "Aye, sir."

"And just last night you went to Mrs. Fallowfield's home, who is the head of the dressmakers' department of Arnison's, and told her something very important, didn't you?"

Toby sniffed back tears. "Aye, sir."

"Now, Toby, I want you to stand up straight and speak up. I want you to tell us all everything you said to Mrs. Fallowfield. Can you do that?"

The boy straightened his shoulders and nodded. "Aye, sir."

Gabriel nodded back and Toby began, "As told Mrs. Fallowfield that As knew who stole t'money from Mr. Arnison's till and who put the oil in the cutting room pitcher sos Miss Ainslie would hurt her hand."

The tears poured down his cheeks, and he wiped his nose on his sleeve, rattling his chains. He glanced at Gabriel, who smiled and nodded encouragingly, and I held my breath.

"It were Miss Salkeld, sir. First, she paid As to put oil in the pitcher, then she paid As to take a certain black box from the men's department to a certain room at the back o' Sutton Yard on Blueberry Lane. As peeked into the box, even when she made me swear I wouldn't. I saw the money inside, sir."

My eyes shot to Mrs. Fallowfield's. She sat forward on her seat and gave me a steady look. This was what she knew all morning.

Gabriel picked up the black box on the table and brought it over to Toby. "Is this the box, Toby?"

"Aye, sir."

Returning the box to the table, Gabriel came back and leaned over to Toby. "You're doing very well, son. Now, tell us when you took the box to Miss Salkeld in Blueberry Lane and what you saw when you got there."

The lad nodded. "As took it just the Friday night before Mr. Soulier died, sir, at midnight, and knocked on the door. Mr. Soulier opened it half undressed, and As saw Miss Salkeld sitting on the bed in nothing but a nightgown, sir." Toby's face lit red as the audience gasped.

There it was. Proof they had been working together all along. A wave of nausea passed over me, and my legs went weak. I held the rail to steady myself. This was why he'd never slept with me. He was sleeping with Eliza.

Gabriel leaned on the rail with both hands in front of the boy. "Now, Toby, you know that putting the oil in the pitcher was a very bad thing to do. You should have gone right to Mrs. Fallowfield or Mr. Arnison and told them what Miss Salkeld wanted you to do, isn't that right?"

"Yes, sir," the lad replied with a sob.

"Now tell us why you didn't do that." Gabriel stood back to allow the room to see Toby's face as he answered.

"As were frightened," he cried. "Mr. Soulier told me he would kill me if As told, sir."

Another rumble went around the room, and I wanted to take Toby in my arms and weep bitterly.

Gabriel turned and looked over the jury. "So Mr. Soulier threatened to kill you, and this is why you waited until last night to go to Mrs. Fallowfield with what you knew, is that right, son?"

Toby tried to compose himself. "Aye, sir," he managed before dissolving into sobs.

Gabriel gave the boy his handkerchief and patted his shoulder, then stepped back. "Your witness, Mr. Edgar."

Mr. Edgar sat silent for a moment, then stood and turned to address the judges. "No questions, my lords."

Chapter Thirty-Two

The next witness was Constable Jackson, and Gabriel went right to work. "Thank you for your efforts to sort out the facts of this case, Constable. I will leave it to you to tell your story and about what you found when you returned to Penrith early this morning."

The constable cleared his throat and stood tall. "I was made aware of Toby Elliot's confession last night and returned to Penrith to see if I could find evidence of his claims, which, of course, I did. I found the room on Blueberry Lane in whose door the third key found in the Souliers' flat fit perfectly, but the room was empty. It was made known to me the room was let by Mr. Crick, the same landlord renting the flat above White Hart Yard to Mr. and Mrs. Soulier."

The room tilted. *Mr. Crick?*

I searched for the man's face where he had been sitting in the gallery all day, but he was no longer to be found.

Constable Jackson ignored the crowd and continued in a firm voice. "A search was then made of Mr. Crick's home in White

Hart Yard, and I found the following." He removed a paper from his pocket and began to read. "'The black box from Arnison's, containing thirty-eight pounds, the exact amount stolen from the till, and letters to Miss Salkeld from Mr. Soulier, promising to take her with him to France after he had accomplished his,' what he referred to as 'tasks,' and swearing his undying love for her."

He paused to take a breath, then read on. "'Also found in Mr. Crick's closet was new clothing, definitely not of a size to fit a man of Mr. Crick's stature, a trunk full of women's belongings, and an empty satchel.'"

But no money.

"While searching Mr. Crick's home, I discovered an iron hook in his closet, of a similar size and mounting to the one on which Mr. Soulier struck his head on when he died."

I clutched at the rail, anxiously awaiting his next words.

"The court should know that the hook in the Soulier's flat was a locking mechanism that, when pushed hard in an upward motion, opens the paneling above to reveal a secret compartment, which is where the defendant claims to have seen her husband removing many pieces of paper and where she also claims, upon opening the compartment when alone, she found a ten-pound note caught between the boards."

The whistles from the railway station sounded outside, and I bit my lip, not wanting to miss a single word.

"Upon applying the same motion to the hook in Mr. Crick's closet, the panel above opened and 584 pounds in notes were found inside, almost the exact amount of money stolen from Barclays Bank and the Bible Church Building Fund combined."

I gasped along with the rest of the court and found Gabriel's eyes.

The constable handed his paper to Gabriel with a nod.

"Mr. Crick has been confined and is available for questioning if the court should so choose."

"Thank you, Constable," Gabriel said. "Your witness, Mr. Edgar."

Mr. Edgar kept his seat and crossed his arms in annoyance. "No questions, my lords."

Gabriel stood boldly and turned to look my way. "The defense calls Mr. Crick to the stand."

He entered in chains, a different man than before. He looked at the ground and had to be assisted up the step of the platform, breathing heavily, leaning on the bar.

"Mr. Crick, you are reminded that you are still under oath in this courtroom," the bailiff called out.

Gabriel stood before him, his face set like flint. "Mr. Crick, there has been clear evidence revealed in this court that you have committed theft and perjury. Is there anything about your testimony you would like to now amend?"

The man snorted defiantly. "Not a word."

There were shouts and insults hurled at him from all sides, but Gabriel went on. "Then you deny that you rented a room of your property to Mr. Soulier in which he kept company with Miss Eliza Salkeld?"

Mr. Crick swayed slightly. "I do not deny it."

"Then you already admit to your perjury in neglecting to tell the whole truth, Mr. Crick. When did you find out about Mr. Soulier's plans to steal from the bank and the church?"

"Not till I found the money," he slurred.

"You lie! You knew about the money, and Mr. Soulier had you in for a nice cut of it—that is why you spied on Mrs. Soulier, because you had to keep her from revealing you and Soulier's plans before they were complete."

Training his arrogant eye on Gabriel, the man shifted in his chains and licked his beefy lips. "Prove it, lover boy."

I wanted to scream!

"You knew he planned to kill his wife and leave her body for you to dispose of after he fled. How much money did he pay you for that service, Mr. Crick?"

Mr. Edgar was on his feet. "I object—Mr. Dalton is putting words in the witness's mouth!"

The short one slapped on the bench. "Order! Mr. Dalton, stick to the facts, if you please."

Gabriel barely nodded. "When you found Mr. Soulier had been killed when his wife defended herself, I'm sure you wasted no time in removing everything from your room in Blueberry Lane and told Eliza Salkeld to get out of town as quickly as she could, isn't that right, sir?"

Mr. Crick's eye bulged with anger. "I'll not say another word, Mr. Dalton. You will have to question me at my own trial to get another word out o' me!"

The clamor of the crowd was almost deafening, and I fought back tears of rage and fear, knowing that without proof of William's plan to kill me, I would hang. I begged God silently to force him to speak.

The magistrates both beat on the bench, but the room was not so easily quieted.

My heart froze, knowing that Gabriel would call me next to the stand and I would have to relive the nightmare all over again in the presence of men who wished for nothing more than my death as retribution for the wrongs done to them.

I bent my head in despair, knowing my life hung by a thread, but a movement caught the corner of my eye. I saw an older gentleman escorting a young woman with a cane to the front of the gallery as another man in a constable's uniform took a packet of papers to the bailiff. I didn't recognize them and thought they looked out of place.

Gabriel and I exchanged questioning glances, then he was

called to join Mr. Edgar at the bench. The magistrates gave Gabriel the documents to read, and he stood next to Mr. Edgar, allowing him to read over his shoulder. I watched as they both blanched, and Mr. Edgar's face went pale. He nodded to Gabriel, who nodded at the judges, then came to me.

"Cairstin," he whispered, and I could hear the raw emotion in his voice. "This is the answer we've been waiting for, my love. Take courage and hold fast!"

He left me, and I stood in disbelief. *The answer? What answer?*

"My lords, the defense calls Mrs. Lydia Soleil to the stand."

Lydia Soleil? Who could she be?

"And I ask the court's permission for her father, Mr. Winston Everwood, to help her speak to the court, as Mrs. Soleil has a speech impediment."

Permission was given, but I pulled at the names of the two in my mind, searching for some connection.

The gentleman helped his limping daughter onto the stand, and the two were sworn in, the lady signifying her consent with a nod. I looked over her slight, lovely form, dressed in a beautiful rich day dress of blue silk with a high lace collar, her raven hair in tufts of curls next to her porcelain face, inside her lace-filled silk bonnet. She was beautiful, and I was positive I had never laid eyes on her or her stately father before.

"I understand," Gabriel began, "the two of you have come with a Constable Mason all the way from London today and have only just now arrived at the rail station next door, is that correct?"

The lady nodded. "That is correct, sir," Mr. Everwood said. "We are only glad that we made it before the proceedings ended, as we are anxious to tell you our story and see if it will shed any light that may be useful, and to know if Mrs. Soulier's circumstances may be able to solve a crime perpetrated on myself and my daughter."

I listened in bewilderment.

"And how is it that you came to have an interest in Mrs. Soulier's case, sir, madam?" Gabriel's voice was softened and edged with compassion.

"We read about Mrs. Soulier in the papers, sir, and one in particular, *The British Daily,* caught our attention, as it included that Mrs. Soulier had been injured by her late husband, with the details of her injuries, and Mr. Soulier was likely killed in self-defense."

The man paused when his daughter pulled on his sleeve and whispered in his ear. He nodded. "You see, there are certain similarities between this case and something that happened in London to myself, the bank I work for, and especially to my daughter, who was grievously used by a man known to us as Mr. William Soleil."

The room rumbled, and something connected in my mind Lydia Everwood . . . Lydia Netherwood. Ah! This was the girl William had been engaged to! But wait—she was being called Mrs. Soleil.

I stepped up to the rail and gripped it with both hands. There she was in the flesh, and she had come to help me!

Gabriel stepped aside and gestured. "Please explain, Mr. Everwood."

The man took a deep breath and nodded to his daughter, then looked at me. "You see, early last year I had a promising young man, Mr. Soleil, working under my supervision as a clerk at Godfrey's Bank in Sussex. I was impressed with his abilities and good manners and had him to my home to dine, where he met my daughter, then known as Lydia Everwood."

The man patted his daughter's hand resting on her cane. "Mr. Soleil seemed to form an immediate attachment to my daughter and soon asked for my permission to court her. Of course, I hesitated to allow a mere clerk to court my daughter, but I could see great potential in him and new I could have influence over his career, and once I found that Lydia was more than amiable to the idea, I relented."

He paused for breath, and Lydia took a handkerchief from her sleeve and dabbed at the tears on her cheeks. I knew what came next and began to cry with her.

"My family devoutly attends our parish church, and during that time a fundraising effort was commenced to add an addition to the church building to house a school for the local street urchins, where the church would provide them with not only a basic education but food and other necessities. It was a project my daughter had long envisioned, and she put her heart and soul into its realization. However"—and at this the man looked at his daughter with a mixture of great love and regret—"after they were wed, and that much too quickly, I admit, Mr. Soleil took my daughter to the opposite side of the parish to live, and we rarely saw her."

Mr. Everwood swallowed, and his gray eyes misted. "Only two weeks after the wedding, my daughter was found nearly strangled to death in their flat, all the money gone from the church's account and many others at the bank."

The court erupted. My eyes found Gabriel's. He was right—this was the answer we had been praying for.

My mother and Rose stood, followed by Annabel, Mrs. Fallowfield, and Mr. Arnison. Soon others joined them, and the room hushed until silence fell and all that was heard were the sniffles of the woman on the stand and the woman in the dock.

Lydia took her father's arm and nodded up at him. At last he was able to continue. "I almost lost my daughter to that man. Thank God he left her for dead when he did. One moment more and she would not have lived to tell the story of how he'd beaten and starved her, how he'd strangled her more than once, kicked her in the ribs and . . . and"—he faltered as his own tears fell—"and held her arms to force his knee into her backside, crippling her for life."

The room reacted, and more people stood to their feet.

I shook like a leaf as I watched and listened, my chest pressed to the barrier.

His voice was rough and quiet as he wiped a tear from his daughter's face. "She cannot talk above a whisper now. Soleil permanently damaged her ability to speak when he crushed her throat with his hands."

Still more people stood, including Mr. Drinkwater. The last man remaining in his seat was Reverend Thomas, whose face twisted with indecision.

I thought my heart would burst.

Mr. Edgar cleared his throat loudly, breaking the spell in the room.

Gabriel nodded to him and stepped aside. "Your witness, sir."

He sighed dramatically as he approached the two. "Well, Mrs. Soleil, Mr. Everwood. We are all very struck by the tragedy of your story, and I am sure Constable Mason will confirm your statements, but there is still no solid evidence that your Mr. Soleil, however similar the name, is the same Mr. Soulier that this court is concerned with. So I ask you, Mr. Everwood, how can you prove that these two men are one and the same?"

I squeezed the railing in front of me as if I could wring the evidence out of the wood, my hands screaming with pain in protest.

After a harrowing pause, Mr. Everwood raised his chin and rallied himself. "There is a chance, sir. My son-in-law not only stole money but an object of great sentimental value to me, the gold watch my dear wife gave me for our twenty-fifth anniversary the year before she died."

My eyes grew wide with revelation. William's watch! *W. E. S.!*

Gabriel dashed to the evidence box, shooting a question over his shoulder. "Can you describe it, Mr. Everwood? Does it have an engraving?"

Mr. Edgar glared at Gabriel's abrupt interruption. "Your Honors, I object!" he shouted, but the short magistrate stopped him.

"Just a moment, Mr. Edgar—let us see what Mr. Dalton is about. Please answer the question, Mr. Everwood."

The room collectively held its breath, listening carefully. "Yes, sir. It has my monogrammed initials, W. E. S., on its cover, and the date of our twenty-fifth anniversary inside—February 4, 1845."

The crowd gasped, Reverend Thomas stood, and I crumbled to the floor.

Epilogue

Spring 1848

As I stand beside the River Eden, my mind is filled with threads of memories, all woven together like a tapestry, weaving a picture of loss, suffering, struggle, and pain with love, faith, hope, and joy.

My brand-new husband stands beside me as we enjoy the view of spring in full bloom, the blossoming trees reflected on the surface of the water, the birds singing in the branches, and the mingling scent of damp earth and freshly cut grass. Across the river from us is our wedding party, enjoying a lovely breakfast feast, talking and laughing like one big, happy family.

I see Mother and Rose dressed in light-blue gowns, my sister looking more like a young woman every day. Mother now and then dries a happy tear, and I catch her smiling upon me constantly. We have been living again behind my tailoring and dressmaking shop in Appleby, but today we are completing our move to Gabriel's new town house in Carlisle, where he is famously known as "The Beloved Barrister," and I will live in the ecstasy of his company till death parts us.

There is Robert and Annabel Nixon sharing a piece of cake, who are expecting their first child in a few months. Robert is now Gabriel's assistant in his new office and has proven to be a fast learner in the ways of the law. Annabel has learned to cope with her burn-scarred hand, even learning to stitch with her left, and we look forward to working together in a little shop of our own next door to our husbands' office, with a sign above the door: "Dalton and Nixon's Dressmakers and Tailors."

Mr. and Mrs. Arnison are chatting, at the long flower-and-food-laden table, with Mrs. Fallowfield, who is, as always, her proper self. After I was acquitted, she confided in me that long ago she ran away from a husband who beat her constantly. Mr. Arnison, who had been kind enough to take her in, never revealed her secret.

On the far end of the table sits Susan Dykes and Joseph Bell, both reestablished in their positions at Arnison's. They have been courting for some months now, and I expect an announcement any moment, which warms my heart. Susan is completely recovered, and Mr. Bell no longer orders fabrics made with Scheele's green, as it has been found to contain poisonous arsenic in the dye.

The day of my trial, once our shackles were removed, Mr. Bell came to me in tears, apologizing that he had let Eliza influence him not to deliver my note from Gabriel that Christmas. His demeanor is completely altered since his ordeal, and he and Susan have become our friends. Eliza Salkeld has never been heard from again.

And then there is Lydia Everwood, whose maiden name was restored when it was found that William Soleil, whose real name was William Solari, had married her illegally after abandoning his first wife, a vicar's daughter in the east side of London. Lydia and I have become dear to each other, and no one knows the waters I have passed through better than she.

With her is her father, Mr. Winston Everwood, who dotes on me like I am another daughter to him. He has become enamored with the railway and steam engines, telling everyone if it weren't for the train from London to Carlisle through Penrith, he and Lydia would never have made it in time to spare my life. They often come to visit to breathe the fresh air of the dells, and we, along with Mother and the Nixons, have been known to talk late into the night about our shared experiences.

I feel a shiver run through me, then Gabriel's arm around my waist. "I know what you're thinking, Mrs. Dalton. 'Look how far we've come from that day.' Am I right?"

Tucking myself into his shoulder, I lay my head on his chest. "Indeed, my love. That, and how very grateful I am to you and to God for this day." Turning to look into his face with my arms around him, I see the mist in his eyes and do not hold back the tears in my own. "Thank you for waiting for me, Gabriel. I wanted to be a whole woman for you, and the time to heal has been a gift."

He touches my face tenderly, a caress I have longed for my whole life. "You are my gift, Cairstin Dalton. God put us together, and I cannot wait to have you all to myself."

He pulls me tightly to him, our hearts beating hard against each other, our lips meeting, and all the world around us fades away.

THE END

Acknowledgments

Editor: *Dori Harrell*
Cover Design: *Roseanna M. White*
Beta Reader: *Karen Laage*
Agent: *Rachel McMillan*

UK Consultant: Gareth Hayes, Appleby-in-Westmorland, UK. I cannot thank you enough for your contribution to this work and for your friendship.

Special Thanks to: Tim and Nigel Scott-Arnison for allowing me to visit and explore every part of their incredible store, which has closed after 283 years of service to Penrith, Cumbria, UK. It was an honor and I hope you will be pleased with my story.

And to my husband, Artine Yapoujian, for allowing me to drag you around looking at old things. I love you all the way.

Also: Karen Lowthrop; Zoe Barkley of Penrith Library; Lucy Richardson; Roger and Jane Storey.

About the Author:

Sydney F. Grey is a Christian historical fiction author whose work blends Regency/Victorian romance, gothic suspense, with themes of faith. A native of Colorado, she grew up among the pine forests of the Rocky Mountains, where her love for stories first took root. Always captivated by British history, Sydney draws on her passion to create richly detailed, faith-driven narratives.

Her debut novel, *Those Who Trespass*, was a double finalist in the prestigious Crown and Selah Awards.

Beyond writing, she is also a fine artist, singer, and vocal coach. Sydney and her husband enjoy traveling, boating, and exploring new trails on their e-bikes.

To Read the Author's Notes:

Visit the website: www.sydsartsongs.com

www.ingramcontent.com/pod-product-compliance
Ingram Content Group UK Ltd.
Pitfield, Milton Keynes, MK11 3LW, UK
UKHW040747150626
13130UKWH00036B/619

9 798993 111940